MURDER
OF A
SUFFRAGETTE

BOOKS BY MARTY WINGATE

LONDON LADIES' MURDER CLUB SERIES

A Body on the Doorstep

A Body at the Séance

A Body at the Dance Hall

MURDER OF A SUFFRAGETTE

MARTY WINGATE

Bookouture

Published by Bookouture in 2024

An imprint of Storyfire Ltd.
Carmelite House
50 Victoria Embankment
London EC4Y 0DZ

www.bookouture.com

Storyfire Ltd's authorised representative in the EEA is Hachette Ireland
8 Castlecourt Centre
Castleknock Road
Castleknock
Dublin 15 D15 YF6A
Ireland

Copyright © Marty Wingate, 2024

Marty Wingate has asserted her right to be identified
as the author of this work.

All rights reserved. No part of this publication may be reproduced, stored in any retrieval system, or transmitted, in any form or by any means, electronic, mechanical, photocopying, recording or otherwise, without the prior written permission of the publishers.

ISBN: 978-1-83525-212-3
eBook ISBN: 978-1-83525-211-6

This book is a work of fiction. Names, characters, businesses, organizations, places and events other than those clearly in the public domain, are either the product of the author's imagination or are used fictitiously. Any resemblance to actual persons, living or dead, events or locales is entirely coincidental.

To Leighton

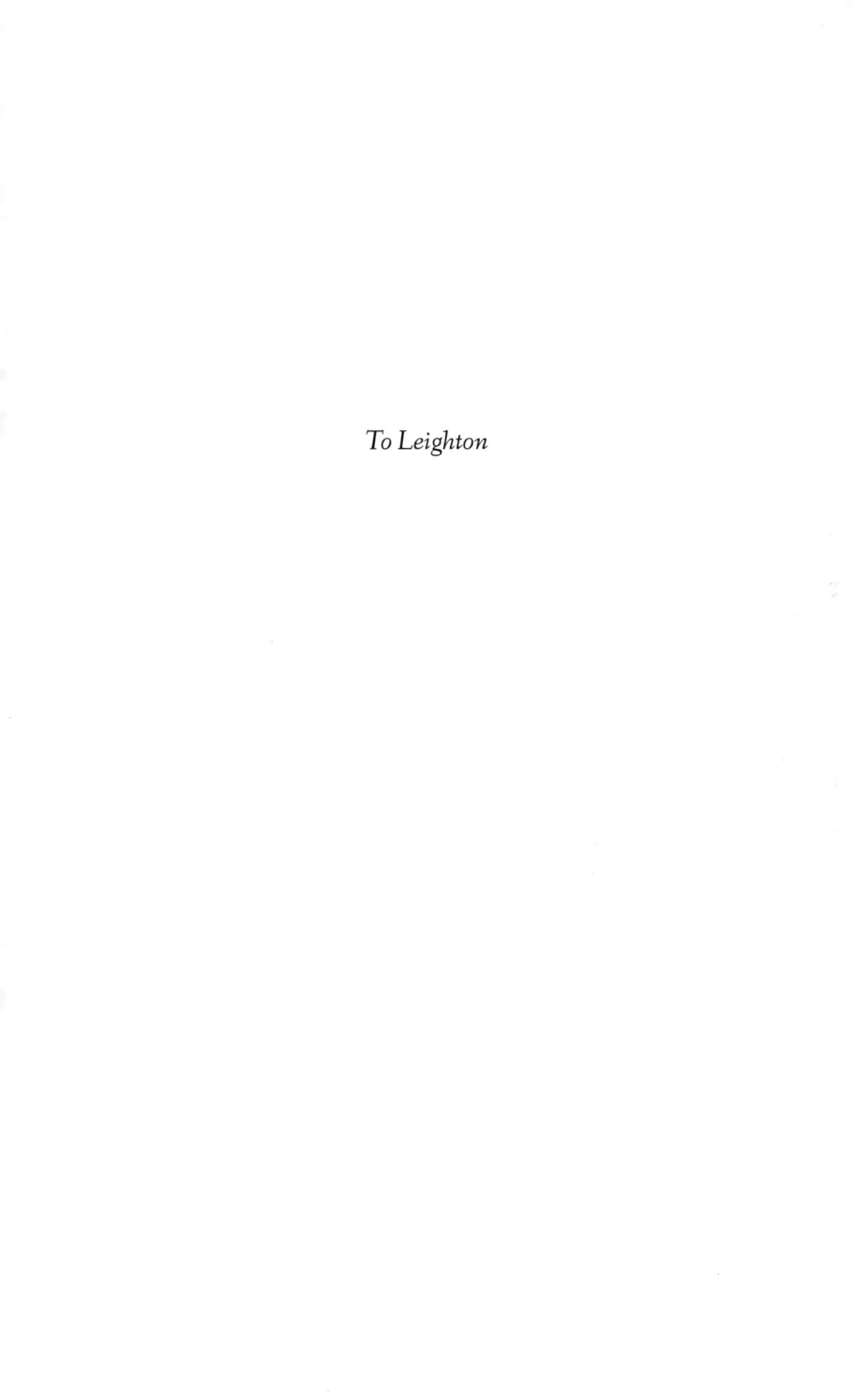

ONE

FELLBRIDGE HALL, SUSSEX

April 1922

Mabel Canning stood eye-to-eye with Dorothea Goose in the chill air of Fellbridge Hall, a great Georgian country house with Regency embellishments, Victorian add-ons and Edwardian modernisations yet still with a touch of the medieval about it.

'I will not wait here in the entrance hall,' Miss Goose declared. A wisp of grey hair had come loose from her bun and she blew it out of one eye, adjusted the wide brim of her straw hat and straightened the faded purple, green and white suffragette sash she wore over her slightly shabby wool coat. She had a weathered face as if she were a farm labourer.

Her shrill voice – too loud to be standing so close – bounced off the flagstone floor and echoed in the entrance hall, empty apart from a small writing desk behind which Mabel had been sitting before she'd had to block Miss Goose's flight.

'Lady Fellbridge knows perfectly well who I am,' the woman continued, 'and of all the women asked to this meeting of minds, I should be allowed through without question.'

'It's a matter of protocol, Miss Goose,' Mabel explained.

'You are not being singled out. Lady Fellbridge has asked me to meet each guest to confirm a few details.'

Dorothea Goose would not be mollified. 'And when did Lady Fellbridge engage you as a private secretary, Miss... Miss...'

'Canning.'

'Canning. I don't remember seeing you before and I am in her ladyship's confidence.'

Mabel had no interest in jockeying for favoured position and so ignored Miss Goose's proprietary air.

'Lady Fellbridge engaged me through the Useful Women agency,' she replied.

'Lillian Kerr's venture?' Miss Goose sniffed. 'I thought that was only for domestic work.'

'Useful Women carry out all manner of work,' Mabel said. 'They act as companions, translate letters, guide foreign visitors around London – as well as wash dogs and collect shopping.'

Miss Goose softened at this concession that had been offered along with a small smile. Mabel steered clear of mentioning the Private Investigations division of Useful Women, which she herself managed and had taken to calling her London Ladies' Murder Club. She had been, in this instance, engaged as private secretary and there would be no need for her other skills.

Lady Fellbridge had put out the call to a select few suffragettes and other supporters of the campaign. Women over the age of thirty had gained the vote in 1918, but the fight would not be over until they were equal to men and had the right to vote at twenty-one. They would choose a leader from among the group during the week and set to work.

'I'm sure I wish Lillian and all her Useful Women the best of luck in this endeavour,' Miss Goose said magnanimously. 'And so I will oblige you and your rules.'

'Thank you, Miss Goose,' Mabel said. 'That's very kind of

you.' Mabel took her seat behind the writing desk, opened the register and confirmed the necessary details. Glancing down at the small leather case with worn corners and a mended handle, she said, 'Binks, the butler, will take your case and show you to your room. You are in the west wing.'

'By the way, Miss Canning,' Miss Goose said as the butler took up her bag, 'I do hope you haven't put Mrs Lotterby in the west wing.'

'You have the rest of the day to yourself,' Mabel said. 'Binks will take a tea tray to your room later. Drinks in the salon at six.'

With that unsatisfactory answer, Dorothea Goose, her chin in the air, followed Binks out, leaving behind a faint scent of camphor.

Not a moment later, Lady Fellbridge came in through the near passage. She held herself erect, moving her tall thin form gracefully across the space. Her manner and appearance belied her age – nearing sixty – and she had her silver hair boldly cut into a short, sleek bob. She smiled.

'Do I detect a hint of camphor?' she asked with a smile. 'So, Dorothea has arrived.'

Mabel nodded just as there came a loud knock at the front door – heavy iron on thick, ancient oak. It echoed around the entrance hall. When Fellbridge Hall had been electrified at the end of the war the newest sort of doorbell had been installed but, although electric lights were a welcome modernisation, the bell was rarely used either because it was unreliable or because no one expected to be heard by any fashion except force.

With Binks off in the nether regions of the east wing, Lady Fellbridge opened the door herself – unheard of in other great houses, but commonplace here.

There ensued a parade of women exiting two taxis that had come from the railway station in Rye. As Lady Fellbridge chatted with the newcomers, private secretary Mabel scurried around confirming the details she'd already entered into the register, while struggling to assign some attribute to each of these women in order to stick name to face.

Miss Lavinia Poppin waved her arms about when she spoke – Mabel would need to take care not to be struck by one of her gestures. Miss Thirza Bass – did she ever blink? Miss Pretoria Fleming-Jones had carefully arranged pin-curls at each ear and across her forehead that had been stuck down with the lady's version of pomade. Those three stood apart in a tight cluster, consulting each other with looks and echoing each other's answers.

As Mabel worked, Mrs Collette Massey followed her around while advising her on how to reorganise the register. Lastly, Mabel spoke to Miss Ruby Truelock. She stood alone, glancing around uncertainly. She appeared to be a good deal younger than the others – younger than Mabel, too. Perhaps not yet twenty and the other delegates were in their forties or older. With her pale skin and pale hair and a pale hat to match, Miss Truelock seemed so nondescript as to disappear. Twice Mabel lost track of her in the group of only six, possibly because the pattern of her red dress with gold trim looked remarkably similar to the wallpaper.

Finally, Mabel raised a hand and called out over the general din of conversation, 'Hello and welcome.'

The women ignored her and carried on talking in raised voices that filled the entrance hall. But Mabel had dealt with worse inattention – those eight-year-old boys in her Sunday school class had been a lesson unto themselves. Lacking a gavel, she rapped her knuckles on the table until the sound cut through the noise and the women paused and looked at her, eyes and mouths open.

'Now then,' Mabel said brightly, putting her hands behind her back and giving her knuckles a rub. 'Binks will show you to your rooms, which are in the east or west wing or the priory gallery and he will take each of you a tea tray. You've time for yourselves until drinks in the salon at six followed by a buffet supper. Until then, Lady Fellbridge encourages you to go out to the gardens or look round the Hall or whatever you wish.'

The butler appeared from the far archway, as another knock on the ancient oak door made everyone jump. As it reverberated, the women looked around their company as if wondering who had been left on the doorstep.

Binks made a half-hearted move towards the door, but Lady Fellbridge got there first and when she opened it, her eyes lit up.

'Annie!' she exclaimed.

On the doorstep stood a short woman perhaps in her middle forties. She'd kept her brown hair long and rolled into a low bun and only a fringe slipped out onto her forehead from under her dinner-plate sized hat. Over her spring wool coat she wore her suffrage sash. Her mouth twisted into a sideways smile, but her face was overlaid with lines of strain and care. Without ceremony she took Lady Fellbridge's outstretched hands and crossed the threshold. 'Emma,' the newcomer said and gave her a kiss on the cheek.

Lady Fellbridge clasped the woman's hands to her chest and with glowing eyes said, 'I'm so glad you've come.'

After this tender moment, Lady Fellbridge stood back and said, 'Look everyone, Annie is here.'

As if on cue, greetings of varying intensities were offered – 'It's been too long,' 'How lovely,' and 'What a surprise.' A faint voice said, 'Are you strong enough?'

Keeping hold of the newest arrival with one hand, Lady Fellbridge said, 'Annie Harkin, this is Mabel Canning.'

'Mabel, what a delight.' Annie grasped Mabel's extended hand with her free one.

'It's lovely to meet you, Mrs Harkin.'

'Oh now,' she said, 'it's Annie. Aren't we all to be on first names?' She paused and looked over those gathered and called,

'Hello, Binks.' The butler nodded once, and Annie turned to the women gathered.

'Look at us all. Thirza, Lavinia and Pretoria – do you remember in 1909 our protest at the lecture given by the Men's League for Opposing Suffrage? And Pretoria – what was it Mr Churchill said about us?'

Pretoria threw out her chest and in a basso voice said, 'These women are marching backward not forward!'

The others laughed and someone said, 'He didn't know which way was up.'

'Collette,' Annie said, 'I remember canvassing with you in Biggleswade to get your husband elected for Labour. He always mentioned suffrage in his speeches.'

Collette, misty-eyed, murmured a reply.

Mabel marvelled at the work these women had done, and how Annie Harkin seemed to be involved in every action.

'And here is Ruby.' The others looked round as if they'd just noticed the young woman before Annie continued. 'This will be a momentous week for the campaign and I'm sure that after all we've been through, we'll be able to stay in the same room for more than five minutes without violence breaking out.' After a moment, there was a titter of laughter.

Lady Fellbridge laughed, too.

At that moment, a woman nearly as wide as the arch on the far side of the entrance hall came striding through it. She wore several layers of variously coloured wool jersey – making her look perhaps broader than she was – and what appeared to be house slippers on her feet.

'You there, Miss Canning!' she bellowed.

'Mrs Lotterby,' Mabel said. 'Is everything all right?'

'All right? How could it be when you have gone and put Dorothea Goose next to me?'

. . .

In the end, Annie Harkin had offered to switch rooms with Diane Lotterby. 'I don't mind Dorothea,' Annie had said and with a stern eye added, 'none of us should mind Dorothea.' That had quieted even the Greek chorus of Lavinia, Thirza and Pretoria. At last the women dispersed to their rooms, finding them with considerable help from Binks, Mabel and Emma.

Mabel herself retreated to her room in the priory gallery where she admired the view of the gardens before stretching out on the bed for a rest. She awoke a few hours later, dressed in a hurry and made her way down to the salon for drinks.

Her frock for the evening was a belted number with a scalloped tunic over the skirt and quite a reasonable neckline for company. Its colour, a sealing-wax red, seemed to suit her brown hair and give her skin a glow so that she hardly needed the face powder and touch of lipstick she applied.

The salon was a more intimate affair than the entrance hall. It had carved cornices and tapestry hangings, and glowed not only with electric lights, but also with candles and a blaze in the Inglenook fireplace along the centre wall.

It looked as if everyone had made it there before her, but the presence of others fell away when she spotted Park Winstone across the room. They hadn't seen each other in a week – he'd been in Paris, where his work with the diplomatic service often sent him. He'd asked Mabel to go with him, and not for the first time, but even though it was her sincere desire to be with Park in Paris – she often dreamed of it – it had never quite worked out. Mabel couldn't abandon one of her Useful Women assignments on what would have appeared to be a whim. The other times he'd asked, just as now with Emma's conference, she'd had other fish to fry.

Now there he stood, his gaze taking her in as she admired him. He wore a black dinner jacket, well-cut in that slimmer look men were wearing. The light reflected off his round-framed glasses, but she knew behind them his eyes held a twinkle. That errant curl that defied pomade fell onto his forehead.

'A drink, Miss Canning?'

The question from Binks at her elbow broke the moment, but she'd barely got out the words 'gin and Dubonnet, please,' when a quavering voice rose above the conversations in the room, drifting on its own current and carrying the scent of camphor.

'Lady Fellbridge?' and then, 'Emma?'

Heads turned towards the door where Dorothea Goose stood with one hand on the doorpost as a support. She had transferred her purple, green and white sash and now wore it over a navy velvet frock, belted with a long jacket and large pockets. Her face appeared ashen against the dark colour.

'Dorothea?' Lady Fellbridge went to her.

'It's Annie,' Dorothea said, breathless. 'I knocked and called out, but she didn't answer, and—'

'There now, Dorothea,' Emma said. 'She must've fallen asleep. She was exhausted after her journey and remember she's a bit deaf in one ear.'

'Shall I go and see about her?' Mabel asked as the other women took up their conversations again. 'Mr Winstone can come with me – I'll give him the cook's tour.'

Park downed his whisky, then he and Mabel walked out the door with Dorothea trailing behind.

'I feel I must accompany you,' she said, her eyes darting to Park and away.

'Of course. Dorothea, this is Park Winstone. Park, Dorothea Goose.'

'Yes, hello, Mr Winstone, pleased to meet you,' Dorothea said. She straightened her suffragette sash. 'Lead on.'

Up to the second floor of the west wing they went.

'The corridor is dark,' Mabel said.

'I switched off the lights as I left,' Dorothea said. 'Little economies help any household.'

It didn't help if you couldn't see. Mabel brushed her arm in a wide arc on the wall until her hand knocked into the box. She pushed the button and electric lights on the wall sprang to life.

Dorothea led them. 'I am at the end,' she said, her voice high and tinny. 'Annie is the end but one. Ruby Truelock and Collette's are just here.' Near the end of the corridor, she stopped. 'This is her room.'

Mabel rapped sharply on the door. 'Annie?' she called out.

'You see—' Dorothy started.

'Annie? It's Mabel Canning. Are you all right?' She took hold of the doorknob, gave a glance back at Park and Dorothea, and went in.

The room sat in darkness, but after a moment shapes and features became clear. A shaft of pale moonlight cut across the floor towards the bed and offered just enough illumination for Park to come behind Mabel and find the switch on the nearest lamp. They all blinked at its brightness.

Annie Harkin, wearing her navy stockingette day dress and suffragette sash, lay still on the bed atop the tousled counterpane. Her eyes and her mouth were open, her arms flung wide.

Dorothea hovered by the door, but Mabel and Park cautiously stepped closer to the bed. A small white feather had caught in Annie's hair. Mabel exchanged glances with Park, who felt the inside of Annie's wrist and nodded.

'She's quite cold,' he said.

Mabel recalled Annie's rather excited arrival and Emma's joy at seeing her old friend and felt a stab of loss for them both. She leaned closer to Annie's face and noticed the bloodshot eyes and a blue cast round her lips.

'Look,' Mabel said. 'What's that?'

Another small white feather, this one stuck at the corner of Annie's mouth.

'This,' Dorothea said with a cry, caught herself and took a deep breath. 'This is what I tried to tell you. Annie is dead.'

Mabel grabbed the pillow next to Annie's head and when she did, a few small white feathers drifted out of a rend in the fabric.

Not just dead, Mabel thought. Murdered.

TWO

From her station at the door, Dorothea said, 'Do you think she had a fit of some sort?'

Annie had been alive and laughing only a few hours ago. Strolling the gardens with an old friend, settling in for what was to be a week where ideas and plans could be exchanged. Now, she lay dead.

Dorothea crept closer and stood behind Mabel. 'She didn't have a strong constitution. Not since... It's just I couldn't tell Emma in front of everyone.'

'Look at this,' Park said.

He held out Annie's hand and Mabel saw another small white feather caught under one of the nails. Had she fought her assailant enough to rip a hole in the pillow?

Dorothea began tugging at the corner of the crumpled counterpane as if to straighten it.

'Come away,' Mabel said, laying a hand on the woman's arm.

Dorothea stuck her hands in her pockets and jerked her elbow away. The movement unbalanced her and she stumbled.

Mabel reached a hand out, but couldn't catch her and as Dorothea fell, she pulled her hands from her pockets, flinging her arms in the air and releasing a cloud of white like a flurry of snow – small white feathers that spun in a slow eddy as they drifted to the floor.

'No!' Dorothea cried, dropped to her knees and began snatching at them.

Mabel knelt, taking Dorothea's wrists. The woman wrenched herself free and swept the feathers trying to get them into a pile and giving a cry when Park moved towards her.

'Where is a telephone?' he asked Mabel, keeping an eye on Dorothea.

Mabel frowned as she thought. 'There's one in the steward's office and in the morning room and in the family's quarters. And perhaps another somewhere.'

'I must tell Emma,' Dorothea said, scrambling up and cramming feathers back into her pocket. 'I must explain.'

Mabel put a hand out to stop her. 'We'll go together,' she said.

'They were everywhere when I walked in,' Dorothea said, looking round the room as if seeing the feathers still suspended in the air. She looked down at her hand where one had stuck to her damp palm. She scratched it off and put it in her pocket. 'I couldn't leave it.'

'Come with me, Dorothea,' Mabel said. She turned to Park.

'I'll stay here,' he said.

Mabel nodded. 'I'll ask Ronald to telephone the police station in Rye – it's closest.'

'Police?' Dorothea said with alarm, pulling away. 'Not the police, please. Why?'

'It's routine,' Mabel said calmly, reaching out her hands.

Dorothea slapped Mabel's hands away and began pummelling her. 'You won't take me, you won't!'

In two strides, Park was there and grabbed Dorothea's arms.

'Aaahh!' the woman screamed and flailed, sending a few feathers up into the air. Then, she sank to the floor. 'No! No!'

Mabel dropped down beside her. 'It's all right, Dorothea. They aren't coming for you.'

Dorothea's shoulders slumped and Park released her gently. 'I'm sorry, Miss Goose,' he said. 'I didn't hurt you, did I?'

The woman, her face grey tinged with green, looked about her. 'I'm all right,' she whispered. 'It's only that...'

Awooooooooo.

The howl echoed down the corridor from a distance. Dorothea froze, but Mabel's heart sang. She leapt up, threw a grateful look at Park and peered down the passageway.

'Gladys?' she called.

Tick tick tick tick. The sound of nails on wood, and then a furry face appeared round the corner at the far end.

Woof!

Gladys came tearing down the corridor and might've knocked Mabel over in her excitement if Mabel hadn't knelt and braced herself.

'Hello, girl,' she said as Gladys covered her with kisses, 'however did you find us?' Gladys, a wriggling mass of toffee-coloured fur with a brown saddle marking, danced in a circle, made throaty noises and snorted before plopping down, her tongue lolling out the side of her mouth in a pant.

'Come with me,' Mabel said, and Gladys followed her into the room.

Dorothea had remained on her knees and gave the dog a wary look.

'Gladys,' Mabel said, 'this is Miss Dorothea Goose. Gladys is Mr Winstone's dog.'

Gladys sat in front of Dorothea and raised a paw.

'Oh.' Dorothea's breathing eased. She studied Gladys' paw

for a moment and then shook it. 'Hello, Gladys, I'm pleased to meet you.'

A feather that had settled on Dorothea's shoulder shook loose and drifted lazily until Gladys snapped it out of the air. Dorothea jumped, but then she laughed. 'Good dog.'

'Now, Dorothea, come with me,' Mabel said again. 'You and Gladys. We must tell Emma. We don't want her to hear what's happened from someone else, do we?'

That brought Dorothea back to the moment. She looked round. 'Emma? Oh poor Emma. We must go to her.'

Park offered a hand to Mabel and the other to Dorothea and helped them up.

'You aren't coming, Mr Winstone?' Dorothea asked.

'It's best he stay here,' Mabel said and left it at that.

But Dorothea's eyes widened and she glanced round the room. 'But, it isn't safe, is it? Not if Annie...'

'Mr Winstone will be all right. It's only that we don't want to leave Annie alone, do we?' Mabel asked in as reasonable a tone as she could. Anything to get the woman moving and leave Park to it.

As a former detective sergeant with the Metropolitan Police, Park knew how to contain a crime scene and how to look for clues. He – as well as Mabel – knew to touch nothing, so as not to compound the work for the fingerprint men. Mabel herself might not have as much experience as the police, but she'd learned a thing or two since she'd joined the Useful Women agency and created its Private Investigations division. She longed to stay with him to get a sense of what had happened and who might've killed Annie Harkin. It must have been someone inside Fellbridge Hall at that moment. One of the suffragettes? But when she'd arrived, everyone had greeted her as a much-beloved worker for the cause. Why would anyone want to kill Annie?

. . .

Dorothea went out the door first and Mabel turned to give Winstone a nod. When she walked out into the corridor and looked to her right, she didn't see Dorothea.

'Dorothea?'

'Here,' came the answer from Mabel's left.

Gladys followed the voice and Mabel followed the dog past the door to Dorothea's own room and to an alcove at the end of the corridor where she stood looking about her. Mabel took hold of her arm.

'We should go.'

With Mabel on one side, holding Dorothea's arm, and Gladys padding along on the other, the three of them made the journey back to the salon without incident. Dorothea had turned quiet and brave as if going to face a dreaded event. As they neared the salon, light conversation drifted towards them.

'Would you like to sit, Dorothea?' Mabel gestured to a chair just outside the door.

'No, Mabel, I don't need to sit,' Dorothea said, a firm set to her chin. 'I'm not an invalid.'

Gladys stayed, but Mabel and Dorothea stepped inside and stopped.

With relief, Mabel saw Ronald – Emma's second son and local vicar – talking with Diane Lotterby nearby.

'Would you excuse us?' Mabel asked Diane, putting her hand on Ronald's arm and drawing him away.

'Ronald,' she said quietly, 'go to your mother and bring her out.'

'Is it time for the buffet supper?' But then he noticed Mabel's face and stilled. Mabel looked across the room and saw Emma staring at her.

Death has a way of speaking without words and in that moment, Mabel understood that both Ronald and his mother knew Annie was dead.

Emma started for them, but as she did, Dorothea stepped out from behind Mabel. She held up a handful of feathers and shook her fist, proclaiming, 'Annie has been murdered!'

Screams erupted and a drinks tray crashed to the floor the same moment that Gladys raced into the salon, chasing and leaping in the air as the feathers, shaken loose from Dorothea's grasp, danced in the currents of panic.

'Annie!' Emma cried out from across the room. She held out her hand towards Mabel then dropped to the floor in a swoon. Ronald raced to her side.

Voices of disbelief and lament filled the room, as if the subject of death warranted as high a volume as possible. The Greek chorus wailed questions in unison to each other: 'What? How could this happen? Our Annie?'

'Binks!' Mabel shouted to the butler above the chaos as he knelt on one knee gathering up broken glass. 'Please take the ladies to the square dining room.'

The butler nodded and herded the women out the door. Gladys had retreated from the fray and now sat near the fireplace at the heels of Cora Portjoy and Skeff. Those two were a sight for sore eyes. Mabel gestured with an open hand that asked them to remain, as she went to Ronald, who had helped his mother to her feet.

'Do you need to lie down?' Mabel asked.

'No.' Emma's voice was little more than a whisper. 'No' – stronger now – 'I want to know what's happened.'

'We need a quiet place where you can sit down,' Mabel said. Emma stood straight and tall, but her pallor spoke of the shock she'd just received.

'I'll take her to the billiards room,' Ronald said.

Good – the closest place with chairs and, Mabel remembered, the fourth telephone.

Mabel stayed behind and went to her friends who had remained by the fireplace with Gladys.

Skeff was tall. She wore her usual trousers and long coat with a tam over the shortest bob cut possible. Cora, not tall, wore a belted wool silk dress of a kingfisher blue that complemented her apple cheeks. They were Mabel's neighbours at New River House in London and, although not Useful Women, were vital members of the London Ladies' Murder Club, which also included honorary members Park and Gladys.

'Annie Harkin was one of the delegates,' Mabel explained. She noticed that Dorothea had sidled back into the salon and went to her, saying in a strong but what she hoped sounded like a sympathetic tone, 'You should go with the others.'

'No, I don't want to go,' Dorothea said with a whinge in her voice. She cut her eyes at the other two as she brushed a few feathers off the mantel and put them back in her pocket.

'Dorothea Goose,' Mabel said, 'these are my friends Cora Portjoy and Skeff.'

'Miss Goose,' Cora said, coming forward, 'I'm so happy to meet you.'

'Suffragette, yes?' Skeff asked, nodding towards Dorothea's sash. She grasped Dorothea's hand and gave it a good shake. 'We owe you a great deal. Did Lady Fellbridge tell you I'm here from the *London Intelligencer*? Do you read the London papers?'

Dorothea's manners overtook her distress and she accepted the diversion. 'I did read *The Suffragette*, of course, and now I subscribe to *The Vote*. I read the *Kent and Sussex Courier* for local matters. Perhaps I have heard of the *Intelligencer*.'

'The *Intelligencer* is my uncle Pitt's newspaper – fair, even-handed journalism, that's what we're known for. I'd be delighted to tell you more about it.'

'Dorothea,' Mabel said, 'would you go with Skeff and Cora? And would you take Gladys with you?'

Reluctantly, Dorothea accompanied Skeff and Cora to the door, but then she stopped. 'You will be gentle with Emma, won't you, Mabel?' she asked. 'It will affect her dreadfully.'

'Yes, of course. And Dorothea, perhaps you shouldn't say any more to the others. Not yet.'

Dorothea put her chin in the air. 'I know how to keep quiet, Mabel.'

'Good. Now, let me point you in the right direction.'

Mabel escorted them partway down the corridor and watched them continue their way to the dining room before opening the door to the billiards room.

Ronald had switched on the wall lights, drawn three chairs together, poured out three brandies and now sat with his mother.

Emma's face remained as pale as her silver hair. 'Oh, Annie! I don't understand, Mabel. She looked well when she arrived – didn't she look well? Is what Dorothea said true?'

Mabel sat and took her drink. 'I'm afraid so,' she said.

'How... how did she die?'

'It looks as if she were smothered with a pillow.'

Emma sat in stunned silence. Mabel saw a look in her eyes as if she were retreating to a safer place. Then, she reached out a hand to her son.

'Darling, you were just a boy the last time Annie saw you.'

Ronald knelt beside his mother and clasped her hands. His dark hair, smooth and thick, contrasted with Emma's silver, but still they were so much alike, Mabel thought. They both had faces that couldn't disguise emotions.

'Not really a boy, Mother,' he said in a kind tone. 'I was twenty and down from Cambridge for my summer holidays. I remember you and Annie and Father having tea out on the lawn every afternoon and Quince running out with umbrellas one day when a storm came up.'

Emma smiled as tears filled her eyes. 'Yes, I remember

that. You didn't know her then, did you, Mabel? You truly were a girl. Wait now, was that the summer we met you and Edith?'

Mabel exchanged looks with Ronald at this mention of his wife – and Mabel's dearest friend – who had died just two years earlier.

'We were fifteen,' Mabel said, 'and Ronald found us trespassing in the rose garden.'

Ronald smiled, his eyes shining. 'Quite full of yourselves, you were.'

For a moment, Mabel lost herself in those memories. She and Edith had grown up in Peasmarsh, the village on the edge of the estate. Returning to work at Fellbridge Hall for a week, with her papa and Mrs Chandekar so near, was rather like a homecoming.

'Who did this to Annie?' Emma asked in a hard tone.

'We'll need to ring the police,' Ronald said. 'And Doctor Finlay.'

'I do not need—' his mother began.

He put up a hand. 'Not only for you, but what about Miss Goose? And any of the others who might take the news badly.'

Emma sighed. 'Yes, all right.'

Ronald crossed the room to a table in half darkness. He picked up the telephone and depressed the hook a couple of times and when the exchange answered, he identified himself and made the request which would soon be all over the parish – police were needed at Fellbridge Hall.

'No?' Ronald said. 'All right, then.' He tapped the hook again and asked the exchange for the doctor and after relaying the news, rang off.

Ronald returned and told them, 'There are only two constables available locally. I'm afraid Sergeant Jesson is ill and can't come out.'

'But shouldn't there be an enquiry?' Emma asked.

'I'm sure there will be, but' – Ronald lifted his eyebrows at Mabel – 'we'll need to let the police sort that out, won't we?'

Not actually a question, Mabel knew – more of a caution. Ronald knew about her private investigations work in London. He should also know better than to think she would let this be. She gave him a benign smile and said, 'Ronald, Park stayed in Annie's room. Would you go up and tell him.'

'Yes, of course,' Ronald said. 'Mother, you should rest.'

Emma had aged beyond her years in the span of only a few minutes, but she rallied herself against his suggestion of coddling.

'Not yet, Ronald. Not when there's work to be done,' she said.

Ronald waited a moment, then, with a nod, he left.

'Who?' Emma asked, when the door had closed. 'Who would do such a thing?'

'Could it be one of the others?' Mabel asked. 'Annie mentioned something about violence.'

'Old resentments,' Emma said bitterly. 'We want the same thing – votes for all, good education for every child girl or boy, a fair chance for everyone. But we each of us hold fast to our own belief of how this should be accomplished. I thought enough time had gone by and... I thought that choosing a leader from among these few...' She clutched at her chest. 'Did I do this to her by calling everyone here? Is this my fault?'

Mabel grabbed Emma's hand and held tight. 'It is not your fault.'

'What do we do now?' Emma asked. 'We can't just sit and be idle until the local constable arrives? Now what?'

They fell quiet, as Mabel carried on a silent discussion with herself. The enquiry should not wait until the next day or whenever the local sergeant could rise from his sick bed or police could be sent from elsewhere. Details – clues – needed to be gathered while they were fresh for the picking otherwise memories fade into nothing or become altered in the mind if left for too long. Action needed to be taken.

Mabel had leapt to her feet before she realised what she was doing.

'I'll conduct the first round of interviews this evening,' she said. 'I'll speak to each of the women. The enquiry begins now.'

THREE

Park had walked into the billiards room as she spoke. She looked across the room at him. Light reflected off his glasses, but that didn't hide the gleam in his eyes.

Emma clapped her hands together. 'Good, Mabel,' she said. 'You're just the one to lead the enquiry.'

At once, Mabel began to retreat from her proclamation. 'Perhaps not lead, but I could get some general information in order. After all, I have the register with everyone's details.'

'Of course you should take the reins,' Park said. 'Who better?'

Later, Mabel would throw her arms round him and express her gratitude for his support. But now—

'Right, well,' she said. 'I'll need someone to sit in with me, but I don't think it should be you, Emma. Do you mind?'

'Not at all,' Emma said. 'They'll speak more freely if they don't have me hovering.'

Mabel next glanced at Park, who shook his head as she had expected. But then, the solution dawned on Mabel, and she saw Park's face light up. They both spoke at once.

'Skeff!'

That settled, Mabel could see her way forward. 'Shall we ask them to come in here to the billiards room?'

'No, use the steward's office,' Emma said. 'It's down the corridor a bit further.'

'Emma, shall we go to the square dining room and you can say a word or two. After that, why don't you have Binks take a tray to your room?'

Emma stood. She'd regained her colour although the strain showed in the hollow look round her eyes.

'I won't desert you quite that soon. I'll go to the dining room, but first I want to see Annie.' Emma held up her hand to stop the protests before they began. 'I won't disturb anything, but I want to see her.'

'I'll come with you,' Mabel said. She turned to Park. 'There are only two constables available locally. They're on their way.'

'Why don't I ring the Met?' Park asked. 'To apprise them of the situation?'

'Yes, do.'

By the Metropolitan Police – Scotland Yard – Park meant Tolly. Detective Inspector Tollerton, that is.

'But that doesn't mean you shouldn't carry on,' Park said. 'There's no point in waiting around for hours. You know what to do.'

His confidence in her settled the butterflies that were flapping round in her tummy. Until this moment, she'd come into murder enquiries in a rather sideways fashion. Now, she would take the helm.

Mabel gave Park's hand a squeeze, then left him to the telephone while she accompanied Emma to Annie's room. After giving Emma time to say goodbye to her friend, Ronald locked the door behind them and they returned to meet Park in the corridor, where the four of them huddled, speaking quietly even though no one else was about.

'Has the doctor arrived yet?' Ronald asked.

'I don't know what good he'll do,' Emma muttered.

Mabel grinned at her. 'You sound like Papa, who thinks no one can measure up to Doctor Ebbers.'

Emma smiled just a bit. 'I must move with the times. All right, Doctor Finlay.'

'He'll have to sign the death certificate,' Mabel said. 'And make arrangements for Annie's body to be taken away.'

'Oh,' Emma said, flagging for a brief moment before regaining her composure.

'I'll stay here tonight,' Ronald said, 'and leave early for morning prayers. What about you, Mr Winstone?'

'I have a room at the pub,' he explained.

Emma shook a finger at Park. 'You should be here,' she said.

Mabel agreed, but her papa might not have done so and it had been easier to tell him Park wouldn't be sleeping at the Hall when he visited. She may be thirty-two years old to the world, but to her papa she remained a girl.

Down the corridor they went, turning a corner one way and the next corner the other way in a zigzag fashion until they reached the small square dining room with one large round table that could still seat twenty at a pinch.

They entered to a heavy silence as if no one had spoken in ages. Along one wall and under the windows a long table had been laid with food for the buffet supper. On the opposite wall, a few chairs had been placed round the fire where Dorothea sat with Skeff and Cora. On the other side of them, Ruby Truelock stood in the shadows. Gladys, stretched out in front of the blaze, lifted her head. The others sat round the table and Diane Lotterby had an elbow propped up on it and her chin resting in her hand.

The butler stood at the end of the buffet as if keeping the food in its place. Mabel had always thought Binks had a timelessness about him, although she knew him to be about her age – in his early thirties. He looked much the same as he had when he'd arrived ten years earlier to be trained up to take over the post of butler from old Quince. Binks' dark hair remained neatly combed, his thick-lensed glasses, lightly tinted blue, pushed up on the bridge of his nose, his collar straight and his jacket buttoned – and yet still he carried about him the slight air of dishevelment.

Collette went to Emma. 'The best way to—' she began, but Emma cut her off.

'Not now, Collette. Do sit down.' Emma straightened herself and addressed the room in a clear and confident voice.

'I'm sure you all realise that because of this dreadful event, the police have been called.'

Dorothea let out a small yelp, and round the room the others glanced among themselves.

'Until then, I have asked Mabel to speak to each of you, only to ask a few questions, so that the police will be that much further along when they do arrive.'

'But you can't think it was one of us?' Thirza asked, her eyes wide. Lavinia and Pretoria repeated the question in a murmur.

'Why would any of us want Annie dead?' Collette asked.

This time, the women's glances shot round the room, landing everywhere but on each other.

'No one is being accused of anything,' Mabel said. 'But everyone's movements must be accounted for so that the enquiry can proceed. What you can recall about the afternoon will go far to finding justice for Annie.'

That last phrase seemed to strike a note among these campaigners, and round the room heads nodded.

'Until you are called, there's nothing else to do but wait,' Emma said, 'so please do let's have our meal.' No one moved. 'Come now – I'll begin.'

. . .

Mabel moved off to stand near the fireplace while Binks uncovered the dishes and a queue formed at the buffet.

Dorothea rose, tugged on her sash, but didn't move until Ruby came out of the shadows and said, 'I'm awfully hungry, Miss Goose, aren't you? Come, let's go.'

Ruby led Dorothea off, then Mabel turned to Skeff and Cora.

'You've your own enquiry now,' Skeff said quietly. 'Well done.'

'*We* have an enquiry,' Mabel corrected her. 'And it's lucky that all members of the London Ladies' Murder Club are here.' When Gladys rose from the hearth rug and shook herself, Mabel gave her a scratch. 'That includes you.'

'What do you want us to do?' Cora asked.

'Right, well,' Mabel said. 'Park is ringing Tolly at Scotland Yard, because they've only a couple of constables available locally. But we don't know when Tolly will be able to get here, so that's why I'm conducting the initial interviews. Skeff, I want you to sit in on them. We'll make it clear you are not representing the press, but helping with the enquiry.'

'Right.'

'And Cora – you have such a kind and generous way about you,' Mabel said.

Cora's apple cheeks warmed at this. Skeff winked at her and said, 'That you do.'

'I don't ask you to be devious,' Mabel said, 'only... listen.'

Cora worked at Milady's, a milliner's on the King's Road, and could work wonders with an old brimmed hat, a length of silk ribbon and a needlefelt robin and could use a hat-fitting as an opportunity for a chat. Her open and accepting nature made it easy for people to talk with her.

'I will do,' Cora said.

'Good, good,' Mabel said, sorting out her next move. 'You two go on and eat. We've an evening before us and you'll need your strength.'

'And you,' Skeff said. 'Take your own advice. Come along now.'

'Just a bite,' she said, 'and then I'll get to it.' Mabel nodded Park and Ronald up to the queue with her.

At the round table, Emma sat with her plate in front of her and hands in her lap as the other women spoke a word or laid a hand on her shoulder when they passed. She looked brave and world-weary, fragile yet strong.

'Did you speak to Tolly?' she asked Park.

'I did. He's sorting it, but I'd say it could be nine or ten o'clock before he arrives, so you've plenty of time to begin.'

Mabel looked down at the buffet table and wondered if cauliflower cheese could subdue her nerves. Then, she noticed Park scrutinising the food. The hot dishes sat over steaming bain-maries – eggs croquettes, lentil rissoles, asparagus and celery covered in fragrant sauces – and dressed salads of broad beans, pulses and spring lettuce from the glasshouses on the estate. Crackers, cheese, apple tarts rounded out the offerings.

'Looking for the joint of beef?' Mabel asked. 'You won't find it here – most of these women are vegetarian.'

'All right by me,' Park said, 'but Gladys will be disappointed.' They looked back at the dog who watched them carefully from the fire.

'You left her in the kitchen when you arrived?' Mabel asked. 'Then I'm sure Deenie found something for her.' But in case, she slipped an apple in her pocket to give Gladys later.

Mabel and Park filled their plates and sat. A chair next to Emma remained empty, as if already a memorial to Annie. There was little talk. Dorothea sat staring at her plate and Emma picked up her knife and fork and set them down several times before even taking a bite.

Mabel took only a few bites before she found herself unable to go on. She wanted to get started. She needed to fetch the register from her room. Who should she question first – did it matter?

Binks had poured out a hearty claret and when he noticed it was going down well, he had gone off to refill the carafe. When he returned it was with more wine and two police constables.

'Police, my lady,' the butler said and went about refilling glasses.

The uniformed men came just inside the dining room and then stopped. They were young and gangly and stood against the wall and didn't speak, as if waiting for their sergeant to begin the proceedings.

Mabel rose and went to them. 'Good evening, I'm Mabel Canning.'

They bobbed their heads. ''Evening, ma'am,' they mumbled.

'And you are?' she asked.

'Ned, ma'am,' said one and coughed.

'I'm Ted,' the other added.

Mabel thought they looked very much alike and, in hopes of putting them at their ease, she asked, 'Are you brothers?'

The pair turned to each other, aghast.

'No, ma'am.'

'Not that we know of, ma'am.'

'Well, shall we call you PC Ned and PC Ted or do you have second names?'

'I'm Ted Scott, ma'am.'

'Ned Cowley, ma'am.'

'Ned Cowley?' Mabel asked, giving the PC a closer look.

Ned couldn't've turned more purple if he were a grape.

'Well, Constables,' Mabel said, 'as your sergeant is under the weather—'

'Sick as a dog, he is, ma'am,' Ted blurted out. He glanced round the room. 'Is his lordship here?'

Emma stood. 'I am Lady Fellbridge, Constable.'

It was Ted's turn to blush. 'Oh, beg pardon, my lady,' he said.

'Miss Canning is my secretary and will see to all necessary arrangements.'

'Thank you, Emma,' Mabel said and turned to the constables. 'A detective will be arriving later this evening from London, but until then, Mr Winstone will look after you.'

In other words, do nothing until Scotland Yard arrives.

As Park went over to the PCs and Emma returned to her meal, Mabel abandoned the idea of eating and went to retrieve the register from her room. Walking across the entrance hall on her return, she heard the sound of a car on the drive and a spray of chippings peppered the panes of the nearest window. Before she could reach the door, the electric bell was pulled followed by the clang of the iron knocker. She opened the door to a man dressed in tweeds and with a deerstalker hat under his arm. He had black hair and a neatly combed black moustache and looked to be nearly fifty. A short scar divided one of his eyebrows. In his hand was a fine leather Gladstone bag, and on his face, a perplexed look.

'Hello,' Mabel said. 'Are you Doctor Finlay?'

He put his hand out. 'I am, yes. Gordon Finlay.'

'Please come in. I'm Mabel Canning.'

Mabel had heard of Dr Finlay, of course, but had not met him. He'd taken over the practice from old Dr Ebbers – who was much missed by her papa – only the summer before.

'Canning, Canning,' Finlay said as he stepped into the entrance hall. 'You aren't Reg Canning's daughter, are you?'

'Yes, I am,' Mabel said.

'Well, now then, pleased to meet you.' He smiled and his right eye drew up in a wink.

'Thank you for coming out.'

The phrase seemed to remind them both of the reason for

his call.

'Yes, dreadful news,' he said. 'Reverend Herringay said one of the ladies visiting for the week has died.'

'Annie Harkin,' Mabel said.

'No, not Mrs Harkin?' Finlay's brow drew up. 'She seemed well enough this afternoon.'

'This afternoon?' Mabel asked. 'Were you here?'

'Yes, Lady Fellbridge called me out,' Finlay said. 'She was worried about her friend's stamina, I believe, but Mrs Harkin assured me she was taking her medication and felt well. Did her heart give out, was that it?'

'No,' Mabel said. 'Well, yes, I suppose. That'll be up to you to say, won't it? I can tell you she died under suspicious circumstances. Police are on their way.'

Finlay narrowed his eyes as if trying to read meaning into Mabel's words, which sounded inadequate even in her own ears, but she didn't want to prejudice the doctor's findings.

The doctor looked around him. 'And where did this happen?'

'She was in her room,' Mabel said.

At that moment, Park and Ronald came into the entrance hall. The vast entrance at Fellbridge Hall was rather like Paddington station – the central place to cross when going from one wing to another.

Introductions were made and Finlay looked at Ronald and said, 'Well, I'd best get to it, hadn't I? I've been told you rang for the police.'

'I rang them,' Park said. 'With Reverend Herringay's permission.'

'Are you police, sir?' the doctor asked Park.

'Not any longer,' Park said.

It was a useful phrase and one that Mabel had heard before. Vestiges of the Metropolitan Police hung about Park although he'd parted ways with the Met before the war. *Not any longer* gave the impression that the relationship continued on some level.

'Well then, Mr Winstone,' the doctor said, 'would you accompany me in case I have any questions.'

'We both will,' Mabel said.

She didn't wait for a reply but held out her hand to Ronald who passed her the key. Mabel walked off, casting a glance over her shoulder to see the doctor following her and Park bringing up the rear. Ronald remained.

'Are you the district's police surgeon?' Park asked as they climbed the stairs.

'I am that,' Finlay said. 'Although, there's little call for me to fulfil that role – apart from the occasional older resident or accident.'

On the first-floor landing they continued up to the second and to Annie's room. Inside, Park and Mabel watched as the doctor set down his bag and looked about the room, eyeing the counterpane in disarray and the pillow with the hole and the few feathers that Dorothea hadn't had a chance to tidy up. Then, the doctor carried out a cursory examination.

'All the signs of asphyxiation, I'm afraid,' he said at last. 'You see the bloodshot eyes and bluish tinge.' He noted that rigor mortis had set in and estimated the time of death at 'a few hours ago'.

It had been two hours since Dorothea had discovered Annie, and her body had been cold then, so that would put her murder sometime in the afternoon while the delegates had been strolling about the Hall and grounds. Everyone had had opportunity.

Finlay *tsked*. 'What sort of world do we live in that someone could do this? She was a friendly sort, and I could see that Lady Fellbridge was quite fond of her.' He snapped his bag closed. 'I'll write up the death certificate and ring for the mortuary wagon for first thing in the morning.'

'Scotland Yard is sending a detective inspector,' Park said.

Finlay looked up and lifted his brows. 'I see. Well then, we'll keep her and await further instructions.'

'Will you carry out the post-mortem examination, Doctor?' Mabel asked.

'I would do, Miss Canning, but I daresay this detective from the Yard will want his own man on it.'

Finished, they filed out and Mabel locked the door.

On the way downstairs, Finlay asked, 'Are you employed here at Fellbridge Hall, Miss Canning? It's only that I remember your father's housekeeper spoke of you living in London.'

'I'm with the Useful Women agency and Lady Fellbridge engaged me to act as her private secretary for the week.'

'And you, Mr Winstone – perhaps you're a friend of his lordship's?'

'I'm a friend of Miss Canning's,' Park said.

'Where was your practice before you moved here, Doctor?' Mabel asked.

'The Borders, Miss Canning,' Dr Finlay replied and with a slight smile added, 'a fierce place as you can imagine.'

She had imagined a slight Scottish accent, and she'd been right, although she'd never thought of the Borders as fierce – not these days. The doctor must have a romantic streak to him. 'How are you finding life in the south?'

'I'm settling in,' Dr Finlay said. 'And every day I thank Doctor Ebbers for retiring. I've been working all my life to have such a fine post.'

They had reached the ground floor and were crossing the entrance hall when Ruby Truelock came running towards them.

'Please come quickly!' she gasped, pulling to a halt. 'It's Miss Goose – she's collapsed.'

FOUR

Ruby spun round and dashed back the way she had come.

'They're in the square dining room,' Mabel called over her shoulder, rushing after Ruby.

Ruby flung open the door with Mabel just behind. Dorothea was sitting on the floor with her back up against a small sofa near the fire, gasping for breath. Ronald knelt beside her and Gladys sat just in front of her with a paw on Dorothea's leg.

'Miss Goose,' Ruby said, wringing her hands, 'are you all right?'

'Dorothea,' Dorothea rasped. 'You're to call me Dorothea.'

'Let's get you up,' Emma said.

Skeff and Cora hurried over and each put a hand under one of Dorothea's arms, pulling her up onto the sofa. Gladys shook herself and trotted over to sit beside Park.

The rest of the women had kept to the other side of the round table. None of them looked frightened or even too surprised.

'Chamomile tea is what you need,' Collette said, giving her instructions from a distance.

The doctor approached Dorothea quietly, set his bag on the floor and knelt in front of her.

'This is Doctor Finlay,' Mabel explained. She approached and sat on the footstool in Dorothea's line of sight. 'Dorothea?'

'Miss Goose?' the doctor said, taking Dorothea's wrist and checking her pulse. 'Can you tell me what's wrong?'

'Nothing,' Dorothea said in a strained whisper. 'Nothing. I couldn't breathe and needed air. I... I had a turn.'

'Well, we all have a turn now and then, don't we?' he asked as if discussing a bad run of luck at whist. He held out his hand. 'Here now, squeeze my hand, will you? Really squeeze. Come on, you can do better than that. Ow!' he said, and Dorothea gave a breathless laugh.

'Never underestimate Dorothea Goose, Doctor,' she managed to say. Her breathing eased and she glanced over her shoulder at the others. 'I'm fine now.'

The doctor stood and brushed off his trouser knees.

'Is that it?' Lavinia asked. 'Doesn't she need something to calm her?'

Dr Finlay looked down at Dorothea. 'Do you feel the need of a draught, Miss Goose?'

'Certainly not,' she replied stiffly, then softened. 'Thank you, Doctor. You have a good manner about you.'

The doctor smiled and his right eye winked. 'Thank you, Miss Goose. It is, after all, my job. But to be certain, let me write you a prescription for something to calm you if you feel the need.'

He sat across from Dorothea and opened his bag.

Mabel had an eye for leather satchels, having bought a small, second-hand one of her own when she had taken on the Private Investigations division of Useful Women. She couldn't help but admire the doctor's – a large Gladstone variety that opened at the top. Its well-conditioned leather sported brass protectors at the corners and a brass plate under the handle with the initials G F.

'That's a fine bag you have,' she said.

'Thank you,' Finlay said and smiled. 'My father gave it to me when I qualified – donkey's years ago that was now, but I've always looked after it.'

Moving the stethoscope to the side, he reached into the pocket for his prescription book and took the fountain pen from his breast pocket.

'It's quite mild,' the doctor told Dorothea. 'You're not to worry about taking it.'

Mabel glanced over his shoulder as he wrote in an irregular, loopy style. Although he didn't write quickly, the words appeared to be in a hurry, dancing up and down in the air above the line. Mabel heard strains of 'Flight of the Bumblebee'. She recalled that Edith had come across a four-hand piano arrangement of the piece and they had done their best to play it, but ended up doubled over in laughter with fingers tied in knots.

Finlay finished writing out the prescription with a flourish. He tore out the paper and handed it over to the patient.

'Did something disturb you, Dorothea?' Mabel asked.

'There was talk of the suffragette campaign before the war,' Ruby said.

'There was talk of going to prison,' Skeff said.

'That was a long time ago, Dorothea,' Thirza called from across the room.

'We didn't mean police were taking anyone off now,' Pretoria added.

Dorothea fingered her suffragette sash and didn't answer.

'Mabel,' Lavinia said. 'Are we to stay here in the drawing room all night?'

It wasn't even nine o'clock, but uncertainty can do odd things to time.

'Yes, when will you begin your interrogation?' Diane asked.

Mabel heard a short gasp from Dorothea.

'A chat,' Mabel said. 'That's all I need. Give me a moment to get myself sorted and we'll begin.'

'Binks,' Emma said. 'Perhaps you'll bring coffee up.'

The butler had been standing against the wall near the door. He nodded and left as the women settled themselves back around the table. Mabel led the doctor out and Skeff, Park and Ronald followed.

The doctor looked at the closed door to the dining room. 'Does Miss Goose suffer from nerves?'

She certainly seemed to, but Mabel was loath to offer a diagnosis. 'Annie's death has affected her.'

'They were suffragettes together?' At Mabel's curious look, he added, 'It's only that I noticed they are the only two who wear the sashes.'

Mabel glanced back at the door, too. 'Yes, they were.'

'Well, that's me away,' the doctor said. 'Please do let the fellow from Scotland Yard know I am at his disposal. I will ring about the arrangements for the body.'

Ronald saw the doctor out as Mabel, Park and Skeff went to the steward's office.

The office, cold as if unoccupied for a good while, had not enough chairs and an abundance of walking sticks, books, maps and shelves holding decades' worth of account ledgers. The walls were covered with various drawings and photographs of places around the estate.

Mabel looked at the desk. Should she sit there as if she were Miss Kerr reigning over Useful Women from her desk on Dover Street or Detective Inspector Tollerton questioning suspects in a murder enquiry? They each had a rather formidable nature.

Mabel banished the niggling worm of fear that she wasn't worthy, walked round the desk and put her register down. 'There,' she said as if she'd climbed Mont Blanc.

'It would be good to check all the entrances to the Hall,' Park said. 'In case.'

In case someone had sneaked in, murdered Annie and sneaked out again.

At that moment, Ronald returned.

'Would you and Park go round to the windows and doors to see if anything looks amiss?' Mabel said. 'You can give Park one of your maps.'

At that, Ronald reddened. 'No.'

'Oh, go on,' Mabel chided. 'It'll give him a sense of the place.'

Mabel had never heard of an actual map of Fellbridge Hall existing – at least, not a proper one. The map that had been copied and recopied over the years the family enjoyed passing around as much for a joke as anything else. It was the map Ronald had drawn for a school project when he had been about twelve years old. A true and accurate map as far as it went, but when the boy had grown tired of details, he had drawn clouds at the edges as they did in ancient times along with the warning *Here be dragons*.

Reluctantly, Ronald rummaged through a drawer, found what he sought and the two men set off.

Mabel looked at Skeff. 'Let's begin.'

In the dining room, the women sat with coffee among the remainders of the meal. As arranged, the cooks had left for the evening long ago and wouldn't clean up until the morning. Little had anyone known that the rest of the evening would be spent among dishes of congealed cauliflower cheese.

'Thank you for staying together,' Mabel said, 'and for sitting through this preliminary interview.' Mabel liked the sound of that – clean, efficient. 'Who would like to go first? Dorothea, how about you?'

Out the corner of her eye, Mabel had seen movement at the table, as if someone had been about to volunteer, but when she glanced over, the trio sat unmoving and Diane Lotterby looked down, worrying a cuticle.

Dorothea stood with dignity. 'Yes, I'm ready.'

'I arrived and you took my details and then I went to my assigned room,' Dorothea said. She sat across the desk from Mabel, and Skeff had set a chair to the side. She had her notebook out and Mabel had her register open. 'Diane Lotterby opened the door of the next room and we... exchanged greetings and she left. Not long after, Annie Harkin came up to the west wing to say she was taking Diane's room.'

'Were you surprised at that?' Mabel asked.

'Not surprised at Diane's reaction – I've grown accustomed to how she and the others are towards me and I have no hard feelings about it. I wasn't surprised about Annie, either. She's always been the generous sort.'

Already Mabel had seen the other women keep Dorothea at arm's length.

'Well,' Dorothea continued, 'bags came and went. It was nearly one o'clock when I went out to the gardens – I needed air. I dislike being indoors for too long at a time.'

Dorothea paused to make sure they'd got that down before she continued.

'As I said, I needed air,' she said, 'and knocked on Annie's door to ask if she'd like a stroll, but she didn't answer. When I went out, I saw Annie and Emma together. I talked with the gardener, Campsie, and then he and I went off to the orchard.

When I got back to my room, Binks was coming out after leaving a tea tray, so I went in for a cup.' She picked at her skirt then clutched her hands. 'I should've checked on Annie then, but I didn't.'

'Why would you feel as if you needed to check on Annie?' Mabel asked.

Dorothea's entire body seemed to shrug. 'Often it's good to have someone near when memories are stirred. Although, other times it isn't.'

'Comrades together,' Skeff said, and Dorothea nodded.

'Did you see Binks leave a tray for Annie?' Mabel asked.

'I asked, but he said he'd left Annie's earlier.'

'And after that?'

'I rested... well, I confess I slept, and while I slept...' Her eyes became glassy and she cocked her head as if listening.

'Dorothea?' Mabel asked.

Dorothea flinched. 'Yes? Oh, yes. I had a dream, which I can no longer recall – and that's a good thing, isn't it, because listening to another person's dream is such a bore. And then, I dressed and before I went down to the salon, I knocked on Annie's door again. Something seemed odd, but I can't quite say what. So I went in and... and there were feathers everywhere,' she finished in a whisper.

The image rose in Mabel's mind.

Dorothea's breathing came quicker again. 'I... I went to Annie and saw she wasn't... that her eyes were open and... and it worried me that her room was in such disarray. I thought if I could just tidy up a bit, then I would ask for assistance.'

'You went directly to the salon?' Mabel asked.

'I went to tell Emma. It's terribly sad. They hadn't seen each other in so long.' She scrabbled round in her pocket and drew out a few more feathers. 'Do you want these? It's what police do, isn't it, collect evidence?'

If they wanted feathers they could collect them from the

salon or Annie's room, but regardless, Mabel searched desk drawers and came up with an empty envelope, and Skeff relieved Dorothea of her burden.

'Lavinia, Pretoria and I walked out to the meadow,' Thirza Bass said, perching on the edge of the chair. 'The daffodils are still lovely even this late and we noticed a few purple orchids. Did anyone see Miss Truelock in the garden?'

'Were you friends with Annie?' Mabel asked.

'Friends?' Thirza said, smoothing out her skirt. 'Acquaintances, certainly. Cohorts in the fight to...' Her eyes darted to Skeff with her notebook. 'Well, really who could say anything disparaging of Annie? Certainly not I.'

'Thirza and I walked through the walled garden and out and away with Pretoria,' Lavinia said when her turn came. 'Is that what you want to know about?'

'What time was this?' Mabel asked.

'Broad daylight, of course. Mid-afternoon. Do you need more than that?'

'Not for the moment,' Mabel said. 'What did you think of Annie?'

'She was... well, one of our heroines, of course she was,' Lavinia said.

Skeff threw Mabel a look as if waiting for the rest of it.

'Although,' Lavinia said, 'I'm sure anyone would tell you that she did act rather the martyr about it.'

'I stayed out in the garden for what seemed like ages with Thirza and Lavinia,' Pretoria said, patting the pin-curls at either ear. 'I longed to explore the bluebell wood that we can see from the terrace, but Thirza and Lavinia had gone on ahead of me.'

'Left behind, were you?'

'Well, it's only that I didn't want to go alone,' Pretoria said peevishly. 'Also, I feel the cold more than most people and so I turned back, found Binks and followed him to my room. I'm not sure I could've found the east wing again on my own.'

'Had you known Annie long?' Mabel asked.

'For ever so long,' Pretoria replied, adjusting a shawl she'd thrown over her shoulders. 'We all of us fought for the vote. I, in particular, led many a protest walk through the city and have worked tirelessly all these years. We any one of us could be a leader, but some of us prefer not to go on and on about our accomplishments.'

'I was having a word with the gardener – this Campsie – about his pruning technique,' Collette said. 'Dorothea was hovering and so I left Campsie to her and went to look at the pots of fuchsia on the terrace.'

'Collette, I'm sure you can give me a circumspect opinion,' Mabel said. 'What did you think of Annie?'

'She was a saint,' Collette replied and pointedly looked at both Skeff and Mabel's notebooks until they both had written the word down. 'A saint. And saints do not compromise, do they? Even when it seems the right thing to do?'

'I walked out the French windows from the square dining room,' Ruby Truelock said. 'It was one o'clock by then. I went into the garden with Thirza and Lavinia, but I don't believe they noticed. They walked off with Pretoria and I stayed behind. The carmine-red tulips are beautiful – tulips were one of my mother's favourite flowers and I want to ask Lady Fellbridge which this one is so that I could plant some in her honour. I came inside at four o'clock. My room is next to Collette's at the opposite end of the west wing from Dorothea and Annie. There was no one about.'

Skeff raised an eyebrow and nodded towards Ruby as if giving her due for a clear and concise report.

'Did you know Annie?' Mabel asked. She remembered Annie acknowledging Ruby's presence.

'I hadn't met her before today,' Ruby replied, 'and we barely exchanged a word, but my mother always said that Annie Harkin held firm.'

'Thank you, Ruby,' Mabel said.

Ruby stood, but hesitated. 'Mabel, later, may I have a word?'

Wasn't that what they'd just had? 'Yes, of course.'

'It's just as well you've saved me for last,' Diane Lotterby boomed when Mabel returned Ruby to the dining room. 'After all, everyone knows that I was the intended victim. Someone is unhappy about my interest in leading us forward.'

'You what?' Pretoria asked. 'Are you calling attention to yourself, Diane? You aren't the only one who could be singled out for her commitment.'

Emma stood. 'Diane, please – you can't accuse an entire roomful of people of murder.'

'Mrs Lotterby,' Mabel said, 'come with me.'

A great deal of hot air had gone out of Diane as, on the way to the steward's office, she started talking.

'I wasn't accusing anyone,' she said, her voice, although low in volume, still gave the impression of booming. 'In truth, I don't know anything about this business, although I'm naturally willing to help out in any way I can. I only meant that squabbles can—'

She cut herself off when Mabel opened the door and Skeff rose.

'Dreadful business, really,' Diane said.

'Please sit down,' Mabel said.

Diane sat and continued. 'If you want to know what I did this afternoon here it is: I put my nose out in the garden but didn't stay. I went back to my room to wait for tea and fell sound asleep.'

'In your new room in the priory gallery,' Mabel reminded her.

Diane's face darkened. 'You see – you believe it's possible, too. Annie was to be in the priory gallery room, and I was to be next to Dorothea. Oh dear me.'

'You've known Dorothea a long time, haven't you?' Mabel asked.

'Oh, I know what you're getting at. Yes, I admit that Dorothea and I had a few angry words years and years ago. I suppose it's possible I upset her when I asked to move, but you see she flies into these rages and wanders about... well, I suppose she doesn't know what she's doing.'

'Are you accusing Dorothea of murdering Annie, thinking it was you?' Mabel asked.

Diane's face went beetroot. 'Certainly not,' she said, but there was a note of relief in her tone, as if happy she had planted that seed. 'It's only that I would challenge anyone to sleep in a room next to Dorothea. It wouldn't be a quiet night.'

'What did you think of Annie?' Mabel asked.

'We were suffragettes together.'

'Did you stay a suffragette?' Skeff asked.

'I gave up the violence. I saw a better way,' Diane said and when Mabel and Skeff were silent, she continued. 'Annie... you see, although Dorothea – for all her faults – has a firm inner belief, she would never boast about what's she done. Annie, on the other hand, wore her accomplishments as a badge.'

Diane returned to the dining room under her own steam.

'Interesting,' Skeff said.

'Yes,' Mabel said, tapping her pencil on the open page of the register, now enquiry notebook. 'Emma had told me they would be choosing a leader for this stage of the campaign from among those attending the conference. It seemed to me when they all arrived that Annie was the mostly like candidate, but now we've learned that not all the women agreed.'

FIVE

Mabel collected the women from the square dining room and led them to the entrance hall with Gladys at her side. Ned and Ted, sitting in chairs against the wall near the door, popped up and tugged on their jackets. Mabel gave them a nod, but Gladys went over and greeted them, then continued to the far archway as if on business of her own.

'Isn't this where we started today?' Lavinia asked. 'I thought you were taking us to our rooms. I've been lost since we arrived.'

Gladys will know her way round quicker than this lot, Mabel thought.

'It isn't difficult navigating the Hall,' she said to the group, 'once you know that the three wings – east, west and priory gallery – are not connected to each other except here on the ground floor. So you will always walk through the entrance hall to get to where you're going.'

'Nothing is connected?' Collette asked. 'All that needs be done about that is to knock—'

'It's a charming relic of the many conversions the Hall has gone through since early Georgian times. Each wing has its own style of carved newel on the staircases making it ever so easy to find your rooms – hazel catkins and nuts for the east wing, oak leaf and acorn for the west and hop and vine in the priory gallery.'

She gestured to each of the arched doorways, feeling very much like a tour guide in the Victoria & Albert Museum. 'Breakfast is at nine o'clock in the square dining room. Sessions begin at ten in the conservatory.'

'Are we to go on as if nothing has happened?' Pretoria asked.

'Yes,' Mabel said. Although Emma hadn't strictly said so, Mabel thought it best to be firm. She was growing weary of acting mother hen. She'd had little supper and desperately needed a cup of tea and time to think. 'We have PCs Cowley and Scott – Ned and Ted – here for the night to keep an eye on things and by morning more police will have arrived. I do hope you sleep well. Good night.'

By some miracle of mind-reading – but most likely after a word from Emma – Binks brought tea to the steward's office along with a bottle of whisky. Mabel scrounged bread, butter and cheese from the buffet table, Cora brought in a rhubarb tart that hadn't been cut and Skeff took a couple of apples from her pockets. When Mabel pulled out a Spratt's dog cake from her satchel and held it up, Gladys danced in a circle until her meal was placed before her on a saucer.

Emma had gone to bed. The constables waited in the entrance hall for the arrival of Scotland Yard and at last, as Mabel tucked into her late supper, Park arrived.

'Well now,' Skeff said, lighting a cigarette, 'here we all are.'

'Indeed,' Mabel said. 'What do we have to report?'

'Ronald has changed his mind and gone back to the vicarage, as there doesn't seem to be any need for him to stay now the police are here,' Park said, pouring himself a whisky and holding out the bottle. Skeff nodded. 'We found no dragons and the doors and windows were locked in the Hall. Ronald says that Binks is the one to close up every night.'

'No likely suspect has raised her hand to confess during questioning,' Mabel said.

'Early days yet,' Park said. 'Police will look into the women's backgrounds.'

'I'd say there are a few with records,' Skeff said.

'Except perhaps Ruby,' Cora said. 'She would've been a girl during the early part of the movement. Her mother, Susan, died just two years ago. She was a suffragist so she didn't participate in violent protests, but she kept quite busy running a school for destitute girls – rather like the ragged schools.'

'You've already learned all that?' Skeff asked.

'Oh,' Cora said, 'it was just a chat. But the thing is, one of those three was listening.'

'One of the Greek chorus?' Mabel asked. 'Lavinia, Thirza or Pretoria?'

Cora lifted a forefinger. 'Thirza, that's the one. She pulled me aside after and said that Susan, Ruby's mother, and Annie Harkin had a falling out over funding for the school.'

Skeff drained her glass. 'I say.'

Cora didn't look entirely happy. 'Ruby is worried about something, but I don't believe it's about her mother's school.'

'Does she want to join the campaign?' Park asked. 'Carry on in memory of her mother as well as herself?'

'Perhaps she wants to lead the delegates,' Mabel suggested, 'instead of Annie or Dorothea or Diane or one of the trio?'

'I'll see what else I can learn,' Cora said.

'So while the Yard carries out its investigation,' Mabel said, 'the schedule should proceed as planned as long as Emma approves. That includes the lecture you're to give, Skeff.'

Emma had wanted the press represented – someone to give a calm and circumspect view of how newspapers had treated suffrage before the war and now after. Perhaps, even, offer suggestions about how best to put their campaign forward. 'We want the sympathy of the public without damage to our members,' Emma had said to Mabel and then had asked, 'what about your friend Skeff?'

'I do confess,' Skeff said, sitting up a bit straighter, 'to being rather nervous about talking to these women who have experienced far more than I have.'

'They need to see the newspapers from the other side,' Mabel said.

Not for the first time, she marvelled at her good fortune to have made such friends with their own special skills. Skeff with her reporter's nose for news, Cora's reassuring warmth, Park's background with the Metropolitan Police – and his other talents, of course.

'So,' Mabel said, 'any first impressions about the women?'

'For having a central goal, they're quite a mixed group,' Park said.

'Yes,' Mabel said. 'Annie mentioned there'd been trouble. Has it come back to haunt them?'

'Miss Goose seems a bit... flighty,' Cora said. 'But then at other times, she's quite down-to-earth.'

'She's changeable,' Park said. 'Turns on a sixpence.'

Volatile, Mabel thought. Prone to outbursts. 'But she and Annie were comrades in arms.' It was a mild protest aimed as much at herself as Park.

'Will Lady Fellbridge – Emma – send her husband a telegram to tell him what's gone on?' Cora asked.

'She may. Yes, probably. Actually, I'm not sure she would want to bother him.'

Lord Fellbridge – Harold Arthur Herringay or Harry to his wife – had always seemed just out of reach of Mabel's knowing, whereas Emma was, as they say, an open book. His lordship would help pay for repairs to villagers' cottages and sponsor the fund for the church roof, but Emma would be at the cottage making sandwiches for the workers and climb the bell tower at the church for the newspaper to get a photo.

Mabel looked at her wristwatch. 'Gone ten o'clock. Off to bed with us all. Gosh' – Mabel looked up – 'I haven't had a chance to ask how you like the place. Is your room all right?'

Cora clasped her hands. 'Oh yes. It's like our dream come to life.'

Skeff, leaning against the deep windowsill, grinned and reached over to put her arm round Cora's shoulders. 'Although on a grander scale.'

'True,' Mabel said. 'The bedrooms are as big as our entire flats, aren't they?' In Islington, their London neighbourhood, Cora and Skeff lived up on the third floor, Mabel on the second and Park and Gladys near the first-floor landing. New River House was a purpose-built set of flats and quite modern, each with its own tiny kitchen and bathroom and piped-in gas. It suited the busy life of a woman or man in 1922 but couldn't be called spacious.

They all rose. Gladys stretched. Mabel brushed a few crumbs off her skirt. 'I suppose we need to see what the morning brings. We'll meet tomorrow evening in my room.'

Cora and Skeff set off to their room in the priory gallery and Park rounded up Gladys and checked with the PCs at the door. Mabel sat behind the desk absentmindedly sipping cold tea and letting her mind take her where it will, tossed and turned by snatches of conversations and looks and emotions – or lack thereof – from the women in response to Annie's death.

Without a sound, a figure appeared in the open door and Mabel leapt out of her chair.

'I'm sorry if I startled you,' Ruby said.

Mabel rested her fingertips on the desk to steady herself, her heart thumping.

'No, you didn't startle me. Come in, Ruby. And well done on finding your way from the west wing. Did you need something?'

'I thought it best to say this when the others weren't nearby.' Ruby looked over her shoulder to the empty corridor. 'I want to help with the investigation. I know I'm not strictly one of your Useful Women, but I do have some skills. For example, no one ever notices me.'

Should Mabel admit this to be true? Ruby did seem to fade into the background.

'It's always been that way,' the young woman continued. '"Oh, little Ruby, where did you come from?" That's what people have always said, because they never realise I've been standing there for ages. I don't mind it. If I'm forgotten about even though I'm still present, I hear things. I could position myself to eavesdrop. Perhaps there's someone you are particularly interested in learning more about?'

Or someone Ruby is particularly interested in learning about, Mabel thought.

'It isn't my investigation as such' – Mabel felt it important to make this point – 'it will be a Scotland Yard enquiry. I am involved because Emma has particularly asked me to be.'

'And because you are good at it,' Ruby said. 'Even though you're never named in the newspaper articles.'

'I've been a part of enquiries.' Mabel preferred that her name not be in the newspaper. Let Useful Women have the limelight – that way, she felt free of the constraints of the public's expectation.

'Do you have a suspect in mind, Mabel?' Ruby asked.

'No.'

'Do you think it odd that Thirza, Lavinia and Pretoria are so close with each other – might they be keeping a secret?'

Mabel heard a voice out in the corridor and hoped it was Park returning. Time to chivvy Miss Truelock off to bed. 'Perhaps they're old friends,' she said. 'Now, Ruby, it is late and—'

'I'll be keeping an eye and an ear out for you. Shall I come to you in confidence to tell you what I see and hear?'

'Ruby, I don't want you to spy on the other women. Everyone is here to work together – now even more so, don't you think?'

'You've solved cases for Scotland Yard,' Ruby persisted. 'I know you have. You will be leading the enquiry, Mabel – you must!'

Her declaration occurred just as Detective Inspector Edmund Tollerton of Scotland Yard arrived in the doorway. He still wore his coat but carried his bowler hat. Although not hard or unkind, he was a man with a serious demeanour – Mabel could count on one hand the number of times she'd seen more than a passing grin on his face.

'Miss Canning?' Tollerton said.

Ruby whipped round.

'Ruby,' Mabel said, 'this is Detective Inspector Tollerton. Inspector, Ruby Truelock.'

'Oh,' she said, giving the impression of a blush even though she remained the same colour. 'Hello, sir.'

'Pleased to meet you, Miss Truelock.'

'Well,' Ruby said, 'I'll say good night to you.' She turned to Mabel and added, sotto voce, 'We'll talk later.' With that, she glided past Tolly as Park arrived.

The two men walked into the office and, as if caught in the current of a stream, PC Ned was pulled in after them.

'Inspector Tollerton, sir,' he said with a frown, 'I don't understand. You said that your constable had driven you and was leaving the car round the side of the Hall. But it wasn't a constable at all, sir, it was—'

From behind Ned came WPC Wardle.

'Hildy!' Mabel exclaimed. 'That is, Constable Wardle, I'm delighted to see you.'

WPC Wardle stood with her usual ramrod posture, carrying her hat under her arm. She had straight brown hair cut in a short bob and was the picture of official police behaviour, although Mabel could see a twinkle in her small dark eyes and knew her to be just as delighted. She gave a small nod.

Mabel looked at Tollerton. 'How did this come about?'

'Detective Sergeant Lett has his hands full with a string of robberies in Holborn,' Tollerton said smoothly. 'I needed a driver and someone to work the enquiry, and I thought Wardle would do as well as any other PC.'

'Perhaps better,' Mabel said. Tollerton scowled at her, but, at the same time, nearly smiled.

There weren't many women at Scotland Yard, but they were proving their worth. Since meeting Hildy the previous autumn on another investigation, Mabel had more than once called attention to how much help she had provided.

Ted came up behind his cohort. 'Did you get the key, Ned?'

'Key!' Ned exclaimed. 'Sorry, Inspector sir, the door to the room is locked and your photographer and fingerprint men need to get in.'

'I have it.' Mabel took the key out of her pocket and handed it over and the two PCs were off like a shot.

Gladys came trotting in and up to Tollerton. 'Hello, girl,' he said and looked round the steward's office. 'Right, are we in here?'

'Yes,' Mabel said. 'Emma – Lady Fellbridge – offered it.' She cleared the desk of her supper dishes as Binks walked in with a small tray holding a new bottle of whisky and glasses.

'May I get you anything else, sir – a sandwich, perhaps?'

'No thank you.'

Binks left and Tollerton went round the other side of the desk and stopped when he saw Mabel's register. She whisked it away. Park poured three glasses – Hildy declined – and they all sat. Mabel reached over for the letter opener and took the apple from her pocket. Gladys sat at her feet accepting a wedge at a time.

'Well, Miss Canning,' Tolly said as he took his notebook out, 'I heard precious little from my superintendent and not much more from Park and so it's up to you to fill in the missing pieces. What are you doing here?'

'Lady Fellbridge engaged me through Useful Women as her private secretary for the week. I know her because before I moved to London I lived just up the road in Peasmarsh. She invited a small group of women she knew from the votes for women campaign before the war.'

'Suffragettes?' Tollerton asked.

Emma appeared in the doorway. 'Yes, suffragettes,' she said. She paused for a moment. Still dressed in the black and silver frock she'd worn for the evening and a picture of elegance. Then, she came in and closed the door behind her as Park, Tolly and Hildy popped up out of their chairs.

Mabel made the introductions, and once everyone settled, Emma continued.

'We need a path to move forward, to ensure Parliament passes an act that would provide the vote for all women over the age of twenty-one. The fight is not yet won. We need equality in all aspects of life – the vote, in politics, in education, in work and in marriage.' Emma smiled and sipped the whisky Park had passed to her. 'And to get down off my high horse, Inspector, let me say how good it is to meet WPC Wardle, working shoulder to shoulder with other police officers.'

Mabel knew and suspected Emma knew, too, that much of Hildy's police work still amounted to making the tea, but it was at least a start.

Hildy said nothing but beamed. Tollerton cleared his throat and carried on.

'I understand Miss Canning and Mr Winstone have assisted this evening and I need to question them. I'm sure you'd rather—'

'Stay,' Emma said. 'I'd rather stay. Also, I think you'll find that Mabel has already carried out interviews for you.'

Mabel's face heated up. She wished she had been able to explain that to Tolly herself. Too late now.

Tollerton gave her a careful look and nodded after which she could breathe again.

'The first round of interviews,' Mabel explained, adding, 'I took notes,' but leaving out the part about Skeff taking notes, too.

'Now Inspector,' Emma said, 'you want to interview me, don't you?'

'Of course.' He took up his pencil. 'First, who was the victim?'

'Mrs Annie Harkin,' Emma said. 'Cheevers before she married. She lived in Little Lever, near Bolton. Manchester, you know.'

'Time of death?'

'Dorothea Goose found her,' Mabel said. 'She's one of the delegates. That was six o'clock, when we were having drinks in the salon.'

Tolly's pencil paused for a brief moment, and then he wrote.

'I left Annie not long past twelve o'clock, after Doctor Finlay had gone,' Emma said. 'She was going for a rest.'

'She was cold when Mabel and I got to her just after six,' Winstone said.

Tollerton didn't speak, but Mabel could almost hear his mind whirring as he sorted out ambient temperature and how long it took a body to cool after death. He nodded to himself.

'The doctor's a local man?' he asked.

'Yes,' Emma said. 'Gordon Finlay.'

'And who is this Dorothea Goose?' Tollerton asked.

A stiff silence ensued.

'She is one of the delegates,' Emma said, her face betraying nothing.

'A suffragette?'

'Annie and Dorothea were ardent suffragettes,' Emma said. '"Deeds not words" – that's what they believed. If you were with Scotland Yard in the years before the war, you may have encountered them.'

Tollerton shifted in his chair but attended to writing in his notebook. 'Did they have a disagreement?' he asked. 'Is Miss Goose prone to violence?'

That was it, Mabel thought – Tolly had overheard Ruby's comment about Dorothea.

One of Emma's eyebrows arched. 'Annie and Dorothea were in Holloway prison,' she said in a matter-of-fact way. 'Violent acts were inflicted upon them. They protested with hunger strikes and were force-fed, then after that, it was in and out and in and out of prison. The Cat and Mouse Act.'

The room, already quiet, seemed to become muffled. Mabel had been not yet twenty when the suffragettes began their hunger strikes and she remembered her papa trying without success to keep the newspaper reports from her.

'It broke Dorothea,' Emma said in a whisper. 'She's recovered over the years, but there is no hiding the fact that it has left her fragile and, at times, changeable.'

'Is she prone to violence?' Tollerton repeated.

'She would never hurt Annie,' Emma said.

Not intentionally. The words came into Mabel's mind unbidden.

'Has she accounted for her whereabouts during the afternoon?' Tollerton looked at Park and then Mabel.

'As well as anyone else has,' Mabel said.

'It might be best to remove Miss Goose from the scene,'

Tollerton said. 'For her own safety as well as others. It might be best to take her into the police station in Rye.'

'You'll arrest her?' Emma sprang from her chair and shouted, 'I won't have it!'

Tollerton stood, too, and Mabel saw sparks of irritation in his eyes as if he had expected this – Lady Fellbridge chucking her weight about.

'None of us have anything to fear if she sleeps here at the Hall tonight instead of in a cell,' Emma said. 'Putting her there could very well cause her to... It would be too much for her, Inspector. She couldn't take it.'

'Lady Fellbridge—' Tolly said.

Emma's steely voice cut in. 'If you feel she's a danger, then I will be her gatekeeper. I'll sleep in her room with her. I will throw a blanket down in front of the door of her room and stay there to make certain she does not go skulking about the Hall. It's either that, or you'll have to arrest me along with her.'

SIX

The air in the room crackled. No one spoke.

Tollerton laid down his pencil. 'There will be no cause for you to sleep on the floor in Miss Goose's room, Lady Fellbridge,' he said, 'but thank you for the offer.'

He said it kindly and although Emma remained straight and tall, she smiled.

'Now,' Tolly continued, 'if you're up to it, would you tell me about the deceased and the others who are here attending your...'

'Meeting of minds, Inspector. These women all worked in one way or another in the campaign to secure votes for women.'

'And were successful,' Tollerton said. 'A good fight.'

Emma sniffed. 'The fight, Inspector, as I'm sure you'll agree, is not over. Not until Katie in the kitchen has the vote. Not until Constable Wardle has the vote.'

'Yes, yes, of course.' Tollerton cleared his throat.

'During the campaign, Lavinia Poppin and Thirza Bass were suffragists, and so staged only non-violent protests,' Emma said. 'Pretoria Fleming-Jones waffled – she went back and forth so many times, I lost count. Diane Lotterby started as a suffragette but shifted to non-violence by 1910. Annie and Dorothea and I were suffragettes.'

Emma drew a photograph from her pocket and passed it to Mabel. The image had to have been twenty years old. It showed a younger Annie, Emma and Dorothea – all wearing voluminous hats with fabric, tulle and flowers piled on top – holding a banner that read 'Votes for Women'.

'What would Cora say about those hats?' Emma asked and gave a small laugh.

As Mabel showed Park the photograph and then handed it to Tollerton, Emma continued.

'You'll find a long list of arrests for those two, but only one for me. We were outside Parliament in one of the many years that promises were made about giving women the vote, but with no results. There was a bit of pushing and shoving, and police were called in. I gave a false name, but someone recognised me, and so I was released, but not those two.'

'Would there have been conflict between them?' Tollerton asked.

'Ill feelings that would give Dorothea a reason to strike out at Annie?' Emma's question seemed harsh on the surface, but her voice carried a mournful note. 'No.'

'And the others?' Tollerton asked.

'Collette Massey sees herself as a bridge between the two groups. She is the widow of Arthur Massey, who represented Biggleswade in the House of Commons until his constituency dissolved a few years ago, shortly before Arthur died.'

'How is Miss Truelock involved?' Tollerton asked. 'She's too young to have been with you then.'

'Ruby's mother, Susan, worked for the vote, but she had started a school in Bolton. Susan was a tireless worker and considered a rebel by local authorities – you'll find she has an arrest record, too.' Emma gave Susan that label with a note of pride in her voice. 'She died two years ago. The Spanish 'flu.'

Emma glanced at Mabel and covered her hand for a moment. It had been just two years ago that Edith died of the same.

Tollerton frowned at the pencil in his hand. 'I started as a PC in 1906,' he said.

A wisp of remembered pain scudded over Emma's face.

Mabel looked over at Park who caught her gaze and held it. He must've joined the Yard during the campaign. Mabel felt both guilty and relieved that she had been busy with life in her village during those years. When the war came, both the suffragettes and suffragists had called off their campaign.

'Miss Goose may remain here in your hands, Lady Fellbridge,' Tollerton said. 'Miss Canning has everyone's details, but I need to question the women further, as well as the servants.'

'I will leave those arrangements with my secretary,' Emma said, nodding to Mabel.

'Is Lord Fellbridge at home?' Tollerton asked.

A bit late to be asking that, Mabel thought, but realised Tolly most likely already knew the answer.

'No,' Emma said, 'he's away in Brussels on business. Inspector, may I send word to Annie's husband?'

'Mrs Harkin was married?' Tollerton scribbled in his notebook.

'Yes,' Emma said. 'Oliver Harkin. He lives in Little Lever – near Bolton. They've been estranged for years, but still he should know.' Emma frowned. 'May I be the one to tell him?'

'Yes,' Tollerton said.

'I'll send a telegram tomorrow. Ronald can take it in to Rye. Also tomorrow,' Emma said, 'we will carry on as planned, but you are welcome to come and go as needed and use this office. In fact, you can stay here at the Hall – we've plenty of rooms.'

'Thank you, but Mr Winstone has made arrangements at the pub.'

'Draker is a better barman than innkeeper,' Emma said. 'It's your choice, but certainly, WPC Wardle doesn't need to put up in a room at the King and Cork?'

Tollerton's head snapped round to his constable as if not until that very moment had he remembered she was a woman. 'Oh,' he said.

Hildy lifted her eyebrows but didn't speak.

'I'll take care of it,' Mabel said.

Emma gave a weary nod and rose. 'May I?' she asked, reaching for her photo. Tollerton pushed it towards her, and Emma tucked it back in her pocket. At the door, she turned and said, 'If you find a locked door and need it opened, look in the desk drawer for the key. Good night.'

Mabel turned to Tolly. 'There's an available room near me in the priory gallery for WPC Wardle. That is, if she wants to stay.'

'Rather,' Wardle said, and then caught herself and looked at Tollerton. 'Sir. If you think it best.'

'If WPC Wardle stayed here at the Hall,' Mabel went on, 'she would be an invaluable source of on-the-ground information for the enquiry... reconnoitring, you know.'

Tollerton frowned.

'Eyes and ears,' Mabel pushed.

'Yes, yes,' Tollerton said. 'No need to over-egg the pudding, Miss Canning.'

Mabel heard a stifled snigger from Winstone.

'Excellent, that's settled,' Mabel said. 'Hildy, Skeff and Cora will be happy to see you.'

'Skeff?' Tollerton asked sharply.

'They were invited by Lady Fellbridge,' Mabel said.

Tollerton screwed up his mouth. 'Well, I suppose it could be worse.'

Mabel knew what he meant. In the grand scheme of the

London press, the *Intelligencer* was a shining beacon of integrity.

'What about the servants?' Tollerton asked.

'There is the butler, Binks,' Mabel replied. 'Campsie, the gardener, has a cottage by the stables. Deenie Pilford and Katie Darling are the cooks. They don't live in but come from the village. I believe there's a day maid.'

'Was anyone else here today?'

'Doctor Finlay,' Mabel said.

'You mean, before he was called here this evening?' Tollerton asked.

'Lady Fellbridge had asked him,' Mabel said. 'I'm not sure Annie was in good health.'

'If that's the case, it would have made her that much easier to overcome.' Tollerton made a note. 'Where are the women?'

'Gone to bed,' Mabel told him. 'But I... er... talked with each of them this evening.'

Now here it was – confess to the police that she had meddled in the proper order of the enquiry.

'Yes,' Tollerton said, 'your interviews.'

'She's saved you time there,' Park said.

Tollerton threw Park a look and then tossed one to Mabel, too. He looked down at his notebook and then at the register Mabel held in her lap.

'All right, then,' he said, 'let's hear what you've got.'

Mabel gave a full and comprehensive report of her interviews with the women and when finished, closed her register, feeling as though she'd offered nothing much to the enquiry. No suspects, motives or clues seemed to leap out.

'I had no more than a quick chat with each of them,' she said to Tollerton.

'First interviews are for skimming the surface,' Tollerton

said, 'unless you happen to catch the murderer holding a bloody knife or... or a bed pillow. You didn't see that, did you – Miss Goose holding the murder weapon?'

'No, we did not,' Mabel said firmly. 'She did have a pocketful of feathers, but that's only because she was distressed when she found Annie and... wanted to tidy up.'

'That's enough for this evening, then,' Tollerton said. 'I'll see the others tomorrow.'

'What about the photographer and your fingerprint men?' Mabel asked.

'They'll let me know what they find.'

'Doctor Finlay was to arrange for the mortuary wagon,' Park said.

'I'll talk with the doctor tomorrow, too.' Tollerton put away his notebook and pencil. 'Where have those two constables got to? I'll set them to keep a watch overnight.'

When they rose, so did Gladys. She gave herself a good shake and led the way out to the entrance hall. Mabel and Hildy followed.

'I have an aunt who was a suffragette,' Hildy said as they walked. 'She handed out leaflets in front of the post office in our town. She was arrested once. Not because she was campaigning for the vote, but because she knocked a drunk fellow on his bum when he tried to kiss her.'

'And she was the one arrested?' Mabel asked, indignant.

'He was head of the parish council,' Hildy replied, then grinned. 'But not for long after that. And she was released the same day.'

Mabel laughed. 'Oh Hildy, I'm so glad Tolly brought you along. You'll love the room in the priory gallery. It's that way' – Mabel gestured as they reached the entrance hall. 'You'll come to a staircase with a newel carved with hop and vine. Go up to the second floor and knock on the first door to let Skeff and

Cora know you're here. You can take the room next to them. I'm the next door down.'

The two local constables came tumbling out of the far corridor that led to the west wing and nearly knocked into the group before they pulled up. They were followed in a more sedate fashion by three men who carried cases and were buttoning up their coats and putting on their hats. One of them nodded to Tollerton who held up a forefinger in response and turned back to Ned and Ted.

'You two, I want someone here overnight, so decide which one will take first watch. Then I'll see you both down at the pub at ten o'clock tomorrow.'

'Yes, sir,' they said in chorus.

'I've two open cases in London,' Tollerton said to Mabel and Park, 'and so my attention may be drawn off now and then. I'm sure the enquiry will proceed regardless.' He gave Mabel a look and she was too stunned to answer before he walked off to his team.

Park leaned over and murmured, 'Well done.' His warm breath on her skin and those two simple words sent a thrill through her.

The two constables played tinker tailor to count out who would go first – a bit useless as there were only two of them, so the person starting would know who would win. But in this case, what would be the prize – to take the first watch or the second?

After only a moment, Ted brushed off his jacket and straightened his hat. 'Right, that's me away. Good evening, ma'am, sir... Constable.' The last address was aimed at Hildy and said with a note of disbelief, but she took it at face value.

'Good evening, Constable,' she called after him.

Out the door, Ted picked up a bicycle left leaning against the side of the building, switched on the lamp at the handlebars and cycled off.

The crime scene men left, although Tollerton kept one of their cases. 'Wardle,' he said, 'are you sorted?'

'Yes, sir,' Hildy said. 'Shall I bring the car round for you?'

'Go on then,' Tollerton said. 'And keep your eyes and ears open around here. You!' Tollerton said, pointing at Ned who had remained a respectable distance away but looked a bit lost without his partner.

'Ned,' Mabel said. 'Constable Ned Cowley.'

'Cowley,' Tollerton said, 'did you lock the door upstairs?'

Ned's hand slapped his jacket pocket. 'No, sir. Sorry, sir, I'll do it now.'

'Wait, Constable,' Mabel said, 'and I'll go with you.'

Ned seemed to shrink back against the gilded wainscot and waited.

'Park,' Tolly said as he walked out. 'Are you ready? It's past closing time, so we'll have to knock up the landlord.'

Park grumbled an unintelligible reply and frowned at Tolly's retreating figure, then he frowned at Mabel. She frowned back. They had had not one minute to themselves in a personal sort of way the entire evening.

The London officers drove off and Wardle pulled Tollerton's car up. When he opened the door, Gladys was first in, hopping onto the back seat.

Mabel and Park, left alone for the moment – apart from Ned across the entrance hall – stepped close to one another.

With a cautious look over his shoulder at Tollerton, Park said, 'Here's the thing. I'll have to take Gladys out early in the morning.'

'Yes, you will, won't you?' Mabel said.

'You wouldn't be able to think of a good spot to make for at, say, eight o'clock or so? You know, for Gladys.'

'As it happens, there's a footpath between here and the pub – a lovely walk along a low wall, over a stone bridge and through the copse at the bottom of this hill. I'm sure Gladys will enjoy it.'

'I daresay she will.' Park gave Mabel a wink and left.

Hildy returned with her bag, said good night and set off. Mabel turned to the lone constable.

'Shall we go, Ned?'

He took off his police helmet and held it over his heart. 'Miss Canning, I'm terribly sorry for what I did' – the words came out in a rush as if a dam had broken loose. 'I take full responsibility for my actions.'

'Ah,' Mabel said. 'Are you confessing to an eleven-year-old crime? To tell me you were the one who loosened my fountain pen so that when I picked it up to take Sunday school attendance, ink ran everywhere?'

Ned nodded and looked down at the floor. 'Eight-year-olds, ma'am, there's no accounting for what they get up to.'

Wasn't that the truth? Mabel realised Ned reminded her of the current scamp in her life – Augustus Malling-Frobisher III, whose mother regularly rang up Useful Women asking for Mabel to either keep Augustus out of or extract him from his latest trouble.

'Well, Ned, now that's cleared the air,' Mabel said, 'shall we go?'

She led the way up the stairs of the west wing. When they reached the second-floor landing, the air turned cold.

She stopped. The door to Dorothea's room stood open and beyond was darkness.

SEVEN

'Dorothea?' Mabel called, rushing into the dark room and feeling for the wall switch. Another wave of cold air came over her and her arms broke out in gooseflesh, but at the same time, she realised the air smelled fresh and of the night.

The light revealed a room empty of Dorothea, her case with the mended handle and her straw hat – and a wide-open window. Empty, but nonetheless, Mabel called again 'Dorothea?' as she rushed over, put her hands on the sill and leaned out. 'Ned, was this door open when you were here with the crime scene officers?'

'No, that is, yes,' Ned stumbled over his words. 'It might've been, ma'am.'

'Dorothea?' she called. 'Dorothea?'

'Should I run after the inspector?' Ned asked.

'No, wait now.' Mabel forced her breathing to slow. She looked out the window into the darkness and then below. In her mind, she saw this side of the Hall as if she stood outdoors.

She remembered there was an old climbing rose growing on the wall from the terrace below. Near the ground, its stem was as big around as Mabel's wrist, but even the woodiest of stems had enormous hooked thorns that would gouge and tear at flesh. She squinted out into the night and saw a dark patch of trees and remembered a footpath outside the low wall. Where did it lead? Had Dorothea escaped out the window – afraid of her own actions or the memories of being locked up?

'Dorothea!' she called out into the night.

From the corridor behind her came a voice.

'Mabel?'

She whirled round to see Dorothea wearing a flannel dressing gown over floral-print flannel pyjamas. She had her hair in a single braid hanging over her shoulder, her bath bag under one arm and a puzzled expression on her face.

Mabel laughed and a sob of relief caught in her throat.

'Dorothea, I thought you'd gone,' she managed to say.

'Out the window?' Dorothea asked.

'Mabel?' Ruby, also in her dressing gown, came up behind Dorothea. 'I hope you don't mind, but I suggested Dorothea move down to the other end of the corridor so that she wouldn't... be alone.'

Be alone next door to Annie's body.

'Thank you, Ruby – that was good of you. Dorothea, did you open the window?' Mabel asked.

'Yes,' Dorothea said, 'when I first arrived. I prefer to have fresh air. I'm sorry I didn't remember to close it.'

'Was it open all afternoon?' Ned asked.

Dorothea gave the constable the once-over. Meanwhile, Ned's gaze went everywhere but to the two ladies wearing dressing gowns.

'Yes, it was, Constable,' Dorothea said. She watched him for another moment and then, perhaps deciding he wasn't a danger, looked back at Mabel.

'You don't think anyone climbed in that way, do you?' she asked Mabel. 'There's a terribly fierce rose on the wall.'

Mabel considered the possibility that someone had climbed

up to the second-storey window into Dorothea's room that afternoon and then sneaked next door to murder Annie. Or, possibly used this as an escape route so as not to be seen. Easy enough to check that theory – who among them had fresh wounds on their hands and arms?

Mabel closed the window. 'It's unlikely, isn't it?'

They walked out and down to the other end of the corridor.

'Dorothea took the room on this side of me, and Collette is in the last room,' Ruby said. 'In case you need to enter it correctly in the book.'

'Can I still see the bluebell wood from my new room?' Dorothea asked when they reached her door.

'Yes,' Mabel said. 'You're still looking west. The wood isn't all that deep at this point. The formal garden at the back of the Hall is round the corner to the left, then on around further is the kitchen garden and beyond that is the orchard. The formal dining room is below you here on the ground floor of this wing.'

'Now Dorothea,' Ruby said, 'if you need anything, you knock on my door.'

'Yes, yes, thank you. Now, good night,' Dorothea said, then looked over Mabel's shoulder. 'Good night to you, too, Constable.'

'Good night, ma'am,' Ned mumbled as he kept his gaze averted.

Ruby looked over at Mabel. 'Remember, I'll be keeping an eye out.' She tapped her forefinger aside of her nose, then followed Dorothea down to their rooms.

'What's that about?' Ned asked.

'She thinks I'm Sherlock Holmes and wants to be Watson,' Mabel said.

'In a play for the theatre, you mean?' Ned asked with a frown. 'Wouldn't you need to be Mrs Sherlock Holmes or something?'

'Ned Cowley,' Mabel said kindly, 'you're in a houseful of suffragettes, so you'd better watch yourself.'

'Yes, Miss Canning.'

Mabel left Ned in the entrance hall and made for the priory gallery wing. No light shone from under Cora and Skeff's door or Hildy's and so Mabel continued to her own room where she was halfway undressed before she remembered her last duty of the day – to tell Binks that Dorothea had changed rooms and that an additional guest had arrived. She pulled her dressing gown over her nightdress, put her shoes back on and set forth, making her way down stairs, along corridors, round corners and downstairs again towards the kitchen.

She had been out and about in Fellbridge Hall late at night before. When Edith and Ronald were married, he would go back to the vicarage when the Christmas ball ended, but Edith would stay and ask Mabel, too. They'd have one of their usual evenings of nonstop talk and occasional silliness, such as the time Quince, the former butler, caught them posing in the room with the white marble statues as if they were part of the display. He had shooed them away with good humour and they ended up in the kitchen cooking scrambled eggs at four o'clock in the morning.

The other nights she'd spent were of a different nature. During the war, Lord and Lady Fellbridge had given over the gallery and the large dining room as a hospital for officers recuperating from injuries – wounds visible and wounds unseen.

Mabel's nursing skills were rudimentary, but she could read to the men or write letters they dictated to their families. She would occasionally take an overnight shift and remembered the dark silence of the Hall punctuated by cries in the night. She paused at the gallery, opened the door and looked into its silent vastness, remembering a certain lieutenant from near Sheffield who spent a month recuperating. They would read *Lorna Doone* together every afternoon on a love seat in the far corner. Cheeky fellow, she thought and smiled.

It was a decidedly different Fellbridge Hall Mabel walked through now. Not nearly as friendly or comforting. Almost midnight, but it felt like three or four o'clock – that eerie part of the night. The darkness seemed darker, the lights left burning had dimmed and it sounded as if the stone and wood were speaking to her in creaks and groans. Such nonsense.

At the bottom of the stairs in the basement, Mabel paused, waiting for her eyes to become accustomed to the darkness. No one was about, which was as it should be. She walked carefully and quietly towards the kitchen.

Mabel blinked down the corridor. The butler's quarters were at the far end, but she didn't see a light and didn't want to bother Binks so late. She would leave him a note.

Just inside the kitchen sat a small table with a candle on it. Mabel struck a match and then carried the lit candle to the desk that resided in the far corner where the cooks kept track of menus and food orders. That's where she would find pencil and paper.

She raised her candle to throw better light.

'What are you doing here?' a sharp voice asked.

EIGHT

'Ahh!' Mabel let go of the candle. It hit the floor and went out.

The ceiling light in the kitchen came on and there was Binks tying the belt of his dressing gown.

'Miss Canning?'

'I'm so sorry,' Mabel said, her heart racing. 'I was looking for a paper to write you a note so that I wouldn't need to disturb you.'

'Oh, never mind about that,' the butler said in a calm and even voice. 'I'm sorry I frightened you.'

'It's been quite a day, hasn't it?' Mabel said. Binks nodded and made a sound of agreement and at that moment, Mabel remembered when Dorothea announced to everyone in the salon that Annie had been murdered cries erupted – and Binks dropped his drinks tray. Perhaps he remembered Annie from a visit before the war.

'Did you know Mrs Harkin?'

The butler looked at her for a moment without speaking. Because his spectacles were both tinted and thick, she couldn't tell if he were considering how to reply or trying to remember.

'Yes. We were cousins.'

Stunned, Mabel groped for a reply, but came up with nothing of any use. 'Oh, I didn't know.'

'There was no reason for you to know, was there?'

'Still, I'm so very sorry. Were you close?' Mabel asked.

'Annie – Mrs Harkin – was older than I am. I suppose you could say she was rather like an older sister to me, but then as the years go on, you drift apart, don't you?'

Mabel picked up the pencil from the desk and turned it round and round in her fingers. As terribly sad as it was to lose a member of the family, there was also the enquiry to think about. Tollerton would want to know this connection.

'Had you seen Annie recently?'

'Not for ages, ma'am,' he replied.

'Did you know she was to be one of the delegates here?'

The pause, brief though it was, called attention to itself. 'Yes, Lady Fellbridge did mention it.'

'I suppose, then, if you hadn't seen her recently, you wouldn't know if anything in particular had been bothering her. Or anyone.'

'Before she arrived today? No, I wouldn't've known.'

Mabel bent over to pick up the candle, waiting for him to say more.

'Did you have a message for me?' Binks asked.

'Yes, yes I did. It's to say that Miss Goose has changed rooms, but only down the corridor. She's next to Miss Truelock now. We didn't want her to feel... alone.'

'Just as well for her, ma'am, I'm sure. We've a girl from the village in the morning who will help with tea and breakfast and the fires. I'll let her know.'

'Also, Inspector Tollerton has left his constable here – that is, WPC Hildy Wardle. She has taken the room in the priory gallery next to Skeff and Cora.'

'I'll be sure to sort out the tea trays,' Binks said. 'Is Miss Goose all right?'

'She was quite affected as you know,' Mabel said, 'but she seems resilient.'

'Was there anything else?'

'No, that's all,' she said. 'Good night.'

On the way back to her room, thoughts flew through Mabel's mind. If Annie had been in her assigned room in the priory gallery, would she still be alive?

What about the women? But then, how could one of the women have sneaked round the Hall bent on murder when they appeared to be lost the moment they stepped out of their rooms? But then, Mabel reminded herself, appearances could deceive.

Mabel left the curtains in her room open, so that she would wake with the light, and the next morning she lay in bed gazing across the room and out the window to incredibly blue skies. Perfect. Throwing off the bed covers, she threw on her dressing gown, grabbed her bath bag and ran for a quick wash.

When she returned, her tea tray sat on the floor at her door and so she took it in and drank a cup while she dressed, then donned her brown coat, gloves and a beret the green of new leaves. Cora had added a sprig of creamy yellow silk primroses to the top. Mabel pulled the beret down to cover her ears and her golden-brown hair burst out the bottom in soft curls. When she looked in the mirror she appeared to be disguised as a woodland fairy.

Outside, her feet crunched on the chippings, but quieted when she stepped off the drive and onto the worn path that led down the hill and towards the pub. Her breath came out in a fog from the cold. There had been a light frost that morning – the sort that made it look as if icing sugar had been sifted on the ground, not the sort that would worry Campsie the gardener.

The Hall disappeared from view where the path turned and went through a small spinney. Mabel looked ahead to the denser copse where the leaves of the beech and oak were beginning to unfurl, showing only a suggestion of green, and the white buds on the hawthorn were still tightly shut. When she reached a scrubby holly, she heard fast footfalls approaching. Quite fast, but not feet – paws.

'Good morning, Gladys,' Mabel said as the dog came out of the undergrowth at the edge of the wood and raced towards her.

Gladys gave Mabel's hand a lick, circled her once, *woofed* and ran back the way she came, disappearing from sight. Mabel continued along the path into the wood and found Park waiting, homburg pulled low on his brow and coat collar turned up. They took gloved hands and Mabel was able to offer a breathy 'good morning' before he kissed her, which nearly knocked his hat off. Cold lips, cold faces, but the touch struck a warmth that stirred her inside. She slid her hands up round his neck as his went round her waist. They'd been apart a week and that had been too long.

Minutes later she looked up at his fogged glasses. 'I missed you,' she said. She rested her head against his chest.

'And I you,' he murmured into her beret. 'What is this on your hat?'

'Primroses,' Mabel replied. 'Cora is a magician with a bit of silk. How is your bed at the pub?'

'Lumpy,' Park said, leading her over to the low wall where they sat with their backs to the sun. Mabel tucked her hand in the crook of his arm and he held it tightly. 'I'm not sure that Draker doesn't store his potatoes inside my mattress. How was it at the Hall? Did you get them settled?'

'I nearly lost Dorothea, but only because she'd moved further down the corridor. Ruby thought of that. There'll be a great deal to do on the enquiry today and when Skeff and Cora – possibly Hildy – meet tonight in my room, you should be there, too.'

She held his gaze for a moment until Gladys barked in the distance.

'Gladys!' Park called and here she came leaping over the wall and tearing across the path to the other side, to return in a moment and drop in front of them, panting.

'You've spent time around the women now,' Park said. 'What do you think of them?'

'They are brave, every one of them,' Mabel said. 'What was I doing all those years ago, but living a quiet life in a village as others fought the fight for me.' She smiled. 'Although, when we were sixteen, Edith and I did send in five pounds each. It took us nearly a year to save up our pocket money. "For the cause" we wrote. We had a lovely letter back from someone in the National Union of Suffragette Societies.'

Park grew restless, putting his hands in his coat pockets, taking them out and leaning over to stroke Gladys. Without looking at Mabel, he said, 'I was in the police cordon that October in 1910. Thousands of women – and men, too – trying to invade the House of Commons.'

'Black Friday.' A riot that had resulted in violence against the women and left two of them dead. She put a hand on his arm. 'Was it terrible?'

'Yes,' Park said with some force. 'And frightening. And confusing. I was brought up believing women were equal – my mother saw to that. I would've quit the Met after that day but for Tolly. You'd think this whole matter would've been settled ages ago, but I know plenty of men who still say you shouldn't have the vote.'

'Do you?' Mabel asked. 'Why don't you give me their names and I'll set Diane Lotterby and her booming voice on them. Or let Collette Massey talk them into a corner.'

A ruckus arose from jackdaws in a nearby ash tree. Gladys lifted her head and *woofed* then put her head down again.

'You'll keep an eye on Dorothea Goose, won't you?' Park asked.

'I will. She seems fragile and changeable, but' – Mabel peered at him – 'not a strong suspect. After all, Dorothea and Annie were both suffragettes. They were in and out of prison together. Comrades. How could she—'

Park took her hand. 'It's as you say, she's changeable. What if being near Annie reminded her of those times and it did something to her mind?'

A cloud covered the sun and Mabel felt cold. She also felt fiercely, albeit unaccountably, protective of Dorothea, whom she had known such a short time. Mabel knew she must not let sympathy sway her. She sniffed.

'I can't feel my toes.' She stood, stamped her feet on the ground and took Park's hand. 'I'd best go back for breakfast. When will you and Tolly be up to the Hall?'

Park stood. 'Depends on how good the breakfast is at the pub,' he said. 'I haven't explained to him that it's mostly vegetarian fare at the Hall.'

'I daresay you could sneak down to the kitchen and Deenie will cook up a rasher for you.'

'That reminds me,' Park said, 'when I took Gladys down to the kitchen yesterday, Deenie told me to advise you to stay out of trees.' He frowned at her. 'Is that right?'

Mabel laughed. 'Deenie and I were at school together and she's always remembered the time we were eight years old and I told her I could see Brighton if I climbed to the top of the school's beech tree. She didn't believe me, so I started climbing and got about halfway up before I realised it wasn't the best idea. I was too afraid to move. Half the village came out to watch Papa climb up to bring me down.'

They stood close, neither moving. 'My room at the pub is upstairs last door on the right,' Park said.

'Is it now?' Mabel asked. 'As if no one would notice me

marching up those stairs from the public bar? Perhaps I should go round the back and climb up to your first-floor window?'

'Well, you did make it halfway up that beech tree—' He stopped and grinned. 'All right. Tolly wants to talk to the local doctor and he's got more questions for everyone at the Hall. In fact, he has questions for you.'

'As I do for him,' Mabel said. The enquiry had resurfaced in her mind. 'Have you brought along a load of reports to write?'

Park wrinkled his nose. 'I have, but that doesn't mean I won't be around. You find things for me to do, and I'll do them.'

She kissed him for that.

'Binks and Annie were cousins,' she said.

'Were they now,' Park said in a speculative manner.

'I remembered when Emma – and Dorothea – announced to the women that Annie was dead, Binks dropped a tray. I asked if he'd known Annie, and he told me.'

'Murders are often committed within families,' Park said. 'Did they know each other well?'

'She was rather like an older sister, he said. But they hadn't seen each other in years.' Mabel thought back to the previous afternoon. 'Annie said hello to him when she arrived. In a pleasant way.'

'Were the cooks at the Hall all day?'

'No, they come and go as needed.' She kissed him. 'And, oh, by the way – I don't think even a murder can get you out of dinner with Papa and Mrs Chandekar this evening.'

'I wouldn't want to get out of it,' Park said, but with a furrowed brow. 'I look forward to meeting your father.'

'Yes,' Mabel said, her voice heavy with meaning. 'And he looks forward to meeting you.'

Cora opened the door to Mabel. She wore a simple day dress in a muted rose shade that brought out the colour in her cheeks.

She had a turban of matching fabric tied at the ear with a sprig of shredded ribbonlike flowers of ragged robin done in silk.

'Good morning, come in,' Cora said.

Their room, much like Mabel's, contained furniture and décor that spanned a century or more. The curtains and the canopy on the four-poster bed which were in a leafy Arts and Crafts style, and a small Victorian cast-iron surround had been installed over the larger Georgian fireplace. Two upholstered chairs were set at each side.

'We're so pleased Hildy is staying next door,' Cora said. 'Will she come to the meeting this evening? Does she know about the London Ladies' Murder Club?'

'I hope she will attend,' Mabel said. 'She may have heard me mention our arrangement in passing earlier in the year – during that other business.'

'The dance hall,' Cora said and nodded. 'She has proved herself to the inspector, hasn't she? She's already gone down to breakfast, but we waited for you to get the cook's tour in daylight.'

Skeff, standing at the dressing table, tucked her reporter's notebook into the pocket of her trousers and tugged at her long coat. 'Better to get our bearings of the place when we can see,' she said as she looked in the mirror to adjust her saxe-blue velvet tam. 'Perhaps we'll have time for a stroll around the grounds later. The pub down the way looked promising.'

'The King and Cork,' Mabel said as she perched on the footstool. 'There's an actual cork oak growing next to it. It's the only one I've ever seen, but I don't believe it's a King Charles oak whatever they say.'

The morning had brought to Mabel a clarity and a sense of near normality – cup of tea, walk in the country, breakfast. At least on the surface. 'You were rather thrown in at the deep end last evening,' Mabel said. 'I'm sorry I wasn't even able to introduce you properly.'

Cora laughed. 'We managed fine. Emma made certain we met everyone, although she had a job of it to pull us away from Collette. She nearly wouldn't let go of Skeff without getting her first name – and I'm not sure Binks won't see if he can get away with "Miss Skeff".'

Mabel had learned when she'd met these two the previous autumn that Skeff eschewed Miss Skeffington and would rather keep her Christian name, Hippolyta, under her hat.

'It's quite a motley gathering, isn't it,' Skeff said, 'but they are all connected through their work and through Emma. And Annie, too, I suppose.' Skeff clapped her hands. 'What a wonderful opportunity you've given us, Mabel. Thank you once again for asking Lady Fellbridge to invite us. Uncle Pitt is quite keen on the serialised articles I proposed. Great strides have been made for women, but we're only partway there and we can't let up now.'

'To breakfast, then,' Mabel said, 'before it's gone.'

As they left, Skeff looked across the room and out the window. 'So, here we are in the priory gallery wing. Was the priory out there?' She pointed to the meadow beyond the formal garden.

'Yes,' Mabel replied. 'It was torn down during the Dissolution of the Monasteries and the stones were carried off to build nearby houses and the like.'

'This house?'

'Er... possibly. Or perhaps the stables.' Mabel searched her mind for more details of Fellbridge Hall's history. 'And also, I believe the place is built on the foundations of a medieval manor.'

'Where is the gallery?' Cora asked.

'It's below us on the ground floor,' Mabel explained. 'There are no first-floor rooms in this wing because the gallery's ceiling is two storeys high. It has beautiful arched spans that make you think you're in church. And paintings on the ceiling!'

Mabel had fond memories of the gallery and the hours she and Edith would spend looking through its eccentric, museum-like collections.

'I suppose they named this wing by association,' she continued. 'The priory out there, the gallery below. Every aspect at the Hall has its charm, but I love it here best, because it faces south and we get good light. Lady Fellbridge insisted that I stay in this wing, and that I should put you here, too.'

'How many rooms are there?' Cora asked as they followed Mabel down the stairs past a series of landscape paintings of what might have been Venice.

'Bedrooms? I'm not entirely certain, because many have been shut up for years,' Mabel said over her shoulder. 'I'm sure there are parts of the Hall I've never seen.'

They paused on the first-floor landing while Skeff peered out of a small iron-crosshatched window. 'That building down there – it isn't the stables, is it?'

Mabel looked out over Skeff's shoulder to the stone building past the kitchen garden. Nearly engulfed by honeysuckle and with slates missing from the roof, it looked a bit like a medieval ruin.

'No, the stables are around the corner. No horses now, only Lord Fellbridge's Wolseley. That building was originally the kitchen.'

'Doesn't look used now,' Cora said.

'It's been shut up for ages,' Mabel said. 'There's an underground tunnel that leads to it, but it was closed off when the current kitchen was installed in the basement here in the house. Was that after Victoria came to the throne?' Mabel asked herself aloud. 'Now, the family mostly uses the smaller square dining room where all our meals will be.'

When they reached the ground floor, they made their way out to the entrance hall.

'I remember seeing this fellow when we arrived,' Skeff said, pointing to a larger-than-life, gold-gilt framed portrait of a seventeenth-century man in a blue and silver brocade coat and a wig that looked as if an entire sheep sat on his head.

'Ah,' Mabel said. 'The first Lord Fellbridge – or possibly not. Historians can't quite make up their minds.'

'The ruling class,' Skeff said, 'could quite muddle up their families, couldn't they?'

Mabel chose the first of two corridors heading towards the east wing. 'Here we go.'

Cora looked back at the entrance hall. 'Oh, I know what's missing – there's no grand staircase.'

'No grand staircase,' Mabel agreed as they took the dog-leg turn. 'With Regency and Victorian add-ons and then modernisation the Hall is a bit higgledy-piggledy. The staircases are in corridors instead.'

The trio of Thirza, Lavinia and Pretoria looked round the corner at the dog-leg, appearing like a three-headed beast.

Mabel took note of their attire – all three wore day dresses of wool crepe with long sleeves and floaty side panels in navy, rose and that grey-brown shade called mole. The real difference in what they wore was that Pretoria now sported a suffragette sash.

'Breakfast?' Lavinia asked.

'Yes, just this way,' Mabel said, and stepped to the side of the corridor along with Cora and Skeff.

'I knew it was this way,' Thirza said as they passed.

'Good morning,' Pretoria greeted them. 'I hope we aren't last in.'

They continued on their way.

'You've known this place your entire life, Mabel?' Cora asked.

'I've known about it all my life,' Mabel said. 'Papa has supplied fruit and veg to the Hall since forever and along the way Lady Fellbridge – Emma – and Mrs Chandekar became acquainted. I've become more familiar in the last... well, nearly twenty years, I suppose,' Mabel said. 'I should be clearer about its history, but when it's so familiar, it's easy to be careless about details.'

'Will we meet Ronald's older brother, the heir apparent?' Skeff asked.

'That's Hal. He's the first son, and so he has the title. He has taken his wife and children off to Devon, and Lord Fellbridge is in Belgium on business.'

'Ronald emits a calm, pastoral aura, don't you think, Skeff?' Cora asked.

'He does,' Skeff said, looking at Mabel in a speculative manner. 'I wonder that after Edith died someone didn't think the two of you might marry.'

A vicar needs a wife. How many times had Mabel heard that around the village after a suitable time of mourning for Edith had passed?

'Ronald is a fine man and a dear friend,' Mabel said. 'But he knew better than to latch on to the idea that we would marry. Although, I believe the village talk might've been the last straw that sent me to London.'

'And we are the luckier for it,' Cora said.

'As is Winstone,' Skeff added. 'He'll be around today?'

'Yes. We are expected for dinner in Peasmarsh this evening. I'll take you two over one day this week, too, so that you can meet Papa and Mrs Chandekar.'

'The greengrocer and well-known wine and cordial maker as well as the legendary ayah,' Skeff said as they reached the square dining room. 'Just think, Cora, this week we're not only meeting those working for votes for women. We're also meeting Mabel's past.'

. . .

Breakfast was well underway in the square dining room when they arrived. Low, everyday conversations and the chink of knives and forks on china gave the impression that life had returned to normal, but Mabel sensed that the topic of Annie Harkin's murder took up a great deal of room even when it wasn't being discussed.

Across the room, she saw Binks setting down a platter of kippers, but when he straightened and turned, it was not Binks, but Campsie the gardener wearing a butler's jacket. Campsie had one shoulder that sloped – a war injury that never stopped him from his work in the garden. But here amid a great many things that could break, he looked a bit nervous. Mabel took up a plate and began to serve herself.

'So, Lady Fellbridge has you working inside today?' Mabel asked him.

Campsie looked down at his own attire. 'Yes, her ladyship asked if I would, and Mr Binks has given me one of his old jackets.'

'It suits you.'

He tugged on the hem of the jacket as his face reddened. 'Lord Fellbridge, he gave me one of his old bowlers and said I could wear it in the garden if I want.'

'You wouldn't want to make a permanent move into the house?' Mabel asked.

'No, no,' Campsie said. 'I don't mind helping out Deenie and Katie, but I'll be back in the garden as soon as ever I can. I've had to scrub my hands about down to the bone to be clean enough for them.'

He held out his hands and Mabel gave them more than a cursory look. They were red as if a stiff brush had been taken to them and had a few scratches and several old scars, but no wounds the size that the climbing rose outside Dorothea's window would give.

'There's tea in the pot here,' Emma called over from the table and so Mabel took her plate and sat next to her.

'How are you this morning?' Mabel asked.

'Oh, you know,' Emma said and busied herself buttering a slice of toast.

Mabel looked round the room and realised that nearly all the women were present, which meant they had been able to find their own way. She was pleased and a bit suspicious. Had no one become lost? She had half-expected she'd need to go in search of one or two of them in the far reaches of the Hall.

Emma's light dimmed. 'The mortuary wagon arrived quite early. They've taken Annie up to London.'

'I'd say Inspector Tollerton will be here before long,' Mabel said.

'I wonder how they fared at the pub,' Emma said. 'Please remind Inspector Tollerton rooms are here for his taking. And I believe I will insist that your Mr Winstone move up – I've already asked that the night nursery be made ready for him. That will suit, won't it?'

Mabel saw the scheming look in Emma's eyes, noted her suppressed smile and was both grateful and a bit embarrassed. She turned her attention to her eggs and mushrooms. 'Yes,' she said. 'It will. Thank you.'

'And that invitation of course includes Gladys.'

'She'll be delighted,' Mabel said. 'Will it be all right if Inspector Tollerton uses the steward's office today?'

'Today and every day until he finds who did this to Annie. It isn't as if we have a steward to turf out – it's only Harry that's ever in there nowadays, so I'll let Binks know.'

'Binks,' Mabel said. 'Binks and Annie were cousins, I hear.'

'Yes,' Emma said. 'I didn't mention that before? I'm so sorry.'

'Binks told me last evening,' Mabel said. 'Were they close?'

'I believe they were at one time. It's how Binks came to us. Quince longed to retire and Annie said that Binks needed to get away from Little Lever for his own good. He'd had a bit of trouble and it was so like Annie to want to see him put on the right path.' Emma's eyes shone with tears.

'Do you know what sort of trouble?'

'No,' Emma said. 'His past didn't matter to us – all we ask is a willing worker.'

'And he and Annie parted on good terms?' Mabel asked.

'Ah,' Emma said with a smile, 'I see even Lady Fellbridge is not excused from the detective's questioning.'

'Sorry,' Mabel said. 'How is he this morning – Binks?'

Emma lifted her hands palms up. 'One is never sure how Binks is. Stoic in the extreme. Annie used to say Binks fights his own wars and keeps his own counsel. It's probably what got him into trouble. And he isn't one for idle conversation. He does his job and either stays in his own quarters or goes down to the pub for a pint – perhaps Draker knows more about him that we do.'

'And now, about Lord Fellbridge' – Mabel didn't believe Emma's insistence on using Christian names extended to her husband – 'does he know what's happened?'

'No, but I'll send him a telegram later. He can stay where he is, because he knows Ronald is here.' Emma lifted her head with resolution. 'Now to begin our day. Binks already has the conservatory set with chairs and there's even a fire going to take the chill out of the air.'

'And here is our schedule,' Mabel said, opening her register. 'After a few words from you, Collette starts out with the potted history of the campaign. I believe things should run fairly smoothly, and I will be there as much as possible, but—'

'But you need to focus on the murder enquiry,' Emma said. 'Do what you can – I'll consider the enquiry as much your job for Useful Women as being my private secretary. I'll ring Lillian

Kerr to let her know your assignment continues in one way or another. I'd say she will want to hear from you, too. Now, you finish breakfast.'

Emma left with the trio. Mabel buttered a slice of toast and turned to Ruby on her other side.

'Has Dorothea come and gone?' she asked.

'I knocked on her door as I left,' Ruby said, 'and she said she would be right down.'

Across the table Collette Massey was telling Hildy the best way to cook a kipper. Ruby dropped her voice and Mabel had to lean in to hear.

'Dorothea had a disturbed night,' she said.

'What – someone came in?'

'No, no,' Ruby said, 'it's only that I could hear her shouting and crying out and wailing. I thought it might be why no one wanted to sleep in the room next to her.'

'I suppose,' Mabel said. It sounded as if everyone knew of Dorothea's sleep habits. Or perhaps only being among these other women is what caused her nightmares. Was Park right and Dorothea should be a suspect in Annie's murder – carried out when the balance of her mind was disturbed?

'She should be honoured, not ridiculed,' Ruby said. 'Think of what she did for us. My mother always said she was a stalwart.'

'Still, if you'd like to move rooms,' Mabel said, 'I can arrange it.'

'No, Mabel, I wouldn't do that to her. I rather feel as if she needs keeping an eye on, so I'll stay where I am.'

'Thank you, Ruby,' Mabel said. 'That's very kind.'

After breakfast, Mabel stopped at the steward's office and found neither Tollerton nor Park, but she did meet Dorothea in the corridor.

'Good morning. Have you been to breakfast?' Mabel asked. Despite Dorothea's weather-beaten complexion, she looked a bit peaky. 'It won't do to skip a meal.'

'It's all right, Mabel, thank you,' Dorothea said, smoothing her sash. 'Mr Binks very kindly brought me toast and an egg as well. He said he thought I might like a lie-in after being the one to... find Annie. I thanked him but did say I would be down for all other meals. I don't need mollycoddling. Hadn't we better go in?'

'Yes,' Mabel said, unable to disguise a smile. She'd happily take orders from Dorothea if it meant seeing the woman so sure of herself. 'It's just ahead there.'

The conservatory sat on the southeast corner of the Hall – an ornate iron-and-glass protuberance making it look as if a piece of the Crystal Palace had moved to Sussex. It held all manner of plants unsuited for the outdoors – ferns, fiddle-leaf figs, orange- and yellow-flowering clivias and small citrus trees in large clay pots.

Away from the glass, the conservatory segued into a music room suitable for small concerts. In the far corner stood a harp that was more conversation piece than musical instrument, and a grand piano upon which Mabel and Edith had delighted in playing four hands. A much better instrument than the old upright Mabel had learned to play on at home, although her sentimental attachment would never allow her to admit it.

When Mabel had moved to London, she had missed the piano almost as much as she missed her papa and Mrs Chandekar. Then, she met Park and he had a portable piano in his flat. It lacked the highest and lowest octaves, but they barely missed them. It meant only that when they played four hands, they must sit quite close on the bench.

The chairs in the conservatory had been arranged in two slightly curved rows facing a tall, carved oak music stand. Dorothea marched up to the front, but before she took a seat, turned to look at the trio behind her. She affixed her gaze on Pretoria who met her gaze at first, then looked down at her sash, adjusting it slightly as if the fit was too tight. Dorothea turned away and Ruby came up to join her. Hildy sat at the other end with Diane. Skeff talked with Emma and, standing apart from the others, Cora with Collette. When Cora noticed Mabel, her eyes grew wide. She put her hand on Collette's arm and guided her to Mabel.

'But I'm about to speak,' Collette said.

'This could be important, Collette,' Cora said.

'Is it about the bucket hat you wanted me to try?'

'No, it's about the car you heard,' Cora said. 'The car that was hidden by the trees and whose engine you heard starting up and roaring off in what seemed to you like a great hurry.' Cora gave Mabel a significant look. 'Yesterday afternoon.'

NINE

'A car?' Mabel whispered as Emma went up to the front. 'Collette, come out into the corridor.'

Collette looked back at Emma who stood at the carved music stand saying a few words. 'I'm about to speak.'

'Yes, of course you are,' Mabel said. 'Only for a moment.'

She got behind Collette and chivvied her out the door.

'You have a lovely view from the west wing, don't you, Collette,' Mabel said. 'Some days it seems as if you could see all the way to... Never mind. Tell me about this car. What you know could be important to the enquiry.'

Collette turned her attention to Mabel. 'Oh,' she said, 'yes, of course. I will do whatever I can, but I do hope I don't have to repeat my testimony again and again. In an enquiry, you should organise your questions so that—'

Mabel swallowed her objection to Collette's use of the word 'testimony' – they weren't in court – and dismissed the idea of explaining that it was the way of an enquiry to be asked the same questions again and again.

'What you saw and heard could be vital, Collette,' Mabel said. 'Vital.'

Collette took a moment to preen and then began. 'From the west wing, I can see a little wood, but there must be a road beyond it.'

'Yes, a road that circles the estate. It goes up into the village and around and back. It isn't a terribly busy road,' Mabel said.

'No one wants a busy road in the country,' Collette said, 'although we must get from one place to the other in some fashion and no one wants to go back to travelling by coach and horse.'

Mabel feared that the woman might start in on the history of transport in England, but instead, Collette glanced at the door to the conservatory and, apparently mindful of her time, continued.

'When I returned to my room yesterday afternoon, I sat at my window and had my tea and heard the car.'

'Did you notice what sort of car?' Mabel asked.

'I didn't actually see, but heard the engine start up and roar off.'

'Do you think—'

Mabel's next question was cut off when Cora came out of the conservatory. Behind her, the others sat waiting and Emma, at the carved music stand, said, 'And now, Collette.'

Mabel stood at the back of the room with her mind wandering far afield while Collette's voice kept her moored to the moment.

'... and our great suffragist leader, Millicent Fawcett. When I joined Mrs Fawcett in the non-violent fight for the vote, I told her the way to go about gathering others to our cause, was to...'

A shadow out on the terrace caught Mabel's eye. She edged her way along behind the women and through the plants, ducking under a tangled vine, until she reached the French windows. The iron handle creaked when she opened it and she winced but pressed on, and once out, closed the door behind her.

Park stood nearby against the stone wall squinting in the sunlight. 'Tolly has something for you to see,' he said. 'Are you free?'

Mabel took his hand. 'I certainly am.'

'Morning, Miss Canning. Morning, sir,' Ned greeted them at the door of the steward's office. He looked far too chipper for being up half the night, but that, Mabel thought, was youth for you.

In the steward's office, a shaft of sunlight cut through the window at Tollerton's back as he sat at the desk. WPC Wardle, notebook in hand, had taken the chair in the corner with Gladys at her feet.

'Good morning, Inspector,' Mabel said. She sat across the desk from him, much as she sat across the desk from Miss Kerr nearly every morning at the Useful Women office in London. She carried with her the register for the meeting of minds, which had already transformed into her notebook on the enquiry. She had stayed awake as long as she could the night before to add details and thoughts of her own, switching off her bedside light only when she could no longer keep her eyes open.

'How was breakfast at the pub?' she asked.

'Filling,' he replied. 'More so than yours, I'd say. Park tells me your ladies don't eat meat.'

'Many don't, but some do eat fish,' Mabel said, 'and so there were kippers.'

Tollerton frowned at her as if about to say how could a fish replace a plate of sausages, but he didn't pursue it and she was glad, because she wasn't certain she could have put up a good argument.

On their way from the conservatory, Park had tempered

Mabel's initial excitement at his words 'Tolly has something for you to see' by adding 'no arrests are imminent, sorry to say.' But what did he have and how long would she need to wait to see it?

'I'll want to see the butler,' Tollerton said.

'Binks,' Mabel said.

'Wardle tells me you know the cook here, Miss Canning,' Tollerton said. 'Cooks, that is. Could you bring them up one at a time?'

'Yes, of course.' Mabel didn't move. 'I'd say they're finishing up with the breakfast things. Meanwhile—'

The telephone on the desk jangled. 'Tollerton,' he answered.

He'd answered as if he'd known the call was for him, and he had been right. Park, Hildy and Mabel sat silently while Tolly mostly listened, interrupting only to ask short questions. Mabel prided herself in being able to fill in the unheard half of a conversation, but in this instance all she could tell was that Tollerton wasn't best pleased.

He rang off. 'How do they expect me to carry out one enquiry if I have two others hanging over my head? I could use two more sergeants up in London if I'm to pay any sort of attention down here.' He gave the telephone a look as if blaming it for his woes.

'Good thing you've got help on this enquiry then, isn't it?' Park asked.

Tolly grunted. 'I've got the fingerprint men coming back this afternoon to take samples from everyone. Will that be a problem?' he asked Mabel.

'I can't imagine it would be.'

'I'll leave Wardle in charge of it,' Tollerton said.

'Then you've nothing to worry about,' Mabel said.

Tollerton drummed his fingers on the desk.

'Tolly,' Park said, 'don't you have something to show Mabel?'

'Right,' he said. He shifted papers around and then picked up and handed over a framed slip of paper secured between two pieces of glass. 'This was under the cup and saucer on Mrs Harkin's tea tray.'

It was a place card that read *Mrs Harkin, priory gallery*. But *priory gallery* had been crossed out and corrected to *west wing*.

'Turn it over,' Tollerton said.

Mabel turned the frame over and read the words on the other side.

Do you remember Agatha Tyne?

Mabel looked at Tolly, then at Park. Her pulse quickened.

'Is it a warning? A call for help?' Mabel looked back at the message. 'Who is Agatha Tyne?'

'Who delivered the trays to the rooms?' Tollerton asked.

'Binks,' Mabel said. 'Annie Harkin's cousin.'

TEN

'Cousin?' Tollerton snapped.

But Mabel's attention had returned to the writing on the slip of paper.

Do you remember Agatha Tyne?

She studied first one side of the note – the label for the tea tray. *Mrs Harkin* with her room corrected to *west wing*. It had been written with a firm hand in a tidy, no-nonsense cursive style that reminded Mabel of a sprightly country dance. Deenie's, no doubt – she was a cheery sort. The correction was in the same hand.

The message on the other side – *Do you remember Agatha Tyne?* – had been written in a different hand. It was a skill of Mabel's – some might say a quirk – to look at a person's handwriting and hear music. The letters here took command rather like an organ voluntary did at the beginning of Sunday services. Strong, determined, calling attention to themselves. *Look here*, they said.

'I don't suppose the hand looks familiar?' Tollerton asked.

'No.' Mabel regretted she hadn't asked each woman to write down her own details, because then she could've compared. 'Mrs Harkin's name was probably written by Deenie – that would be easy to check. What does it mean?'

'We'll know that when we find who wrote it,' Tollerton said. 'There's no one here by the name of Agatha Tyne?'

Mabel shook her head. 'No. Someone was sending Annie a message?'

'Or was she leaving a message for someone?' Tollerton asked.

'It could've been left as a distraction,' Park said.

'That would need a bit of nerve, wouldn't it?' Mabel asked. 'After smothering Annie, the murderer takes the time to leave a false clue? He must've been plenty sure he wouldn't be disturbed.'

'I want to see the butler now,' Tollerton said.

'Binks?' Mabel asked. 'I don't think Binks killed her. They were family, how could—' She stopped herself before either Tolly or Park reminded her that a murderer was more often than not a family member. 'I'll find him for you. I wonder if Deenie saved the labels for the trays – it would do to check the others for messages.'

The telephone rang and Tollerton cursed it.

The conversation was short and, once again, heavy on the other side. Tollerton stood as he replaced the earpiece on the hook. 'I've got to go to London, but I'll be back by the end of the day. That means hold off with the butler—'

'I can talk with Binks,' Mabel said and before Tolly could object, she hurried on. 'I won't put the screws on him. I'll only ask those preliminary sorts of questions. And I can talk with Deenie and Katie.'

Tollerton reached for his hat and stuffed his notebook into his coat pocket before answering.

'You're not in charge, Miss Canning,' he reminded her.

'Heaven forbid,' was Mabel's reply.

'Wardle, you can take me to the station and then come back here. Don't let Miss Canning get carried away.'

'Sir,' Hildy replied, but she smiled behind Tollerton's back.

'And Winstone—'

'Yes, guv?' Park asked in a meek voice.

Tollerton snorted a laugh. 'Find something useful for Ned and Ted to do. Right, Gladys, it's up to you – keep an eye on this lot.'

Woof.

When Hildy and Tollerton had gone, Mabel turned to Park.

'Collette Massey heard a car yesterday afternoon.'

'On the drive?'

'No,' Mabel said. 'On the road that's just beyond the wood on the west side of the Hall. It was after she'd gone to her room from the garden. She heard the engine start up and the car roar away.'

'Where does the road go?' Park asked.

'It rather circles the estate,' Mabel said. 'Through the village, down by the church and around. You could take Ned and Ted out for a look.'

'Right,' Park said. 'I need to sort my own business out and then I'll find them. You'll wait until I return to talk with the butler?'

Mabel had a free hand and Park had never tried to stop her from carrying out what she could do for an enquiry, but she knew that didn't keep him from feeling protective at times. She felt protective of him.

'Binks is harmless,' Mabel said. 'But yes, I'll wait if I can.'

. . .

In the meantime, Mabel returned to the conservatory to find that things were ticking along in her absence – Collette had finished her talk and Binks had brought in the coffee.

Mabel took a cup and a slice of seedcake and explained to Emma that Inspector Tollerton, nearly overwhelmed with cases, had gone to London for the day.

'But you will continue with the enquiry,' Emma said with no question in her voice.

'Yes,' Mabel said, 'I will.' She then sought out Skeff. 'I'm sorry I'll miss part of your talk.'

'You've heard me rehearse it plenty of times,' Skeff said. 'You carry on as you must.'

They both turned to see that Pretoria had broken away from the other two members of the Greek chorus and stood talking with Cora, who gestured around Pretoria's head as if administering some sort of blessing. Most likely the conversation concerned hats, but Cora might be eliciting a bit of useful information to share later.

Mabel finished her coffee, left the meeting of minds to its own agenda and went down to the kitchen with her register and a sharpened pencil. The place teemed with activity – a complete contrast to the evening before when Mabel had crept down in the dark. Pans rattled, the tap gushed, pipes clanged and the enormous kettle's low moan slowly grew into a whistle as it worked itself up to a full boil. Deenie stood at the sink with her back to the room and at the table sat Ned and Ted over plates of eggs, bacon and a mountain of sausages. At their feet, chin resting on the table, sat Gladys, her eyes darting back and forth between the constables' bounty.

'What's this about?' Mabel asked.

Ned and Ted leapt from the table with knives and forks in hand. A small piece of egg jumped off Ned's fork and landed, as it happened, on Gladys' outstretched tongue.

'Breakfast,' Ned confessed, his face gone beetroot. 'It's only that Mrs Pilford offered.'

'And Miss Darling offered, too,' Ted added.

'We couldn't turn down their kindness, could we?' Ned asked. 'It wouldn't be polite.'

'Well,' Mabel said, 'I'd say you'd better kindly and quickly finish up and hightail it to the entrance hall. Mr Winstone is looking for you – on Inspector Tollerton's orders.'

The two plopped down in the chairs and in the matter of seconds, managed to shovel in a mountain of food. Deenie looked over her shoulder with a grin and Mabel could only watch with amazement.

Mouths full, the constables sprang up, grabbed their helmets and bolted for the door, Ned arriving first.

'Cowley!' Ted called and when Ned turned, his partner tossed a sausage at him.

But Ted had not given a thought to what lay between them – Gladys. With exquisite timing, she leapt in the air, snatched the flying sausage and, as they say, hit the ground running, her paws barely touching the floor as she flew out the door.

'Blimey,' Ned commented as the constables followed.

'Well, Deenie,' Mabel said, settling in at the table and eyeing one of the overlooked sausages. 'How are you and Katie faring here at the Hall?'

The cooks had taken the post two years earlier when the former cook at the Hall retired. They both lived in the village – Deenie Pilford's husband ran the garage and Katie Darling, unmarried and unrepentant, and her two young children lodged with Katie's aunt Janet who had the telephone exchange two doors down from Canning's Greengrocer.

'We're all right,' Deenie said. She sat, too, and pushed the sausage plate closer to Mabel then wiped her damp hands on her apron.

Deenie had black hair that she kept well away from her face

with a scarf wrapped round and tied at the back and the tail tucked under, and that clear porcelain skin that made her eyes – as blue as the morning's sky – stand out. The last time Mabel had seen Deenie was the end of summer – a reminder that since the war, life seemed to move quickly.

In the scullery, the door to the larder opened and closed followed by a *thunk* and a shout of 'You won't get the better of me, you!'

'Katie!' Deenie shouted. 'Company!'

Katie Darling stuck her head round the corner. She wore a large, old-fashioned mob cap that covered all her hair and left her round face looking like the man – or woman – in the moon.

She showed a toothy smile that included two slightly prominent front teeth and said, 'Sorry – we've a swede left in the garden over the winter. It's as big as your head and I have no idea what we'll do with it.' And then, as an afterthought, added, 'Hello, Mabel, how are you?'

'I'm well, Katie. And you?'

'Robbie's got the croup and Bets won't eat anything that isn't covered in strawberry jam. I can't tell you how wonderful it is to leave them with Auntie and come up here to the Hall. Although, you know, sad under the circumstances today.'

The circumstances. 'Yes, it is a terrible thing,' Mabel said. 'You two were both here yesterday, weren't you? I need to confirm everyone's whereabouts.'

'Confirm our whereabouts?' Deenie said. 'Oooh, Mabel, don't you sound official.'

'It's part of the enquiry,' Mabel explained. 'Every detail must be gathered.' *Because therein may lie a clue.*

Katie had paled. 'What have *we* got to tell them? We've got nothing to tell them. Deenie?'

'Oh now, Katie,' Deenie said, 'Scotland Yard doesn't care who your latest conquest is.'

'I'm off men,' Katie said with a firm chin.

'What about Campsie?' Deenie asked.

Katie's resolution melted. 'Ah, Campsie,' she said, her cheeks flushing pink. 'He's different.'

'So,' Mabel interrupted, opening her register. She'd forgotten how these two could go on. 'What time did you arrive yesterday?'

'I came up right about ten o'clock,' Deenie said. 'The church bells were ringing, so I remember that.'

'Katie?'

'I was just behind her,' Katie said. 'I couldn't get away from home fast enough. Auntie Janet can keep those two in line, but they walk all over their mum, let me tell you.'

'And were you down here in the kitchen the entire time?'

'No time for frolicking, I can tell you that,' Deenie said. 'First, we had sandwiches to make and the tea trays to sort out.'

Yes, the tea trays, Mabel thought.

'And all the dishes for the buffet supper to start on,' Katie added. 'I was knackered.'

'What time did you leave?'

'It was about one o'clock,' Deenie said, 'but I couldn't be certain because I didn't hear the bells.'

'The trays were ready for Binks by then?'

'All but for boiling the water.'

'Did you see him around?' Mabel asked.

Deenie shrugged. 'He came down early on to tell me Mrs Harkin and Mrs Lotterby had swapped rooms. The rest of the time, he was somewhere – he always is. Down the corridor to his rooms? The other way and up the stairs? He doesn't exactly announce himself when he walks by.'

'Ned told me there's a woman policeman here,' Katie said.

'WPC Hildy Wardle,' Mabel said. 'She's a fine officer.'

'Fancy that,' Katie mused, 'working with all those fellows.'

'Ready to join the police, Katie?' Deenie asked. 'Think of the benefits.' Katie made a face at her and laughed.

'Did you see anyone else coming or going?'

Deenie's face furrowed in concentration. 'No, no one. I heard the doctor drive in. You can't miss his arrival in that car of his. He didn't stay long.'

Dr Finlay had come to see to Annie at Emma's request, Mabel thought. Not that it did her any good.

'Anyone else?'

'Once I went out of the kitchen and I saw a lady looking down the stairs at me' – Deenie glanced at Mabel. 'I thought she was one of yours.'

One of hers. Mabel had already sensed she had taken on the role of mother hen to a brood of chicks.

'Can you describe what she looked like?' Mabel asked.

'She looked rather ordinary,' Deenie said. 'Normal. It didn't seem as if any part of her stood out, so I can't really say. But younger than the others.'

'Ruby Truelock,' Mabel said.

'Don't you want to know who I saw?' Katie asked.

'Who, then?'

'I saw Deenie,' Katie said and began ticking off the list on her fingers, 'and we heard the doctor in his car, and when we came back later, I saw Gladys the dog and that Mr Winstone who brought Gladys down to us.' Katie gave Mabel a significant look out of the corner of her eye. 'Well done, Mabel.'

'Thank you, Katie,' Mabel said. 'When did you come back to prepare the buffet?'

'Deenie and I walked back together at four. We came straight to the kitchen to cook and get the water boiling for the bain-maries. Once the supper was set up, we left. That was about six o'clock. That's what Lady Fellbridge had told us to do – you can ask her.'

'We'd packed up and gone by the start of the dinner,' Deenie said. 'That was the arrangement with Lady Fellbridge – that we'd clean up last evening's dinner things this morning. I arrived before seven o'clock to be met with Binks telling us such awful things. That's all we know.'

'Did you see anyone else?'

'No,' Deenie said.

'No,' Katie said.

Mabel wrote in her notebook and the cooks watched in silence. She looked at them and after a moment said, 'Are you certain?'

Katie put a finger in the air. 'Wait now, I saw one of your ladies, too, Mabel. But it was earlier on when we were here midday. I forgot, sorry.'

And that's why, Mabel thought, *an investigator must ask the same questions over and over.*

'What did she look like?' Mabel asked.

'Well, she was standing at the halfway landing up the stairs and the light was behind her, so I couldn't see much,' Katie said. 'She wasn't too tall. Nor too slim. She asked for Mr Binks, but he wasn't about.'

Not too tall and not too slim. Annie Harkin, looking for her cousin? The description could also do for Diane Lotterby.

'Right,' Mabel said, closing her register and standing. 'That's all for now.'

'For now?' Deenie asked. 'What else could we have to tell you?'

'Something may come to you,' Mabel said. 'Do either of you know an Agatha Tyne?'

She was met with blank looks.

'Is she one of your ladies?' Deenie asked. 'We don't have her on the list.'

'Deenie,' Mabel said, 'did you write out the ladies' names on slips of paper for the tea trays yesterday?'

'Yes. Lady Fellbridge had left instructions because some of the ladies are a bit finicky – no butter here, no piccalilli there, extra cress, only egg yolk. We had to keep things straight.'

'Did you save them?' Mabel asked.

'The papers? Yes. In case we needed them again. The one didn't come back from Mrs Harkin, but I suppose that doesn't matter now.'

'May I see them?'

'Yes, sure,' Deenie said with a slight frown. She took a small wooden box from the shelf and held it out.

It didn't take Mabel a moment to inspect them. No other had a message on the back.

'You'll excuse me, won't you,' Katie said in an officious manner. 'I've the chickpeas to soak.'

Deenie sighed. 'Chickpea loaf with beetroot sauce, Mabel – how does that sound?'

'Interesting,' Mabel said.

'I've had a time with the menus – all this vegetarian business. Broad beans in parsley sauce, potted lentils, curried lentils, lentils and potatoes au gratin. Pease porridge can go only so far, you know.'

Coffee had finished in the conservatory and the women were beginning to settle themselves for the next talk – Skeff and the role of the newspapers in the campaign for the vote. As Binks cleared the coffee things away, Mabel sidled over to Emma.

'Do you know Agatha Tyne?'

Mabel had a long list of people to ask that same question of, and she realised she'd better get to it.

'No,' Emma said, but with a frown. 'Should I know her?'

'Not necessarily. Also, Emma, do you have a sample of Annie's handwriting? It would be helpful.' Helpful how, Mabel didn't explain and she was relieved that Emma didn't ask.

'Yes. Would you like me to get it now?'

'Not this minute, but when it's convenient. Now, I'd like to speak with Binks.'

'Of course,' Emma said.

Mabel had thought it through – Park had taken Ned and Ted out on the grounds and there would be no point in waiting for him, because by then the butler would have lunch duties to attend to. Mabel could well ask Binks a few questions on her own. She caught him in the corridor with the trolley of dishes.

'Binks, if you have a moment, could I have a word?'

'Yes, Miss Canning, of course.'

Mabel nearly sighed with relief. Of course Binks would talk to her – what objection would he have? When Hildy came down the corridor, returned from dropping Tollerton at the station in Rye, she said, 'Constable Wardle will be there, too.' Hildy held up and waited. 'We'll go to the steward's office.'

'Shall I bring coffee?' Binks asked.

Mabel sat behind the desk and shuffled a few sheets of paper aside, uncovering a surprise – the glass-framed note from Annie Harkin's tea tray the previous afternoon. Had Tolly left it on purpose for Mabel?

Hildy took the chair to the side with her notebook. They had declined coffee, but nonetheless, the butler remained standing as if ready to serve.

'Binks, thank you for coming in,' Mabel said. 'Inspector Tollerton has been called away to London and will be back this evening. I'm continuing with the enquiry.'

Binks nodded. Mabel opened her register to a fresh page, turned it round on the desk and held out a pencil.

'Would you write down your details for me?' Mabel asked. 'Name, previous place of residence. It's fine if you'd like to sit down.'

Binks took the pencil, hesitated for a moment and then sat. He didn't labour over his writing, but he did take his time.

When he'd finished, he pushed the register over and laid the pencil on the desk.

Mabel studied not the words he'd written, but his hand. It had a slow and steady pace, the letters carefully set down. It reminded her of the Chopin prelude that repeated an A flat over and over. It was not the hand that wrote the note found on Annie Harkin's tea tray. Next, Mabel handed Binks the glass-covered slip of paper.

'I understand the tea trays yesterday afternoon each had a place card of sorts. Here is the one for Annie's room. Turn it over and take a look.'

Binks took off his spectacles and Mabel was startled to see that the butler's eyes were different colours – one more green than blue and the other more blue than green. The difference wasn't marked and the light-blue tint of his lenses made it so that she'd never noticed – not that Mabel had ever made a habit of gazing into the butler's eyes.

He held the glassed-in paper quite close and looked down at it for the longest time without speaking. Finally, he handed it back to Mabel and put his glasses back on.

'Did you notice this yesterday?'

'No, ma'am, I did not.'

'It was tucked under the saucer.'

'I hadn't collected the tray from the room, ma'am.'

The tray hadn't been collected from Mabel's room either. She had noticed a day maid scurrying around earlier – but there was a great deal of work for one young woman.

'Do you know what the note means?' Mabel asked. 'Could Mrs Harkin have written it to you?'

'I don't know why Mrs Harkin would write a note to me,' Binks said.

'You were cousins,' Mabel pointed out.

'Yes, ma'am. Our fathers were brothers and we lived close.'

There, Binks had offered an actual piece of information instead of having it dragged out of him. There's keeping yourself to yourself, and then there's being stubborn on purpose.

'Aren't you Cheevers, then? Wasn't that Annie's name before she married?' Mabel asked.

'Yes, Cheevers was my surname, ma'am,' Binks said. 'But my father died, and my mother married again and I took my stepfather's name.'

'This Agatha Tyne,' Mabel said, pointing at the note, 'perhaps it's someone the two of you knew in Little Lever.'

'I wasn't much more than a child, ma'am.'

Mabel waited for him to say more and in the silence, heard Hildy writing in her notebook. Mabel jotted down a few thoughts in the register. 'Did anyone come near the trays after you'd set them up?'

'Deenie and Katie set the trays up. Then they left for the afternoon, and I brewed the tea and took the trays up to the rooms.'

'Back and forth and up and down that many times?' Mabel asked.

'I use the trolley, ma'am. Put several trays on and leave it at the bottom of the stairs to each wing.'

'Still,' Hildy said, 'you were away from the trays and someone could've got to them.'

'I suppose so,' Binks said.

'Were the trays all the same?' Hildy asked.

'No,' Binks said. 'Her ladyship had left instructions for each lady visiting – what sort of sandwich or if they prefer their tea a certain way. That's why the trays had bits of paper on them with the ladies' names. Just as that one does.'

'And you didn't notice the paper with Mrs Harkin's name on it had writing on the back?' Mabel asked.

'I had no cause to look.'

'Mr Binks,' Hildy said, 'have you ever had any run-ins with the police?'

He turned to Hildy, his look unknowable behind the tinted lenses. 'Yes, Constable,' he said, 'I have.'

ELEVEN

'Binks was cautioned for violence outside a drinking establishment in Little Lever in 1911,' Mabel told Park. They stood on the terrace outside the conservatory. Gladys had stuck her nose in the yew, given a *woof* and now pursued a squirrel down the length of the hedge.

'Violence?' Park asked.

'He broke a man's nose,' Mabel said. 'It wasn't long before he came here. He gave that information up voluntarily.'

'It looks good, doesn't it?' Park asked. 'Makes him appear honest and forthright. It's a good ploy to give up one thing to hide something bigger.' He took his spectacles off and polished them with his handkerchief. 'His eyesight – did that happen during the war?'

'No,' Mabel said. 'It was ages before he came here. I remember Edith telling me that he'd been hit on the head by a loose slate falling off a roof when he was about sixteen. He's worn those thick tinted glasses ever since. He seems to manage all right.'

At that moment a bee wandered between them, making for a pot of campanula, and Mabel waved it away. Campsie, walking up from his cottage at the stables, saw her movement and waved back. He wore Binks' cast-off jacket and Lord Fellbridge's bowler hat that looked – even at that distance – as if it had seen better days.

'Campsie the gardener,' Mabel said. 'He's probably helping with lunch.'

'What about him?' Park asked.

'I haven't interviewed him yet,' Mabel said. 'Several of the women put him in the garden for most of yesterday afternoon. Dorothea, in particular, spent time with him.'

'Has he been here long?' Park asked.

'Since he was a boy. He had worked his way up to under gardener before the war. He was injured in 1915. His shoulder healed poorly, but he begged Lady Fellbridge to take him back and here he is head gardener. Now, he's the only gardener. I'll chase him up about where he was all afternoon.'

'At least you have something to go on,' Park said.

'These first interviews are the tip of the iceberg, aren't they?' she asked.

'I noticed someone has joined Miss Goose in wearing a suffragette sash,' Park said. 'Who is it?'

Mabel glanced back into the conservatory. 'Pretoria Fleming-Jones. Emma said she had gone back and forth between being a suffragette and suffragist. But now, donning her sash, is she making a bid for leading the group? Perhaps she believes that Dorothea needs competition. I'll find out. Come on – let's listen to the rest of Skeff's talk.'

They went into the conservatory and settled in chairs at the back. Cora sat in the middle chair of the front row wearing a bicorn hat the colour of twilight and smiling up at her partner. If Skeff began her lecture with a bit of nerves, she had shed them now and spoke to the women in a way that both entertained and informed. As she told the story of the campaign as it had been covered in the press, Skeff poked fun at the 'rags' of the day and even told a story or two of her uncle Pitt, ending with the passage of the Representation of the People Act.

'... and that day in November 1918, Uncle Pitt ran into the pressroom at the *Intelligencer* and shouted, "Stop the presses – Parliament has just declared that women are people, too!"'

Skeff finished to enthusiastic applause, then, chairs scraped as everyone stood and began to share their own stories of that day.

When Ronald looked in from the terrace and caught Mabel's eye, she and Park went to meet him. From his coat pocket, Park pulled out the map of the Hall.

'You aren't still using that, are you?' Ronald asked.

'This is a charming and nearly historic document,' Mabel said. 'And quite accurate in its own way, although perhaps a new version is needed. I'll have a word with your mother and then arrange for Miss Kerr to find one of the Useful Women who can draw an accurate and detailed floorplan of Fellbridge Hall.' Mabel, an evangelist for Useful Women, never passed up an opportunity.

'It's quite a map for a twelve-year-old,' Park said. 'I found everything easily – apart from the dragons.' Park tapped it. 'Fellbridge Hall seems just the sort of place to have hidden rooms.'

'What,' Ronald said, 'you mean the priest hole? I don't think I put it on my map.'

'You *do* have a priest hole, then?' Park asked.

'It's what we called it,' Ronald said. 'Ours is more a child's cubby and Victorian, too, so not old enough to be an actual priest hole. It's under the stairs in the nursery wing. It doesn't lead anywhere and once you're inside, you can't get out on your own – I found that out when Hal closed me up in it.' Ronald sighed and added, 'But I suppose that's what older brothers are for. Father is the one who knows about all the hidden bits of the Hall.'

Emma approached. 'Hello, love,' she said to her son, and Ronald kissed her. 'Will you stay for lunch?'

Ronald and Emma moved off to follow the others out of the conservatory. Park stayed, pulled his notebook out and flipped a page. 'There are French windows all round the ground floor – the conservatory, gallery, library and formal dining room. And they all use old keys that are easy to jimmy.'

'So anyone could get in any time?' Mabel asked just as the rest of the London Ladies' Murder Club came out onto the terrace.

'Good, here we are,' Mabel said. 'Can we take a moment to go over the enquiry? Cora, I saw you talking with Pretoria.'

'Bluebells,' Cora said. 'She wants to add bluebells to a bicorn hat.'

'Did she say why she's wearing a suffragette sash?' Mabel asked. 'She didn't have it on yesterday. Is it a challenge to Dorothea?'

'I'll ask,' Cora said.

'Good,' Mabel said. 'Now, we don't have much as far as suspects go. Hildy and I have had a word with Binks. I see no motive to murder his cousin. He told us he'd been arrested in 1911 for a brawl outside a pub in Little Lever. Skeff, could you look into any local newspaper reports? That wasn't long before he came here.'

Skeff frowned. 'Yes, leave that with me.'

'We need to find out who Agatha Tyne is,' Mabel said, and explained about the note on the tray.

'*Do you remember Agatha Tyne?*' Skeff repeated. 'Perhaps this brawl Binks was in had something to do with her.'

'Quite possible,' Mabel said. 'Could you keep an eye out for her name in regards to Binks? But if Agatha Tyne is a suffragette, then we'd best ask each woman. Cora?'

'Yes, I'll do that,' Cora said.

'Good. Now.' Mabel steeled herself. 'At the moment, the

only other suspect we have is Dorothea, because of her opportunity and what has happened to her in the past... and... her volatile nature.' She didn't like speaking the words, but there it was.

'Mabel?'

Mabel jumped. Where had Ruby come from? Had Mabel mistaken her for a fern in the conservatory? How much had she heard?

'Yes, Ruby, were you looking for me?'

'Did you notice Pretoria wearing a suffragette sash today?' Ruby asked. 'She wasn't wearing it yesterday.'

'I did notice,' Mabel said.

'It's only I thought it a bit curious,' Ruby said. 'Yesterday, only Mrs Harkin and Dorothea wore their sashes. Will Emma choose a leader from the group now that Annie is gone? Do you think wearing a suffragette sash will sway opinion? I have my mother's sash with me.'

'Are you interested in leading the campaign?' Mabel asked.

'I?' Ruby asked, hand to her chest. 'No, it isn't that. It's only I would... want to show my support for the cause.'

Until that moment, Mabel had thought Ruby wanted only to help with the investigation. Did the young woman want to show support or did she see herself as the vanguard of a new, younger spirit marching into the campaign? But would she murder for the chance?

'I can't imagine wearing a suffragette sash would be a requisite,' Mabel said. 'Thank you for keeping me abreast of your observations, Ruby, but please don't go out of the way to...'

'Snoop?' Ruby asked. 'But it's what we do as investigators, isn't it?'

After a pause, Skeff said, 'Well, to lunch?'

. . .

Skeff and Cora took Ruby with them, but Hildy stayed behind to examine the map. Park held it out and shifted it to align with where they stood. Mabel looked down at it and then out to the landscape – the formal garden, the kitchen garden and, as the land fell away, the derelict old kitchen nearly swallowed by honeysuckle. Ronald had included the old kitchen, but it was not much more than a green blob. Mabel tapped on the map.

'There's a tunnel between the old kitchen out there and the house,' she told Park and Hildy. 'It comes up somewhere next to the formal dining room.'

'A tunnel?' Hildy repeated.

'It's closed up,' Mabel said. 'Hasn't been used in ages. I've never seen it.'

'It would be worth a look,' Park said.

'Right,' she said, 'let's go.'

At Mabel's command, Gladys, who had been sunning herself on the terrace, popped up, shook herself from nose to tail, and followed them into the conservatory, out the door and down the corridor.

As they crossed the entrance hall, Mabel said over her shoulder, 'We'll need candles. There should be a few in a drawer of one of the sideboards. Lord Fellbridge keeps candles in every room for emergencies. He never quite trusted the electrics.'

They arrived in the formal dining room on the ground floor of the west wing, and Mabel took a moment to look round. The long table could seat sixty and along the walls were side tables and wall mirrors that displayed soup tureens, platters and coffee services in several different antique bone china patterns.

Park waited near one of the French windows with Gladys snug up against his leg and away from the breakables. Hildy, hands behind her back, gazed up at the bigger-than-life painting hanging over the fireplace – an early eighteenth-century Lord and Lady Fellbridge and their five children with an out-of-scale landscape of the estate seen through the window behind them.

The room brought back memories for Mabel. Ronald and Edith's wedding dinner had been held here as well as late suppers at Christmas balls, but none of those occasions had involved going through the tunnel out to the old kitchens.

'The door has got to be here somewhere,' Mabel said, hands on her hips.

They checked all available alcoves, tapped on panels and tried to turn various pieces of decorative woodwork to release a latch, but could find no door, secret or otherwise.

'Doesn't seem likely the murderer stole in through the old kitchens and then into the house, does it?' Hildy asked.

'You're right there,' Mabel said. 'I believe that door is bricked up.'

'I'll take a look at it to make certain,' Park said.

'Good, thanks,' Mabel said. With a last look at the room, they left.

Luncheon – known as 'lunch' in London – was served as a buffet as the Sunday evening supper had been. This style of eating could become quite a thing, Mabel thought as she stood in the queue. Skeff continued to receive high accolades for her talk, answering questions and discussing salient points over bowls of nettle soup. Binks stood at the end of the buffet table, keeping an eye on things. He seemed innocuous, placid. What could prompt him to kill his cousin?

Mabel let the conversation flow around her as she ate her lunch. Pretoria squabbled with Thirza and Lavinia about the bluebell wood, saying the two hadn't waited for her so that they could see it together. They denied it, but she swore she'd seen them. Diane bemoaned the hole mice had eaten into a silk turban she'd put away in her wardrobe at home. 'Camphor will keep them away,' Dorothea told her.

Park excused himself – one of his never-ending reports to write – and left with Gladys for the Cork.

'See you later,' Mabel called after and he gave her a wink.

Diane Lotterby spoke after lunch. Mabel had the distinct impression Emma had arranged the speakers just so that Diane's booming voice would keep everyone awake. She reported on the campaign in her district where they had arranged a series of afternoons called Tea and Talk, and had invited women who normally could not attend anything because they were keeping house and children. The church hall had filled because of the remarkable stroke of genius by one of the committees who arranged to have several nannies take all the children away on a picnic. It had resulted in good support for the cause and an increase in membership in the local chapter of the Women's Freedom League. Still, Diane's voice seemed to hammer on Mabel's ears and she rose and slipped out, meeting Ned in the corridor.

'Well-timed, Miss Canning. Inspector Tollerton is ringing for you.'

'Is he?' Mabel thought this could be either good news or Tolly was ringing to remind her not to overstep her bounds.

'Ah, good,' Tolly said when Mabel answered. 'I'm stuck here for the rest of the day, so I thought I'd see what you've got for me.'

Surprised, pleased and a bit apprehensive, Mabel opened her register and gave Tolly the important points.

'... and I spoke with Binks.' She waited but heard no complaint and so told him about the butler's run-in with police. 'Skeff is looking for a newspaper report.'

Tollerton was silent for a moment, but over the line Mabel heard a page turn and realised he was taking notes.

'Anything else?'

'This morning, Miss Fleming-Jones was wearing a suffragette sash,' Mabel said.

'Is that significant?'

'The aim of this week is to select a leader to resume the votes for women campaign. I believe Emma thought everyone would accept Annie, but now that she's gone... it could be seen as throwing her hat into the ring.'

'Any of the others show interest?'

'Well, Ruby might be considering it.' Mabel shook her head in disagreement with herself. 'Or, she might want to fit in with the others. Or wear her mother's sash as a show of respect.'

'Right,' Tollerton said. 'I'll try to get back this evening.'

'I do hope you can. Lady Fellbridge will have a place for you here at dinner,' Mabel said. 'You'll have Hildy there, and Cora and Skeff, so you'll have someone to talk with.'

'Yes, fine. I'm sure the kitchen at Fellbridge Hall roasts a fine joint.'

Mabel decided not to mention the chickpea loaf.

TWELVE

Holding onto her straw hat against a gust, Mabel took off down the drive. She told herself that the evening ahead was only a casual gathering, but she didn't believe that. She loved her papa and Mrs Chandekar and – *go on, admit it, Mabel* – she loved Park Winstone and she wanted everyone to get along. Papa hadn't cared much for the other men Mabel had kept time with. She hadn't cared for them much either, so it didn't matter, but now it did.

She took the footpath that led up to the road and into the village where Canning's Greengrocer sat on a corner proudly proclaiming its existence in gold and green lettering on the window. Under the window were crates of oranges, stalks of rhubarb, bundles of asparagus spears and a veritable mountain of cabbages. When she stepped inside, the bell above the door jingled and Reg Canning looked up from stacking coins on the counter. He wore a white apron over his shirt and tie so that he offered a tidy appearance even if he was sweeping up onion skins and clumps of dirt that had sloughed off the potatoes.

'Hello, Papa.' She went to him and kissed his cheek.

This visiting every few months – the last time had been

Christmas – had had a startling effect on Mabel. When she'd arrived on Friday, she'd noticed his dark hair marked with grey at the temples and the lines at the corners of his eyes. When had they appeared? He was only fifty-five. When she was in London, in her mind's eye, she saw him as he had been when she was ten – thick dark hair with a single distinct wave to it. But his piercing eyes could still nail you to the spot as they had when she'd been caught stealing a slice of treacle tart from the larder, and he'd never lost the smile that assured you he found humour in nearly every situation.

He squeezed her shoulders and gave her his best try at a stern look. 'I have half a mind to lock you in your room and not let you go back up there.'

'And what will you do with the other half?' she asked him, following their usual script. 'Oh Papa, what's happened is a one-off. It's Fellbridge Hall not Whitechapel.'

Mabel had taken the time earlier to telephone Mrs Chandekar and had been prepared for her papa's reaction.

'How is Lady Fellbridge?' he asked.

'Annie was her dear friend, but she's being brave.'

'That's to be expected. Go through before Moti comes looking for us,' he said. 'I'll finish here and close up.'

'Leave the door unlocked for Park,' Mabel said.

'Humph. Couldn't even escort a lady to dinner?'

'I've come early, you might notice, to lend a hand,' Mabel called back as she went through the passage that led to the cottage.

Some greengrocers may live above their shops, but not at Canning's in Peasmarsh – they had an entire cottage behind. Reg had bought the going concern thirty-three years ago, sight unseen, and made all the arrangements by post from India. In the beginning, the negotiations had been for his new family – wife and baby on the way – but had ended as the home where he would bring up a motherless child. Not that Mabel had ever felt the lack and that was because of Moti Chandekar, baby Mabel's ayah who became their housekeeper as time went on.

In the kitchen, a fresh pot of tea sat on the table. 'Hello, love,' Mrs Chandekar said. She took Mabel's face in her hands and kissed her cheek. 'Is Mr Winstone not with you?'

'He'll be along. What can I do?'

'There's nothing to do but to sit and have a cup of tea,' Mrs Chandekar said and set about pouring two cups.

Mabel could only ever remember Mrs Chandekar wearing English clothes, but she always had at hand a long silk paisley scarf in vibrant colours to wrap round her shoulders. Today it was purple, and it set off her dark skin and jet-black hair, now shot through with silver and pinned back in a neat bun. Her age – somewhere in the vicinity of fifty – did nothing to diminish her beauty.

Mabel missed having a mother – but in an abstract way. Emotionally, that role had been filled by a young Indian woman who had appeared one day at the Army Service Corps office in answer to an English newspaper advertisement for an ayah. Over the weeks of the voyage to England, her initial intention of returning to India with a different British family had weakened and then she had given it up altogether as ayah and baby bonded and Reg Canning's anxiety over rearing a child on his own diminished.

After tea, Mabel laid the table in the dining room and went to the kitchen where the aroma of rich spice made her mouth water.

'I'll send Papa back here and wait for Park myself,' she said. 'There's no need to frighten him the moment he arrives.'

Once she'd shooed her father off, Mabel stood at the window and watched the nearly deserted street that ran through the village. The garage lay over the road to the right with a few more shops – butcher, fishmonger, newsagent. No baker in the village, but her papa ordered in bread from Rye, delivered fresh every morning for his customers. Canning's was on a well-positioned intersection. One road led down to the church while the other that Mabel had walked on came up from the King and Cork. Fellbridge Hall lay just beyond the pub. The road went through the village and all the way to Rye.

Staring out the window made Mabel nervous, and so she took up the broom and swept the floor with a bit too much vigour, knocking over a sack of seed potatoes under the counter. She crawled underneath to collect them and that's when she heard the bell jingle and saw a familiar pair of boots walk in with four furry paws just behind.

Park bent over, looked under the counter at Mabel and called out, 'Shop!'

She giggled as she backed out and, still on her knees, rested her arms on the counter.

'Yes, sir,' she said. 'See something you'd like, sir?'

He put his elbows on the counter, leaned over and, in a low voice, said, 'I see something under the counter I'd like.'

They kissed until Gladys *woofed* and a voice boomed at the back door.

'Did someone call "shop"? Shop's closed – did you not see the sign?'

Park shot upright, whipped his hat off and held it to his chest while putting a hand out to help Mabel up. Once she was standing, he let go of her hand, but otherwise didn't move, looking as if he were ready to face a firing squad.

Reg Canning seemed to have grown both taller and wider and now filled the doorway. He'd taken off his grocer's apron and put on his coat along with a fresh collar. He had a fierce look, which Mabel did her best to ignore.

She brushed her skirt off. 'Papa, this is Park Winstone. Park, my father Reginald Canning.'

As calm as she had intended to be, still she ended the short introduction a bit breathless, as well as a bit annoyed. After all, at thirty-two years of age, she had the right to see whom she pleased. Reg would disagree – she was his only daughter, as he'd reminded her when she'd arrived on Friday, and so he had a duty to be concerned.

Reg Canning gave Winstone the once-over as if he were judging a delivery of suspect cauliflower.

'Very pleased to meet you, Mr Canning,' Park said, extending a hand.

'And about time, I'd say,' Canning replied and shook. 'What with all that's gone on.'

'Park isn't responsible for my private investigations,' Mabel said. 'And this is Gladys,' she added. 'Say hello, Gladys.'

On cue, the dog trotted over to Mabel's papa, sat and held out a paw.

Reg looked down his nose at Gladys. 'Trying to butter me up, are you?' Gladys replied with a throaty comment. 'I thought as much,' he said, but shook the paw regardless.

'Shall we go back?' Mabel asked.

'Let me just put the lock on the door,' Reg said, 'although I suppose it's too late now.'

Mabel laughed. Her papa gave her a stern look which she knew he didn't mean. Park, his eyes wide, shot her a look of apprehension.

Gladys' nose led them to the kitchen and Mabel made the introductions. Mrs Chandekar took Park's hand and said, 'You're very welcome.'

'It's kind of you to ask me,' Park said. 'I've heard a great deal about you, of course.'

'We haven't heard nearly enough about you,' she replied with a smile. 'You realise you're on trial this evening, don't you? Not with me, but it's difficult for Reg. Now, Gladys, have you found your supper?'

Gladys had surreptitiously scooted her way over to the hob

where there lay a small dish covered with a cloth. She stretched her nose up as near as ever she could get to it.

Mrs Chandekar stroked the dog's head and said something to her in a low voice. Gladys looked at her with adoring eyes. 'Chicken without the spices for you,' she said, set the dish on the floor and whisked off the tea cloth.

Using the cloth, she opened the oven door and was about to lift a large earthenware baking dish out of the oven when Reg walked in.

'Here now.' He hurried forward and used the cloth to retrieve the dish. 'Shall I take it through?'

'Yes, thank you,' she said as he went off.

'Glass of something?' Reg called from the dining room.

'You go on,' Mabel said to Park. 'We'll be right behind you.'

Park straightened his collar and set off. Mrs Chandekar closed the oven door and Mabel checked the potatoes, then they followed.

Mabel's papa stood at the sideboard, holding a bottle of nearly clear liquid in one hand and an empty glass in the other.

'Drink, Mr Winstone?' he asked.

Mabel gasped. They'd arrived in the nick of time.

'Papa,' she said sharply. 'That isn't your parsnip cordial, is it?'

'Why shouldn't it be my parsnip cordial?' Reg asked. 'There's nothing wrong with it.'

'Isn't there?' Mabel asked. 'At the very least, it's an acquired taste. You shouldn't force Park to drink it.'

'I'm not forcing him to drink it,' her papa said with far too much innocence. 'Would you like something else, Mr Winstone?'

'No, sir,' Park said. 'I'll take the parsnip cordial.'

'Well,' Reg said to his daughter, 'there you are, then.' He poured the small glass to the brim. Mabel winced as she watched Park take a swig.

It was a moment before he swallowed, and then a moment after he swallowed as he tried not to cough. After that, he inhaled deeply and drank the rest down in one go.

'What do you think, Mr Winstone?' Reg asked solicitously.

Park held out the empty glass and, in a strained voice, said, 'I think I'll have another.'

Reg narrowed his eyes, but then shrugged as if he knew he'd been beaten – at least in this first skirmish.

They sat at the table in the dining room, which Mabel remembered they'd never used much except for company. Once Gladys finished her supper in the kitchen, she joined them, settling in a shaft of evening light from the window.

They ate a casserole of chicken that had simmered in a blend of spices Mrs Chandekar mixed from ingredients Reg ordered especially for her. Conversation during dinner began with the weather and moved on to Mabel telling a light-hearted story about a recent Useful Women assignment that concerned picture hanging.

'And what is it you do for the diplomatic service, Mr Winstone?' Reg asked.

Mabel wasn't certain Park's usual explanation – *I read other people's letters* – would fly with her papa, and Park must've sensed this, too, because instead he told a story of tracking down black-market traders from the war. She saw grudging respect in Reg's face and almost a nod of approval.

'Please do have more,' Mrs Chandekar urged Park, who needed little encouragement to take his third helping.

'I don't see why you're staying up at the Hall,' Reg said to Mabel. 'We aren't that far away here.'

'I need to be on hand at all times, Papa – as I've already explained. It's my job.'

'Yes, yes,' he muttered. 'And you, Mr Winstone – you aren't staying at the Hall, are you?'

A slight pause ensued. 'I put up at the pub last night, sir,' Park said.

'Emma insisted that Park stay at the Hall tonight,' Mabel said.

'Why?' Reg asked. 'Are you in danger up there? You said police had everything in hand.'

Had she said that?

'No one is in danger,' Mabel said. 'Ronald is keeping a close eye on things, too. It's to... assure the women that everyone is safe.'

'I don't know why Lady Fellbridge puts on these meetings or lectures or whatever they are,' Reg grumbled.

'And yet you're happy she does,' Mrs Chandekar said, 'especially when you receive her orders for your fruit and veg.'

Reg grinned at the housekeeper and Mabel grinned at Park.

'It's a meeting of minds,' Mabel said. 'Restarting the campaign for the vote and increasing education for all.'

'Well,' Reg said to his daughter, 'you just remember we're not far away, so there's no reason you couldn't pop down now and then.'

'How is Binks getting on with the extra work?' Mrs Chandekar asked, easing them onto what she must've thought was safer ground.

'Binks gave Campsie one of his old jackets to wear and so Campsie is helping out indoors,' Mabel said.

'Lady Fellbridge hasn't asked Binks to drive any of the ladies round, I hope,' Reg said with a laugh.

'Binks drives?' Mabel asked. 'Can he see well enough to drive?'

'He doesn't seriously drive,' Mrs Chandekar said.

Mabel raised a questioning brow.

'He takes Lord Fellbridge's old Wolseley out on a Sunday afternoon,' Reg said, 'drives up and through the village and back round to the estate. Just a big circle. He's been doing that for – how long, Moti?'

'It was last year sometime his lordship taught him to drive,' Mrs Chandekar said. 'He's always looking for something Binks might be interested in – otherwise, if he's not butlering, he's sitting down in his quarters all on his own or at the pub nursing a pint.'

Conversation turned to the growing number of automobiles in London, adding to traffic congestion with trams, buses and horse carts, but Mabel's thoughts stuck on the Wolseley and Binks driving out on a Sunday afternoon in a big circle round the estate. That must've been the car Collette had heard but did not see out of her window.

They finished with rhubarb pudding and custard after which Park said, 'That was a fine meal, Mrs Chandekar.'

'Always a fine meal at this table,' Reg said. 'Now, Gladys, you wouldn't want to go for a walk, would you, girl?'

Walk was one of Gladys' favourite words. She *woofed*, stretched and trotted over to the table.

'Mr Winstone,' Reg added, 'care to come along?'

Park rose. 'Yes, sir.'

Mabel watched them go, hoping that Gladys would use her indescribable ability to oil any situation. She turned to Mrs Chandekar.

'Oh dear.'

'Well, it was to be expected, wasn't it?' Mrs Chandekar asked. 'Your father wants to know what Mr Winstone's intentions are. Do you know?'

'No, I don't know what his intentions are,' Mabel said. 'I don't even know what *my* intentions are.'

'Not even an inkling?' Mrs Chandekar asked.

'No. Yes. Possibly.' She began to collect the dishes. 'Papa does remember how old I am, doesn't he?'

'Of course not,' Mrs Chandekar replied. 'To him, you will forever be a ten-year-old girl who climbed too high up in the school beech tree and had to be rescued.'

They left while it was still light. The men shook hands and Mabel kissed her father and Mrs Chandekar. Gladys accepted scratches behind ears with her usual aplomb, then snorted and trotted off ahead of Mabel and Park.

'That went well,' Mabel said, linking her arm through Park's as they walked down the road. Park made an unintelligible reply. 'What did you two talk about on your walk with Gladys?'

Park looked at her out the corner of his eye. 'Oh, you know – the price of tea in China. That sort of thing.'

'That bad, was it?'

'I suppose we won't know for certain until next time I visit and we see if he offers me parsnip cordial.'

They stopped on the side of the road long enough for Mabel to kiss him. 'You are intrepid.'

On they went, turning off onto the footpath toward the Hall, Gladys zigzagging ahead of them in the dying light of the spring evening. Where the footpath split, they took the left fork towards the King and Cork.

'Am I really to be in the nursery?' Park asked.

'Ostensibly,' Mabel said. 'But now that you've walked all the corridors of the Hall, I'm sure you can find your way round with no problem.'

When they reached the pub and walked in, he asked, 'You wouldn't want to come up while I pack my bag, would you?'

Mabel looked round, spotting three men and two couples whom she knew and greeting them with little waves. 'I think Gladys and I will wait here,' she said. 'Look, there's Binks.'

The butler sat in a corner near a lamp with a half-full pint glass in front of him, his bowler hat beside him on the settle and a newspaper in his hand. He looked up and they exchanged 'evenings'.

Draker, behind the bar, nodded to them. He was a thin man who always seemed to be polishing something – the cloth running over the bar, the hand pumps, the lid to the jar of pickled eggs. 'Evening, Miss Canning, Mr Winstone,' he said. 'Drink?'

'No thank you, Mr Draker,' Mabel said. 'I'm just waiting for Mr Winstone.'

'I'm moving up to the Hall this evening,' Park said, 'and am just going to collect my things.'

When Park went off to his room, Mabel asked Draker, 'Has Inspector Tollerton returned?'

The barman picked up a glass, held it up to the light, found it wanting and got to work with his cloth. 'He rang a bit ago and said to keep his room but he wouldn't be back until tomorrow.'

Mabel considered this as giving her a free hand in the investigation and, as Draker moved off to serve a customer, she set about trying to pick out a distinct line of enquiry to follow.

It was Ronald who opened the door when they arrived back at the Hall.

'Your mother suggested Park stay and she's put him up in the nursery,' Mabel said before they got any further than the entrance hall.

Ronald didn't blink an eye. 'Yes, yes, you're very welcome.'

'How is your mother?' she asked.

'You know how she can be,' Ronald said. 'Sad one minute, practical the next. She had me go straight into the post office in town to send Mrs Harkin's husband a telegram.'

'Poor man,' Mabel said.

'Yes,' Ronald said. 'Even though they had been estranged for so long, such news can be a shock. Well, Mabel, you'll show Park to his room?'

'I will. We saw Binks at the pub.'

'He'll be back at closing time to lock up,' Ronald said.

'Papa and Mrs Chandekar told me that Binks drives,' Mabel said. 'That was a bit of a surprise.'

Ronald clicked his tongue. 'Father thought it would give Binks an interest, that perhaps he'd like to learn about automobiles. I think Binks takes the Wolseley out just to make Father happy. He never goes far. Well, I'll say good night.'

Ronald went on his way to the family rooms on the first floor of the west wing, and Mabel led Park the opposite way, to the first floor of the east wing. The nursery scullery, the night and day nursery rooms, and the nursemaid's bedroom occupied most of the corridor. The nursemaid's bedroom had been turned into a project room for the boys as they grew older and now was filled with half-built models of ships and the like. Mabel opened the door to the night nursery, switched on the light and stood back.

'Here you are,' she said.

The room consisted of two short beds, a round table about two feet high, and four chairs to match.

'I feel like Gulliver,' Park said. 'Did Lady Fellbridge do this on purpose?'

'I believe she did,' Mabel said. 'This way, you can tell people you're staying in your own room when actually you're in mine.' She switched off the light. 'Just in case word got back to Papa. Come on, let's go.' Park caught her round the waist, and she added, 'They'll be waiting for us – the murder club, that is.'

They didn't stop to make cocoa, but Mabel nipped into the billiards room for a bottle of brandy. Then, she led Park to the priory gallery staircase and up two flights. She tapped first on Cora and Skeff's door and then Hildy's. 'Bring your own glasses,' she said and soon the five of them were settled in Mabel's room on chairs, footstools and the dressing table bench all pulled round the unlit fireplace. Gladys hopped up onto the bench window seat.

'Once again, Skeff, well done on your talk,' Mabel said as she opened her notebook and took up her pencil.

'She's an historian, aren't you?' Cora asked. 'You show how newspapers are woven into the events of our time. She knows so much more than just the *Intelligencer*.'

'Well,' Skeff said, reddening. 'A reporter is only as good as her next story.'

'Hildy, how did fingerprinting go?' Mabel asked. 'No one put up a fuss?'

'Have you ever tried to herd a flock of chickens?' Hildy asked. 'You get them going in the same direction and suddenly one breaks this way and another breaks that way. Mrs Massey remembered she had a letter that needed writing and Miss Poppin required a cup of tea to take a pill and... well that's the way it began. Then, Miss Goose stepped forward to go first. I believe she rather shamed them into it. Miss Truelock didn't show at all and I had to go and find her.'

'Where was she?' Mabel asked.

'In the kitchen talking with Mrs Pilford and Miss Darling.'

'Why?' Park asked.

'She said she was waiting because she wanted a word with the butler. She apologised for forgetting.'

Ruby had been loitering around the kitchen the previous afternoon, too. She had given what had sounded like a careful account of her time while Annie Harkins was murdered, but hadn't mentioned this.

'We gave our prints willingly,' Cora said. 'Although I had a time washing the ink off after.'

'Inspector Tollerton said he wanted the cooks' prints, too,' Hildy said. 'At dinner, there was some talk of inky prints on the chickpea loaf.'

'Chickpea loaf?' Park asked.

'A lucky escape on your part,' Mabel said.

'Once they were all in the salon,' Hildy said, 'Mrs Massey tried to tell the fingerprint man how to go about using the ink. But in general, although no one was best pleased, none of them protested. They don't seem terribly worried about what happened to Mrs Harkin. In regards to their own safety, I mean. They aren't happy about it, I don't say that, but you'd think with no murderer found they'd be concerned. It's as if they think, well, this is what the murderer came to do and now, job done.'

'Perhaps they don't realise that they are each of them a suspect,' Mabel said.

'Fingerprints may show something,' Park said. 'They'll be comparing them to what was found in Annie Harkin's room.'

'Skeff?'

'No newspaper in Little Lever,' Skeff said, 'so I'm onto the Bolton paper now.'

'I've more of my own work to do tomorrow,' Park said, 'but I haven't finished with the footpaths yet.'

'Yes,' Mabel said. 'Walk through the bluebell wood out to the road. That's where Collette heard the car.' She turned to the others and, hoping it didn't sound as if she were joining up the dots, added, 'Binks drives.'

'Does he?' Skeff asked.

'We just heard this from my papa and Mrs Chandekar,' Mabel said. 'He's usually out and about on a Sunday afternoon, but I doubt if he had the time yesterday.' She made a note to ask him. When she looked up, Skeff, too was writing as were Park and Hildy. Cora stared off into the middle distance with a slight frown.

'It's odd, isn't it,' she said. 'About Ruby in the kitchen. Why would she want to talk with Binks?'

Mabel nodded and made another note.

'Hildy,' she said, 'any word on Inspector Tollerton?'

'A quick conversation on the telephone. He's up to his ears in cases in London and not best pleased about it. He'll be down for certain tomorrow.'

'Well, we'll see what we have for him by then,' Mabel said. 'Cora, what about Pretoria wearing a suffragette sash?'

'I've a brief report about that,' Cora said. 'I made a comment about it and she became a bit... huffy, saying no one could fault her for her commitment to the cause and perhaps it was time for her to be more forthright with her beliefs. Then she asked me about bluebells again. If she wants to see the bluebell wood, she should go and see it.'

Mabel tapped her pencil on her chin. 'Ruby asked me about wearing a sash. She's brought her mother's along with her and now she seems keen to show her colours.'

'She's wanted to help you with the enquiry,' Park said, 'but perhaps she wants to keep close to you for some other reason.'

'For what reason?' Cora asked.

'Exactly,' Mabel said. 'Right, let Ruby keep an eye on the enquiry. Meanwhile, I'll be keeping an eye on her.'

Skeff peered into her empty brandy glass. 'Full day tomorrow, it sounds. We'd best be off.'

The women said their good nights and left. Mabel, on the footstool, smiled at Park who stayed perched on the edge of the dressing table bench. Gladys stretched and sighed in her sleep.

'I promise,' Mabel said, reaching a hand out to him, 'the mattress on my bed doesn't feel as if it's filled with potatoes.'

THIRTEEN

The next morning, Park and Gladys were up and away when Mabel returned from having a wash.

As she dressed, Mabel contemplated her day and the questions she would ask. She had barely met Annie Harkin before the woman was murdered and now wished she'd known her longer. Had Annie said or done something to one of the women attending this meeting of minds that would cause them to lash out? It could've happened years ago and only now, seeing Annie again, brought the long dormant resentment to the surface. Were they jealous of her closeness with Emma and that she was considered the presumptive leader of the campaign?

Annie had been suffocated. A pillow put over her face until her weak heart gave out with the struggle. Could the method of her death be significant? Had someone wanted to stop her from talking?

Mabel picked up her register-turned-enquiry notebook and set off for breakfast.

. . .

Ruby Truelock waited at the bottom of the staircase on the ground floor, clutching her hands at her waist.

'Good morning, Mabel.'

'Good morning, Ruby. I was just going to breakfast. Have you been?'

'I have,' Ruby said, 'but I'll walk with you, if that's all right. Do you have an assignment for me today, Mabel, or shall I gather any general information I can and turn it over to you later?'

'No, there will be no need for any listening in,' Mabel said.

'You know more than you are saying about the investigation, don't you?' Ruby asked.

'An investigator always gathers rather than disseminates,' Mabel said in a vague fashion.

'You don't want to let your suspect know that you know?'

Mabel didn't care for the searching look Ruby gave her. 'You have your talk scheduled today.'

'Yes,' Ruby said, apprehension replacing scrutiny.

'I'm sure you'll do well,' Mabel said and then added, 'Ruby, why were you looking for Binks on Sunday afternoon?'

Ruby gave Mabel a blank look and then said, 'Did you know they were related – Mrs Harkin and Mr Binks?'

'Yes, I did.' Mabel stopped outside the square dining room. 'Who told you?'

'I heard it mentioned,' Ruby said. 'I thought, in case it was relevant to the enquiry, I'd better let you know. Now, I must get my notes together.'

Only Thirza, Lavinia and Pretoria – with her suffragette sash – were left in the dining room.

Was she displaying the courage of her convictions, or could it be Pretoria's way of throwing her hat in the running to lead the next wave of the campaign? That field seemed to be getting crowded.

Mabel approached the buffet to find it nearly empty. She gathered what she could and had just sat down with the scrapings off the scrambled egg platter and the last slice of toast when Dorothea appeared at the door wearing her straw hat and her sash over her coat.

'Oh Mabel,' she said, putting one hand on the doorpost and one hand to her chest.

Mabel dropped her toast and leapt up. 'Dorothea, are you all right?'

'I heard something,' Dorothea said faintly. 'I heard something from Annie's room.'

The Greek chorus paid them no mind as Mabel went to Dorothea and led her to a chair. 'But you couldn't have heard something from Annie's room. You moved, don't you remember?'

'No, no,' Dorothea said. 'It was Sunday afternoon. I had fallen asleep and had a dream, but now I'm not certain that it was a dream. I believe it was real.'

Mabel sat next to her. 'All right. What did you hear?'

Dorothea took a quick breath and then another, then her face drew up in anguish. 'Scuffling,' she said and pressed a fist against her mouth to stifle a sob. 'A muffled voice? "You!" and "trust" or perhaps "trusted". I didn't realise... I had dismissed it, because... you see, I sometimes have nightmares as if I'm back there again.'

'In Holloway?' Mabel asked, hoping it wouldn't send Dorothea over the edge.

'Yes,' Dorothea said, now calm. 'Annie had it as bad as I did, but she never had nightmares. Still, it was why she didn't mind being next to me. She never woke up shouting and trying to throttle the pillow as I do, but at least she understood.'

Mabel should've been elated – here was another clue to

explore – but instead, she saw a vision of Dorothea, in the middle of a nightmare during an afternoon nap. Not knowing what she was doing, she stumbled out of her own room and into the next one, smothered Annie then stumbled back to awaken later and find Annie dead. Could she be hanged for this? Mabel recalled Dorothea's pocket full of feathers.

At that moment, the Greek chorus made a show of rising and excusing themselves. As they made their way to the door Pretoria asked no one in particular, 'Is there time to see the bluebells before the lecture? I've yet to have the opportunity.'

'Oh Pretoria,' Lavinia said, 'you're not still going on about that, are you? We didn't go out to the bluebell wood without you.'

'It's all right if you did,' Pretoria said loftily. 'You don't have to pretend.'

At that, a single bell was struck. Mabel abandoned what little breakfast she had on her plate and went off to oversee the day of talks.

Ruby did an admirable job of telling the story of her mother, Susan's, ragged school in Bolton. By all accounts – and exemplified by Ruby's anecdotes – Susan had been determined to let no destitute girl go uneducated and had been fearless when it came to confronting angry fathers who would rather send their girls to the factory. When she finished, Ruby answered one or two questions, the bell clanged and the door opened to Binks bringing in the tray of coffee. Mabel got in the queue just behind Ruby.

'You'd no need for nerves,' Mabel said, 'you did a fine job.'

Ruby blushed and it brought a bit of colour to her face. 'I did it for Mother.'

'Do you teach at the school?'

'Not since she died,' Ruby said. 'I don't do well with a great deal of commotion around me – the children were too much. Mother left the school in competent hands, although funds remain an enormous concern.'

'Was Mrs Harkin involved in your mother's school?' Mabel asked. 'She lived so near and they knew each other from the campaign.'

Ruby busied herself adding a spoonful of sugar to her coffee, drizzling the milk and slowly stirring the mixture. Without looking up, she replied, 'I don't remember that she was. Did Emma say something about that? Or one of the others?'

Behind them, Diane Lotterby cleared her throat – a signal to move the queue along. Ruby walked off and Mabel poured her own coffee, sloshing it into the saucer in her haste to get out of the way.

Next, Collette Massey would speak on her husband's work for the campaign in the House of Commons, and in the afternoon... who was it? A quick check of her agenda told her Pretoria would discuss employing the best of the suffragette campaign – 'Deeds Not Words' – and the non-violent strategies of the suffragists to obtain the vote for all.

She left them to it and went to the steward's office, striding in to find PC Ned Cowley sitting behind the desk, arms spread to clasp the corners as if he was about to pronounce judgement.

At the sight of Mabel, he sprang from the chair, knocking his custodian helmet off the desk in the rush.

'Inspector Tollerton, Miss Canning,' he blurted out. 'He rang.'

'And told you to take over the enquiry?' Mabel asked.

'Lord no, ma'am. He's told me to make myself available to you or Lady Fellbridge or Mr Winstone or the Reverend. He's asked Mr Winstone to keep an eye out and says that it's good the ladies are staying in a group with their talks and such, because there's no... no...'

Ned's face screwed up in thought, then his eyebrows jumped. 'Indication! He said there's no strong indication as to where the murderer came from and so we are all to be vigilant. He's said WPC Wardle is constable in charge while he's away, but if any questions come up about the enquiry, we are to ask you. He said he'll try his best to return later today and I am to keep on my toes.'

'Well, Constable Cowley,' Mabel said, 'thank you for that report.'

Ned grinned and nodded.

'Here you are, Constable,' said a sugary voice behind Mabel. It was Katie Darling with a tray of tea and cake and her mob cap set slightly awry. When Katie saw who sat behind the desk, her sweetness evaporated.

'Where's Constable Scott?' she asked.

'Ted's gone home,' Ned replied, tugging on his jacket in an officious manner. 'I'm on duty the rest of today. Can I help you with anything, Miss Darling?'

Katie looked down at her offerings and with a note of resignation said, 'Oh well, I suppose you could have this.' She set tea and cake on the desk. 'I'd best go back to the kitchen. Deenie's struggling with something called mushroom meringue.'

Katie left. Ned remained at attention, but Mabel saw him eyeing the tea. 'When you finish that,' she said, 'it's back to the entrance hall with you.'

'Yes, Miss Canning.'

The rest of the morning proceeded as scheduled. Mabel was attentive and alert through Collette's effusive description of her late husband and their quiet life in Biggleswade that she had forsaken in order to join the campaign.

At lunch, Mabel heaped macaroni cheese onto her plate leaving just enough room for a lentil croquette and a small roasted beetroot. She found it difficult to join in normal conversation and only listened as Dorothea waxed poetic about Campsie's cutting border that promised peonies the size of cricket balls and Pretoria nattered on about – dear God – bluebells.

The women rose to serve themselves steamed jam pudding and Skeff, at the end of the queue, leaned down to whisper something in Cora's ear. Cora, in return, blushed and laughed.

Mabel heard a small sigh and looked over at Emma who watched the two with tears in her eyes. She glanced over and said, 'I wish we had been that brave – Annie and I. To live as we pleased.' Emma shook her head. 'But then, I wouldn't have Ronald and Hal, and I can't bear the thought of that.' She laughed and the tears tumbled out. 'It makes no sense, does it?'

Mabel had no words of comfort about lost love, but Emma didn't seem to expect them. She reached in her pocket and drew out an envelope.

'An old letter from Annie,' she said. 'You wanted to see her handwriting.'

'Yes,' Mabel said, grateful to be brought back to the enquiry, 'yes, I did. Thanks.'

She looked at the writing – a strong, firm hand that brought to mind the sounds of an organ voluntary at the beginning of a church service. It was the same hand that had written *Do you remember Agatha Tyne?* on the tea tray place card.

So then, it had been Annie sending a message.

Mabel heard next to nothing of Pretoria's talk in the afternoon, her mind whirring.

Had Binks not recognised his cousin's hand? Mabel would give him that – it had been a good few years and perhaps they'd never corresponded – but if Annie left the note on the tea tray it must have been for him. She sensed a stubborn streak in the man. He fought his own wars, but did he know who to fight over this Agatha Tyne and refuse to tell the enquiry?

Tea had been served, but Mabel went instead to the steward's office to ring the pub. Had Tollerton returned?

Before she reached the desk, the telephone rang, and she jumped.

'Fellbridge Hall, Mabel Canning speaking.'

'Miss Canning, this is Miss Kerr at Useful Women.'

The fact Miss Kerr would need to identify herself in such an official fashion sent a shiver of fear down Mabel's spine.

'Yes, Miss Kerr?'

Miss Kerr cleared her throat. 'Augustus Malling-Frobisher has gone missing.'

FOURTEEN

'Augustus?' Mabel echoed. She sank down in the desk chair. 'How do you know?'

'The maid rang to pass on the news from his school, St Botolph's. You know it? Didn't you visit him there?'

'I was there for Parents' Day in January,' Mabel said weakly. 'It's just up the road near Tunbridge Wells. Does his mother want me to go and search for him?'

'That may not be necessary,' Miss Kerr said. 'Apparently he's on his way to you.'

'Here to Fellbridge Hall?'

'This is what I know. It is half term and Augustus has stayed at school with a few other boys.' *Abandoned*, Mabel thought. 'He didn't turn up for breakfast and was nowhere to be found on the school grounds. The assistant head rang his mother and his friend Walter. Your name was mentioned by both. Does Augustus know where you are?'

Mabel sighed. 'I may have mentioned it a few weeks ago when I escorted him to Victoria Station after he made a surprise visit home hoping his father was visiting from Australia.'

She surveyed her surroundings, half expecting to find Augustus smoking in the corner.

'Should we inform the police?' Miss Kerr asked.

'Let me take care of that,' Mabel said. 'We've got two constables here from the police station in Rye.' She offered this knowing Augustus could run rings around Ned and Ted.

'Very good,' Miss Kerr said, the words rushing out in relief. 'I will tell Mrs Malling-Frobisher I am leaving the matter in your capable hands. She already fairly begged me to do just that. Now, Miss Canning, can you tell me anything about your current circumstances? Lady Fellbridge did ring yesterday.'

'We have yet to solve the murder, but we are making progress in the enquiry,' Mabel said. 'As the police would say, it's early days yet. Did you know Annie Harkin?'

'I knew of her,' Miss Kerr said. 'Such a loss. Now, you will let me know about Augustus.'

'I will.' *The little blighter*, Mabel thought, but with fondness.

She replaced the earpiece on the hook only for the telephone to jangle at her.

'Fellbridge Hall, Mabel Canning speaking.'

'Mabel dear,' Mrs Chandekar said. 'There's someone here who would like to speak with you.'

There was a shuffling and a clatter and then a chipper voice said, 'Hello, Miss Canning, it's Augustus.'

Mabel returned to the conservatory to find Campsie gathering plates and cups and Dr Finlay sitting at ease with tea and Madeira cake. He rose when Mabel appeared.

'Good afternoon, Doctor.' She looked round the room. 'Are we all well?'

'The good doctor had come to see me,' Dorothea said, straightening and adjusting her sash. 'I'm afraid you've made a trip for nothing. I'm well as can be. I was out in the garden first thing this morning asking Campsie for work and I'll go out again this afternoon.'

Doctor Finlay took the rebuff in his stride. 'Very good, Miss Goose – nothing like a bit of fresh air to clear the head.'

'Would you like a fresh pot, Miss Canning?' Campsie asked as he picked up the tray.

'No, thank you.' Mabel turned to Emma. 'I must go up to the shop for a bit – I've a visitor waiting for me – a young boy who is one of my frequent assignments from Useful Women.'

'Is it your Augustus?' Emma asked.

'Do you know about him?' Mabel asked.

'You didn't think you could leave the village and everyone would forget you?' Emma asked with a smile. 'Your father has a story to tell every customer and Moti shares your news with me. They are quite proud of you, even though they miss you. We all do.'

Mabel's chin quivered. She missed many things about Peasmarsh – Papa, Mrs Chandekar, Ronald, Edith – no hope there – the hop fields in July, someone else cooking for her. But if she returned to Peasmarsh, even more would she miss Park and Gladys, spending evenings with Cora and Skeff, the excitement of London, Miss Kerr and the variety of Useful Women assignments. Perhaps most of all, she would miss the London Ladies' Murder Club.

'Yes,' Mabel said, 'Augustus got it in his mind to come for a visit. I'll go sort something out and will return... as soon as I can.'

'Bring Augustus with you if you like,' Emma said. 'I'd love to meet him.'

Mabel laughed, but then sobered up. Was the boy to stay?

'It's too late in the day to send him back to school,' Mabel said. 'If Papa and Mrs Chandekar don't mind putting him up tonight, perhaps he can spend the day here tomorrow. I will go first thing after breakfast and collect him.'

'Well,' Finlay said, 'I shall be on my way, too. May I give you a lift to the village, Miss Canning?'

'Yes, thanks,' Mabel said. 'Emma, I'm sorry to miss the discussion, "The Promontory View – Whither Next?" I should be here to assist you.'

'We'll manage just fine.' To the others she said, 'I'll go and gather my notes and so we'll have a few minutes before we begin. Take a turn round the garden if you like.' Then she cast a pensive look over the women. Mabel realised that this was to be when a new leader would've been selected. Had this been the moment Annie would've taken the reins? Would the discussion build into confrontation?

Emma left and the rest of the women followed with the trio trailing behind and Pretoria's complaints rising above them like a cloud. 'They'll have gone over by the time I see them – excluded as I was from your jaunt.'

'Pretoria, we did not go to the bluebell wood without you,' Lavinia said with exasperation.

Pretoria harumphed. 'Perhaps it was a badger I saw rustling in the hazel.'

'Are you comparing me to a badger?' Thirza asked and the argument continued as they drifted down the corridor.

With the doorway clear at last, Mabel walked out followed by Finlay.

'Good thing you're coming along, Miss Canning,' the doctor said as they went. 'Lord Fellbridge has given me a tour of the Hall and all its eccentricities and I must say it's a fascinating old place, but I'm not entirely certain I could find my way anywhere on my own.'

'You're not alone there,' Mabel said. 'It's only because I've been coming up here for so many years that I know the place.'

'You were great friends with Reverend Herringay's wife, weren't you?'

Mabel paused at the dog-leg. 'Edith. Yes. Did Ronald tell you about her?'

'No, it was Janet Darling, the font of all Peasmarsh knowledge,' Finlay said and guffawed. 'God knows what secrets I've told her – she could squeeze blood out of a stone.'

They continued down to the entrance hall and encountered Binks crossing towards them. He had his glasses off and as he walked, he polished them with a handkerchief and didn't seem to notice Mabel and Finlay until he was nearly upon them.

'Miss Canning, Doctor Finlay,' he said. 'Do you need anything?'

He stopped and looked at them expectantly as he put his glasses back on.

'Err...' Finlay said faintly as he looked at Binks' different-coloured eyes – one more blue than green, the other more green than blue. 'Ah, no, thank you.'

'We're just off to the village,' Mabel explained.

The butler looked from Mabel to Finlay as if awaiting further direction, but when none came, he gave the impression of a bow. 'Good day.'

Finlay and Mabel watched him go.

'It's unusual, isn't it, Doctor?' she asked as she pulled open the ancient oak door and they walked out onto the doorstep. 'Different-coloured eyes.'

'Yes, certainly uncommon,' he said.

'I'd never noticed with the lenses in his glasses being coloured.'

'Has he worn glasses all his life?' the doctor asked.

'No, only since an accident when he was sixteen,' Mabel said. 'Or so I'm told.'

'Yes, well, poor lad,' Finlay said. He gave another look back into the entrance hall, then turned to Mabel. 'How have the staff fared with the death of Mrs Harkin? I've called on the ladies, but perhaps I should see to the others as well?'

'It's unsettling for them, of course, but it really only touches Binks, because he and Annie Harkin were cousins.'

'Cousins,' Finlay echoed. 'Odd, isn't it, that her death happened here? Do you believe Binks has an idea of who might've done this?'

If he does, Mabel thought, *he hasn't said so to me.* Then it occurred to her that here at hand Mabel had an expert to answer one of her questions.

'Binks drives, did you know that?'

Finlay frowned. 'Does he see well enough for that?'

There you are then. 'Everyone says he does. It was Lord Fellbridge who taught him and lets him take the Wolseley out. He doesn't go far – around the village and back again to the stables where the car's kept.'

'Is that so?' Finlay asked with some amazement. 'It shows you what a person is capable of if he puts his mind to it, don't you think? Well done, Binks.'

Eight-year-old Augustus sat at the table in the cottage's kitchen with his legs dangling over the edge of the chair seat and his school cap on his knee. He smiled, displaying a fine set of front teeth – but the smile wobbled a bit at the corners.

'Are you surprised to see me, Miss Canning?'

Mabel, determined to remain in a position of authority until she'd had her say, stood over the boy and took on a serious tone.

'You know, don't you, that it isn't going to do either of us any good if St Botolph's and your mother decide I'm not a good influence on you. What if they say, "Oh, we can't ask for that Miss Canning at Useful Women – she'll just get him into trouble"?'

The smile wavered and melted, as did Mabel's heart.

Mrs Chandekar poured the tea. 'Augustus came into the

shop a while ago and introduced himself to your father in quite the proper fashion.'

Mabel sat, squeezed Augustus' arm and smiled. 'Well, so – how was your journey?'

He beamed. 'I took a bus from the crossroads near school this morning. It was going all the way to Rye, but not through Peasmarsh, so I got off early and the driver gave me directions and I walked the rest of the way.'

'You've been travelling all day?' Mabel asked. 'And didn't the driver wonder why you were on your own in your school uniform?'

'I told him I was coming to visit my auntie,' Augustus said, a note of apprehension creeping into his voice.

'I'm always delighted to see you, Augustus,' Mabel said, 'but did you really think it would be a good idea to come and visit without telling your mother?'

Augustus' forehead knitted with worry. 'Mother said it would be better if I stayed over at school this half term, because any day now she will be welcoming a new member of the family.' He watched Mabel carefully as if waiting for comprehension to dawn, then he whispered, 'A baby.'

A baby? Augustus' father lived in Australia, although Mabel remembered he had been back for a visit in… September. And here it was barely six months later. Oh dear.

'Will you send me back to school?' Augustus asked.

What else could she do? Not today – it was too late for that and so perhaps one night at the greengrocer's would work. Augustus was her responsibility, though, and so she couldn't foist him off on Mrs Chandekar or her papa for the rest of the week. But Mabel had a murder enquiry to conduct and she couldn't spend her time showing the boy the sights of Sussex. Then she had a vision of him knocking about nearly empty St Botolph's. Staying over at school during half term should be reserved for students whose families lived abroad and truly had nowhere to go, not those who had to travel only a short train journey up to London.

'Before we decide anything,' she said, 'I'd better have a cup of tea. Have you eaten?'

'He was famished when he arrived,' Mrs Chandekar said as she popped the lid on a tin of jumbles, 'and so he's had a ham sandwich and the last wedge of treacle tart.'

Regardless, he attacked the biscuits with relish.

Mabel shook a jumble at him. 'They're best dunked first,' she said, watching him fight with one as he tried to take a bite.

'It's all right if they knock out a couple of my milk teeth in the back,' Augustus said.

Reg came down the passage from the shop and stood in the doorway of the kitchen with his hands on his hips and looking as ferocious as he could.

'Well now, is this rapscallion eating me out of house and home or have you saved one of those biscuits for me?' he demanded.

Augustus froze with half a jumble sticking out of his mouth. He chewed and swallowed in an instant – possibly swallowing one of his milk teeth, too – and offered Reg the plate. 'I haven't eaten them all, Mr Canning. I was saving the last one for you.'

'Reg,' Mrs Chandekar said, 'why don't you show Augustus what it's like to be a grocer. You might have a bit of work for him to do.'

Augustus hopped off his chair. 'Can I wear an apron like yours, Mr Canning?'

Man and boy went off to the shop and Mabel put her elbow on the table and dropped her chin in her hand. 'What am I to do?'

'Do you want to send him back to school?' Mrs Chandekar asked.

'I couldn't do that,' Mabel said. 'How depressing. But I must ring his mother and say he's been found and is well.' She went no further, but turned a quiet, serious gaze on Mrs Chandekar and waited.

'You don't think I know that look of yours.' Mrs Chandekar shook a finger at Mabel and laughed. 'All right – he can stay here and sleep in your room.'

The clouds cleared from Mabel's thoughts and she clasped Mrs Chandekar's hand and gave her a kiss on the cheek. 'You wouldn't mind? Papa wouldn't mind? At least for tonight. I'll come for him in the morning.'

'It's perfectly fine. The boy would get lost in Fellbridge Hall,' Mrs Chandekar said.

Mabel thought that, like Gladys, Augustus would learn his way round Fellbridge Hall faster than anyone there.

Mabel went to the telephone in the passage and looked out to the shop. Augustus had donned one of Reg's aprons that had been shortened by rolling it at the waist so many times that the boy looked as if he'd wrapped a bicycle tyre round his middle. He stood on a crate counting onions and stacking them into a pyramid.

She rang Miss Kerr first and after that, Mrs Malling-Frobisher, who gushed with gratitude at Mabel's report of Augustus being found and never once said 'send my son home'. Quite the opposite, because 'this was a difficult time' she expressed thanks at Mabel's offer to look after the boy for the rest of the week.

That settled, Mabel helped Augustus collect the onions that had rolled around the shop floor after the pyramid collapsed. They played three rounds of the Counties of England card game, which Mabel had played as a child, then sat down to an early supper in the kitchen whereupon Augustus fell asleep over his plate of shepherd's pie.

Mabel rose to go, thinking that she could just make drinks in the salon before the evening meal was served at the Hall. The disturbance woke Augustus up.

'I'll come for you tomorrow morning,' she promised him.

'What will I do at Fellbridge Hall?' he asked.

What indeed.

'Perhaps you can help Campsie in the garden.'

'I don't know how to garden,' Augustus answered with a sorrowful look.

'You could help Mrs Pilford and Miss Darling in the kitchen.'

'I don't know how to cook.'

'How are you at sitting still all day long and reading a book?' Mabel asked, one hand on a hip.

Augustus' face fell.

'Sleep well,' Mabel said, and gave him a kiss on the forehead.

She left through the shop door and Janet Darling, Katie's aunt, leaned out the window two doors down and waved. Mabel returned the wave but didn't stop. Janet sat at her telephone exchange board with not only a good view of what went on in the village, but also with the knowledge of who rang whom – although rules of conduct forbade her from sharing anything she heard. Doctor Finlay had remarked that Janet Darling could get blood out of a stone, and Mabel knew that wasn't far wrong.

Two sherries in the salon went to Mabel's head and having already had a meal with her family, she kept to cheese, crackers and fruit. While the others ate their dinners, Mabel asked what she'd missed at the end of the day.

According to Skeff, the discussion that afternoon on who would lead the final votes for women campaign had been unremarkable. No decision had been made. Instead, Emma had sent them off to contemplate the skills needed for leadership and they would discuss it all again the next day. Emma looked a bit fretful and Mabel worried that the meeting of minds was losing its focus with the murder enquiry hanging over everyone's head.

The women found their own occupation for the evening. Skeff went off for a few games of billiards after the meal and Cora had promised millinery consultations to Collette and Diane. Hildy joined the trio for a hand of bridge. Ruby knitted while Dorothea read a copy of the *Gardeners' Chronicle*. It was all so normal that Mabel's mind felt fuzzy – drifting among the murder enquiry, the suffragettes, Winstone and Augustus.

She retired early and Park, after taking Gladys for a run, joined her. As weary as she felt, Mabel couldn't sleep, Instead, she stared at the dark ceiling, her thoughts churning. A woman had been murdered and how far had she come in finding out who had done it? The only thing for it was to question each of the women again the next day. *Describe your movements Sunday afternoon. Do you know Agatha Tyne?*

'The same questions over and over,' Park murmured, 'it gets results.'

'Have I been speaking aloud?' Mabel asked.

He pulled her close. 'You're thinking about what might have stirred up long-buried emotions.'

Old resentments. Who would want to hurt Annie Harkin? What secrets lay in her past?

There were no lectures scheduled for Wednesday morning and the women were taking advantage of this each in their own way. Most were staying in for a quiet time, but the trio had voiced a desire to go into town and Hildy, who still had use of the police vehicle, offered to drive. Not only drive, of course, but listen in for any comments that might relate to the enquiry.

Just after breakfast, Mabel kissed Park. 'I'll meet you and

Gladys at the shop. And don't worry – it's too early in the day to be offered parsnip cordial.'

As she headed out the door, Skeff caught up with her.

'I've got something for you. About Binks.'

Mabel, standing in full sun on the forecourt, suddenly felt cold.

'About the pub brawl in 1911?' she asked. 'Was it more than that?'

'No more than a brawl,' Skeff said, 'although by all accounts Binks started it. What you'll find interesting is who he attacked – it was Oliver Harkin. Annie's husband.'

Stunned at Skeff's announcement, for a moment Mabel couldn't answer. At last she came out with, 'He never said. Does this make him look more guilty for Annie's murder?' She shook her head. 'I'll speak with him again later. Thanks, Skeff.'

As Mabel passed the car, she looked in to see Thirza and Lavinia with Diane.

'Didn't Pretoria want to go into town?' Mabel asked.

'Pretoria,' Lavinia said with a click of the tongue, 'has gone to see her bluebell wood.'

They motored off and Mabel stood thinking for a moment. Emma had told her from the start what a private person Binks was, but wasn't this carrying it a bit too far? Unless he had more to hide than a punch-up with the murder victim's husband.

She put those thoughts aside and started down the footpath at an ambling pace. The morning sun shone through fresh green leaves, creating a serene atmosphere that cleared her mind. It was a new day and she would make progress on the enquiry as soon as she returned to the Hall and found something to occupy Augustus. What a surprise for Tolly if she had the entire enquiry wrapped up even before he could make it back to Sussex.

Eventually, she came to the road with the pub down to her right, Mabel turned left to head towards the village.

She hadn't taken many steps when, behind her, there came the sound of an approaching engine. She moved to one side, giving the driver plenty of room to pass and turned round to see who it was.

The next moment, over the rise appeared a large black automobile – a Wolseley. But instead of keeping to the other side of the road, the car veered. It sped up and – no mistaking it – came straight at her.

FIFTEEN

Mabel leapt off the road, tripped and crashed through the cow parsley, tumbling down the slight incline and coming to a rest against a beech. For a moment, she lay dazed among a few bluebells, the sky above her reeling. She thought she heard the car pause and she scrambled up, but her head spun and she lost her balance and fell onto her bottom as the engine roared and the Wolseley took off. With great effort, she clambered up to the road on all fours weakly shouting a few choice words. Mabel saw the back end of the car as it swerved wildly, negotiated the corner poorly and disappeared from sight. She lay back on the verge and closed her eyes, taking deep breaths. In the distance, she heard a *thump*.

There came a bark. Mabel opened her eyes. She propped herself up on her elbows to see Gladys approach at speed and dance round her. Mabel sat up and saw Park directly behind. One look at her and his smile vanished. She straightened her cloche and scrambled to her feet.

'A car,' she said before he could even ask. He helped her up and she pointed back towards the Hall. 'It came up heading for the village. He nearly knocked me off the road.' She swayed and

Park grasped both her arms as she sank slowly to the ground again.

'Nearly?' Park said angrily.

Something dangled at the edge of Mabel's vision. She shook her head. 'What's that?'

Park knelt and pulled a broken stem of bluebells off her hat.

She took the flowers and stared at them. They reminded her of Pretoria.

'Are you all right?' Park asked. 'Can you walk or shall I go and ring for the doctor?'

'No, I'm not hurt,' she said. She took his hands and stood. 'I tripped and that sent me tumbling.'

Park glanced across the road. 'There's plenty of room for a car to go by.'

'Yes,' Mabel said. 'But it was as if...' She looked up at Park and his eyes burned through the last vestiges of clouds in her mind. 'It was as if he were aiming at me.'

'Did you get a look?' Park asked. It was a police question, but the tight grip on her hands and flush of anger on his face revealed his emotions.

'It was a Wolseley.' For a brief moment the driver's face, like a spectre, floated behind the windscreen and her heart sank. 'A man,' she said. 'He might've worn a bowler hat and he might've had spectacles on.'

'Tinted blue?'

'I don't know,' she said with exasperation. 'Am I filling in the blanks because I'd just learned that Binks takes the Wolseley out? Why would Binks want to run me down?' Mabel asked.

'Because you suspect he killed Annie.'

'Do I?' Mabel asked herself aloud. 'What motive does he have?'

'A long-standing family dispute?' Park suggested.

'Remember he has violence in his past. Seeing her again brought it all back.'

'Yes,' Mabel said. That reminded her she had something to tell Park. What was it? In the stillness of the moment, what came to Mabel was the sound she'd heard after the car roared off.

'He may have hit something after he passed me,' she said. 'Up around the turn. Come on.'

She grabbed her satchel in one hand and Park's hand in the other and they took off, Gladys running ahead of them so that when they'd turned the corner, the dog had arrived first to investigate what looked like a bundle of clothes at the side of the road, but which turned out to be a man.

Mabel gasped and ran towards him, Park following quickly behind. Gladys whined as she sniffed the fellow, but Park put a hand up and the dog retreated and sat down.

The man lay on his back, his arms flung out. Several feet away, a small suitcase had burst open and nearer, a Panama hat lay in the grass. Park knelt and, frowning in concentration, felt for a pulse. He lifted one of the man's eyelids with his thumb and, as if he'd flipped a switch, the man opened his eyes and began flailing.

'Where is he?' he shouted. 'What sort of driving is that?'

Mabel dodged his wild movements. Park tried to grab the man's wrists but got knocked in the chin for his troubles.

'Argh – highwaymen?' the man shouted. 'You'll have nothing off me!'

'Sir!' Mabel shouted in his face. 'Sir, we're only trying to help.' The man quieted as he squinted at her. 'Are you injured?' she added.

'Er...' The man patted his chest with both hands as if to verify. 'No, I don't believe so.'

'What is your name?' Mabel asked and he returned a vague look.

'Do you know your name?' Park asked.

'My name?'

He looked about fifty years old. His dark suit and dark coat were worn but well-kept. He had no remarkable characteristic that would make him stand out – apart from the fresh cut on his forehead. It didn't look deep. Mabel took the man's handkerchief out of his pocket and dabbed the wound.

'If you don't remember your name, sir,' Park said, 'perhaps you have a wallet with identification?'

'Of course I know who I am,' he said, sounding miffed, 'but if you need proof I'll show you.'

He stuck his hand in his pocket and pulled out a bacon roll. From several feet away, Gladys licked her chops. Back into the pocket went the bacon roll and out of the other pocket he pulled an overly stuffed wallet and began riffling through it. As he did so, several bits of paper slipped out and fell to the ground, including an old photo. Mabel picked it up.

It was of a bride and groom. The bride sat on a chair, staring out at the camera, wearing a simple white dress and a veil that hugged her head and flowed down nearly to the floor. It must've been taken twenty years ago, but Mabel still recognised Annie Harkin.

Standing next to Annie in the photo and wearing a top hat, was the same man in front of them now.

'You're—' Mabel began.

'I'm Oliver Harkin.'

Oliver Harkin insisted he could walk, and so they made for the shop, Park keeping a firm hand on Harkin's elbow. Mabel slipped the Harkins' wedding photo in her pocket and carried the small suitcase. Gladys trotted alongside them. As they went, Mr Harkin asked as many questions as did Mabel.

'What happened to my Annie? Did you catch the man?'

'Mr Harkin, have you just arrived?'
'Murder! Where are the police?'
'Is Lady Fellbridge expecting you?'
'How is a person not safe in such a big house?'
'Had you seen Mrs Harkin recently?'

It was an unsatisfactory interview, to be sure.

When they walked into the shop, Reg was nowhere to be seen. Augustus stood on a crate wearing his modified grocer's apron and holding two stems of rhubarb as if they were drumsticks as he beat out a passable tattoo on the countertop.

'Good morning, Augustus,' Mabel said.

The boy's gaze darted from Mabel to Harkin to Park – and then stopped when he saw Gladys.

'You have a dog!'

Mabel set Harkin down on a stool. 'Yes, this is Gladys, who belongs to Mr Winstone. Mr Winstone, this is Augustus Malling-Frobisher.'

'Hello, Mr Winstone, pleased to meet you,' Augustus said, climbing off the crate. He had eyes only for the dog. 'Hello, Gladys.'

Gladys offered Augustus a paw, which sent the boy over the moon.

'And this is Mr Harkin,' Mabel said.

Reg appeared out of the passageway. 'What's this about?' he asked. Catching sight of Harkin, he went straight to him. 'Are you injured, sir?'

'He nearly hit me,' Harkin declared. 'I'm lucky to be alive.'

'We'll find the doctor for you, Mr Harkin,' Mabel said. She noted a slight shift in Harkin's tone from befuddled to more than annoyed, yet not quite irate. 'Perhaps we should move you into the sitting room.'

As Park led Harkin towards the sitting room, Mabel said, 'Augustus, take Gladys back to see Mrs Chandekar and ask her for tea.'

Boy and dog trotted off and Reg put a hand on his daughter's arm.

'It's that business at the Hall, isn't it?' he asked.

'Possibly,' Mabel said, 'but I don't actually know at the moment.' She went to the telephone in the passage, glancing further along into the kitchen to see Mrs Chandekar spooning tea into the pot and speaking in a low, calming voice while Augustus and Gladys sat patiently watching.

After trying the surgery and several patients, Janet reported that the doctor couldn't be reached and so she would leave a message for him at the golf course. Yesterday, Mabel had seen a set of clubs in the dickey seat of his car and wondered if he always carried them around. She asked Janet for the Hall next, and Hildy, returned from ferrying the women to and from Rye, answered. Mabel gave her a brief account then asked her to come to the shop and fetch Oliver Harkin.

'Don't mention Harkin to anyone yet,' Mabel added. 'I want to see Emma first.'

While waiting for Hildy, Mabel sent Augustus and Gladys out to the yard to throw a ball. Park had remained with Harkin in the sitting room, and Mabel walked in to hear a more subtle form of questioning.

'Long journey,' Park said conversationally. 'Did you come into Rye station this morning?'

Harkin didn't answer. He'd taken the bacon roll out of his pocket and had almost finished eating it. As he popped the last bit in his mouth, he looked into his teacup and sighed. Mabel offered to add a tot of parsnip cordial to it and the man didn't say no. It didn't help much – Harkin turned morose, muttering 'My poor Annie' but little else.

Mabel went back into the shop.

'Papa, before we arrived, did you see a car go by?'

Reg squinted towards the shop door. 'I saw Binks driving by in the Wolseley.'

Mabel's heart sank. 'Going which way?'

'Coming from the Hall – or the pub. I couldn't say, could I? Moti!' Reg called. 'Can you come out a moment?'

When Mrs Chandekar came into the shop drying her hands on a tea cloth, Mabel asked, 'Did you see a car go by earlier?'

She nodded. 'Not too long before you arrived, Binks drove by in the Wolseley.'

Mabel sighed.

'Did Binks hit that man?' Reg asked.

'I'm not sure he was actually struck by the car. He might've fallen getting out of the way.' Much as she had done, but best not to mention that now. She turned to Mrs Chandekar. 'Are you certain it was Binks?'

Mrs Chandekar gazed out the window to the street, then turned to Mabel and frowned. 'It looked like Binks.'

Mabel had offered only the bare minimum details of the event to Reg and Mrs Chandekar – promising a full explanation later. They took her on faith and she loved them for it.

When Hildy arrived, they trooped out to the car. Harkin understood they were going to Fellbridge Hall, and that calmed him. He sat between Mabel and Park on the journey, while Augustus and Gladys hung over the seat, the boy peppering Hildy with questions.

'Are you a real policeman or is it just a costume? Do you have a truncheon to beat robbers and thieves with? May I see it? I think I might want to become a policeman, you see, and I might need the practice.'

'You have to go to school to join the Metropolitan Police,' Hildy said. 'Did you know that?'

That fact quieted the boy for the rest of the journey. Upon

arrival, Gladys hopped out of the car and trotted off with purpose round the side of the Hall and in the direction of the kitchen. Hildy escorted Harkin to the steward's office with Augustus in tow, and Mabel asked Park to find Binks.

'I don't want him to know about Harkin yet. I want to be there when they see each other. Perhaps he should stay in his quarters.'

Park nodded. 'I'll see to it. And I'll check on the Wolseley – see if the engine is still warm.' He gave her hand a squeeze and they went off.

Mabel stood in the entrance hall alone. It was too early for lunch in the square dining room and no meetings had been scheduled for the morning. The Hall felt deserted. Mabel knew she must find Emma first and tell her about Oliver Harkin before anyone else got wind of his presence.

But before she could move, Collette appeared from the far corridor that led to the west wing.

'Have you seen Emma?' Mabel asked.

'I've seen no one,' Collette replied. 'Dorothea and that little Ruby are in the garden with Campsie – I do wish he would listen to me about pegging the ramblers. Diane is' – Collette waved vaguely above her head – 'talking with Cora about hats. Skeff was interviewing Emma about our hopes and plans, but that was earlier. Pretoria – well really. You'd think she would never see another bluebell again if she didn't see these. I told her she should wait until May and the countryside would be covered with them as it always is, but did she listen? No, she went off straight away this morning.'

'Mabel?' Emma came out of the salon. 'Mabel, where is your Augustus?'

'He's with Hildy.' *And Oliver Harkin.* 'I need to have a word with you.' Mabel crossed the entrance hall and took Emma's elbow to guide her back into the corridor. Best not to let anyone overhear who had arrived. Not yet.

But they'd not gone a step before Harkin's voice echoed in the corridor as he burst into the entrance hall with Hildy behind him.

'Why am I being held?' he demanded. 'Am I under arrest?'

'Oliver!' Emma exclaimed.

'Oliver!' Collette echoed.

'Oliver? Oh, dear.' Dorothea had come into the entrance hall wearing dungarees, her suffragette sash and a straw hat. Ruby stood just behind her, and Dorothea put an arm out as if to bar the younger woman from going further.

To keep her from seeing Oliver Harkin? With that one protective movement of Dorothea's, Mabel, who had honed the ability to interpret actions into words, saw the story written in the faces of everyone present – shock, fear, longing, resentment.

Ruby Truelock and Oliver Harkin looked so incredibly alike with their pale colouring and hair to match. Now, both sets of eyes widened at the sight of the other as high colour rose on their cheeks. It was unmistakable.

'Ruby,' Oliver began, but choked up.

Ruby took a step back then two steps forward, breaking through Dorothea's barrier. 'Mr Harkin, is it?'

'Ruby, please,' Harkin said, 'you know, don't you? You know that I'm your—'

'Father?' Ruby said in a biting tone.

And there it was – the truth.

'Yes!' Oliver said with fervour. 'I'm your father – won't you call me that?'

'How can I call you father when you were never one to me?' Ruby's voice took on a taunting tone. 'Excuse me, sir – have we met? I don't believe so.'

'Stop it, please!' Emma said.

She moved between them and held her hands up like a referee keeping opponents separated in the world's largest boxing ring. In one corner was Oliver Harkin, estranged husband to Annie and estranged father to Ruby Truelock. In the other corner, the abandoned daughter, now wearing her mother's purple, green and white suffragette sash with her chin jutted out as if to dare the man she'd never known to speak another word.

'It was your mother's decision – she pushed me out of your life!' Harkin said.

'How dare you even mention my mother!' Ruby shouted. 'And what did your *wife* think about all this? I asked her and she wouldn't tell me anything.'

'Come along, both of you,' Emma said, directing them into the salon. 'You don't need an audience for this.'

Collette turned to go, then paused as if about to offer instructions on reconciliations, but instead shrugged and continued on her way. Dorothea patted Ruby's arm. 'I'll be in the garden if you need me.'

Emma herded Ruby and Oliver off and the others had gone, but Mabel didn't move, watching the retreating figures.

'Hildy,' she said, 'would you keep an eye on them?'

'Will do.' Hildy moved off to stand outside the door of the salon.

As players who enter the stage just after a clamorous battle scene, Skeff and Cora walked into the entrance hall and took in the quiet.

'What have we missed?' Skeff asked.

Mabel frowned. 'Just then, Ruby said Annie wouldn't tell her anything. But Ruby told me she'd never met Annie before Sunday and gave the impression they hadn't spoken. Why has she kept that conversation under her hat?'

'Why, indeed?'

Mabel filed that question away to be drawn out later.

'But the bigger news is that Oliver Harkin has arrived – a surprise visit as far as I can tell' – then she remembered the

Wolseley nearly running both of them down – 'although that remains to be seen. And it turns out, he's Ruby's father.'

'Oh that,' Cora said.

'Did you know?' Mabel asked.

'Diane told me the story,' Cora said.

Mabel looked past Cora. 'Is Diane with you?'

'She's gone for a lie-down,' Cora said, 'and to decide whether or not to remake a knitted bucket hat she only finished last month.'

'Diane knew Oliver was Ruby's father?' Skeff asked.

'Apparently they all know,' Cora said, 'but no one ever speaks about it.'

'Well done, you,' Skeff said and gave Cora a quick kiss.

'Oh now,' Cora said with a giggle. 'Sometimes people want to talk, but they don't know they want to until they're trying on a hat.'

'Has Ruby always known Oliver was her father?' Mabel asked.

'No,' Cora said. 'At least, the women believed Susan kept it from her daughter.'

'I wonder when she found out,' Skeff said.

Long enough ago to turn bitter at the deception, Mabel thought. Whose honour had been protected by keeping this secret from her daughter? Had it not, instead, led to a girl growing into a young woman and now full of anger towards her father, his wife and even her own mother?

Cora looked round the empty entrance hall. 'It's awfully quiet, isn't it? You'd think there'd be more commotion over Mr Harkin's appearance.'

Only at that moment did Mabel realise it certainly shouldn't be quiet – not with Augustus Malling-Frobisher in residence.

'Where is Augustus?' she asked.

'Accounted for,' Hildy answered from her post guarding the

salon door. 'He's in the steward's office, staying where he's told, unlike Mr Harkin.'

'Alone?'

'I left Constable Cowley with him.'

Good. That would give Mabel time to talk with Binks.

'Have any of you seen Pretoria?' Cora asked. 'That's who I came to find. I've managed to sew together a cluster of silk bluebells for her picture hat. She was ever so keen to have them.'

'Perhaps she's gone out to see them in situ,' Skeff said.

'I believe she's rather enjoying niggling Thirza and Lavinia, saying she was left behind when they went to view the bluebells,' Cora said.

Hildy shook her head. 'I've heard that business, but they swear they didn't go without her Sunday afternoon. Bluebells are the reason she didn't go into town with the other two this morning.'

'If she didn't see the other two, I wonder what she did see,' Skeff said.

'How long has she been gone?' Mabel asked.

A moment of silence followed during which a wave of unease swept over Mabel.

'There aren't that many bluebells to see,' she said. 'I'll go and look for her.'

She left by way of the conservatory, out onto the terrace and down into the garden striding with purpose at first but by the time she cleared the formal hedge, she ran, dashing across the strip of meadow before the wood began. She saw a low, brown figure racing towards her through the grass and cow parsley and realised it was Gladys. Mabel held up. The dog arrived and circled her, barking and herding Mabel off in the direction she had intended to go – the bluebell wood.

Dappled, late-morning light filtered through the fresh beech canopy and picked out the spots of blue in the spring grass. A footpath ran through the wood to the road on the other side, but

Gladys veered off it to the right to a recently-made path of crushed grass and flattened bluebells. Mabel saw large footprints – perhaps a man's boot – and smaller ones. She avoided them and picked her way through and when Gladys stopped ahead and sat down, Mabel crept forward a few more steps.

In a patch of sunlight ahead, Pretoria lay amid the bluebells, her arms askew as if warding off a blow or sending one of her own.

'Pretoria?' Mabel whispered, but without expectation of an answer. The blood that had seeped onto the blades of grass and into the ground below her head wasn't fresh, but rather drying and sticky-looking with several flies showing interest. The spit-curls she kept so tidily stuck to her face had become dislodged and formed a soft brown halo round her face. Her suffragette sash had been cinched round her neck like a bowtie. Mabel rubbed the gooseflesh from her arms. Two suffragettes murdered.

But why? And who would be next?

SIXTEEN

'Mabel!'

Mabel tore her gaze away from Pretoria's body and the suffragette sash tied round her neck flecked with blood.

'Park! Here – over here!'

She didn't move from the spot and when Park approached Mabel held up her hand and he stopped.

'It's Pretoria,' she said. 'She came out this morning sometime and no one noticed how long she'd been gone. Look there where someone has walked – see the prints.'

They circled the body with care, looking for any signs of who had done this but found nothing. Park walked out towards the road on the other side of the wood and returned with little news.

'The layby is packed dry dirt and no discernible tyre tracks,' he said, polishing his glasses with his handkerchief before putting them back on. 'Doesn't mean there hasn't been someone there.'

Mabel frowned at Pretoria's body – hoping anger would stave off her tears. 'All she wanted to do was look at the bluebells.' She sniffed sharply. 'Was it the same person she saw on Sunday afternoon when she thought Thirza and Lavinia had come out without her? Was it the same person who murdered Annie?'

'Does this confirm it's someone from outside the Hall?'

'It would seem to – but what if that's the point? To turn our attention elsewhere, to an outsider, and away from the murderer who is actually inside the Hall?' *And who would that be?* 'What about Binks?'

'Constable Scott showed up for work,' Park said, 'or for a cup of tea with Katie, I'm not sure which. I've left him guarding Binks' door. Binks says he's been repairing a shelf in the pantry all morning and Deenie confirms that, but not with a great deal of confidence. I went down to check the Wolseley. It's where it should be now, but it's been driven – there was still a bit of warmth to the engine.'

'We'll have to ring Tolly – he'll have to come down now.'

'With the whole team, I'd expect,' Park said. 'Including someone to make a cast of those boot prints. Is the doctor on his way?'

'Janet's looking for him, to come and check on Oliver Harkin. Now this. Bluebells,' Mabel said. 'No, this can't be all over bluebells.'

'Can't it?' Park asked. 'I've seen worse.'

'I wonder did Pretoria know about Harkin being Ruby's father?' Mabel asked. 'It sounds as if all the women did. Only I can't imagine knowing that would be reason enough to get her murdered.'

'Perhaps it has nothing to do with some secret in the past,' Park said. 'Perhaps someone doesn't like suffragettes. Any suffragette.'

'Oliver Harkin himself? How did he react to Annie's involvement in the movement all those years ago? That could be part of why they separated.' Mabel squinted towards the Hall.

'What if Harkin arrived before today? I want to talk with him again.'

'You go on,' Park said. 'I'll stay out here.'

'I'll send Ned to you.'

Gladys had been nosing round at a safe distance along the footpath and began growling and pawing at a clump of grass. She caught something and trotted up to them with a pair of spectacles, one of the wire temples between her teeth.

Park pulled out his handkerchief and took the glasses from Gladys. The lenses were thick.

'But not tinted like Binks',' Mabel pointed out. She looked down at the dog. 'Good girl. It's just as I'd thought – a disguise. Now if only you could find us a discarded bowler hat we might be able to discover who was pretending to be Binks this morning.'

'Oliver Harkin couldn't try to run himself over,' Park pointed out.

'Yes, so at least he's got an alibi. But what if Ruby knew her father had arrived and she'd gone off to give him a scare? Would she think to try and look like Binks?'

'Miss Canning,' Ned said, 'it was my turn and he's jumped two of my men and now wants to be crowned.'

PC Ned Cowley and Augustus – former and current scamps – sat hunched over a small table in the steward's office where a draughts board had been laid out. The constable was playing black and the boy playing white. There was a sizeable stack of captured black pieces on Augustus' side of the board.

'It wasn't your turn yet, Constable,' Augustus explained. 'I had three jumps to make and it's all legal. Isn't it, Miss Canning?'

The players looked to Mabel for an answer. She was taken

by how alike they were and decided she might need to make sure they didn't spend too much time in each other's company.

'You didn't go backwards, did you?' Mabel asked.

'No,' Augustus said with astonishment.

'Well, Ned, he's got you there. Now, I'm afraid you'll have to abandon your game. I have an important job for each of you. Ned, take Augustus to Deenie in the kitchen. Ask her to please keep an eye on him till I get there. Then go out to the wood on the west side of the Hall, because—'

Mabel held up in the nick of time, feeling Augustus' keen gaze on her. She would have to think of a way to explain Pretoria's murder to the boy later. In the meantime – 'Because, Ned, Mr Winstone is waiting for you there. Now, Augustus – your job is to stay in the kitchen and wait for me. Right?'

They were off like a shot, allowing Mabel a moment to compose herself before she sat at the desk and rang the exchange.

'Scotland Yard, Janet. Detective Inspector Tollerton.'

She'd done her duty – related all the news necessary. Tolly was all business as Mabel had filled in as much as she could about Binks, the resurgence of suffragette sashes and the suspicions of the London Ladies' Murder Club. They rang off at last. Mabel thought she had at least two hours before the police arrived, and so she planned her next moves in the enquiry.

Mabel emerged from the steward's office, down the corridor and into the empty conservatory. She needed to find Emma before anyone got wind of Pretoria's murder, but out the windows, she caught sight of Campsie as he walked along the lower path below the terrace, coming up from the stables to the kitchen to help with lunch. He wore Binks' cast-off jacket, but now with a flat cap.

Mabel went out to the terrace and called, 'What's happened to your bowler?'

Campsie touched his flat cap. 'That bowler hat of mine,' he said, shaking his head. 'It's turned up missing, it has. I must've taken it off somewhere in the garden and left it.'

'When did you see it last?'

'Oh, I don't know. Might've been yesterday.'

'Are you sure no one took it?'

Campsie laughed. 'Walk into my cottage and steal that old bowler and walk out? I can't see the point of that, can you? You wait now, it'll turn up peeking at me from under a cabbage leaf or something.'

Mabel studied Campsie for a moment. The man seemed without guile.

'Campsie, do you drive?'

'Drive?' the gardener echoed. 'No, I don't. Never have and never want to.'

'Did you hear anyone take the Wolseley out this morning?'

'No, ma'am,' Campsie replied. 'I've been weeding the asparagus bed most of the morning. Miss Goose is sowing another bed of peas and then digging compost in for the leeks. I'd forgotten how nice it is to have an extra pair of hands.'

'What about Ruby – has she been helping this morning?'

'I haven't seen Miss Truelock.' Campsie gave Mabel a nod. 'I'm to help with luncheon, and so I'd best be off before I'm missed.'

The kitchen would be busy, but Mabel needed to see Binks – and check on Augustus, but just as she intended to sweep out of the conservatory, Emma swept in.

'Oh, Mabel,' Emma said, her face drawn with anguish.

For a moment Mabel thought she'd already heard about Pretoria, but then Emma continued. 'I should've explained about Oliver long before this. It was a poorly kept secret – I still don't know how Ruby found out, but I'm surprised she learned it only recently. But I can't believe this had anything to do with Annie's death.'

Emma took Mabel's hands and, heaving a great sigh, led her to the small sofa where they sat.

A sense of dread crept over Mabel. 'You haven't left them alone together, have you – Oliver and Ruby?'

'No, she shot out of there the moment he started talking. I asked Hildy to take Oliver to the billiards room to keep the steward's office free for you. He seems a bit bewildered. What a fine mess this is.'

'So,' Mabel said. 'The argument Susan and Annie had all those years ago wasn't about funding for the school.'

'No. Annie and Oliver's marriage was... he loved her and she was quite fond of him. Each of them knew where the other stood, but still they decided to make a go of it. They had both made compromises, and Annie would've welcomed a baby. They did try. Then Oliver and Susan started their affair. It went on for some months, apparently, until Susan knew for certain about the baby. That's when she broke it off with Oliver.'

'It's an odd time to end the affair, just when she might need help,' Mabel said.

Emma gave half a shrug. 'Becoming pregnant brought Susan to her senses. She didn't want to be tied to a man, but she did want her baby. Annie was hurt and reacted badly to the news and so decided she wouldn't have Oliver back.'

'But that left Susan to manage alone,' Mabel said.

'Susan was a resourceful woman,' Emma said with a smile. 'Ruby was looked after by a mother of one of the school children.'

'Yet Harkin stayed near?' Mabel said.

'He never left Little Lever – his one act of defiance – but

never revealed himself as Ruby's father. Annie and Susan had been great friends, but this was a break neither of them could surmount. But Annie seemed finally to have come to terms with it. I believe it's what she wanted to talk with me about.'

'When she arrived here?' Mabel asked.

'Yes. After the doctor had gone Sunday afternoon, Annie told me, "So much time has gone by and yet I see it still so clearly. I can't let it die with her."' Emma glanced up at Mabel. 'Annie had written to tell me when Susan died. It happened two years ago, as we were here grieving Edith.'

For a moment in the quiet, the sound of Edith's name spoken inside in Fellbridge Hall brought it all back to Mabel as clearly as if it had happened only moments ago.

Mabel imagined Ruby's shock, heartbreak and, perhaps, anger at discovering who her father was. Did she blame Annie for standing in the way? Had Ruby come to Fellbridge Hall to confront Annie – or to kill her?

As if she'd been summoned by Mabel's thoughts, Ruby herself marched in through the French windows off the terrace.

The young woman had changed – perhaps the appearance of her father had taken hold of her very core and created a steely resolution. No one would dare lose her in a crowd now. The inward transformation had been paired with only one outward change. She had donned a suffragette sash.

Ruby's gaze darted about the conservatory, then she said, 'Mabel, Mr Winstone and Constable Cowley are in the bluebell wood. They told me to keep clear. What is it? What's happened?'

With a jolt, Mabel thought of Pretoria lying dead, her suffragette sash wrapped round her neck in a garishly comic fashion.

Squabbling voices were heard in the corridor, the door flew open and in came Diane Lotterby, Collette Massey, Thirza and Lavinia with Skeff and Cora trailing behind them.

'I tell you something is wrong,' Thirza said. 'She stayed back because—'

'She didn't want to shop,' Lavinia broke in, 'and she was a bit put out with us but for no reason at all.'

The all stopped when they noticed the others.

'Emma,' Thirza said with relief, 'would you intercede for us? You know how Pretoria can get something in her head and not let it go.'

'Pretoria—' Mabel's voice rose above the others and they all looked to her.

'I have terrible news,' Mabel said in a quieter voice. 'Pretoria is dead. Someone attacked her in the wood this morning.'

Wails rose from the two remaining members of the trio, drowning out the others' exclamations. Thirza swooned and Cora took her arm and led her to the sofa. Skeff tried to quiet the others whose voices grew louder and louder trying to be heard over each other.

Emma grasped Mabel. 'Pretoria!' she sobbed. 'But why?'

Ruby drew closer to them. 'Who would want to hurt her?'

'Who would want to hurt Annie?' Mabel asked, and Ruby drew back. The din continued, covering their conversation. 'Ruby, you said that you'd never spoken to Annie Harkin, but that's not true, is it? Why didn't you tell me?'

Ruby frowned. 'We had only a brief exchange. It was nothing. Then the doctor arrived to see her. Remember, Emma?'

Mabel clapped her hands and shouted over the clamour, 'Quiet, please!'

She was met with looks of astonishment, but at least they'd gone silent.

'Inspector Tollerton is on his way. While we wait, lunch should go ahead as usual.' It occurred to Mabel this was how events proceeded on Sunday after Annie's body had been found. 'I'm sure the meal is nearly ready, but I'll let Deenie and Katie know.'

Mabel raised her eyebrows at Skeff, hoping she understood the request. *Keep an ear out for what they say.*

Skeff nodded back. *Understood.*

Before Mabel went to the kitchen, she stopped by the billiards room, knocking once before opening the door to find Oliver Harkin sitting in a leather wingback chair with a whisky in his hand and Hildy applying a plaster to the cut on his forehead.

He raised his eyebrows at Mabel and then winced. 'She wants nothing to do with me,' he said morosely. 'My own daughter. I've made a dog's breakfast of things, but it wasn't all my fault.'

'Mr Harkin,' Mabel said. 'You know Mr Binks, don't you?'

'Where is he?' Harkin said, his eyes turning dark and beady. 'I'd like a word with him.'

'Would you now?' Mabel asked. 'What about?'

'About?' Harkin asked. He looked down into his drink. 'It's a private matter.'

'There's nothing private in a murder enquiry,' Mabel said.

Harkin took a sip of his whisky. 'I don't understand, Miss Canning. I've got a WPC keeping an eye on me. It's good to have police here, don't think I'm complaining, but what do *you* have to do with all this?'

'I'm a private detective through the Useful Women agency in London. Lady Fellbridge has employed me to carry out an enquiry into Annie's death alongside Scotland Yard's investigation.'

'A lady detective?' Harkin asked.

'Exactly that,' Mabel replied. 'Do you know Agatha Tyne?'

He frowned. 'Never heard of her. Who is she? A friend of Annie's? Is she here?'

'When did you arrive, Mr Harkin?'

'You know when I arrived – you were in the car with me.'

'I don't mean when you arrived here at the Hall and you know it,' Mabel said. 'You're being obtuse.'

'I want a word with Binks.'

Mabel fumed on her way down to the kitchen. Harkin would have a word with Binks when she said so, and not before – and she would be present when it happened. Let him put that in his pipe and smoke it.

She nodded to Constable Scott who stood at Binks' door at the end of the corridor and then walked into the kitchen where the cooks were hard at work on luncheon. A cacophony of sounds met Mabel – chopping, sizzling, the tap flowing, the kettle boiling, pots clanging – along with the aroma of pastry and butter and all manner of vegetables stewing or roasting. Mabel spied an onion tart cooling and a platter of steaming spinach covered in breadcrumbs. She couldn't help but think a bit of bacon would make it all the better.

She looked round and saw only Deenie and Katie.

'Where is Augustus?'

Katie, intent on piping potatoes around the edge of a dish of lentils, jumped in alarm.

'Oh Mabel,' she said, 'you nearly frightened me to death. I didn't see you there.'

'Augustus?' Mabel repeated.

'Over there,' Katie replied, nodding to the far corner as she went back to her piping.

But the corner was empty.

'Over where?' Mabel asked.

Katie looked and then did a double-take. 'He was just there,' she said. 'Deenie, wasn't Augustus just there?'

Deenie, who had had her back to them as she sliced bread, paused and turned, knife in hand. 'Yes, he's—' She pointed with the bread knife to the empty corner. Deenie looked under the table and then walked into the far pantry and back out again. 'Where did he go?'

'All right,' Mabel said, 'everyone stay calm.' Her heart paid no attention to this advice and ran off at a gallop.

'I told him to stay put,' Katie said. 'I should've known better – my Bets can vanish in the blink of an eye. Augustus!'

Mabel rushed out of the kitchen.

'Constable,' she called to Scott, 'have you seen a young boy come out of the kitchen?'

'I saw a young boy go into the kitchen, Miss Canning. Ned brought him down.'

'But he didn't come out?'

'No,' Scott said, shaking his head. 'Unless, that is, he came out the moment I took Mr Binks in a cup of tea.'

Augustus needed only a moment to vanish – Mabel could testify to that. But where had he gone?

'Miss Canning!'

She whirled round to see the boy barrelling towards her.

'Where were you?' Mabel demanded, unable to keep the shrill tone out of her voice. 'You were to stay in the kitchen. This is no time to be sneaking off.'

'There you are!' Katie said from the door of the kitchen wagging an accusatory finger at him.

'I didn't sneak!' Augustus looked from Mabel to Katie and back. 'I was *underfoot* – that's what my mother says – and so I thought I would go sit on the stairs out of everyone's way. Then, halfway up, I noticed a door and so I opened it and there's a flower garden!'

The fire in Katie's eyes went out and the corner of her mouth lifted. 'Oh,' she said. 'It's Campsie's garden that he planted for me.'

'I'm sorry I frightened you,' Augustus said, hanging his head. He looked up at Katie with one eye. 'I like your garden, Miss Darling.'

Katie clicked her tongue. 'Sorry I let him slip off, Mabel.'

'Well, present danger is over,' Mabel said, and Katie retreated to the kitchen.

Mabel looked past Augustus to the end of the corridor and the bottom of the staircase. 'So, the door wasn't locked?'

'No, ma'am,' Augustus said. 'But you can lock it if you like — there's a key on the wall.'

Mabel climbed the stairs to the turn halfway up. There was a door deep in the alcove and a key hanging on a nail. A skeleton key, same as used on the French windows throughout the Hall. Easy for a person with one key to get in through many doors.

The door opened onto a small secluded patch of ground where servants could get a breath of fresh air without being seen. A brick wall enclosed the fourth side of the garden with a wooden gate at one end.

A garden had been planted and now, in late April, spears of foxglove shot through low mounds of lungwort, dog-tooth violet, lily-of-the-valley and clumps of heart's ease. A bench sat among cow parsley that was nearly in bloom. It looked so peaceful that Mabel longed for a moment to sit there and think.

'Gladys!' Augustus called.

Here came the dog through the garden gate, racing across and bounding up the steps to greet them, licking the boy's face, snorting and shaking herself.

'Miss Canning,' Augustus said, 'may Gladys come indoors?'

Gladys could do as she liked, but Mabel didn't say that aloud, afraid that the boy would believe he had the same permission.

'Yes, Gladys, come in.'

They went back to the kitchen. 'Deenie,' Mabel said, 'Binks was in the pantry all morning fixing a shelf?'

Deenie shrugged. 'As far as I know. I'm not his minder.'

So, it could very well have been Binks driving the Wolseley. Murdering Pretoria. Binks, the scapegoat?

'I need a few sandwiches and a couple of bottles of beer,' Mabel said.

Augustus gasped. 'Are we going on a picnic?'

Mabel took Augustus up to the square dining room. Campsie followed them in with another tray of lentil-related dishes and laid them on the buffet table. The women had started to gather but instead of queueing stood in a cluster as if remembering there was safety in numbers. When the metal top of the bain-marie slipped and clattered onto the table, Thirza jumped and Lavina gave a little squeal. Mabel offered what she hoped looked like a reassuring smile and then introduced Augustus to Skeff and Cora.

'Miss Skeff,' Augustus observed, 'you're wearing trousers.'

'That I am,' Skeff said. 'Do you like them?'

'Yes, ma'am. You look... dashing.'

'She does, doesn't she?' Cora asked him with a wink.

'Who is this fellow?' asked Dorothea, coming up behind them in her dungarees.

Mabel made the introductions and with his usual scampishly fine manners, Augustus replied, 'I'm very pleased to meet you, Miss Goose.' Then he noted, 'You're wearing trousers, too.'

'I'm wearing trousers, young man, because I've been in the garden digging compost into the bed where the leeks will be planted out.' She smiled down at him. 'Gardening is a dirty business, you know.'

'And no one minds?' Augustus asked.

'The trousers?'

'No, ma'am, the dirt.'

'Not a bit,' Dorothea said. 'Dirt, mud, whatever – it's expected of a gardener.'

'I'd like to be a gardener,' Augustus said.

'Would you? Well, why don't you come out with me later and we'll try you out on chopping weeds.'

Mabel hadn't seen Dorothea in such fine fettle – it must be the fresh air and sunshine that made her blossom. Even the slight scent of camphor had dissipated. But then, she glanced up and Mabel saw the worry in her eyes.

'Best to keep the boy busy and away from what's happened, don't you think?' she asked.

'Yes,' Mabel said with relief. 'Thank you.'

'Oh,' Dorothea said, waving her hand, 'who is this joining us?'

A bumblebee had come in from the open window, bobbing up and down as it made its way to the buffet.

'Shall I find a jar and capture it?' Augustus said.

'You'd put him right out again, wouldn't you?' Dorothea asked. 'We wouldn't want him harmed.'

'Yes, Miss Goose, I promise,' Augustus said. 'I'd catch him and take him straight out.'

But Mabel saw the many possibilities between those two actions – upturned bowls of lentils and pickled beetroot strewn across the room and perhaps an upturned table to boot.

The bumblebee veered off course and instead buzzed out the window, perhaps fearing the same catastrophes.

'There now,' Mabel said with relief, 'all taken care of.'

When they reached the food, Mabel pointed out the selections. Augustus had no interest in lentils or chickpeas, but he took a plateful of cauliflower cheese and a large slice of rhubarb tart.

Mabel left the boy under Skeff and Cora's watchful eye and went downstairs. She sent Constable Scott out to the murder scene with a basket of beef sandwiches, sausages and bottles of beer and the message that Scotland Yard was on its way.

'And come straight back to the Hall, please.'

Scott left with Gladys following on his heels.

With Scott gone, Mabel knocked on the door of Binks' private quarters and asked him to join her in the billiards room. They walked in on Hildy watching Harkin tap a cue stick on the rim of the table.

'They may call it a billiards room, Constable,' Harkin said, 'but this is a snooker table and there's no mistaking it. You see—'

'Oliver!' Binks said, and Mabel could see his eyes widen behind the thick lenses.

Harkin turned to them, pointed the cue at Binks and said, 'So they've got you at last.'

SEVENTEEN

'Do you know what's going on here?' Harkin asked Binks, swinging the cue around as if to take in the Hall or all of Sussex. When Hildy took a step back to avoid being struck, he added, 'Pardon me, Constable.'

'Was Lady Fellbridge expecting you, Oliver? That is, Mr Harkin.'

'Go on with you, Binks. We've known each other's secrets too long for this "Mr Harkin" business.'

'Secrets?' Mabel asked, raising an eyebrow.

Harkin reddened. 'Oh now, Miss Canning, you can't pick at every word I say. You know what I mean.'

Maybe she did. Maybe she would keep an extra keen eye on Oliver Harkin.

'I said nothing to Emma about coming,' he continued, 'because she would've told me to stay away from my daughter and I won't do that any longer. No one can persuade me to do that now.'

'Not even your daughter herself?' Mabel asked. 'Will you force your fatherly attentions on her?'

'She and I – we're all we've got left,' Harkin said.

'Mr Harkin, you wanted to talk with Binks,' Mabel reminded him.

'I wanted to offer my condolences,' Harkin said.

'And I to you,' Binks replied.

Mabel doubted very much that was all Harkin had wanted to say, but neither man looked willing to say more. Time to poke the bears.

'There was another murder this morning,' she announced.

Harkin shouted, 'No!' He threw the cue stick onto the table and lunged forward as if to make a break for it. Mabel leapt back, but Hildy was on him in a flash, and Harkin found himself face-down on the green baize of the snooker table. She kept hold of him as he struggled and sobbed, 'Not my Ruby!'

Beside her, Binks breathed hard. 'Was it, Miss Canning?'

'Not Ruby,' Mabel said. 'One of the other suffragettes. Miss Fleming-Jones.'

Harkin let out a moan of relief. Mabel thought it was quite a show – he'd seen Ruby no more than half an hour ago.

Binks shook his head. 'Here inside the Hall?'

'In the bluebell wood,' Mabel said, and the butler squinted his eyes and looked at the wall as if he could see all the way out to where Pretoria's body lay.

'That has nothing to do with me,' Harkin said. 'Can you not let me up – I'm not going anywhere. Not when I've come this far.'

Mabel nodded at Hildy, who let go of him. 'Did you know her?' Mabel asked. 'Pretoria Fleming-Jones.'

Harkin straightened, tugged on his jacket and rolled his shoulders back. 'I suppose I did. I knew them all years ago.'

'Have you ever been here to Fellbridge Hall, Mr Harkin?' Hildy asked. 'Before today?'

Harkin's gaze darted round the room. 'You aren't going to collar me for something I didn't do.'

Out the window Mabel heard the roar of an engine and the

scattering of chippings as the car came to a sudden halt. The doctor had arrived.

'Lunch is being served as a buffet, Mr Harkin,' she said. 'Would you like to join the women or would you prefer to take your meal in here?'

No surprise that Harkin chose to eat alone. She asked Binks to make up a plate for him. She hoped he enjoyed his chickpea loaf.

'But I thought I was here for a fellow who'd had a road accident,' Finlay said as Mabel walked him out to the murder scene.

'There's been another death,' Mabel said.

'Death?' Finlay asked sharply.

'Murder,' Mabel said and explained briefly. 'Inspector Tollerton is on his way.'

An air of gloom hung about the bluebell wood that no amount of dancing sunlight could banish. Mabel's heart went out to Pretoria, and she hoped that the woman had had a chance to enjoy the flowers before... a sob caught in Mabel's throat and she coughed it away. But surely even a private detective is allowed some emotion at the loss of a life.

Mabel and Finlay went first to Park at the edge of the wood.

'Rum business,' Finlay said by way of a greeting. He set down his Gladstone bag and went to examine the body.

'Stay clear of the trampled ground if you can,' Park called.

Finlay stopped and looked down at his feet. 'Yes, all right.' He edged his way round to the body.

Ned stood well away – he was looking a bit green about the gills. Gladys had eaten her sausages and gone off on her own business.

'You don't have a spare sandwich going, do you?' Mabel asked Park.

He rummaged in the basket. 'It's no good pushing yourself to the brink,' he said, coming up with a pickle. 'Sorry.'

'No, it's all right,' she said. She took a large bite of the pickle and her face drew up in reaction to the brine. 'I'll have an extra slice of cake at tea. Perhaps I'll eat the entire cake.' She took Park's hand and he rubbed his thumb lightly across her knuckles.

'What did you make of Harkin?' he asked.

'He seems truly sorry about what Ruby has been through, but secretive in other ways. He'd been talked into keeping quiet about his daughter, but perhaps he'd grown tired of other people telling him what to do. He was keen to talk with Binks.'

'What about?'

'I don't know – they wouldn't say with me there. Harkin reacted badly when he heard about a second murder, afraid that it might be Ruby. He wasn't thinking straight, I suppose.' Mabel finished off the pickle. 'Are you and Ned all right out here?'

'Oh, we're grand,' Park said. They glanced over at Constable Cowley, who sat propped up against a beech with his head back and his eyes closed.

'I'm going into town,' Mabel said, drawing the Harkins' wedding photo from her pocket. 'I'll ask at the station if anyone remembers seeing Harkin come off the London train this morning.'

'Does Harkin know you kept the photo?' Park asked with a grin.

'I've only borrowed it,' Mabel explained. 'No harm done. You'd've done the same.'

'I would've,' Park agreed.

'Well now,' Finlay said, returning to them. 'I stepped as carefully as I could, Mr Winstone, and I've disturbed the body as little as possible. It looks very likely to be a blow to the back of the head – there was a great deal of blood. The... er...' – He pointed to his own nondescript grey necktie – 'doesn't seem to be too tight.' He coughed.

For a doctor who had surely seen a lot of death in his profession, he seemed awfully squeamish, Mabel thought. And then she realised that he'd probably rarely, if ever, seen murder. Mabel now had to use two hands to count the number of murder victims she'd encountered. That gave her pause.

'I'm sure the inspector will want to see Miss Fleming-Jones just as you found her, Miss Canning,' Finlay continued as he regained his composure. 'I believe I'll go up to the Hall and look in on Lady Fellbridge and Miss Goose and the others. And what about this fellow you rang about?'

'It's Oliver Harkin,' Mabel said. 'Annie Harkin's husband.'

Finlay's brows shot up. 'Mrs Harkin's husband... and he was struck on the road today?'

'Mr Harkin wasn't actually struck,' Park said.

'He nearly was,' Mabel said.

Finlay frowned. 'But if he wasn't injured, why did Janet ring for me?'

'We thought it would be best to have him looked at,' Mabel said.

'Didn't the driver stop?' Finlay asked.

'He didn't stop for Mr Harkin,' Mabel said, 'and he didn't stop for me.'

'You?'

Mabel told her story without emotion. Already in her mind, she had seen that Wolseley coming at her so many times it had worn out its fright.

'Well, I'll be blowed,' Finlay said. 'What about you, Miss Canning? Were you injured?'

'No,' Mabel said, 'only surprised.'

'Who was the driver?' the doctor asked.

'The driver has not been identified,' Mabel said and then added, 'Not yet.'

'Ah,' Finlay said, 'well there's a bit of good news at last. When you say "Not yet", Miss Canning, it tells me you may have an idea who it was.'

'It's no use to speculate,' Mabel said. 'I'll walk up to the Hall with you, Doctor.'

She gave Park a look and he raised his chin in acknowledgement.

They went in through the conservatory where Finlay said, 'I would like to see Miss Goose if that's possible. I admit to being worried about her nerves – how has she taken Miss Fleming-Jones' murder?'

'As well as can be expected,' Mabel said. Actually, Dorothea had taken it better than the others.

They made their way to the dining room where Binks stood against the wall keeping an eye on the buffet table. He gave them both a nod. The women looked up in fear from their plates as if Mabel were there to announce yet another death.

Finlay glanced round the room and when Mabel followed his gaze she saw that another suffragette sash had appeared – Diane had joined Ruby and Dorothea. Was she, too, declaring her intentions? Was it a show of solidarity with Pretoria and Annie? Were they all daring the murderer to take another of them?

'Ah, Miss Goose, there you are,' Finlay said and smiled. He took the chair next to Dorothea.

'I'm quite well, Doctor, and I don't need to be fussed over,' she said stiffly then softened. She set her knife and fork on her empty plate and smoothed down her sash. 'Really, you're very kind to look in on me, but there's no need.'

'Now, Miss Goose, you've not filled that prescription I gave you to help quieten your nerves,' Finlay said, shaking a forefinger at her in mild reproach.

'I'm afraid I have mislaid it,' Dorothea said. 'I'm sorry.'

'It's no bother for me to write another.' Finlay set his Gladstone bag on the empty chair next to him and went to open it, but his hand hovered over the brass latch, and then he said, 'But then, would that really do any good?'

'I'm sure you know best, Doctor,' Dorothea said indulgently, 'but I am well. So well, in fact, I have regained my memory about Sunday afternoon.' She lifted her chin. 'I'll have a word with you about that, Mabel.'

The room had grown quiet and Mabel felt as if every ear had turned to hear what Dorothea had remembered.

'If you've remembered something, Miss Goose,' Finlay said, 'you must inform the inspector.'

'Mabel is conducting the enquiry, Doctor,' Dorothea said with a small smile. 'Surely you've noticed that.'

'Dorothea, why don't we go out onto the terrace and have a word?' Mabel suggested.

'I would do, Mabel,' Dorothea said, 'but I have more urgent matters to attend to. Greenfly have attacked the early planting of peas. It's such a chore to knock the little buggers off the stems, but we must dispatch them immediately. I'll catch you up later.'

Emma came in and the doctor rose to talk with her as the others re-started their conversations. Dorothea leaned over to Mabel.

'I didn't mislay the prescription,' she said. She patted her pocket and Mabel heard the crinkling of paper. 'I don't need it and it's only for valerian – I can buy that on my own. I have it with me, thinking I would bury it in the compost heap, but I don't want to hurt the doctor's feelings.'

'Burning a hole in your pocket, is it?' Mabel asked, smiling at Dorothea's desire to keep the doctor from getting his feelings bruised. 'Here, give it to me.' Before Mabel put it in her own pocket, she looked down at the irregular loopy hand that seemed to dance above the lines. 'Are you sure you don't have a moment to tell me what it is you've remembered?'

Dorothea pulled a face. 'I may have over-egged the pudding there. I don't know if you've noticed, Mabel, but the others have always looked on me as a bit odd. No, no,' she hurried on, sensing Mabel's protest, 'I'm accustomed to it after all these years. But also, I've learned to try to appear as run-of-the-mill as possible. So, instead of saying I was having wild dreams while next door Annie... well, instead I'd prefer to put it about that I'm more in control than that.'

Mabel tried to hide her disappointment. 'You don't remember what you heard?'

Dorothea lifted a forefinger. 'Now, I do believe those disjointed words I reported hearing earlier weren't a dream. But as to who was saying what...' She shrugged.

Augustus, who had been sitting between Cora and Skeff, had slipped off his chair and sauntered over to the doctor's bag. He put a finger out as if to touch the brass detailing and the initials G F.

'Hello there, young man,' Finlay called, coming over.

Augustus snatched his hand away from the bag. 'Hello, sir. I'm Augustus Malling-Frobisher. I'm a friend of Miss Canning's.'

Mabel didn't believe that being her friend would grant Augustus immunity for pawing at the doctor's bag, but it was, after all, a fine bag.

She introduced him and they shook hands.

'My father gave me this bag when I qualified,' Finlay said. 'A reward for my hard work.'

'I won a prize for spelling once,' Augustus said, then added with incredulity, 'they gave me a dictionary!'

Mabel laughed and the doctor guffawed, his right eye drawing up in a wink. Binks came to the table and leaned over, offering one of his abbreviated bows.

'Doctor Finlay, would you care for coffee?'

'Yes, Doctor, stay for coffee,' Mabel said as she rose. 'Are you finished with your lunch, Augustus? I've an errand in town. Perhaps we can talk Constable Wardle into running us in.'

'No need for that,' Finlay said, popping up from his chair. 'I'm happy to take you as long as the boy doesn't mind sharing the dickey seat with my golf clubs.'

They looked in on Oliver Harkin before they left and found him continuing with his snooker tutorial for the benefit of Constable Wardle.

'Now, Constable,' Harkin said, handing her the cue, 'hold the cue stick steady and try to hit the white ball. Don't worry about any of the others yet.'

Hildy glanced over at Mabel, the doctor and Augustus, and then said, 'All right, Mr Harkin, I'll give it a try.' She accepted the cue stick, leaned over the table and took aim, smacking the cue ball, which then struck a red ball that ricocheted off one side of the table and into a pocket on the other side.

Augustus hooted and clapped while Mabel swallowed her snigger.

'Mr Harkin,' Mabel said, 'Doctor Finlay is here to take a look at your head.'

'My head?' Harkin touched the plaster on his forehead. 'Oh yes, that.'

'I hear you were nearly knocked down in the road, sir,' Finlay said as he peeled back the bandage.

'The car missed me, but just,' Harkin said. 'Don't know I deserved that when all I wanted to do was come pay respects to my Annie.'

'It's not much more than a scratch,' Finlay said, peering at the wound. 'Good dressing, though. Who put it on?'

'I did, sir,' Hildy said.

'Well done, Constable,' Finlay said, sticking the plaster back in place. He looked down at Harkin. 'I doubt you'll have any reminder – not like the one I've carried since I was a boy.' He tapped the short scar that ran straight through one of his own black eyebrows. 'Old wounds, eh?'

There was a brief moment of silence as if to acknowledge this statement, then Augustus stuck his leg out and pointed to his knee. 'I have a scar from last year when I tried to climb the statue of George IV in Trafalgar Square on a school trip. That was before I met you, Miss Canning.'

To which, Mabel could only say, 'Thank God.'

'There's been an incident,' Augustus said to Mabel as they walked out onto the forecourt. Then he added, his voice heavy with significance, 'A murder.'

'Who told you that?' Mabel asked.

'I didn't eavesdrop!' he proclaimed. 'At least, not on purpose. But Mother never tells me anything, and so I taught myself how to listen when no one thinks I'm listening.'

Mabel considered this one of her special skills, but it wasn't something she could condone in an eight-year-old.

'It's truly terrible, what's happened,' she said, 'and everyone's quite upset. But I don't think it's anything you need dwell on and I intend to keep you out of the fray. You must do your part to stay well away from it.'

'Yes, ma'am,' Augustus replied in such an obedient tone that Mabel immediately worried.

The boy climbed into the dickey seat and found a space between golf clubs and the doctor's bag. Mabel handed him her satchel.

'Mabel!' Skeff called from the doorstep. Mabel hurried over.

'Good news,' Skeff said, grabbing Mabel's arm. 'Agatha

Tyne – I've found her death notice from twenty-two years ago. She died in Little Lever.'

'That's where Annie was from,' Mabel said, her whispered voice quivering with excitement. Had she and Oliver married by then? 'Binks was there, too – or Cheevers, I suppose he would've been at the time.'

'She died at the canal,' Skeff said, 'and the coroner left the verdict open. I've got a fellow going to the county offices to look up the coroner's report. He'll ring me first thing tomorrow and read it out and we'll have the details.'

Mabel squeezed Skeff's arm. 'Brilliant! Keep this on the q.t. – we don't want Binks getting wind of it.'

'Right you are.'

'Miss Canning?' the doctor called.

They'd found Agatha Tyne! Mabel walked on air to the doctor's two-seater. So, twenty-two years ago they were all there – Annie, Susan Truelock and Binks were there. Where was Oliver? What had happened? And what did Agatha Tyne's death have to do with the suffragette murders at Fellbridge Hall?

EIGHTEEN

'I was noticing, if you don't mind my saying so,' Finlay said as they motored down the lanes, 'that these deaths seem to have stirred up a renewed fervour among the ladies. With the wearing of the sashes, I mean.'

'They're suffragette sashes, Doctor,' Augustus said from his perch in the dickey seat. 'Miss Goose is a suffragette and she went to jail.'

Mabel frowned. 'Did Miss Goose tell you this?'

'No, Miss Truelock told me, but Miss Goose was there and heard it and she didn't say it was a story.'

'Miss Goose is a brave woman,' Mabel said. 'She stood up for what was right – is doing so even now. All the women at the Hall worked in their own fashion for votes for women.'

'Mrs Chandekar told me that there is a lady who lives in London and her name is Sophia Dupleet Singh and she's an Indian princess and a suffragette,' Augustus said with wonder in his voice. 'At the same time!'

'"No vote, no census",' Mabel said. 'That's what Princess Sophia wrote on her 1911 census form. She also wrote "As women do not count, they refuse to be counted." Mrs Chandekar and my friend Edith and I learned all about the princess. She's quite a woman.'

'Can I be a suffragette?' Augustus asked.

'Well, now, Augustus,' Finlay said, 'that doesn't seem quite proper, does it?'

'You can certainly support the cause in many ways,' Mabel said. 'Boys and girls today will grow up in a world where everyone is equal, and we must all do our part to make it so.'

Augustus was quiet for the rest of the journey and when they arrived at the surgery, he climbed out of the dickey seat with a pensive look.

'If I'm a suffragette, will I need to wear a sash?'

'Sashes are optional,' Mabel said. She dusted herself off as she took in the house. It had been known as Dr Ebbers' place for most of her life and the garden looked the same as it always had – comfortably unkempt with primroses and bleeding hearts and stems of campanula piercing cushions of phlox. When Finlay opened the door and invited them in, Mabel found the indoors looked much the same, too.

'We don't want to disrupt your day, Doctor,' Mabel said standing in the entry. 'We'll be on our way.'

'Stay for a cup of tea, at least, then you can be off on your enquiry. I'm sure you remember your way to the surgery, Miss Canning. Go through.' He left his bag at the door and continued back to the kitchen. 'I won't be a moment.'

The surgery and living quarters were under one roof in the cottage, which had been given by Lord and Lady Fellbridge to the physician in residence. It made the post of district doctor all the more attractive.

In the surgery, Augustus, keeping his hands behind his back, began an examination of the old prints on the wall, the books on the shelf and the doctor's implements lined up on a high shelf. Mabel noticed the desk looked tidier than it had with Dr Ebbers, but nothing else had changed except the framed certificate on the wall. The University of Edinburgh stated in scrolly writing that it had 'resolved to offer Gordon Finlay the degree of medicine'.

'Here we are now,' Finlay said, coming in. He set the tray down on the desk. 'I'm sorry I was late going out to the Hall. When Janet rang round I was between calls – on my way to Mrs Varnell. Do you know her?'

'Yes, I remember Mrs Varnell,' Mabel replied as she poured out the tea for them. 'How is she?'

'I'm afraid she's not coping well on her own,' Finlay said, stirring sugar into his tea. 'She had already forgotten I'd been round yesterday afternoon and I'm sure she's already forgotten about this morning, too. She has a daughter in Yeovil and I'll be talking with her soon.'

Augustus watched and waited and when this exchange ended, he changed the subject. 'When you operate on someone,' he asked Finlay, 'how big a knife do you use?'

'Augustus!' Mabel said.

Finlay tried to cover his laugh. 'You're best asking a surgeon a question like that, young man, not a country doctor.'

After that, they made short work of the tea. As Mabel and Augustus stood on the doorstep, ready to be off, Finlay said, 'Miss Canning, about Miss Goose.'

'What about her?'

He dropped his voice as Augustus wandered out to the road.

'I'm concerned. She's a kind woman and proud, there's no question about that. I doubt she's had an easy time of it and I feel as if there's something brittle inside her. Seeing the others again, these feelings could've risen to the surface and caused her to snap. What do you think?'

The proliferation of suffragette sashes worried Mabel and she couldn't deny that she'd had the same thoughts about Dorothea, but she was loath to admit to them. But what else could connect the murders of Annie Harkin and Pretoria Fleming-Jones? Had Agatha Tyne been a suffragette, too? Her death had been more than twenty years ago, and that would be before the active campaign – Deeds Not Words – kicked off. But even then, women were coming together.

Mabel realised Finlay was watching her, then seemed to take her frown as a reply. He held up his hands and exhaled with exasperation.

'The thing is,' he said, 'a doctor can't see inside someone's head – more's the pity. I hope it isn't so, but at the same time, I hope that everyone at the Hall is taking care.'

Mabel and Augustus walked down to the station where she showed the Harkins' wedding photo to the station master.

'Have you seen this man getting off a train?' she asked.

The station master shook his head and referred her to the porter, who had his hands full of suitcases for the first-class passengers of a train nearly ready to depart. While Mabel and Augustus waited on the platform for him to finish, she caught the boy eyeing the left luggage cart at the end of the platform.

'I don't need to hold your hand to keep you from slipping away and smoking, do I?' she asked.

'No, Miss Canning,' Augustus said. 'I've given up cigarettes. My dad says next time he visits from Australia, I can try out one of his cigars.'

Augustus' father had given the boy a sword for his eighth birthday – a real sword – and so a cigar didn't sound out of character. But Mabel didn't have time to voice an opinion, because the porter had seen the train off and now approached.

'Did you seen this man come in on a London train?' she asked, showing the wedding photo of Oliver Harkin. 'He's older now, but still looks much the same.'

'Oh aye,' the man said. 'Asking which way to Fellbridge Hall.'

'Yes,' Mabel said, 'that would've been him. He arrived this morning?'

'Morning? No, ma'am, he came in last evening, he did. Early evening train – the 7:07 as I recall.'

'Did he now,' Mabel muttered.

'How are you, sonny?' The porter nodded to Augustus.

'I'm fine, sir,' Augustus said. 'Do you blow the whistle for the train to start?'

'No, I'm the man who shifts the bags and trunks and whatnot from where they are to where they're supposed to be – that's what I do. I help the ladies off the train, and I give directions to anyone who asks.'

'Do you know where he went?' Mabel asked. 'This man you saw arrive last evening?'

'You see now, sonny, here's a good example,' the porter said. 'This man was asking the way to Fellbridge Hall, ma'am. When I told him, he asked me for the nearest hotel.' The conductor pointed up the hill.

'The Mermaid?' Mabel asked.

'Couldn't do better,' the porter said. 'He had only the one case and so there was no need to send anything on. He set his Panama hat on his head and off he went.'

'Thank you, sir,' Mabel said. 'Right, Augustus, off we go, too.' She put her hand on the boy's shoulder and turned him round.

'Is this fellow you're asking about to do with that business up at the Hall?' the porter asked. 'The murder of that suffragette?'

Mabel should've known word had travelled about Annie's death, but still it was a jolt for her to hear *that business* referred to by a stranger. No doubt news of Pretoria's murder wouldn't be far behind.

'Thank you for your help,' Mabel replied.

Up the hill to the Mermaid they hiked, passing white or pink houses with scrubbed doorsteps where clusters of tiny daisies pushed their way out of cracks in the flagstone. The street was narrow and the cobbles formidable. Mabel kept to the pavement, but Augustus went back and forth across the street and still arrived at the door of the hotel before she did.

The public rooms of the Mermaid – the only rooms Mabel had ever seen – had dark, shiny wood panelling, luxurious velvet curtains hanging on golden rods and a comforting scent of old fires from the cold grates. Mabel had celebrated her tenth birthday at the Mermaid and she still remembered the cream buns and how many of them she and Edith had eaten.

Now, the man at the desk looked up at Mabel and then down at Augustus, who stood nose-to-bust with the carved stone statue of a Greek goddess.

Mabel introduced herself, showed the old wedding photo and explained her connection to both Oliver Harkin and to Fellbridge Hall. 'It's only that Lady Fellbridge did expect him yesterday and we were a wee bit worried, as you can imagine. The porter at the station said he might've come this way.'

The man turned a page in the register and said, 'Yes, Mr Harkin. He stayed only for the one night. I'm uncertain when he – here, Lottie!' he said to a young woman passing by with a tray of drinks. 'Do you remember Mr Harkin? I believe he had a hearty breakfast before he left this morning?'

'That was Mr Harkin, was it? He not only ate a hearty breakfast,' Lottie replied without stopping, 'but I believe he took away a bacon roll in his pocket when he left.'

Identified by a bacon roll.

Lottie paused in the doorway. 'By the time he finished his breakfast, he'd missed the early bus and didn't care for the price of a taxi, so struck out on foot.'

Mabel and Augustus took the afternoon bus back to Peasmarsh and on the journey, Mabel tried to fashion this new information into some sort of evidence as to Harkin's guilt in the death of his estranged wife. He appeared to be off the hook for Pretoria's murder, because he'd been eating his hearty breakfast and then walking at least as far as the village before he was nearly run over.

Still, he had lied about his arrival. Why?

And could there be two murderers?

She tried with little success to convince herself that the afternoon had not been wasted, even if it did produce no new leads. In an enquiry every possible question must be asked and answered. Still, she felt let down, and then realised that her low spirits could be because she'd had no lunch. She suspected that teatime might be flying past her, too. Augustus, on the other hand, enjoyed every minute of the journey, asking a continuous stream of questions about the town, the river, the old tower and the Battle of Hastings.

They alighted in the village and, as the bus turned the corner and went on its way, Mabel waved to Janet Darling, who sat in the window of her cottage at the exchange board. Janet returned the wave and opened the window as if to speak, but one of her telephone lines rang. Mabel thought Janet would certainly want to be filled in on the details of the day and was glad to escape that questioning.

When they walked into the shop, Reg looked up from a crate of beetroot.

'Well now,' he said, eyeing Augustus up and down, 'I'd wondered where my assistant had got to. You'd best get your apron on and get to work.'

Augustus hopped to it. Mabel gave Reg a grateful smile and a quick kiss on the cheek, but before she could turn away, he caught her hand and gave her a look that told her he had seen how weary she felt.

'I only need a cup of tea, Papa,' she explained. He looked unconvinced but didn't argue and Mabel continued down the passage to the kitchen.

A cup of tea and a ham sandwich. She felt better after the first bite and when Mrs Chandekar sat across from her at the table, she told her about Pretoria. They commiserated about the strain on Emma and how both murders were affecting the spirits of the women. Mabel went on to explain her suspicions about Oliver Harkin and how Binks denied he'd been out driving that morning.

'Yes, I meant to tell you,' Mrs Chandekar said. 'I know I said it looked like Binks drove by, but even as I said the words I knew that wasn't right. In my mind, I've watched the Wolseley drive by again and again and you know, I don't believe it was Binks after all.'

'How did you come to that?'

'It was a Wolseley, that's true.' She wrapped her shawl round her shoulders and frowned into the distance. 'It could even be Lord Fellbridge's, although I couldn't tell you that for certain. The driver wore a bowler and spectacles, but...' She took a breath. 'I saw him from the side, you know, and this person was hunched over the steering wheel, raising his shoulders and thrusting his chin forward' – she did as she described – 'the way one might expect Binks to drive, because he doesn't see well. But that isn't how he drives. Binks sits tall in the seat with his shoulders back just as he always holds himself. He's quite an upright fellow.'

True. No one could accuse Binks of sagging shoulders or poor posture. But where did this leave them? Someone had donned a bowler hat and thick spectacles and taken the Wolseley out so that people would think it was Binks driving. Not to run down Oliver Harkin – no one knew he was coming.

To hit her? Was Mabel getting too close to the truth? She hoped that wouldn't occur to Mrs Chandekar or her papa.

'Could it have been a woman?' she asked.

'Well,' Mrs Chandekar said, drawing out the word. 'I suppose so – with her hair pushed up inside the bowler. Are you thinking of someone in particular?'

Mabel shook her head. 'It's just something to consider.'

Did Ruby drive?

Out in the shop, the bell above the door jingled and there came a loud *woof!* followed in the next instant by a crash and a series of thuds. Mabel looked down the passage and saw an enormous cabbage roll across the floor with Gladys in hot pursuit. At the shop door, Park stood with hat in hand looking at Reg with apprehension.

Park made it safely past Reg, and Mabel led him into the dining room where he told her that Tollerton and his scene of crime officers had arrived, and the mortuary wagon had come and taken Pretoria away.

'Tolly won't go back to London tonight,' Park said, 'and so there'll be plenty of time to talk with him.'

Mabel thought there would be little for her to do at the Hall while Scotland Yard worked the scene except to get in the officers' way and, as Reg and Mrs Chandekar both took it for granted Mabel and Park would stay for an early evening meal, they did. Fish pie for the people and a dish of specially cooked mince for Gladys. Conversation stayed well away from murder but did wander into flights of fancy as Augustus regaled them with stories of his father, who sounded partway between a pirate and the next prime minister.

As the boy began work on a mountain of rhubarb pudding, Mabel said, 'The doctor told me he'd been out to see Mrs

Varnell this morning. She'd taken a turn apparently and didn't remember he'd been stopping in every day.'

'Did she?' Mrs Chandekar said, frowning. 'I'm sorry to hear that. He's good with the old ones, Doctor Finlay is.' Mabel's papa rolled his eyes, but the housekeeper ignored him. 'I'll take her a plate of gingernuts – those are her favourites.'

'They're my favourites, too,' Augustus said.

'Well then I'll leave a few back,' Mrs Chandekar replied.

'Miss Canning,' Augustus said, 'I can go up to the Hall tomorrow morning on my own. I know the way.'

Mabel gave him her look she reserved for the most wayward eight-year-olds. 'Under no circumstances are you to leave here without Mr Winstone or me coming for you.' She watched and waited as the boy took this in.

He sighed. 'Yes, ma'am.'

Gladys had fallen asleep by the front window, but now as they all rose she did, too, shook herself and trotted to the door.

They said their good nights and Mrs Chandekar led Augustus upstairs. Reg followed Mabel and Park out the kitchen door to the yard and as far as the road where they stopped, and he took a deep breath.

'I don't like what's going on up at the Hall,' he said, 'but I know, too, I can no longer put my foot down and stop my daughter from doing what she will. Not that I ever could, really. So, it's down to you, isn't it, Mr Winstone, to see that nothing happens to her.'

'Mr Canning,' Park said, 'I would protect Mabel with my life.'

For a moment, Reg regarded Park as if assessing the truth of this statement. Then he gave a single nod.

Mabel, for her part, wanted to say she could protect herself thank you very much, but the flippant reply didn't make it out past the tears that threatened. She had the sudden knowledge that she would do the same for Park.

'Good night, Papa,' she said. 'I'll see you in the morning.'

She and Park held hands as they strolled along the road with Gladys crisscrossing in front of them. There would be work to do when they reached the Hall. Perhaps Tolly would have news for them. She had some of her own for him.

Mabel spoke her thoughts without preamble. 'What about Oliver Harkin?' she asked. 'What will Tolly do with him?'

'Tolly asked him to stay close and Emma offered a room,' Park said, 'but Harkin said he'd put up at the pub for the night. He isn't under arrest.'

'Yet. Let's see if he's at the pub now,' Mabel said. 'Because I have a few more questions for him.'

Mabel told Park what she'd learned about the timing of Harkin's arrival as they continued down the road to the King and Cork. They walked into the pub to find a moderate crowd – the usual locals in their usual places, including Binks with his bowler hat on the settle beside him and pint on the table. The only difference was that this evening, he wasn't alone. Sitting across from him was Oliver Harkin.

They had their heads together and took no notice of who'd arrived until Mabel walked over and said, 'Good evening.'

Binks rose in a sedate fashion and nodded.

Harkin, on the other hand, nearly knocked his glass over as he leapt up.

'I've done nothing wrong,' he said. 'There's no law against having a pint with an old friend.'

It hadn't occurred to Mabel to call Binks and Harkin old friends.

'Well, if you'll excuse me,' Binks said, 'I'll be on my way. Mr Winstone. Miss Canning. Good evening, Oliver.' He drained his glass, took his hat and left.

'Mr Harkin,' Mabel said calmly. She saw him twitch. 'Could we have a chat, do you think, just the three of us?'

'Yes, all right,' Harkin said. He looked down into his glass.

'Another, Mr Harkin?' Park offered.

Harkin sighed. 'No thank you, sir. I'd better keep my head about me.'

'Oh, go on then, Mr Harkin,' Mabel said, 'have another. This isn't an interrogation. I'll have a sherry.'

Whisky, sherry and a pint of the mild. They adjourned to one of the back rooms at the pub for privacy and settled round a table. No fire had been lit, but regardless, Gladys settled on the hearth.

'What were you and Binks discussing, if you don't mind my asking?'

'Annie,' Harkin said. 'We were talking about Annie.'

'It must've been a shock for you, receiving the telegram with the news about Annie,' Mabel said. 'You must've made your mind up to come down to Sussex quite suddenly. When was it that you arrived in the district?'

Harkin looked round him as if searching for the answer.

'Because you weren't straight with me before, were you?' Mabel persisted.

'I didn't lie!'

'No, you didn't lie,' she said, 'but you evaded the truth with a smart retort.'

Harkin took a deep drink, set his glass down and wiped his mouth with the back of his hand. 'When the telegram came on Monday from Emma – Lady Fellbridge – about Annie, well, I was that torn up with grief. But after a while, out of that, came the thought of Ruby. You see, I knew she would be down here with the others. They all know I'm Ruby's father and have for donkey's years. What if someone slipped? What if Susan had already told her?'

'How did you know the women were coming to Fellbridge Hall?' Park asked.

'Annie told me,' Harkin said. 'We'd had the occasional conversation since Susan died, you see, and... well, I thought it only fair, at last, for Ruby to hear from me. So, I made a decision and got on the train.'

'But when you got off your train in Rye, you didn't go to the Hall,' Mabel said. 'Why not?'

'I'm a coward, all right?' Harkin shouted and Gladys gave a *woof* in her sleep. 'There' – he dropped his voice – 'I've said it. I took a room at the Mermaid and waited until this morning before I had regained my nerve and started off, only to be nearly run down by some fool on the road.'

'Miss Canning was nearly run down, too,' Park said in a hard tone, 'just before you.'

'Were you?' Harkin asked eagerly. 'Did you see the driver?'

'Did you?' Mabel asked.

Harkin watched her for a moment. 'You think it was Binks – he said as much. The question you should be asking is who would want you to believe that?'

Mabel had her suspicions, but she wasn't about to tell them to Harkin.

'But you and Binks had a public brawl,' she pointed out.

Harkin shook his head. 'That was a long time ago now, Miss Canning, and there was no harm done. Binks could be a bit of a hothead when he was younger, and a... conversation got out of hand.'

'Outside a pub,' Mabel added.

Harkin gave a single nod.

'What was it about?'

'Well, what do you think it was about?' Harkin said. 'He'd finally heard that Susan's little girl was mine and he didn't take kindly that I had done that to Annie. He didn't know the... extenuating circumstances, if you will. Not that that excuses my behaviour! And, well, he threw only the one punch. He couldn't blame me any more than I'd already blamed myself over the years. I was in the wrong. But that's not on Ruby – she's a fine girl and always has been.'

'And that's why you didn't bring charges up against him?' Mabel asked.

'That's Annie's doing. She said what Binks needed was a place he could live a quiet life – and that's what she found for him. He's done well with the butlering, hasn't he?'

'Why wait until now to contact your daughter, Mr Harkin?' Park asked. 'You don't live far apart and you've come all the way to Sussex to meet her.'

'If you'd known the two of them – Annie and Susan – you'd understand that I've been caught between two forces stronger than I was ever prepared to fight. You've already seen evidence that I'm not the most forthright character God ever made. They said it was best for Ruby and I didn't dare put a foot wrong.'

'You make it sound as if Susan and Annie were still friends after your affair,' Mabel said.

He winced at the word *affair* as if all these years later he regretted it afresh.

'Nothing's ever that cut and dried, is it?' Harkin said. 'Susan was a strong-willed woman and had no intention of ever marrying – she had made that quite clear to all concerned. But the trust she and Annie had as friends was gone and that never came back. Even so, for Ruby's sake they would talk every now and then. Annie liked the girl, but from afar, you see. Everyone talked to each other, except to me.'

'Do you think yourself ill-used by women, Mr Harkin?' Mabel asked. 'Ill-used by the suffragettes?'

'What?' Harkin asked. 'No, you can't pin that on me. I was a supporter of the campaign from the start – Annie could tell you that.' He stopped and his face darkened. 'The others can tell you. They all remember.'

'I'm very sorry about Annie,' Mabel said – a late condolence, but it hadn't occurred to her to offer it to Oliver who now seemed more to be pitied than suspected. She pulled the wedding photo out of her pocket. 'I borrowed this earlier. I hope you don't mind. It's only that, in a murder enquiry every possible line must be pursued.'

Harkin stared at the image and his eyes filled with tears.

'She was a joy to be around,' he said. 'And even after I found out that we weren't as… compatible as a married couple usually is, still I always wanted her company before anyone else's.'

Mabel and Park left Harkin to the rest of his pint and walked up to the Hall, pausing on the doorstep as Gladys made an inspection of a nearby patch of lawn. Park took Mabel in his arms and she rested her cheek on his chest for a moment, then looked up, took his spectacles off and said, 'Did you notice Papa didn't offer you parsnip cordial?' He grinned and kissed her and for just a moment Mabel's mind and body were filled with more pleasant thoughts than murder. Then, PC Scott opened the door.

'Detective Inspector Tollerton is waiting for you both in the steward's office.'

Tolly sat behind the desk wearing his coat, with his bowler hat on a shelf. He rose when they came in.

'Good, good,' he said. 'We'd best get to it. Where's Wardle?'

'Here, sir,' Hildy said, coming in behind Mabel and Park with a tray holding a bottle of whisky and six glasses.

'Who else are you expecting?' Mabel asked.

'Mr Harkin's staying at the pub, but I wouldn't be surprised if he didn't march in,' Tolly said, pouring four glasses and handing them round. 'He seemed reluctant to go and in a hurry to leave – in equal measure. I got an earful from him about someone trying to run him down.'

'Whoever it was aimed at me first,' Mabel said. 'Do you want to start with that?' At a nod, Mabel told her side of the story. 'To begin with, we thought it was Binks – the car was seen passing the shop. But Mrs Chandekar has had second thoughts and I believe she's right.'

'But that means someone wanted you to believe it was Binks,' Tollerton pointed out. 'Who?'

Mabel skirted the answer. 'Campsie, the gardener, has an old bowler that's gone missing. Anyone could've walked into his cottage and taken it, added these spectacles' – Park shook them out of his handkerchief and set them on the desk – 'and driven the Wolseley out and about without anyone knowing the car was even gone. Everyone knew I was walking down to the shop to collect Augustus.'

'No prints were found in the car or on the hand crank,' Tollerton said. 'If not Binks, who?'

Mabel wondered if she should have another whisky to get through this. 'I've been thinking about Ruby. She only found out about Oliver being her father recently, or at least since her mother died two years ago – I'm a bit unclear on that, but will find out. Misplaced anger could've driven her to kill Annie, but I don't know why she would attack Pretoria. Unless Pretoria had found out how Annie died. What have you found out about how Pretoria died?'

'Miss Fleming-Jones died from her head injury probably early this morning. The suffragette sash round her neck was... I don't know. Decoration? Did Oliver Harkin feel himself hard done by as far as suffragettes are concerned?' Tollerton asked.

'His grief seems genuine,' Mabel said, but tentatively. She'd been taken in before. 'Also, he has a firm alibi for this morning – he was eating breakfast.'

'But no alibi for Mrs Harkin,' Tollerton said.

Mabel frowned. 'Could he have followed Annie down, murdered her Sunday afternoon and then rushed back to Little Lever to receive Emma's telegram the next day? He knew Ruby would be here. Perhaps he believed that if Annie and Ruby settled their differences, he would still be out in the cold. That might've angered him.'

Tolly gave her a nod.

'He told me he'd arrived just this morning,' Mabel said, 'but he was at the Mermaid last night. He said he was trying to gin up his nerve.'

Tollerton frowned. 'If he lied about one night, perhaps he lied about more. We've nothing to hold Harkin on, but I'll have someone check on who signed for the telegram Lady Fellbridge sent him on Monday.'

'It seems far-fetched,' Mabel said and then held up her hand. 'No, you're right – eliminate every possibility.'

'We've just come from the pub,' Park said, 'where we walked in on Harkin and Binks in conversation.'

Tollerton's brows raised. 'About what?'

'Their grief at losing Annie,' Mabel said.

'And you believed that?'

'Yes.' She heard a defiant tone sneak into her voice.

'Did you learn anything else from him?'

'Hildy, you kept an eye on him in the billiards room for a while,' Mabel said. 'Did he say anything to you?'

'Mr Harkin said nothing to me,' Hildy replied. 'He was too bent on teaching me how to play snooker until I won the first frame.'

They drank in silence for a moment, then Mabel nearly dropped her glass as she exclaimed, 'Agatha Tyne! Skeff has found her – she told me as I was on my way to check Harkin's alibi.'

'Agatha Tyne?' Tollerton asked as if he'd forgotten all about her.

'The name isn't familiar to any of the women,' Mabel said. 'Cora's been asking around, but I will go back to each of them again just to see if I get a different answer. Agatha Tyne died twenty-two years ago in Little Lever – the inquest declared an open verdict.'

'Which means there was doubt in the coroner's mind,' Park pointed out.

'Skeff has someone who will read the entire coroner's report to her tomorrow,' Mabel said.

'Good,' Tolly said. 'That's good. So, until tomorrow.' He downed his whisky and the rest of them followed suit.

The next morning, Park kissed Mabel behind her ear and murmured something. She sighed, for a moment half-awake, and then drifted off again, awaking fully to a clatter of dishes at the door. Park and Gladys were already gone. Mabel sat up and winced at the twinge in her shoulder. For a moment she couldn't think where that had come from, then, she recalled her tumble off the road when the Wolseley had come at her.

That seemed ages ago now, but it had only been the previous morning. Annie dead on Sunday. Pretoria dead on Wednesday. And now, Thursday, suffragettes seemed to be coming out of the woodwork – Diane had donned her sash and Ruby wore her mother's. Mabel couldn't forget Dorothea and her ordeal in prison. Was this week – this meeting of minds – causing her mind to snap? Would another of the women be targeted next or – a shiver ran down Mabel's spine – would the murderer be more careful the next time he aimed at her?

She had a sudden desire to throw the blanket back over her and hide for the day, but her common sense took over and she leapt out of bed. Yes, danger was present, but a private detective forged ahead no matter what.

But not before a cup of tea. Mabel brought in the tray and threw open the curtains. The light that came through the window was diffuse and grey – hardly like a morning at all, at least not the sunny sort they'd been having. She downed her tea, took her bath bag and set off for a wash. By the time she returned, the sun blazed through the window. Then, as she dressed, a sharp shower began beating on the glass. Spring had turned tricksy on them.

As she pulled on a stocking, she recalled the words Park had murmured to her – he had a bit of his own work to do but would be around when needed. She had her own work, too – practical work. Emma intended to start up the meetings again, as scheduled. At least that way all the women would be in one place, and their attention turned from murder back to the campaign.

It was time for her no-nonsense day dress, a lightweight wool in navy blue with a square white collar and trim. She added a navy cloche with a single white silk rose pinned at the ear. She went to the window and saw blue sky and piercing sunshine and decided she also would need her coat and an umbrella.

Everyone else in the priory gallery wing had gone down before Mabel – Skeff and Cora had knocked, but she hadn't been ready yet and told them so. She'd heard Hildy join them and Diane call out in her booming voice for them to wait up.

When Mabel opened her door, the corridor was dark, but she thought that must be because the sun had been so bright in her room. When she closed the door, she realised that the corridor lamps were not switched on and it reminded her of Dorothea switching off the lights in the west wing.

Mabel blinked, waiting for her eyes to adjust to the dark – there were no windows in the corridor and so she needed to make her way to the stairs at one end or the other, then she'd see her way. She put a hand out on the wall. That's when she heard the footsteps.

They were down to her right – light footfalls on the wood floor at the top of the stairs, she thought. Had Cora forgotten her hat or Skeff his reporter's notebook?

'Who is it?' she called. 'Can you switch the light on?'

No reply came. Without knowing why, Mabel held her breath. She told herself how absolutely ridiculous and unfounded her fear was, but she didn't listen. She tiptoed down the corridor to her left, being sure to stay on the carpet runner, afraid to put a hand out to the wall lest she knock into a table or the frame of a painting.

She heard movement behind her and then she ran. The end of the corridor seemed miles away and instead of trying to make it to the landing – and perhaps being pushed down the stairwell – she lunged for what she could finally discern in the dark: a doorway.

She turned the handle, fell into the room and slammed the door behind her.

Fumbling for the lock, she realised it would be a skeleton key and what good would that do to protect her against whatever was out there? But then – a key turned on the *outside*. She was being locked in.

She rattled the door handle and, in the distance, she heard voices and laughter.

Pounding on the door, Mabel called out. 'Skeff? Cora? I'm in here! Let me out!'

Their footsteps thundered down the corridor to her, but it took several minutes for a skeleton key to be located in one of the other bedroom doors before Mabel was released. In the meantime, she flew to the window and threw open the shutters. Whoever had trapped her might've gone down the nearest stairs – two sets to the ground floor – and out. But which way? The library French windows?

But she couldn't see that corner of the Hall from the priory gallery – the view from these rooms went out south, across the terrace, the formal gardens, the meadow and beyond. Whoever it was, had no doubt gone off to the right through the bluebell wood and would be long gone before she could follow.

Or the person hadn't left the Hall, but merely blended back into the morning activities as if nothing were amiss. Mabel paced up and down the room as the thoughts swirled in her head. When she heard the lock turn, she flew to the door as it opened.

'There!' Skeff said.

'How did this happen?' Cora asked.

'Did you see anyone?' Mabel asked. 'As you ran here?'

They shook their heads.

Mabel's hands trembled with spent fear – or present rage – and she rubbed them on her face to disguise it.

'Oh Mabel,' Cora said. 'You should sit down.'

'No,' Mabel said. 'No, I'm fine.' She leaned against the doorpost behind her and gave them an account of the event, short-lived though it was, and counted herself lucky that Diane Lotterby wasn't with them or the news would've been boomed throughout the Hall.

'It doesn't make sense – why would someone take the chance of being caught, knowing we are all watching out?' Although not watching out enough, apparently, Mabel told herself.

'It makes sense if one of the others wants you stopped,' Skeff said fiercely. 'You're the lightning rod for the enquiry, Mabel – all the women know that, but perhaps one of them is worried about how much it is you know or suspect.'

'It's lucky you two appeared,' Mabel said. 'Otherwise...' No need to go further there.

'You've no idea who it was?' Cora asked. 'That is, what about Binks? Is he off your list of suspects?'

'The list changes depending on which murder you mean,' Mabel said.

'You'd better tell the inspector,' Cora said.

'Yes,' Mabel said, feeling a bit foolish. 'I will tell him the moment I get back with Augustus.' She held her hands out, palms up. 'Look I'm unhurt. There's an inspector and three police constables on hand. I believe we're well protected.'

'Apparently not,' Skeff said. 'I think we should be sure none of us is alone.'

'Yes, good idea. Well then,' Mabel said, 'it's off to breakfast.'

Her head was clear by the time they arrived in the square dining room. Mabel picked up a slice of toast and sat down next to Emma.

'Are you off to collect Augustus?' Emma asked.

'I am. I won't be long.'

'Don't hurry back,' Emma said. 'We can manage.'

'You'll be together in the conservatory this morning?' Mabel asked.

'We will,' Emma said. 'We'll attend to business as best we can.'

Mabel checked the library French windows before she left. They were locked shut.

Not an hour later when Mabel walked into the shop, she found Augustus perched on a stool at the end of the counter wearing his rejigged grocer's apron and with an orange in each hand.

'Good morning, Miss Canning,' he said. 'I'm picking out the oranges with too many soft spots so that they can be sold for juice. Also' – he whispered loudly – 'Mrs Chandekar is baking gingernuts. I can smell them.'

Reg stood at the other end of the counter going over orders.

'There are child labour laws, you know,' Mabel said to him.

'I'm teaching the boy a trade,' Reg replied with mock indignation.

'And you,' she said to Augustus. 'We need to get back to the Hall as soon as we can.'

At her words, the light outside vanished and the skies opened up. For a moment the three of them watched out the window as the rain fell so hard, it bounced off the macadam.

'Although,' Mabel said, 'I suppose I could take time to have a proper breakfast.'

'Mr Canning, this one is awfully soft.' Augustus held an orange out and kneaded it as if it were a ball of yarn. 'Could I eat it? I can pay for it – I have sixpence in my school bag.'

'You might as well have it – we'll consider it your wages,' Reg said, shaking his head as if astounded at his own generosity.

In the kitchen, Mrs Chandekar put the kettle on as Mabel cut an X at the top of the orange. She sat Augustus at the table with a tea cloth tucked into his shirt. Conversation was impossible while the boy made a racket with his orange, and so Mabel set about cooking herself an egg. By the time it was ready, Augustus had finished, washed his hands and face and returned to his grocer duties.

'How is everyone this morning?' Mrs Chandekar asked. 'How is Mr Harkin?'

Mabel dipped a toast soldier into her egg. 'Everyone at the Hall is... on edge.' *Or is that only me?* 'Mr Harkin stayed at the Cork last night. He's quite a character,' she added.

'In a good way or a bad way?' Mrs Chandekar asked as she took a sheet of gingernuts out of the cooker.

'In an odd way,' Mabel said.

A loud *crack* sounded followed by rolling... was that thunder?

No, not thunder. Mabel looked down the passage and saw an avalanche of carrots and onions rumble across the shop floor.

The next second, the bell above the door jangled, a woman squealed and Reg shouted, 'Look out!'

Mabel ran out to the shop in time to see Augustus standing with his hands on his hips in a sea of vegetables. He looked up at the customer and said, 'Are you making soup today, ma'am? We've a special going.'

Augustus worked diligently to restore order to the shop and even swept the floor when the vegetables had been returned to their proper crates.

'I don't know when I've seen the shop floor this clean,' Mrs Chandekar said as she handed Augustus a tin of gingernuts. 'Now remember, these are for the ladies, too.'

'Thank you, Mrs Chandekar,' the boy said, holding the tin as if it contained great treasure. 'I promise to share.'

'The boy's a good worker,' Reg said, 'I've the taxman coming today, otherwise I wouldn't mind if he stayed. I might've let him see to the till.'

Augustus gasped. 'Could I do it tomorrow, Mr Canning? I won an award for my sums.'

'We'll see about that,' Mabel said. 'Now, we'd best be on our way.'

They walked out of the shop and down the road. The skies had cleared and the world glistened with raindrops captured on the tips of leaves and grass blades. The sun was nearly blinding.

'I want to know where you are at all times today,' Mabel said. 'No wandering off. If I'm not nearby, you must tell Skeff or Cora. Right?'

'I'll sit and read all day,' Augustus said, holding up the copy of *Kim* he'd found in Mabel's bedroom. 'You won't even know I'm around.'

But it turned out he had more plans than reading a book, and as they walked, Mabel let the boy natter on about his day.

'Miss Goose says I can tie up the peas and Constable Cowley promised I could stand watch at the Hall, although not on my own. Mrs Pilford and Miss Darling are making bread and they'll let me punch it down, but they said that means only one punch, which is a shame, because I might want to be a boxer and would need the practice.'

Just before they turned off onto the footpath, Mabel heard an engine coming their way and without thinking, she grabbed Augustus, pulled him off the road and into the cow parsley, holding him against her in a tight grip while her heart thumped. Then over the rise came a green van with gold lettering on the side that read 'Terry's Pork Pies.' She gave a breathless laugh.

'Delivering to the King and Cork,' she said, ostensibly to Augustus, but actually to herself. 'That's all – just a load of pork pies.'

No PC waited for them at the entrance to the Hall, and when they walked inside, their footsteps echoed in the quiet. Mabel considered the time – she was later than she'd intended and now coffee may be finished. Had the women made a decision as to who would lead them in the campaign or had two murders dampened their spirits to go on?

'Well, Miss Canning,' Augustus said, 'where shall I begin?'

At that moment, Ruby came rushing out of the corridor that led to the conservatory.

'Mabel!' Her brows furrowed with concern and she was out of breath. 'Have you seen Dorothea? I've been all over and can't find her. It's only that, we've no meeting before lunch and I thought she'd be out in the garden, but she isn't there.'

'Well, the weather,' Mabel pointed out. 'If she were in the garden, she's probably had to dash for cover. Have you seen Campsie? He'd know.'

'I don't know where Campsie is. Dorothea had wanted to go over the names of the roses with him, but I thought perhaps they'd finished and she'd gone up to her room to rest and so I went up to our wing. I knocked on her door, but there was no answer. Then, I thought I saw someone at the end of the corridor, but it was dark ...' Panting, Ruby put her hand out and pointed to nothing in particular, but as if she still saw the figure.

'Who did you see?' Mabel asked, trying without success to hold down the fear that rose up, that threw her straight back into her own dark corridor. 'Was it Collette? She's on your wing, too.'

'Collette? No, I don't believe so. I thought it might be Campsie come up to find her, but that makes no sense. Perhaps it was Binks.'

'Binks? Are you sure?' Mabel asked. Had Binks been after her that morning and now gone for Dorothea?

'I couldn't see well,' Ruby said, 'because the lights in the corridor had been switched off. Dorothea switches them off, and Collette or I switch them back on again. I knocked and knocked on her door and I... knocked on the door of the room she started in.' *The room next to where Annie was murdered*, Mabel thought. 'Both rooms were empty. I went back out and looked in the kitchen garden and back to our wing. Back and forth, back and forth.' Ruby's voice had risen as she spoke and she ended in a whisper. 'She isn't anywhere.'

Mabel put a hand on Ruby's arm and felt the young woman tremble – or was she trembling herself? *Not Dorothea,* she thought. *Please not Dorothea.* To have come so far through such turmoil in her life.

'Of course Dorothea's somewhere,' she said to Ruby.

'Shall I look for Miss Goose for you?' Augustus asked in a burst of enthusiasm.

'No,' Mabel said, and then grabbed the boy and gave him a hug, which startled them both. 'But thank you for the offer.'

The door opened bringing with it a fresh breeze along with

Park and Gladys. The dog *woofed* and danced around the boy and Mabel, who gave her a scratch behind the ears.

'Ruby is looking for Dorothea and can't seem to find her,' Mabel said to Park in what she hoped sounded like an even voice.

He saw through her in a second. 'When did you last see her?' he asked.

'Ages ago,' Ruby said and then paused. 'An hour? Possibly more.'

'Tolly hasn't come up from the pub yet,' Park said, 'but there should be one of the PCs around.'

'I'll go look for Constable Cowley for you,' Augustus said. His eyes were wide as he looked from Mabel to Park and back.

'You will not,' Mabel said. 'You will stay—'

Woof!

They all looked down at Gladys. The dog cocked an ear then whipped her head round towards the door in the far corner of the entrance hall. They followed her gaze but saw nothing. Mabel listened hard and heard nothing. But Gladys heard something.

Barking, the dog flew like the wind, her nails scratching on the stone, and through the arch to the west wing.

'Gladys!' Mabel and Park called at the same time, but the dog paid no heed and disappeared into the staircase corridor.

They took off after her – Mabel in front, Ruby next, Augustus and Park last. When they reached the bottom of the staircase, they caught only a glimpse of Gladys on her way up.

Augustus shot past Mabel in hot pursuit.

'Augustus!' she called.

Aoooooo! Gladys' howl echoed in the stairwell.

Up the stairs they went, stopping abruptly at the first-floor landing where Gladys was carrying out a thorough inspection of the space, sniffing the skirting boards, starting up a step to the second floor, and spinning round again.

'What is it, girl?' Park asked.

Gladys followed her nose and zigzagged across the floor, whining and fretting until she stopped in the alcove where Mabel had found Dorothea that first evening. Gladys snorted and then she barked. She looked at Park and back at the wall and barked again.

Park dropped to his knees and laid his hands on the panelling.

'Listen!' Augustus whispered.

They leaned towards the wall and when there came a knock, Mabel nearly jumped out of her skin. The voice that followed was muffled and weak.

'Help! Please! Help!'

'Dorothea!' Ruby threw herself against the wall. 'Dorothea!'

For it was Dorothea, Mabel recognised her voice and, even though muffled, she also recognised the panic it held.

Park cut his eyes at Mabel. 'Priest hole?'

'Dorothea,' Mabel called, 'we're here. Are you all right? Can you get out?'

Even as she said the words, she knew the answer was no. Ronald had said as much, and he'd learned it firsthand. There was no way out. But they could get in.

Dorothea's voice rose in tenor and fear. Her words became unintelligible and the beating on the wall grew fainter. Mabel trembled as if Dorothea's panic was contagious.

'She hates being in a small space,' Ruby said, wringing her hands and near to tears. 'Because of prison.'

'We'll get her out,' Park said. 'There's a lever or knob to make it open.' He ran his hands over the wall and along the wainscot at the edge of the panels but found no carved rose or other ornament that might disguise a latch.

Dorothea wailed and she drew such laboured breaths they could hear her through the wall.

'We're here,' Mabel said, her voice thick. She pounded on the panelling. 'It's all right.'

It wasn't all right, not for Dorothea, inside her worst nightmare. They heard a choking sound, all went silent, and then there came a *thud*.

NINETEEN

'No!' Ruby screamed, beating on the panelling. 'Dorothea!'

'Here! Look here!'

Augustus had kept out of the way, standing near where a single curtain panel had been hung to close off the alcove from the corridor. Now he leapt up and down while continuing to call out, 'Here! Here!' as he pointed up to the curtain-rod. There, barely discernible in the dark, was what looked like a circular knot protruding from the wood.

Park reached up and tried turning it one way or the other or pulling it out or... he pushed it in and a lower section of the panelling next to Mabel popped open with a *click*. She caught a whiff not of camphor, but a sickly-sweet odour – ether.

Gladys shot past everyone into the space and to Dorothea who had collapsed in a heap. The dog put her nose on the woman, *woofed* and licked her ear. Dorothea shrieked as she awoke, her arms flailing, but Gladys persisted, and Dorothea sat up, laid her hands on the dog and became still. She patted the rough brown coat and in a wobbly voice said, 'Oh Gladys, it's you, isn't it? Well done, girl.'

Augustus was second in before Mabel could grab hold of him.

'Augustus,' Mabel said, 'come out of there.'

'Is that the boy?' Dorothea asked, blinking into the light.

'Yes, Miss Goose, it is I, Augustus,' he said, looking eye to eye at Dorothea. 'Are you all right?'

Ruby leaned against the panelling outside the door of the priest hole and sank to the floor. 'Oh, Dorothea!'

Dorothea squinted back against the dim light behind them. 'Oh now, look what a fuss I've caused,' she said, wheezing. 'Dear boy, I hope I didn't frighten you.'

'No, I wasn't frightened,' he said, although Mabel had never seen him so pale.

'May I help you out, Miss Goose?' Park asked, no doubt mindful of the last time he'd tried to assist Dorothea.

'Thank you, Mr Winstone, but I can manage. You go on, Augustus.' She shifted onto her knees, but the ceiling was low – the place looked like a child's cubby – and she had to crawl to the opening. Then she said, 'Well, perhaps your hand?'

As she rose, Dorothea held tight to Park with one hand while Augustus held the other. Mabel stood and leaned against the wall, needing a bit of support herself as the fear that had galvanised every muscle in her body began to drain away. Gladys came trotting out behind Dorothea with a snort of success.

'What happened?' Mabel asked.

'Attacked,' Dorothea said, spitting out the word. 'I was attacked from behind and… a hand put over my face and held there. I could barely breathe and when I did… the odour… That's the last thing I remember.'

She swayed, but Park held on.

Ruby scrambled up. 'Dorothea, you must rest,' she said, her face full of anguish and her eyes filled with tears. 'And see the doctor. Mustn't she see the doctor, Mabel?'

'I daresay I need a word with Inspector Tollerton,' Dorothea said, 'but I do feel a bit peaky, so perhaps a visit from the doctor wouldn't go amiss.'

'We'll find the inspector and I'll telephone for Doctor Finlay,' Mabel said.

Dorothea freed herself of support and brushed off the bib of her dungarees, but then froze and looked down.

'Where is my sash? Who has done this?' Dorothea said, her face breaking out in blotchy beetroot red spots. 'Who has taken my sash? I won't have it – I won't have such a thing happen!'

Ruby fingered her own sash as if confirming she still wore it.

'We'll find it,' Mabel said. 'First, Dorothea, let's go to your room.'

Dorothea allowed herself to be chivvied up the stairs to the second floor and along the corridor to her room.

Gladys trotted in directly to the window seat, jumped up and stretched out. Augustus sat with her. Park had stayed behind but now joined them in the room as Ruby and Mabel got Dorothea settled sitting up in her bed and muttering about her sash.

'I didn't see a sash,' Park said.

'I will not be silenced!' Dorothea declared with fervour.

'You must rest.' Ruby patted Dorothea's arm and plumped her pillows, as she continued to speak in a low voice. 'Lean back now. Don't worry.'

'I'll ring down the pub for Tolly,' Mabel said.

'Good,' Park replied. 'I'm going back to the priest hole – it's bigger than it looks. The ceiling is low at the front, but higher as it goes back. There could be a way out.'

She laid a hand on his arm. 'Park.' She needed to tell him she'd been chased down the corridor that morning. She hadn't been caught, but that had been only by a stroke of luck. But then she thought that could wait. 'You'll need a candle,' she said and crossed to the dressing table and opened first one drawer then the other. 'Ah, here they are.'

She handed a candle and matches over and Park headed for the door, but turned back. Gladys raised her head and watched him. 'Stay here, girl.'

'I'll come and help you search,' Augustus offered.

'Augustus,' Mabel said, 'we'll leave that to Mr Winston. I want you to come down with me and Ruby to find Lady Fellbridge.'

Ruby looked up, alarmed. 'No,' she said. 'I can't. I need to stay here. You go down.'

Mabel could not put into words or even come up with a logical reason in her own mind why she didn't want to leave Ruby alone with Dorothea. But neither did she want to leave Dorothea completely alone.

'Augustus and I will stay with Miss Goose,' Park said in a reasonable tone, 'until the two of you return with Lady Fellbridge. She would need you both, wouldn't she?'

'Yes, of course,' Mabel said with relief. 'That's what we'll do. Dorothea, we won't be long.'

'Perfectly fine, Mabel,' Dorothea said, her voice still rough. 'I'm in good hands.'

Mabel and Ruby hurried down to the entrance hall, but when they stood on the stone floor, alone, Mabel paused.

'Have you seen Mr Harkin today?' she asked.

'No,' Ruby said. 'Why?'

'Don't you want to?'

Ruby's face looked thunderous. 'Mabel, the three of them conspired to keep the truth from me. My entire life I've never known who my father was. What would it have hurt? Mother was too proud for her own good. "We can do this ourselves, Ruby love" she'd say when I asked about my father. Mrs Harkin told me she'd promised Mother to never to say a word, but now I find out that all these women' – she swept her arm in a wide arc – 'have always known. Why not me?'

All these women – that included Pretoria, the second murder victim and Dorothea, nearly the third. Had Ruby's fury been kindled by her mother's death and then burst into flames here at Fellbridge Hall?

But where did Mabel fit into that line of enquiry?

'There's no going back to change what was said or wasn't said,' Mabel said. 'You can't undo the past, you can only decide how to carry on.'

Ruby lifted one sceptical brow, but didn't speak, because Emma came into the entrance hall. While the three of them were alone, Mabel gave a quick explanation.

'Dorothea is unharmed, although she was frightened, of course,' Mabel concluded.

'Was it the murderer?' Emma asked in a hoarse whisper.

'We can't say for certain,' Mabel said. 'But it does seem likely.'

Emma looked about the entrance hall as if she didn't know the place. 'Why now and why here? Could this be coming from within the group instead of without? Is it one of the other women?'

'It's possible,' Mabel said, highly aware that a likely suspect stood beside her. 'I'm sorry to say it, but it's true. But we'll find the murderer, Emma – make no mistake.'

'Why would the murderer leave Dorothea in the priest hole?' Emma asked.

Mabel had wondered the same thing. How was it that Dorothea had escaped Annie and Pretoria's fate?

'I might've disturbed whoever did it,' Ruby said. 'I might've seen someone in the corridor. It was dark.'

Unless Ruby herself attacked Dorothea and then made up the convenient tale as cover.

'I don't understand how she was subdued,' Emma said. 'Dorothea is quite strong.'

'Ether,' Mabel said. 'I could smell it.'

'Ether,' Emma muttered, as if it were an epithet. 'We've probably a bottle here in the Hall.'

'It could've come from anywhere,' Mabel replied, 'but I will mention that to the inspector. Dorothea's in bed and resting – although I'm not certain how long we can keep her there. Park and Augustus are looking after her.'

'And Gladys,' Ruby added.

'Yes, and Gladys,' Mabel said. 'Gladys found Dorothea for us. Her exceptional hearing, no doubt. Now, I'll ring Doctor Finlay.'

'The inspector is looking for you,' Emma said.

'He's arrived? Why don't you and Ruby go back up to Dorothea?'

'Shall I go with you, Mabel?' Ruby asked. 'To give my account to the inspector.'

'No,' Mabel said. She needed to have a private word with Tollerton. 'No, thank you. Go be with Dorothea.'

Emma hugged herself as if she had a chill. 'I can't stop thinking that none of this would've happened if I hadn't brought them all together.'

'It's none of your doing,' Ruby said with such force that Mabel flinched. 'You can't be blamed for others' actions now or in the past.'

Emma studied the young woman, then took her arm and led her towards the west wing. 'We've all done you a disservice, Ruby. But won't you talk with your father?'

'No, I will not,' Ruby said.

Mabel continued to the steward's office and arrived as PC Ned Cowley came out and closed the door.

'There you are!' Ned exclaimed. 'Inspector Tollerton has been—'

'Yes, thanks.' She gave one knock on the door and received a barked reply that might've been 'go away' or 'come in'. As she couldn't tell which, she went with what she wanted it to be, opened the door and stepped in.

'There's been an incident,' she said.

'Another?' Tolly said.

'Not another murder,' Mabel hurried on, 'and actually, two incidents this morning here in the Hall. First, to me.'

'What's happened to you?' Tollerton asked, his face like thunder.

'Someone was in the priory gallery corridor this morning,' Mabel said. She told him her story quickly. 'Skeff and Cora were to hand and that was that.'

Tollerton narrowed his eyes at her as if he were about to argue with her offhand story, so Mabel carried on to the end of her brief encounter and when she'd finished, said, 'And now, Dorothea.'

'Miss Goose?'

'Dorothea was attacked in the house and locked in one of the priest holes. It may have happened more than an hour ago. She's all right, only shaken, although I came to ring for the doctor, just for peace of mind. She didn't see who it was. She's quite willing to talk with you. They're all up in her room on the west wing – down the other end from where Annie's room was.'

'Neither you nor Miss Goose caught a glimpse of who it was?'

'No, and neither of us could see if the person ran down the stairs and out of the Hall or... went about her business somewhere within the Hall.'

Tollerton's gaze bore a hole through her. 'Miss Truelock?'

Mabel nodded. 'Ruby is quite interested in all aspects of the case. We need to confirm her whereabouts this morning. She's given her own account of Dorothea's attack as a witness.'

'Right,' he said and was out the door before Mabel turned round.

'Cowley,' he shouted at Ned, who stood on duty. 'Cowley, find Scott and Wardle. West wing. Now.'

Mabel closed the door behind them, took the seat at the desk and rang the exchange.

'Hello, Janet, I need the doctor at Fellbridge Hall.'

'Again?' Janet asked with a sharp intake of breath. 'Oh Mabel, not another of the ladies, is it? Another... murder?'

She couldn't blame the woman – not with all that had gone on. 'No, it isn't. But I do need to speak with the doctor.'

'Yes, yes. Wait now,' Janet said. 'He has surgery hours on Thursday mornings, so you may just catch him in.'

No such luck, but Janet promised to keep trying, saying she would start at the golf course. Mabel looked behind her as a ray of sun pierced a heavy cloud. That's dedication for you.

In Dorothea's room, Mabel found Park gone, Emma perched on the edge of the bed and Ruby at its foot as Tollerton tried to explain to Augustus why he couldn't stay.

'But Gladys and I saved Miss Goose, and she's allowed to stay and so I should be, too,' the boy said with an eight-year-old's reasoning.

'You did save her,' Mabel agreed, 'and we are all grateful. But now, it's a police matter and the room is becoming a bit crowded. Let's you and I go down and wait for Doctor Finlay.'

'Run along, Augustus,' Dorothea said with all good cheer. 'And don't you forget, you've promised to chop weeds. I won't let you off the hook.'

'Lady Fellbridge,' Tollerton began.

'I won't say a word, Inspector,' Emma said. 'But I'm staying.'

Tolly must've understood that the subject was not up for

debate, and he took the wise course. 'Yes. Right. Now, Miss Goose,' he said. 'Can you tell me what's happened.'

Mabel herded Augustus towards the door as Dorothea replied.

'My sash, Inspector. *My sash*' – she beat her chest on each word – 'is gone. He took it. He didn't take Annie's sash. He didn't take Pretoria's. Why did he take mine?'

Her words hung in the air. Without explicitly saying so, Dorothea had made it clear what had been in Mabel's mind – the person who locked her in the priest hole was the person who had murdered Annie Harkin and Pretoria Fleming-Jones. Dorothea said *he*, but was she sure of that?

Pretoria's suffragette sash had not been taken, but the murderer had left it round her neck as if it were a grotesque message. Mabel's mind flashed on Ruby rubbing the cloth of her own sash. Had she donned her mother's sash not as a statement of solidarity, but as a ruse?

'Are you certain it was a man?' Tollerton asked.

But before Dorothea answered, the three constables came hurrying down the corridor.

Mabel pulled Augustus out of the way. She longed to stay, but for the moment her duties lay elsewhere.

The constables stopped in the doorway. Tollerton gave them a brief explanation and said, 'Get the women in the conservatory – Wardle, ask Skeff to keep an eye on them. All three of you, search the bedrooms, the servants' quarters, the kitchen, the conservatory – all the rooms. Look for a suffragette's sash and for any signs of ether.'

Cowley, Scott and Wardle were off as quickly as they'd arrived, leaving Mabel and Augustus exposed.

'The doctor?' Tollerton reminded her.

'Yes. Off we go, Augustus.'

. . .

No sign of the doctor yet, and so they had to cool their heels in the entrance hall. Mabel paced, but Augustus sat in the chair underneath the portrait of the first Lord Fellbridge.

'This isn't very important, waiting for the doctor,' the boy said, kicking his dangling legs back and forth. 'Mr Winstone is searching for clues and Inspector Tollerton is questioning the victim.'

'He also serves who stands and waits,' Mabel reminded the boy.

'I'm sitting and you're walking,' Augustus pointed out.

Mabel stopped and laughed. Then she heard the roar of an engine and the scattering of chippings and opened the door as Finlay took his bag out of the dickey seat. He looked down at a paper in his hand and then stuffed it in his jacket pocket.

'Doctor,' Mabel said, 'I'm so sorry to call you away.'

'No, no, Miss Canning,' Finlay said. 'I was to collect an order of linen bandages at the chemist, but that can wait. What's happened?'

'It's Miss Goose.'

His face fell. 'No, not Miss Goose. Is she...'

'She's all right,' Mabel said quickly. 'She'll tell you she's perfectly fine, but still, we thought it best you take a look. We should go up.'

They walked in and across the entrance hall. 'This way, sir,' Augustus said, leaping forward. 'I'll show you. I know the way because I was the one who saved Miss Goose.' He looked back as they climbed the stairs. 'Well really, Gladys saved her first, but I was second.'

'Gladys is a dog, is that right?' Finlay said, following the boy. Over his shoulder he said to Mabel, 'Can you tell me what happened?'

Augustus answered with gusto. 'Someone grabbed Miss Goose and stuffed her in the priest hole, but Mr Winstone and Miss Canning will catch him, because he's caught a diamond thief before and Miss Canning is always solving murders for Scotland Yard.'

'Augustus!' Mabel said.

At the first-floor landing, Mabel noticed the curtain had been drawn across the opening to the alcove wherein lay the priest hole – that is, the Victorian fancy of a priest hole.

They continued up to the second floor and reached Dorothea's room. Finlay strode directly to the bedside, displacing Ruby who had to take a step back. Park had returned from his exploration and he stood near the fireplace, arms crossed and leaning on the wall with one shoulder. He caught Mabel's gaze and held it for a moment.

Emma had remained at Dorothea's other side with Tollerton at the foot of the bed. Gladys, still on the bench seat under the window, raised her head at the new arrivals. Mabel and Augustus stayed in the corridor out of the way.

'Well, Miss Goose,' Finlay said, 'here we are again, and still you look as fit as a flea.'

Dorothea laughed and gave a small cough. The doctor carried out a brief examination – he felt his patient's forehead, took her pulse and asked her if she played golf – during which time Park made his way out to the corridor.

'You found something,' Mabel whispered.

His brows jumped but he said nothing.

Right, Mabel thought, time for everyone to move along so that they could have a quiet word with Tolly.

'I'll have Binks bring a tray up,' Emma was saying, 'and I'll stay with you.'

'No, no,' Dorothea said as she swung her legs over the side of the bed. 'I am going downstairs to have tea. I'm not an invalid. Are you coming, Emma? Ruby?'

Emma looked to Tollerton who rubbed his forehead.

'Yes, all right, go ahead, Miss Goose,' he said. 'But could I ask you to keep someone with you for the rest of the day?'

'I'll stay with her,' Ruby said. 'I won't leave your side, Dorothea.'

'An admirable offer,' Dorothea said, 'but I doubt you'll say that when I start shovelling horse manure into the leek beds.'

'I'll shovel the horse manure, Miss Goose,' Augustus said.

'That would be right down your street, young man,' Dorothea said with a smile.

'Well, gentlemen,' Finlay said, 'and ladies, of course. I daresay you don't need me any longer, and I do have other patients. I hope you'll find the miscreant who attacked Miss Goose.'

They filed out of the bedroom, down to the ground floor. The women, except for Mabel, continued to the conservatory. Tollerton and Park headed to the steward's office. Augustus and Gladys loitered under the first Lord Fellbridge's portrait.

'I don't see how she can take shock after shock like this,' Finlay said as he watched Dorothea go.

'She has amazing stamina,' Mabel replied.

'Yes, yes.' Finlay looked round the entrance hall. 'Well, Miss Canning, it's been a pleasure.'

Mabel watched him leave thinking that it hadn't exactly been a pleasure, but thought the doctor might be looking ahead to the golf course. She turned to Augustus and considered her next task – keeping the boy out of mischief. Could she talk him into going back to the shop? But salvation arrived in the form of the Reverend Herringay walking in the door.

'Ronald!' Mabel exclaimed.

'Mother rang,' Ronald said. 'I thought I'd better come up. Are you all right? Shouldn't there be more police around?'

'Ronald, this is Augustus Malling-Frobisher. Augustus, meet Reverend Herringay.'

'How do you do, Reverend.'

'Ah, yes, Augustus,' Ronald said.

'Your reputation precedes you,' Mabel said at the boy's

raised eyebrows. 'Now, would you take Gladys out the front door – she may need a minute or two in the grass.'

They stood on the doorstep and watched the boy and dog. 'Ronald,' Mabel said, 'Augustus needs some sort of occupation and needs an eye kept on him. You're the only one I can trust.'

Ronald narrowed his eyes at her. 'Are you all right, Mabel? I know I'm not supposed to worry and that you are capable and competent, but I do worry.'

'I am all right,' she replied.

Of course he would worry. Mabel and Ronald were each other's connection to Edith – dear friend for her, wife to him. They relied on each other's memories. Mabel knew that if something happened to Ronald, she would feel as if she'd lost Edith again, too.

Ronald sighed with resignation.

Augustus and Gladys came racing towards them and in the door.

'Augustus,' Mabel said, 'I'd like you and Reverend Herringay to go to the conservatory. Skeff and Cora are there with the others.'

'I'm supposed to chop weeds for Miss Goose,' Augustus said, as if he sensed he was being shunted off onto a sideline. 'And there's horse manure, too.'

'And you will get to the horse manure – later. Now, you need to go to the conservatory.'

Augustus screwed his mouth up to one side. 'All right,' he said.

'I'm very glad you said yes,' Ronald told him. 'I'm having a bit of trouble with my sermon for Sunday and could use a few ideas. It's about Daniel in the lion's den.'

'I know that story,' Augustus said, brightening. 'But, Reverend, have you ever thought how much more exciting it would be if instead of a lion, there was a dinosaur in the den?'

'Oh, I don't think that would work out,' Ronald said as they walked down the corridor. 'You could never fit an entire dinosaur in one of those dens.'

Gladys took a few steps as if to follow Ronald and Augustus, then stopped and looked back at Mabel.

'Go on, girl,' Mabel said. 'Watch out for them. Be vigilant.'

No constable stood at the steward's office door, and so Mabel walked directly in.

'Here she is,' Tollerton said, standing behind the desk and gesturing at Mabel as if introducing the next singer in a revue but looking too annoyed for that to be true. 'I've got the idea Park doesn't know about your incident. I didn't want to be the one to explain.'

Park had leaned against the windowsill, but now bolted upright. 'What happened?'

'I haven't had a chance to tell you,' Mabel said. 'There's been too much going on. And I'm all right – I'm not hurt. I wasn't attacked.'

The beetroot shade of Park's face told her she was making it worse, not better.

'Someone was in my corridor this morning. It was dark, I felt as if I were being chased and ran into an empty bedroom and whoever it was locked me in and must've been scared off by Skeff and Cora. There. That's it. That's all.'

Park took a slow breath. 'Man? Woman?'

'I didn't see. But I'm unharmed,' Mabel insisted. 'Untouched. Now, sit down.'

The three of them settled round the desk.

'We've got two murders and Dorothea's attack,' Mabel said.

'Two murders and two attacks,' Park corrected her.

She conceded with a nod. 'Were they all committed by the same person?'

'Were the two attacks meant to be murders, as well?' Tolly asked.

Park kept still as a statue.

'Both attacks – my possible attack, that is – were interrupted,' Mabel said. 'Skeff and Cora for mine, and Dorothea's attacker may have heard Ruby coming.'

'By Miss Truelock's own account,' Tollerton said.

'How could Ruby know about the priest hole?' Mabel asked.

'The attacker not only knew about the priest hole,' Park said, 'but also how to get in and out. First of all, there's a small leather strap on the inside of the door, so it can be pulled closed if you're inside. At the back where the ceiling is raised, there's a door hidden behind a panel. There's a press latch on the panelling to open, but no strap on the inside of that door to close it.'

'Miss Goose didn't realise there was a way out at the back?' Tollerton asked.

'She didn't have time to look round, because she'd been knocked out with ether.' Mabel frowned. 'There was no trace of ether around Annie or Pretoria – although the smell could've dissipated by the time we found them. I didn't smell ether from whoever it was in the corridor.' She turned to Park. 'What was behind the door?'

'Stairs – steep, narrow and winding,' he said. 'They go to the ground floor where there is a bookcase door in the corner of the library.'

'The library has French windows,' Mabel said. 'It's an escape route.'

'All the French windows use skeleton keys,' Tollerton said, 'and they're no good to anyone except a thief or a murderer.'

'And they are no doubt plentiful,' Mabel said. 'Emma mentioned there were keys in the desk.'

Tollerton looked in one drawer after another, then yanked

on the large bottom drawer, pulled out a metal box and set it on the desk. Inside the box was a motley collection of keys from a large, rusty specimen that might've hung off the rope belt of a monk a few centuries earlier to a few more modern Chubb keys – but the majority were skeleton keys. Tollerton slammed the lid down. 'Damn.'

'The hidden stairs are an escape route,' Park said, 'but not just for Dorothea's attacker today. Here's what I found at the bottom of the stairs just inside the bookcase door.' He reached into his jacket pocket, pulled out his handkerchief and unfolded it. There lay three white bed pillow feathers.

'Feathers from Annie's pillow,' Mabel whispered. 'There were feathers everywhere – the murderer must've tracked a few out without knowing.'

'So the murderer knew how to get in and out of the Hall,' Tollerton said.

'It could still be someone among the women or staff,' Mabel said. 'It isn't difficult to get around outdoors without being seen. Keep to the far side of the hedge, skirt the orchard and stay hidden behind the brick wall – that way, you can go from the bluebell wood on the west side of the Hall to the servants' garden near the kitchen on the east side and no one would catch sight of you. Also, the stables – now the garage for the Wolseley and Campsie's cottage, are beyond, where the land falls away.'

'Prints,' Tollerton said, drumming his fingers on the desktop. 'We should get fingerprints inside the priest hole and in the library.'

'You'll find mine, too,' Park said, 'but I was careful as I could be and used my handkerchief.'

'We've got the prints of everyone here. I'll get the men back to see what they can find. Two attacks today – the murderer is getting bold. I don't want a third.' Tollerton pulled the telephone closer, picked up the earpiece and hit the hook a few times. When Janet came on the line, he asked for Scotland

Yard. Hearing the urgency in Tollerton's voice, Mabel imagined that the fingerprint men would be on their way back down to Sussex by the time he rang off.

A thrill went through Mabel – an unwieldy mix of excitement and fear. They were near, but the murderer could be nearer still.

'We'll need to compare what they find in the hidden staircase with what we have. No prints for the murder in the bluebell wood – not even on the spectacles Glady found – but we could identify what we found for Annie Harkin, at least,' Tollerton said. 'We'll put a stop to this now.'

They all three jumped at the urgent rapping at the door. WPC Wardle burst in with PCs Cowley and Scott crowding behind her.

'We've found a suffragette sash,' Hildy told them. 'In the butler's quarters.'

TWENTY

Mabel leapt up.

'Binks?'

Surely not Binks.

'Where was it?' Tollerton asked as he came out from behind the desk.

'Sir—' Hildy began.

'Lying at the bottom of his wardrobe,' Ned told them.

'Hardly the best hiding place,' Park said.

'Sir—' Hildy tried again.

'He could've been in a hurry,' Scott offered.

'Bring him up,' Tollerton said.

'Sir!' Hildy's voice cut through like a knife. 'There's something else. We also found a large wad of cottonwool and there's still a trace odour of ether on it.'

'In Binks' room?' Mabel asked, aghast.

'No,' Hildy said. 'In Ruby's. It was under her bed as if it had been discarded in a hurry. Like with the sash, it was a rather obvious place to leave a clue.'

'Possibly, but still I'll want to talk with each of them,' Tollerton said.

'Also, sir,' Hildy said, 'Mr Binks is gone.'

'Gone?' Tollerton said.

'No one has seen him since just after breakfast.'

'You've just searched the Hall,' Tollerton said.

'Yes, sir,' Hildy said. 'Every room, every wardrobe.'

'There's another priest hole,' Mabel said. 'It's in the nursery wing.'

'I had the nursery wing, Miss Canning,' Ned told her, 'but I didn't know about another hidden place.'

'Reverend Herringay is in the conservatory – he can show you,' Mabel said.

Tollerton nodded. 'Check there, Cowley, then meet us out on the forecourt. Scott, come with Mr Winstone and me. We'll spread out and see what we can find. Wardle, get them all into the conservatory – cooks, gardener, the lot. Make sure Miss Truelock is there. I'll deal with Binks first. You're officer in charge inside the Hall.' Tollerton looked round their party as if counting noses. 'Mr Harkin should've arrived by now – he told me he'd be here after he finished breakfast.'

'That could take a while,' Mabel said.

'Haven't seen him, sir,' Hildy replied. 'Lady Fellbridge asked me about him, too.'

'I'm not finished with him,' Tollerton said. 'He knows that.' He snatched the telephone as if he wanted to strangle the machine. In less than a minute, Janet had connected him to Draker at the King and Cork to learn that Oliver Harkin was not in his room, not in the bar – nowhere on the premises. And his bag was gone.

'Harkin and Binks,' Park said. 'Are they in this together?'

'They'll have been gone hours now,' Tollerton said.

'They've absconded?' Mabel asked. It all sounded too far-fetched. 'Wouldn't someone have noticed them striking out on their own? I'll ring the shop and ask Papa and Mrs Chandekar if either has been seen walking by. I'll ask Janet Darling, too. Then...' Her voice petered out.

'What is it?' Park asked.

'This morning,' Mabel said, 'when Augustus and I were walking back here to the Hall, a van for Terry's Pork Pies went by – coming from the direction of the pub. If Binks and Harkin didn't want to be seen, I wonder did they catch a lift into Rye? Once there, they could be on their way anywhere.'

'We'll spread out over the grounds,' Tollerton said, then added bitterly, 'There aren't enough of us.'

'Skeff can help,' Mabel said. 'She could ring Terry's Pork Pies and the railway station and the like.'

Tollerton gave her a hard look and she thought he would say he didn't want a reporter involved in a murder enquiry, but instead he nodded. 'Good. Go fetch her.'

Mabel went to the conservatory. She had a brief thought that, if they had to stay together in one place, at least it was in this large cheerful room with sun streaming in through the French windows and a grand piano. At that moment, she longed to sit down and play.

She slipped in quietly and for a moment no one noticed. Thirza and Lavinia sat together and were keeping their eyes down and their hands busy with tatting. Diane stood among the ferns while Collette told her the best recipe for orchid food. Dorothea, on the sofa, had Ruby on one side and Emma on the other and Augustus sat on a footstool by the fireplace reading *Kim*.

Mabel leaned over the small table where Skeff and Cora were chatting and in a low voice said, 'Skeff, anything from Little Lever yet?'

Skeff shook her head.

'Tolly would like a word with you. He needs a bit of help.'

Skeff left quietly without notice.

But Dorothea had been watching. 'Mabel – what is it?'

And with that, she had everyone's full attention.

'It's nothing, Dorothea,' Mabel said. 'That is, Inspector Tollerton has asked us to wait here in the conservatory.'

Thirza and Lavinia put down their tatting and gave Mabel mournful looks.

'Why?' Thirza asked.

'Police have business on the grounds,' Mabel said. 'We don't want to get in their way.'

Lavinia's hand went to her mouth as she gasped. 'They've found Pretoria's murderer?'

'Not yet,' Mabel said.

'We didn't mean anything, you know,' Thirza said. 'We all three of us were fond of a jest, weren't we, Lavinia?'

Lavinia nodded as if she knew what Thirza meant. Mabel did not.

'What was the jest?' she asked.

'About the bluebells,' Thirza said. 'She kept saying we were out there on Sunday afternoon and we said we weren't.'

'Were you?'

'No, we weren't,' Lavinia said with a sad smile. 'That was the jest.'

'She seemed quite positive she'd seen someone on Sunday afternoon,' Mabel said. 'If it wasn't you two, then who was it?'

The question hung heavy in the air.

'Perhaps she saw the same person in the bluebell wood yesterday morning,' Mabel said, 'and that made her realise it wasn't you two at all.'

Thirza sucked in her breath and Mabel realised that she should've been speculating with Park or Tolly and not to the other women, any one of whom could be the murderer's next target.

'She couldn't've mistaken the murderer for me!' Lavinia said indignantly. 'The very idea.'

'Until this is cleared up,' Mabel said, continuing her announcement, 'we must all stay together.'

'How long will that be?' Diane asked.

'I don't know,' Mabel said with some impatience. 'Annie and Pretoria have been murdered. Dorothea was attacked in the west wing, right under our noses.'

The women's eyes widened as they looked to Dorothea, as if it had just been called to their attention that one among them had narrowly escaped being the next victim.

'That was dreadful, Dorothea, just dreadful,' Diane boomed. 'I wish there was something we could do for you. Perhaps thinking of gardening can ease your mind. I say – I've brown spots on my privet hedge. Would you know anything about that?'

'Dorothea,' Thirza said, 'in a quiet moment, perhaps we can have a chat about my peonies. They haven't bloomed for ages.'

'I have an old rambler that's quite got away from me,' Lavinia said. 'Will you explain how Campsie has trained them here?'

'Dorothea,' Collette said, 'can you tell me how to keep the whitefly from my geraniums?'

Collette's astonishing turnround of asking for instead of handing out advice gave pause to the entire group.

'Well now,' Dorothea said, 'I'm happy to answer each of your questions. I don't suppose we could go out and—' She looked to Emma.

'Mabel?' Emma asked.

'I'm afraid it's best we stay indoors,' Mabel said. 'Until... until Inspector Tollerton says otherwise.'

'Ruby said the police went to search the butler's quarters,' Collette said. 'Is he staying indoors, too?'

'Binks is not under arrest,' Emma said in a firm voice.

No, he isn't under arrest, but he has escaped.

Mabel glanced at the quietest woman in the room – Ruby. She was the very picture of misery – her pale features had crept towards pallor, her eyes had a pinched look and her hands fidgeted in her lap. Was it the culmination of events she had observed or had she had some hand in these deaths?

'I saw him,' Diane said, waving out to the terrace. 'From the French windows here – he was walking out beyond the formal garden, but I saw Binks in his bowler hat.'

'When?' Mabel asked sharply.

'I don't know,' Diane said. 'An hour ago? More? After we'd heard about what happened to Dorothea.'

Mabel looked out in the direction Diane had indicated. No one had seen Binks since after breakfast and here it was nearly lunch. Diane might've seen Campsie. Perhaps the old bowler hat Lord Fellbridge had given him had turned up. Or could it have been Binks going off to the bluebell wood or sneaking in the Hall and up the stairs to attack Dorothea? Regardless, he was long gone now.

Hildy came in. 'Mabel, Mrs Pilford and Miss Darling ask could they bring up cold dishes for lunch in case we're here for a while?'

Mabel looked to Emma who nodded. 'I don't see why not.'

While lunch was being set up, Mabel called Ruby to the far side of the conservatory behind what looked like a forest of pelargoniums.

'The constables found a wad of cottonwool that smelled like ether under the bed in your room,' Mabel said. 'It was ether that knocked Dorothea out.'

Ruby swayed and Mabel grabbed her.

'Who put it there? Who?' Ruby's voice was choked with anger. 'I would never hurt Dorothea. Why would I do that?'

'Ruby, don't you think the others regret keeping the secret about your father? That perhaps even your mother regretted it?'

'It's too late for regrets,' Ruby said.

Dorothea walked to the French windows a few feet away and opened it a couple of inches.

'Dorothea,' Mabel began.

'It isn't against the law to want a bit of fresh air,' Dorothea said. 'I'm not trying to do a bunk.'

Mabel smiled. 'You're feeling all right, then?'

'One must always go forward.' Dorothea looked at Ruby out of the corner of her eye. 'Wouldn't you say?'

'Dorothea,' Ruby said, 'I would never hurt you.'

'Of course, you wouldn't,' Dorothea said. 'I know that.'

'Ruby,' Emma called, holding an arm out. 'Come have lunch.'

Ruby took a deep breath as if gathering her strength for a coming storm and went in. Mabel and Dorothea remained, both looking out to the terrace and beyond.

'Mabel,' Dorothea said, 'about remembering that dream I had or thought I had on Sunday afternoon when Annie was killed.'

'Yes?'

Dorothea sighed. 'These days have been difficult for me, but I'm truly well and I don't want everyone worrying. The doctor does tend to hover – as does Emma, bless her.'

Mabel waited a moment, but nothing else was forthcoming. 'And so, you haven't remembered anything else? For certain?'

'Yes, I may have.' She turned to Mabel with a puzzled expression. 'The details have been just beyond my reach and so I've been telling myself "Remember, remember" until it finally came to me that *that* is what I remembered.'

Oh dear, she's more befuddled than ever.

Dorothea looked at Mabel intently. 'I heard Annie say "Remember."'

'Remember?' Mabel whispered. She felt hot and cold at the same time. 'Did she say "Remember Agatha Tyne?"'

'I didn't hear that,' Dorothea said. 'I'm sorry – it's as I told Cora, I don't know Agatha Tyne.'

'It's all right, Dorothea,' Mabel said, patting the woman's arm absentmindedly. But surely it had to be about her. Annie had left the note under her teacup. *Do you remember Agatha Tyne?*

Had the note been to enlist Binks' help or in hopes that whoever collected the tray – Deenie or Katie or the day girl from the village – would pass the note to Lady Fellbridge and alert her to...

But Emma had no idea who Agatha Tyne was. Soon, though, Skeff would have the details of the coroner's report. Soon they would all know.

Mabel tried to create the scene Sunday afternoon with Annie and her murderer. 'Dorothea, did Annie say "I remember" or "We remember"?'

Dorothea mouthed the words as if trying them out to see which fit, but she shook her head. 'We?' She said the word tentatively. 'No, I can't say. I'm sorry, Mabel. I might've made something out of nothing.'

'Not a bit of it. Every tiny detail helps.' But the frown remained on Dorothea's brow. As a distraction, Mabel asked, 'What is your garden at home like?'

The frown vanished. 'A bit of a hodge-podge,' Dorothea said. 'In an odd sort of way, my garden and the Hall are much alike – both made over many years and with their own special quirks.' She smiled at Mabel. 'I miss it.'

Mabel thought about the Hall and its idiosyncrasies. She thought about the times she and Edith would walk the corridors, posing below pictures of portraits, making up stories about the shepherds and shepherdesses painted on the ceiling in the gallery. The gallery had been one of their favourite rooms and Mabel had yet to visit it since her arrival. Part of the reason was that she had stayed busy, but another part was because it held so many memories. But now, it was as if she heard it calling her. She left Dorothea looking out the windows and went to Emma.

'I've forgotten my register in my room and I'm going to fetch it,' Mabel said. 'I've made so many notes, it might do to look them over.'

'Here, I'll go with you,' Emma said. 'Or take Hildy.'

Hildy sat at one end of the table keeping an eye on things while at the same time chatting with Campsie who had come in to oversee the cold lunch in place of the missing Binks.

'There's no need to bother either of you,' Mabel said. 'The Hall has been searched, remember, and now the grounds are being searched. It isn't as if I don't know my way round. I won't be in danger.'

Augustus, standing in the queue, watched Mabel going to the door and she was about to admonish him to stay in the conservatory when Cora pointed to a dish of lentils that had turned bright pink from the slices of beetroot lying atop them and said something to the boy, who giggled. As quiet as she could, Mabel left, closing the door behind her. What would Augustus' mother say about Useful Women now, with her son dropped into the middle of a murder enquiry? Or would she only be relieved he wasn't underfoot?

Mabel saw no one and heard nothing but her own footsteps as she made her way to the entrance hall and then to the corridor that led to the gallery. She swept open the double doors, stepped inside, closed them behind her and paused. Before her was a long room with an arched ceiling two storeys high. Glass cabinets that ran down the middle of the room held collections from previous Lord Fellbridges or their offspring – here a display of Roman glass and pottery, there Anglo-Saxon silver jewellery studded with garnets. Mabel thought she remembered a letter written by Charles II to the first Lord Fellbridge in one of the cabinets.

In the far corner stood an array of early-Victorian taxidermy – birds, stoats and even a badger. Throughout the room were antique globes and ancient weather-observing tools. 'Barometers Through the Ages' Edith had dubbed them.

Mabel felt Edith's presence strongly here – the hours they had spent laughing and reading and talking about how amazing it was that Edith had married a vicar who was also the second son of Lord and Lady Fellbridge. 'I would've had him even if he had been a peddler,' she would say, and Mabel knew it to be true. So had Ronald.

Why had Mabel come into the gallery? Had she expected a revelation – for Edith to send her a message telling her where Binks was and if he'd murdered his cousin and Pretoria? Or perhaps Mabel expected to find the butler himself sitting stoically in the corner next to the stuffed owl, waiting for someone to come for him. She and Edith had mostly kept their distance from the animals – several of them had bald patches on their fur and looked pitiful rather than scientific. But they both had been fascinated with the insect collection.

Mabel went to a large cabinet of wide, shallow drawers, pulled one open and found row upon row of bees, hornets and wasps, all pinned and labelled. She heard a buzzing and waved away the... she looked round at the empty room. *Letting your imagination run away with you.*

She closed the drawer and then a map on the wall caught her eye – twelve-year-old Ronald's drawing of the Hall. Now, as an adult, he might be embarrassed at his childish attempt to map his home, but at the time, he must've been proud enough of his accomplishment, because he had made several copies, and his mother had this one framed and hung on the wall for all to see. Mabel studied the map, then turned to go out the way she'd come. But she'd taken only a step before she stopped and went back to the map to peer more closely at it.

Here she saw what must have been an addition to later versions of Ronald's map – an ink line that ran from the door of the gallery near where she stood straight out of the Hall across the terrace and the formal garden and directly to one of his warnings at the edge of the map: *Here be dragons*. The line stopped at the now bricked up old kitchens.

Mabel's mind whirred. She had walked in at the far end of the gallery. Here where she stood now were the doors that led out and into the library.

The gallery and library were separated by a short passage of only five feet or so. One walked out the door of the gallery and then in the door of the library. On the left between the two doors was a ponderous carved mahogany side cabinet and on it sat a tall, elegant blue-and-white eighteenth-century chinoiserie. Mabel remembered that distinctly, because she had bumped into the cabinet once and nearly sent the vase crashing to the floor.

She went to the door of the passage, opened it and frowned. Here between gallery and library, the cabinet sat not on her left, but on her right. Had she remembered wrong? And it wasn't flush against the wall, but with one corner awkwardly sticking out.

There was no light in the short passage, and so she went back to the gallery and, after a minute or two, located a drawer with an assortment of Victorian glass ink stands – and candles. She lit one, secured it in a brass holder and carried it carefully back to examine her mistaken memory. When she bent over the place on the left in the passage where she thought the cabinet should've been, she could see the marks from it having been dragged across the wood floor. The cabinet had been shifted in what looked to be a haphazard fashion. Why?

She shot up again and looked directly in front of her at the door to the library.

'Dear God,' she said aloud. At that moment, she recalled having heard that the library and the formal dining room had been switched. When? Certainly not in her memory. During the Victorian improvements? Fifty or sixty years ago, this passage lay between the gallery and the dining room. Servants came from the kitchens, which were in a separate building, down a tunnel and up the stairs.

She had taken Park and Hildy to the new formal dining room to look for the entrance to the tunnel, but that dining room formerly had been the library and today's library had been the dining room. Her head spun, but one thought was clear. The tunnel came up where she now stood.

Who would remember this change? Like the priest holes, the knowledge of the tunnel might've been lost to the annals of time except to the one person who needed to know the Hall inside and out in order to do his job – the butler.

Mabel held the candle close to the wall and saw a door between two sets of panelling. The door was ajar.

She glanced back into the gallery. Should she find Park? But he and the police were spread out over the estate.

What if Binks was holding Oliver Harkin captive?

Or what if Oliver was exacting revenge on Binks for killing Annie? It was as if Mabel heard Edith loud and clear. 'Don't wait – go!'

Mabel pulled open the door, held up her candle and stared into the inky darkness beyond.

She moved cautiously into the dark, pressing one hand on the side of the tunnel and holding the candle out and to the side so that the bright flame wouldn't blind her. A few steps in she came to stairs. Down she went, then paused at the bottom. The stairs and the floor were flagstone, although now covered with a generous layer of soil and dust that softened the sound of her footfalls. Iron brackets had been affixed to brick walls on both sides and there were still the stubs of candles at the bottom of a couple. Mabel scratched at the hard wax to loosen the wicks and then lit them.

She pictured what was above where she stood – the edge of the gallery and the terrace. As far as she could see – not far – the tunnel led straight out. Who would know about this place? The kitchens were closed long before Binks had arrived, but had he found them on his own and was hiding out? If he wanted to escape, why stop so close to the Hall? There would be only one way to find out.

The land beyond the formal garden fell away and so the old kitchen building sat low on the landscape and, covered with wild honeysuckle, it appeared as nothing more than a mound of green from the Hall or out on the terrace. Mabel had walked down a good long flight of stairs to reach the tunnel, and so the path ran straight and even to meet the kitchen door. Soon she saw a dim light ahead and slowed. When she heard a voice, she stopped altogether.

Listening hard, she could tell only that it was a man speaking. She tiptoed further until she came to a wide door standing open. Beyond, inside the kitchen, scattered beams of light fell from missing slates in the roof and long tendrils of honeysuckle hung down through the holes. Binks sat strapped to a ladder-back chair, his head lolling to one side and blood dripping from his forehead onto his jacket. His spectacles were gone and his eyes were closed. Pacing back and forth in front of him was Doctor Gordon Finlay.

TWENTY-ONE

'It was poor judgement on your part, Gerald, you must see that,' Finlay said in a reasonable voice.

Mabel held back behind the door to get her bearings. What was this? Doctor Finlay had captured the escaped Binks? What were they doing in the old kitchens? She glanced round at the enormous scullery sinks on one side, ovens on the other and in the middle, a work table, its surface rotted through in the middle and missing a leg. Opposite to where she stood was an open fireplace so big Mabel could've walked into it and in front of the fireplace a spit that took up the entire wall from floor to ceiling. It had rack after rack of spikes to hold the meat and a pulley and wheel to rotate the entire contraption for even roasting.

To one side, the doctor's fine Gladstone bag sat open on the frame of a chair missing its rush bottom. Dark felted cloth was stuffed into the top of the bag and several pieces of parchment paper were scattered across the floor. Mabel, still halfway behind the door, squinted at the closest one. It looked like a university degree diploma, but she couldn't read the words. She leaned closer and her movement caught the doctor's attention.

'Miss Canning!' His face was flushed and his collar askew.

He threw out his arms as if in welcome and she saw that he held the missing table leg. 'Thank God, you're here. I wasn't sure what to do – this certainly is not my remit, capturing a murderer.'

'What are you doing here?' Mabel asked, looking round at the cobwebs in the corner, the boarded-up windows and the dust motes dancing in the rays of light.

'Well may you ask that,' Finlay said. He was breathing hard but laughed and his right eye winked. 'Mr Binks here needed a doctor, he said. Come to the old kitchens, he said. I'm afraid I was a bit too trusting on that account, but a doctor must go to his patient. When I realised I was trapped, I feared for my life, I can tell you. You, Miss Canning, have saved the day. Where are the others? Inspector Tollerton and his constables?'

'They're out on the estate—' Mabel stopped. Perhaps she shouldn't've admitted that.

'They're looking for Binks?' Finlay asked eagerly. 'Well, he's been found, hasn't he? You go, Miss Canning – find them and tell them the murderer is here.' He pointed to Binks with the table leg and Mabel saw blood on the end of it.

'Did you hit him?' she asked. Her candle had stayed lit and the flame danced as her hand shook. She set it on the ledge next to her.

'He attacked me!' Finlay said, his voice high and shaky. 'He lay in wait as I arrived.' Finlay gripped the piece of wood in his hand, as if judging its worth as a cricket bat. 'He tried to use this on me as a weapon and I took it off him.'

'Why?' Mabel asked. 'Why would Binks ask you here? Why would he attack you?'

The butler stirred and moaned.

'Binks?' Mabel asked and drew near.

'Run, Miss Canning,' Finlay said. 'Run and bring back your inspector and your Mr Winstone. He's a wily one, this Binks, and I don't want you to be in danger.'

'Doctor Finlay—' Mabel began.

'Risley,' Binks said, his voiced slurred. He coughed. 'His name is Archibald Risley.'

'You see what I mean, Miss Canning,' Finlay said, raising the bat as if to strike again. 'I believe Binks has quite lost his mind.'

'He's no doctor,' Binks said and nodded towards the parchments on the floor. 'Only pretends to be.'

She kept her eyes on them both as she took a few steps and retrieved one of the papers. A degree bestowed from the University of Edinburgh. It was identical to the one at Doctor Finlay's surgery – standard printed parchment with the same formal wording and the details filled in by hand. But this degree had not been granted to Gordon Finlay, rather to George Fairclough. She picked up another to Gilbert Figgit and another to Granville Frye.

The names and other details were in the same hand as on the certificate at the doctor's surgery and the same hand that had written the prescriptions for Dorothea's valerian. An erratic script that seemed to dance above the line. Frantic music played loud in Mabel's mind – 'Flight of the Bumblebee.'

Finlay moved towards her suddenly and Mabel jumped back.

'Now, now,' Finlay said, sounding out of breath. 'There's nothing to this. Another of Gerald's tricks, that's all.'

'He murdered Agatha Tyne,' Binks said.

'She slipped and fell into the canal,' Finlay said sharply, as if correcting a child.

'She didn't – you knocked her on the head and pushed her.'

'We were engaged!' Finlay shouted. 'She was to be my wife.'

'Until she joined up with the suffragettes. You didn't like that, did you?'

'Agatha Tyne died in Little Lever years ago,' Mabel said. 'The coroner declared an open verdict, but Skeff... Skeff has a copy of the coroner's report.' A stretch of the truth, but only a little one and the declaration made the doctor flinch. 'Annie wrote you a note, Binks. "Do you remember Agatha Tyne?" it said.'

'Annie recognised you, Risley,' Binks said, struggling with the words.

'But you didn't recognise him?' Mabel asked.

'Before all this,' Binks said, 'I'd only caught sight of him once when he visited his lordship. I couldn't see past his dyed black hair and moustache and that scar above his eye. Scars are telling, Miss Canning. Scars are permanent. Did you do that to yourself, Risley, as part of your disguise?'

'You aren't a doctor?' Mabel asked, trying to keep up with the exchange as facts and guesses ricocheted around the room.

'Of course I'm a doctor,' Finlay said harshly. 'You've seen my qualifications. And my bag. What he says is a lie and he must be stopped.' He spun round to Binks and raised the table leg.

'This bag?' Mabel asked and strode over to it. 'Having a doctor's bag doesn't make you a doctor.' She dug a hand in the bag and came up with what at first had looked like dark felted material. She unrolled it and it became a bowler hat. 'And do you carry around extra pairs of spectacles too – *Doctor*?'

'Doctor's assistant, that's what he was,' Binks said. He blinked as a drop of blood landed in his eye. 'Agatha Tyne cleaned for Doctor Formby. Once you murdered Agatha, you needed to get away and you stole that bag from the doctor. G F – Griffith Formby. Part of your disguise.'

'My father gave me that bag when I qualified!' Finlay shouted.

'Annie recognised you, and so you smothered her.'

'She wouldn't stop talking!' Finlay leaned on the table leg as if it were a cane. His breathing came out like a wheeze. 'The world has gone mad when a woman doesn't remember her place.'

'How many other people have you killed to keep your secret?' Binks' voice rose.

'I'm a good doctor!' Finlay screamed in Binks' face.

'You're a murderer,' Binks replied.

Finlay, changing like the wind, threw himself back to lean against the sinks on the other side of the room and in a calm voice said, 'Don't be so melodramatic, Gerald.'

'I saw what you did to Agatha there on the canal path. You were arguing and you picked up a rock and struck her then pushed her in the canal – you murdered her. But no one would listen to me,' Binks said. 'Could've been an accident, they said. She could've slipped, hit her head on that rock and fallen into the canal. You acted the heartbroken fiancé well. Annie believed me, but even she couldn't convince them I was telling the truth.'

'They knew better than to believe you or your self-appointed caretaker,' he said with a sneer. 'You were a trouble-maker, a rogue, a... hoodlum. Fatherless child running wild. You weren't to be trusted.'

'And then you disappeared,' Binks said, 'taking Doctor Formby's bag along with you. That raised a few eyebrows, but still you got away with it for a long time, Archibald. But no longer.'

'You didn't recognise Binks here at the Hall?' Mabel asked.

'I should've done,' Finlay said. 'A young scoundrel grown up to be an untrustworthy servant. It wasn't until I saw those eyes – the eyes of a devil – that I wondered. Then, here came this message.'

From his pocket, Finlay pulled a piece of paper and threw it at Binks. Mabel sidled over, keeping an eye on the table leg that Finlay still held, and picked the paper up.

I remember Agatha Tyne. Come to the old kitchens from the door near the library.

It was Binks' writing – even and quiet and repetitive. Mabel heard that Chopin prelude with the A flat repeating over and over.

'Binks, why didn't you say something to Inspector Tollerton? To me?'

'No one listened before,' Binks said, his words starting to slur again. 'Why would they listen now? I needed proof. I needed Risley alone and to keep him here long enough to get the truth out of him. Then I'd get your Inspector Tollerton to listen to the confession.'

Annie had known her cousin well. Binks fights his own wars and keeps his own counsel. But it hadn't been the best of plans.

Binks closed his eyes and his head dropped. If he'd had no evidence all those years ago about what Finlay had done, what did he have now except perhaps proof that this Risley fellow had impersonated a doctor. You didn't hang for that, did you? Perhaps Binks had thought to settle this score himself, for Annie's sake.

Finlay stirred and Mabel thought it best to keep him talking.

'Did you try and run me over?' Mabel asked.

'You were meddling, Miss Canning. I'm sorry to say my aim was off. Either that or you're too agile for me.' He brushed an imaginary speck off his sleeve and looked down at the table leg he held. 'But as you weren't struck, I thought at least you could be witness to how reckless an idea it was of his lordship's to allow a blind butler behind the wheel of his Wolseley.'

'What about Oliver Harkin?' she asked.

'That was a lucky happenstance for me! It made it look all the worse for Gerald – running down the estranged husband of his dead cousin. Too bad I missed him, too.'

'No one believes it was Binks driving,' Mabel said. 'You stole Campsie's hat.'

'The bumbling gardener in a bowler? He didn't even know it was gone, did he?'

'And when you missed me with the Wolseley,' Mabel said, 'you tried again inside the Hall.'

'I had you' – he wagged a finger at her – 'or nearly. But I heard voices, so the least I could do was delay your escape.' His voice dropped. 'There was someone else for me to attend to.'

'Dorothea?'

'Another insufferable suffragette. How proud she was in her sash.' He tapped the table leg on the stone floor. 'She knew something. She heard something. I could get back to you, but Miss Goose I needed to nip in the bud. *But again I was interrupted!*'

Binks stirred briefly.

'And left the cottonwool in Ruby's room,' Mabel said, 'and Dorothea's sash in Binks' wardrobe to mix us up. In and out of the Hall you went, practically at your leisure. But you were grasping at straws – you were losing and you knew it.'

Finlay advanced on her holding the table leg out as if it were a fencing foil and Mabel backed away, knocking into the side of an empty Welsh dresser.

'You murdered Pretoria,' she said. 'Why?'

Finlay stopped and lifted his chin as if in acknowledgement of a great feat. 'Bloody suffragettes and their bloody sashes – they are everywhere and I am only doing my part in the fight against their outlandish demands.' He laughed, then sobered up. 'Apparently, she had seen me on Sunday afternoon as I left through the wood after dealing with Mrs Harkin, and when she saw me again yesterday morning – coming for the Wolseley – she said, "Oh it wasn't Thirza and Lavinia, it was you!" Well, I couldn't let that pass, could I?'

Binks moaned and Finlay – Risley, whoever he was –

watched the butler as he tightened and loosened and tightened his grip on the table leg.

'How have you got away with being a doctor when you never were?' Mabel asked.

Finlay turned to her in surprise as if he'd forgotten she was there.

'I have a very good bedside manner and you don't need much more than that. I'm just as good as any other doctor and don't you listen to anyone who says otherwise.'

'So, you've had trouble in previous posts?'

'That's it – I've had about enough of this.' Finlay turned away.

Mabel had been weighing her options. She could've made a run for it while they were talking, but would Finlay have caught up to her in the darkness of the tunnel? Even if he had let her run, Binks would be as good as dead and then Finlay might easily slip through their fingers before Mabel could find Tollerton or Park.

Now, she threw a glance over her shoulder. How long had she been stalling Finlay? When would someone notice the door between the gallery and the library stood open? Who would come for them?

In the second she took her eyes off him, Finlay rushed her, the piece of wood held high over his head, ready to strike. But he didn't have a straight route and so when he ran one way round the table, Mabel ran the other, reaching out to grab a battered kettle left on the hob. He was upon her in an instant, and she threw the kettle at him, but he dodged and swung the bat. Mabel felt the wind stir as it missed her shoulder by an inch and hit the table instead.

The table broke in two, cloven in the middle with the bat stuck between. Finlay yanked it out, but Mabel grabbed hold too, and they fought for control of it in front of the spit. Finlay jerked it out of her hands and Mabel staggered, stumbling on top of the collapsed table.

'Too late for heroics, Miss Canning,' he said. 'I must finish up here and be on my way.' He raised the bat again.

But a sound caught his ears. He paused and looked towards the mouth of the tunnel with a frown. Mabel heard it, too.

Aooooooooo!

TWENTY-TWO

Aooooooo!

Gladys' howl grew closer, and Finlay looked right and left for an escape. In a flash the dog raced into the kitchen and straight at him. Once again, he raised the table leg high and swung it back and forth. The dog, bobbing and weaving like a boxer, barked and growled but did not back down. Mabel grabbed at the weapon and at last caught hold with both hands. Finlay braced himself and wrenched it hard to dislodge her hold, but at the same time Mabel let go and his momentum sent him flying backward. He hit the spikes on the spit, screamed and dropped the bat.

Mabel rushed at him without thinking. He grabbed both her wrists and they wrestled as he tried to push her onto the spikes. Gladys barked and snapped at his legs.

'Get off!' he shouted and kicked at the dog, catching her under her belly. She became airborne, then landed hard, missing the rubble from the table. Her nails scritched on the stone floor as she spun in a circle.

Mabel stomped on Finlay's foot. He grunted and let go of her, and she was on him in an instant, screaming at him and beating on his chest so hard that he collapsed, gasping for breath.

Someone grabbed her from behind and pulled her off.

'Mabel,' Park said, kneeling behind her, 'Mabel.'

'He attacked Gladys!' she shouted as Finlay scrambled up and made for the tunnel.

Binks put his foot out and Finlay went flying, falling flat on his face and at the feet of WPC Wardle who emerged from the tunnel at top speed and skidded to a halt.

Tollerton came next, followed by Ronald and after him PCs Cowley and Scott.

'Mabel?' Tolly shouted.

She pointed at Finlay, who struggled to raise himself up onto his elbows. 'It's him, it's the doctor. He's the murderer.' Not a doctor, but she couldn't catch her breath to say more. 'Park, is Gladys all right?'

Before Park could move, Gladys leapt to her feet and went for Finlay. She didn't touch him, but, teeth bared, she set up barking at top volume an inch from his face. No one even bothered to quiet her. Finlay cowered with his hands over his ears.

'Cuff him, Wardle,' Tollerton said.

When Hildy pulled Finlay's hands behind him, he flinched. 'There's blood on his shoulder, sir.'

'We fought and he fell against the spit,' Mabel said, and could feel Park's grip on her shoulders tighten. 'He battered Binks with the table leg.'

Ronald went to the butler and began working on the leather straps that held him to the chair.

'We'll need a doctor,' Tollerton said and then frowned.

'No doctor,' Binks said. Quite right, there was no doctor.

'I don't suppose we can use what was in the doctor's bag,' Mabel said. At the mention of his Gladstone bag, Finlay began to writhe on the floor and cry out. Hildy put her foot on his back, Gladys growled and he stilled.

'There'll be bandages and such in the Hall,' Mabel said.

'Shall I go look?' Hildy asked Mabel and then looked at Tollerton. 'Sir?'

'Yes, go on.' Tollerton glanced at the bag, then at the parchments scattered across the floor. 'Wait, what's all this?'

'He was never a doctor,' Mabel said.

'He was an assistant,' Binks whispered.

'It looks as if he made up his own degree certificates to suit,' Mabel said, 'as long as the initials were the same as on his precious Gladstone bag. You can match his writing with this.' She drew Dorothea's prescription for valerian out of her pocket. She had been carrying it around, just as Dorothea had, thinking to dispose of it, but perhaps unconsciously, Mabel knew it would be needed. 'He murdered both Annie and Pretoria. He tried to run me down and nearly had the chance to murder Dorothea.'

Tollerton took the prescription and tucked it into his pocket. 'Wardle, before you go, collect all that. You two take Finlay up to the steward's office and keep him there.'

Ned and Ted pulled Finlay to standing. He struggled for a moment, but then gave up.

'Inspector,' Binks said, holding the handkerchief Ronald had given him to his wound, 'he took my spectacles. They're in his pocket.'

Tollerton nodded to Ned who stuck a hand in one pocket of Finlay's jacket and then the other. He pulled out the glasses and handed them to the butler.

'His name is Archibald Risley,' Binks said as he put on his glasses. His voice rose as the constables started towards the tunnel with their prisoner.

'Cowley,' Tollerton called, 'don't let the ladies see him. Take him around...' He glanced over to Mabel.

'Ned, turn left at the top of the stairs and go through the

library,' she said. 'Then you can cross the entrance hall and get into the steward's office down the corridor.'

'Yes, Miss Canning, will do.'

'Well, Mr Binks,' Tollerton said, 'I look forward to hearing the details. Can you walk back to the house?'

'Yes, sir,' Binks said. He stood, swayed and sank back onto the chair.

'Here now, Binks,' Ronald said. 'I'll give you a hand. Mabel, are you all right?'

'I am,' she said, although her legs felt like jelly. 'You go on.'

When everyone had left and it was only Mabel, Park and Tolly, she sat down on Binks' chair and closed her eyes. She felt Park's hands on her shoulders and she leaned against him. She opened her eyes and Gladys came to her, resting her chin on Mabel's knee. Mabel gave her a scratch behind the ears and kissed her head. Tears sprang to her eyes and she blinked them away.

'These are the old kitchens?' Tollerton asked, gazing at the spit. 'Looks more like a torture chamber.'

Mabel felt a sudden fit of giggles coming on and had to swallow and cough to regain her composure, remembering she still had responsibilities.

'Where is Augustus?' Mabel asked.

'Collette Massey took charge and has been teaching him the piano,' Park said.

'Poor fellow,' Mabel said.

'Are you ready?'

'Yes.' She stood. Gladys shook and trotted to the door of the tunnel.

Mabel saw that her candle she'd left on the ledge had gone out. 'I don't have a match.'

'We don't need a candle,' Tollerton said. He pulled out a small box, threw a switch and a beam of light emerged – an official Metropolitan Police electric torch.

'Could I get one of those?' Mabel asked as they walked down the tunnel.

'How is Finlay responsible for all of it?' Tollerton asked, ignoring her question. She would enquire about the torch again later.

'It all has to do with something he did in Little Lever years ago,' Mabel said. 'Skeff should have the coroner's report by now and that'll tell us more, but apparently he murdered Agatha Tyne, the woman he was to marry, because she was a suffragette. He has a very low opinion of the movement, because it had caused Agatha to develop opinions of her own. Binks – Gerald Cheevers then – saw him strike her and push her in the canal. Binks was a bit of a handful at the time and no one believed him except Annie. The coroner left the verdict open. Archibald Risley stole the local doctor's Gladstone bag and... well, we'll have to fill in those blanks as we can.'

'It must've been a shock for Finlay – Risley – to see Annie Harkin and Binks after all this time,' Tollerton said.

'Yes, just when he'd hit the peak of his fake career and was able to play golf every day,' Mabel said. 'I had begun to worry that Ruby Truelock had run off the rails and was responsible for all this. She's not well. Was Ruby in the conservatory?'

'No,' Tollerton said. 'It seems Miss Truelock has gone.'

They received a great welcome when they arrived at the conservatory – the only thing missing was a brass band. Augustus sounded two chords on the piano and then jumped off the bench and came running but had to stand in line as Emma was first to throw her arms round Mabel. Cora beamed from the back of the group and Skeff held up her reporter's notebook – containing details of the coroner's report, no doubt. The women all spoke at once, and Mabel could only smile and nod.

'Look now,' Collette said, 'one of the cooks brought up tea. Shall I pour?'

'Ladies' – Tollerton's voice rose over the din – 'you will hear details of what has happened in due course. I can tell you that Mr Binks has been injured but is recovering, and we are questioning someone else in relation to Mrs Harkin's death.' He frowned. 'And the death of Miss Fleming-Jones. And the attempted murder of Miss Canning.'

There were a few gasps at that.

'And Dorothea's attack, too, I hope,' Diane boomed.

'But who is it?' Thirza asked.

'It's that charlatan of a doctor, isn't it?' Dorothea said. She received shocked looks and added, 'It was Katie Darling when she brought in the tea who told me. She'd just seen the two constables leading him into the steward's office.'

And that's how news travels in a village.

'You're free to leave the room,' Tollerton said, as if neither confirming nor denying Dorothea's statement would make it go away. 'But not the Hall, because—'

'You'll have more questions for us,' Emma finished.

The women drifted towards the door, chattering among themselves – all except Dorothea, who made for the French windows, sunshine and the gardens. She pulled her straw hat down to secure it and Mabel noticed a cluster of silk celandine on the brim – Cora's touch. Dorothea was alone, and even though her attacker had been arrested, Mabel worried. They'd all grown accustomed to Ruby watching out for her.

But Ruby had gone. 'Not vanished. She's left.' That was as much as Tolly had explained when she'd enquired further.

Mabel followed Dorothea out.

'The nerve of the man,' Dorothea said. 'Trying to make me out to be mad, was he? Well, he couldn't pull one over on Dorothea Goose, could he?'

But he had – and on Mabel, too. No need to point that out now.

'Dorothea, what about Ruby? How is she?'

'Poor girl,' Dorothea said, taking a few deep breaths of fresh air. 'Look what we've done to her.'

'It wasn't your secret to tell, though, was it?' Mabel said.

'I don't suppose, but I doubt that makes much difference to her.'

'Do you think she'll ever let Oliver…'

'What?' Dorothea asked. 'Be a father? She might eventually entertain the idea, I suppose. But she'll be all right. We'll all see to that now.'

A thought occurred to Mabel that perhaps it hadn't been Ruby looking after Dorothea as much as the other way round.

'Do you know where she's gone?' Mabel asked.

Hildy came out on the terrace. 'Mabel, Mrs Chandekar is on the telephone for you.'

A stab of panic caught Mabel in her tummy. 'Where's Augustus?'

'Mr Winstone has taken him down to the kitchen and Miss Darling has promised to watch him like a hawk.'

'You go to the telephone, Mabel,' Dorothea said. 'I'm going to check on that early yellow rambler in the walled garden. It's nearly May and there could be a rose or two open already.'

Mabel headed for the billiards room, wondering if news of what had transpired at the Hall had already reached the village. She needed to get her story straight – not that she would ever lie to her papa or Mrs Chandekar, but a great deal of worry can be avoided by the choice of one's words. And there's no sense in worrying about something that has already happened.

There seemed to be a great deal of racket in the corridors and echoing across the entrance hall – voices calling out, even laughter – a welcome change from the deadly silence of late. Mabel smiled as she closed the door and settled at the table.

Lifting the earpiece, she leaned closer to the candlestick base. 'Mabel here. Is everything all right?'

'Shouldn't that be my question?' Mrs Chandekar asked. 'We've been ringing and ringing, and Reg was just about to take off up to the Hall and see what the problem was.'

'Oh, everything is fine,' Mabel said offhandedly, but then added with more weight to her voice, 'We caught him. And it wasn't Binks. It was Doctor Finlay.'

She heard Mrs Chandekar catch her breath. 'Well, I can hardly believe it. I'm very glad it wasn't Binks, although now we'll have to put up with a fair amount of Reg saying "I told you so" as he never cared for Doctor Finlay all that much. We will expect the entire story at dinner this evening – you'll bring the others, too? Not the ladies, but you know – your club and the inspector, of course. And anyone else you like.'

'Yes, thank you, we will all be there, but there's some work to be done here before we can get away.'

'Of course,' Mrs Chandekar said. 'In the meantime, Mabel love, Ruby is here.'

'Ruby?' Mabel shouted, startling herself. 'Ruby is there? How? How did she even know where to go?'

'She tells me she's been watching you and listening carefully, and she had decided that Canning's Greengrocer in Peasmarsh was just the place she could go to have a quiet think about things. Reg found her standing at the door of the shop and brought her in. He's busy with customers otherwise he would be telling you about it.'

'Is she all right?'

Mrs Chandekar made a noncommittal sound. 'She will be. She told me her story. It's been quite a shock for her, learning who her father is.'

'How did she learn?' Mabel asked. 'Did someone let slip?'

'Only a few months ago, someone at the school came across a box of Susan Truelock's personal papers,' Mrs Chandekar said, 'and gave them all to Ruby. In the box were letters Oliver Harkin had sent to Susan asking after Ruby and expressing the desire to meet his daughter at last.'

'And now she's learned that everyone else has known for ages. Look, I'll be right up to fetch her,' Mabel said.

'No need, she's fine here for a while. How is Augustus?'

There's a question needed answering. Mabel said he was well but knew she had better check on him and soon, before the cooks got distracted with dinner preparations.

For it was nearly that time, although not quite yet for Mabel and the other members of the London Ladies' Murder Club – nor for Scotland Yard, she reminded herself. There was the enquiry to wrap up.

The moment they rang off, the room grew dark and Mabel went to the window in time to see a flash of lightning. The next second, thunder boomed and here came the rain once again. Mabel thought she needed a few minutes in a quiet place before rejoining the others, and the billiards room would do for her, so when the door behind her opened, she turned to beg off whatever was needed of her. But it was Park and she realised that had been her real wish all along.

They met in the middle of the room and were silent in each other's arms for she didn't know how long. At last she looked up at him.

'Ruby isn't lost,' she said. 'She went down to the village and Papa took her in and she's been with Mrs Chandekar. She's all right.'

'I hope Reg won't put me back on parsnip cordial after all that's happened.'

'He couldn't possibly do that,' Mabel said. 'You saved us and captured the murderer. How did you know where we were?'

Park laughed. 'As much as I would like to take the credit –

especially if it would put me in good stead with your father – I'm afraid I can't. The second Tolly opened the door to the gallery, Gladys took off straight through to the other end of the room. By the time we got to the stairs she was down the tunnel ahead of us – so we all know who saved you.'

Mabel kissed him. 'But where would Gladys be without you?'

'She would be hunting rats on a farm near Rouen,' Park said.

'Really? I never knew.'

'I was there two years ago – for the service. The farmer had taken in a dog left behind after the war. She'd just had a litter, and he offered me one. I looked down at this mass of toffee-coloured fur, and Gladys was the only one who looked back. I tucked her in my jacket and off we went.'

Mabel's chin quivered and tears fell as exhaustion, fear and elation collided with tenderness. 'Don't mind me,' she said as she took his handkerchief from his breast pocket.

'I mind you very much,' Park said and kissed her tear-stained cheeks.

They looked into each other's eyes for a moment, then Mabel said, 'Is Tolly questioning him – this Risley?'

'He is,' Park said. 'Want to go listen at the door?'

'Yes, I do.'

PC Cowley stood at attention outside the steward's office. Park left Mabel there and went off to see how Binks was faring.

'Well, Ned,' Mabel said, 'do you know how it's going?'

Ned shrugged. 'Constable Wardle is in there taking notes. I never thought I'd work with a lady policeman, but I've got to admit, she can hold her own.'

And some, Mabel thought.

At that moment, Katie Darling appeared carrying a tray of tea and fruitcake.

'I'll take that in if you like, Katie.'

'Can't I go in?' Katie said. 'I'd like to have a word with this murdering doctor – to think I let him treat my little ones when they've been ailing.'

'Did he give them medicine?' Impersonating a doctor must be against the law, Mabel thought. In addition to murder.

Katie frowned. 'I've thought about that, Mabel, and I've got to say, he's never done much of anything – good or bad. Takes their temperature, gives them a boiled sweet. He's been fairly useless.'

'He could've done a great deal of harm,' Mabel said, taking the tray from Katie. 'And he may have elsewhere.'

She knocked once, opened the door and went in.

'She attacked me, this Annie Harkin,' Finlay was saying, 'and that's all I will say. Well, you know those suffragettes – no regard for life or limb, theirs or anyone else's. I was only defending myself.'

Hildy raised her eyebrows in greeting and Mabel smiled in return. As she set the tea and cake on the bookcase, she saw Finlay's gaze dart to her and away.

'Thank you, Miss Canning,' Tollerton said in a that'll-be-all tone of voice.

'You're welcome,' Mabel said, ignoring the unspoken command. 'Shall I pour?'

Tollerton sighed and continued with the interview. 'We will take your fingerprints, Mr Risley, and compare them to those we found in the priest hole, in the hidden stairwell, and on the French doors of the library as well as Mrs Harkin's room.'

Finlay brightened. 'I was called there in an official capacity, Inspector.'

'If you aren't actually a doctor,' Mabel said, 'you aren't official.'

Tolly threw her a look, but she saw a rare twinkle in his eye as he continued.

'We also have questions for you about events in Little Lever, Lancashire, some twenty-two years ago concerning Agatha Tyne, a woman who cleaned for Doctor Griffith Formby and was, at the time, your fiancée. Events for which there is a witness.'

Mabel set tea and a slice of fruitcake in front of Tollerton and stole a glance at Finlay, who had turned beetroot red.

'That damned Gerald Cheevers or Binks or whatever he calls himself,' Finlay said with a growl. 'He's a liar.'

'We have questions about your whereabouts in the intervening years. And don't think we can't track you through not only your appearance, but also that fine Gladstone doctor's bag. I have a feeling, Mr Risley, that no matter what name you used, you left a lasting impression wherever you went.'

TWENTY-THREE

In the kitchen, Augustus, Katie and Campsie were having their tea, Gladys was stretched out in front of the range and Deenie leaned against the sink mixing mustard.

'Everything all right here?' Mabel asked.

Augustus had just inserted an entire gingernut in his mouth and so nodded his head vigorously but had the good sense not to try to speak.

Mabel went to Gladys. 'What about you, girl?' she asked. 'No worse for being kicked by that bad man?' Gladys stood and with a firm hand, Mabel stroked the dog from nose to tail. She didn't flinch. 'Good,' Mabel said. Gladys stretched, snorted and settled down again. 'You deserve something special for your tea, I'd say.'

'I might have a sausage on hand,' Deenie said, and Gladys' head whipped round.

'It was the doctor, Miss Canning?' Augustus asked. 'The doctor did all those terrible things?'

She couldn't keep it from him, but what would this murder-savvy Augustus think? Would his mother now insist that Mabel be struck from the Useful Women roles? Who would look after her son – none of the other Useful Women would touch an Augustus Malling-Frobisher III assignment with a bargepole. This would be a discussion to have with Miss Kerr if the need arose.

'Police are looking into all the details,' Mabel said. 'I'm sure you understand that we should let Scotland Yard carry on.'

'Does that mean I should ask Detective Inspector Tollerton my questions?'

'Well, Augustus, I'd say you could give it a try.'

Terribly sorry about that, Tolly.

'Well, Aunt Janet never liked him,' Katie declared.

'I miss Doctor Ebbers,' Campsie said. 'He was a good egg.'

'Oh yes,' Katie said and smiled at Campsie. 'Doctor Ebbers was a gem, wasn't he?'

Deenie rolled her eyes.

'I'll be back for you in a bit,' Mabel said to the boy as he reached for another gingernut.

When she stepped into the passage, she joined Tollerton and Hildy coming down the corridor.

'Where have you left Finlay – Risley?' Mabel asked.

'In the steward's office,' Tollerton said. 'Both Cowley and Scott are watching him.'

'Plus, he's handcuffed to the chair,' Hildy added.

'The local sergeant is finally well,' Tolly said, 'and they'll be able to lock Risley up overnight at the station.'

Binks' door stood wide open and when they looked in, he was sitting in the armchair by a freshly lit fire, which crackled and hissed. He had a makeshift bandage wrapped round his head and little colour in his face. Park stood at the desk in the corner looking through a ledger.

'Come in,' Binks said, struggling to rise.

'You stay where you are,' Emma said, bustling past them all to reach the butler. 'I don't want you taxing your strength until I've seen to your injuries.'

'See here, my lady,' Binks replied, sounding if not hale and hearty, at least more spirited than he had when he was tied to a chair in the old kitchens, 'you shouldn't be fussing over me.'

'I'll fuss if I need to fuss, Binks,' Emma said, all business. She set down a bowl of steaming water and a pile of fresh linen strips and began to unwind the makeshift bandage. 'Who put this on?'

'It was the young constables, my lady. It took both of them.'

'Well,' Emma said, softening, 'that was kind of them.' Mabel saw Emma's eyes glisten and knew her to be on the edge of emotions that could pivot from anger to joy to tears in an instant. She'd been there herself.

'Mr Binks,' Tollerton said, 'are you able to answer a few questions?'

'I am, sir.'

While Emma carried out her ministrations, the others gathered round the fire. Deenie came in with a tray laden with tea, sandwiches and cake.

'Having a party, Mr Binks?' she asked. 'There's a first.'

When she'd gone, Park held up the ledger he'd been reading and said, 'Binks was telling me he knew about the tunnel from the log kept by Farrer, the butler before Quince.' He gave the book to Binks. 'Is this the one?'

'Yes, sir, it is.' Binks patted the leather-bound book. 'All butlers keep a log, although some, like Mr Farrer there, treat the entries as a chance for a bit of fanciful writing. I've always enjoyed reading his. He was butler when the old kitchens were closed off and the library and formal dining room were switched.'

'Did you ask the doctor – that is, this Risley fellow – to meet you there?' Tollerton asked.

'Yes,' Binks replied. 'I wanted a quiet word with no one to overhear us until I was sure about what I thought I knew. You see, I hadn't recognised him at first. He's fair-haired naturally –

perhaps he's gone grey now, I wouldn't know. He didn't have the scar, but he's always had that odd bit with his right eye. When he smiles, it sort of winks at you. But he'd been up to the Hall only once that I recall since he moved here last year and I hadn't even answered the door to him. Lord and Lady Fellbridge, you see sir, are rather free in that aspect of service – they never mind doing their bit.'

'A title doesn't make us unable to open a door when we hear a knock,' Emma said. She'd cleaned off Binks' wound and was now putting on a fresh dressing.

'We showed you the note Mrs Harkin had left on her tea tray,' Tollerton said. 'And you knew she had written it to you.'

'I did know that, sir.'

'You should have told me then,' Tollerton said.

'But I didn't understand what Annie meant. I thought she might've been telling me that Risley had returned to Little Lever, and now that she was here, she'd tell me about it. I didn't recognise Risley as Finlay. Not at first.'

'I don't think he recognised you either,' Mabel said. 'When he saw your eyes, that gave him pause, but I thought it was only because of how unusual it is.'

Binks removed his glasses and blinked at the others to show his eyes – one more blue than green, the other more green than blue.

'Old Doctor Formby thought nothing of my eyes,' Binks said. 'But I remember they made the doctor's young assistant shiver. "Evil" he said then, and he said it again now.'

'Was it seeing that precious bag of his?' Mabel asked. 'Is that what you recognised?'

'Yes, Miss Canning. Doctor Formby's bag. When he left, he took that Gladstone bag with him. At first, the doctor hadn't quite believed me about what Risley did to Agatha – no one did, truth be told – but after the young man he'd trusted had scarpered, it knocked him for six. He died not long after and no one took over the surgery. The mill was in trouble and it was a bad time for the village. People had other things to worry about.'

'You testified at the inquest?' Tollerton asked. 'We'll have a copy of the full report.'

'Oh yes, I testified,' Binks said. 'But everyone knew what sort of lad I was then – the sort that couldn't quite be trusted. Risley, on the other hand, was smooth as silk. He had been out seeing to Doctor Formby's patients and knew exactly what time he was here or there to the minute. Most folks can only tell you what they did in general "I went to the shops after breakfast" or "I came up from the stables when I'd finished milking." And so they believed him and not me.'

'You should've said something when you knew it was him,' Tollerton said.

'I didn't know for certain until I saw that bag and I got a good, close look at him – then the penny dropped. Still, I wanted to talk it through, and when Oliver showed up, I thought well, here's the fellow to help me out.'

'Did Mr Harkin know Agatha Tyne?' Mabel asked. Because he had denied it to her.

'No,' Binks said. 'He heard about her in passing later. Oliver didn't come to Little Lever until after Agatha was killed.'

'Then why did you think he might help you?'

'Only because he's known me for so long and, begging your pardon, my lady, but I felt as if he was someone I could speak with freely. So the two of us went off to Rye this morning.'

'Did the driver of Terry's Pork Pies van give the two of you a lift into town?' Mabel asked.

'He did, ma'am. He's a good lad,' Binks said. 'Oliver and I spent the morning at the Mermaid, making a few phone calls as we could, asking again about Risley to see if we might pick up a trail.'

'Mr Harkin took his suitcase with him,' Tollerton said, 'and checked back into the Mermaid. Mr Binks, it wasn't up to you to look into the matter, that was for the police.'

'But what evidence did I have of who he was and that he'd murdered Agatha Tyne? No one believed me then, why would they now?' Binks asked. 'Who would know he was Archibald Risley? It would be only my word against his. No, I needed to get him to admit what he'd done. I'm sorry you were caught up in it, Miss Canning, I never meant for you to be hurt, although I'm very glad you found us.'

'I am, too,' Mabel said. It seemed a bit of the impetuous nature of Gerald Cheevers still lived inside Binks and the butler had not taken the time to think his plan through. What good would a confession have been from Archibald Risley down in the old kitchens with no witnesses?

'Risley was right in one thing,' Binks said. 'I was a bit wild when I was young. My father had died and my mother had enough to do to put food on the table and I was often left to my own devices. Annie took me under her wing, always looking to set me on the right path. She was like that – generous with a lively spirit.'

Emma clicked her tongue. 'This Risley's lived a good life while other people have paid the price for him.'

'The coroner left the verdict open on Agatha Tyne,' Mabel said. 'He won't escape that now – nor can he escape from what he did to Annie and to Pretoria.'

By early evening, order had been restored to the Hall. Police had, mostly, left. Binks insisted on serving dinner and Campsie insisted on assisting him. Deenie had promised a mouthwatering meal starting with celery ice and finishing with apple crumble with, no doubt, many lentil delights between.

Mabel expressed regret to Emma at missing dinner in the square dining room.

'Papa and Mrs Chandekar are expecting us, you see,' she explained. The 'us' referred to Park, Skeff, Cora and Augustus plus the inspector and WPC Wardle. 'But we'll stop for drinks in the salon first.'

Mabel had saved her best dress for the last evening and here it was – although the week had ended in a fashion no one had expected.

She wore a golden yellow taffeta with cap sleeves and a dainty scalloped over-tunic. Cora had added straw-braided flowers to the tunic and given Mabel one of the new-style headbands in satin. Mabel would need to wear her coat when she went out – the end of April, even in the south of England, could in no way be mistaken for summer.

When Mabel walked into the salon, Emma said, 'Here she is. To Mabel!' and raised her glass.

The others followed suit and repeated the toast. 'Mabel!'

'Oh, please,' Mabel said. Her face hotted up and she fanned it with one hand while accepting a glass of champagne with the other.

'Yes, all right,' Emma said. 'But we did want you to know how much we appreciate what you've done. There, that's finished.'

The women returned to small conversations and Mabel took a sip of champagne. 'Thank you,' she said to Emma. 'Now, what is the consensus? Who will lead the campaign forward?'

'The morning was a waste as far as making a decision,' Emma said. 'We couldn't concentrate. Tomorrow's the day – we'll spend the morning discussing the possibilities and come up with a plan – each woman to her own specialty. I plan to make the Hall available for monthly gatherings to go over our progress.'

Diane called Emma over just as Collette came up to Mabel. 'I wanted to be sure and tell you that the car I heard on Sunday afternoon was not a Wolseley. I know that because my late husband had a Wolseley and I know the sound perfectly well. The car I heard was that man's two-seater.'

'Thank you, Collette. I'll pass that on to Inspector Tollerton.' Mabel was happy that they had Risley with much more solid evidence than this after-the-fact detail.

She turned to Dorothea, nearest to her.

'Sherry is all right,' Dorothea said, looking down into her own glass, 'but I do prefer something a bit closer to the garden. I make a herbal cordial of my own that's won best in the village show these last five years running and they sell a bottle or two at the shop.' She shook her head. 'Of course, I do live in quite a small village.'

'It sounds delicious,' Mabel replied. 'I hope I have the opportunity to taste it one day.'

'We each of us are connected to the other now, aren't we?' Dorothea asked. 'Because of what's happened. We can only hope for good and useful things to come out of such a week.'

'May I visit you in... in...' *Oh dear,* Mabel thought. *Where was it Dorothea lived?*

'Snave,' Dorothea said. 'As it happens, I've just recently advertised for a companion. I could do with the company and – I have to admit – a bit of help in the garden.'

Mabel appreciated how difficult a decision this could be for a woman such as Dorothea – independent, strong-willed – but she very much hoped Dorothea wasn't implying Mabel could fill the post. She took a swig of her champagne for courage, but before she could answer, Dorothea continued.

'I've brought this up with Ruby,' she said. 'I believe it would be good for her – out on her own, but with someone at hand for support, if you will.'

'What a fine idea,' Mabel said, much relieved. 'What does she think?'

'There's time for her to decide. First, she must come to

terms with her father.' Dorothea's hand went up to smooth her suffragette sash which, of course, was not there.

'Your sash,' Mabel said.

'The inspector will return it when he can. I carry my conviction that the vote is the right of every man and woman no matter what I am wearing.' She clicked her tongue. 'Imagine that man thinking he could plant clues by throwing my sash in one place and cottonwool in another. He was seen! Not only by Ruby in our corridor but by Diane when he was out beyond the garden. He thought he could point the finger at Binks by dressing like him when the entire morning Binks was with Oliver in the Mermaid making telephone calls and seen by every mother's daughter.'

Park came to the door of the salon, his hands on Augustus' shoulders. Hildy stood behind them and Gladys behind her.

'We're off now,' he said.

'Right,' Mabel said. She turned and glanced over, catching Skeff and Cora's attention. They nodded, and the needlefelt blue tit atop Cora's straw hat nodded, too.

'We'll see you there,' Mabel said to Park and Hildy. 'Augustus – with me.'

'Will Gladys come with us?' the boy asked.

Woof.

TWENTY-FOUR

There was not a cloud in the sky as they walked up to the village, although the grass was still quite wet and so everyone but Gladys stayed to the path and the road.

'Will you tell Mr Canning that you captured a murderer?' Augustus asked Mabel.

'Not the minute we walk in, I won't – and neither will you. A good dinner guest offers polite conversation topics, something the host might enjoy hearing about.'

Augustus nodded and went quiet the rest of the walk while Mabel, Cora and Skeff talked about going back up to London the following day.

Reg had started lowering the window shades by the time they arrived – closing time – but stopped to be introduced to Skeff and Cora and shake hands with both Gladys and Augustus.

'I learned how to play the piano today,' the boy said. 'Would you like me to play something, Mr Canning?'

'As soon as I finish closing up,' Reg said, 'I'm all ears.'

'Augustus, take Skeff and Cora through to the sitting room, please,' Mabel said. When they'd disappeared through the passage with Gladys on their heels, Mabel gave her papa a kiss. 'Before you ask, I'm fine. Binks is all right, too. We're all fine.'

A string of jarring chords came from the sitting room, and Mabel cringed. Gladys trotted back out to the shop.

'I never liked him,' Reg said. 'That so-called doctor.'

'Yes, so I've heard,' Mabel replied. 'But you didn't like him because he wasn't Doctor Ebbers. Still,' she said, 'you sensed something was off, and so you must have a bit of detective about you. Perhaps that's where I get it from.'

Mabel went back to the kitchen where Ruby was chopping cabbage as Mrs Chandekar opened the oven, releasing a cloud of steam fragrant with thyme. Mabel's mouth watered for whatever was cooking.

'Has everyone arrived?' Mrs Chandekar asked.

'Skeff and Cora and Augustus. The others are on their way.'

A bit of colour had come into Ruby's cheeks and her eyes had lost that worried, pinched look. She put down the knife and wiped her hands on her apron.

'Mabel, I'm sorry if I worried everyone. This morning, it seemed like the end of things for me. I had thought meeting Mrs Harkin would help me make sense of what happened and then she was gone. And suddenly there was Mr Harkin, my... and he seemed not as I imagined at all. I was so confused. I went for a walk and found myself in the village. Your father and Mrs Chandekar have been so kind. They've asked me to stay to dinner. Is that all right?'

Mrs Chandekar could work miracles just by listening, Mabel knew that. 'Of course it's all right,' Mabel said. 'But the others are leaving tomorrow, and I know they will want to see you before you go.'

'I want to apologise to them, too, and also,' Ruby said, 'I want to have a word with Dorothea. You see, I may go to visit her. She's advertised for a companion. She shouldn't be living on her own, and I think I might be able to help.'

To the benefit of both of them, Mabel thought.

'What about your father?'

Ruby shook then nodded her head. 'Dorothea says that there's a lady in her village who takes in paying guests. I suppose he could visit. If he liked.'

'What will you do at Dorothea's?' Mabel asked.

'Work in the garden,' Ruby said. 'I've always felt quite drawn to flower gardens. Looking at them, at least.'

'Are you giving up on being a detective?'

Ruby blushed. 'Oh, that. It's only that I thought you might know something about my father and so if I kept close to you, I'd learn more about him.'

The shop bell jangled and Mabel peered down the passage to see that the police car had arrived and Reg had opened the door to Hildy, Park, Tolly – and Oliver Harkin.

'Good. That's good,' Mabel said quickly. 'So, you won't mind, will you, that we've invited your father this evening.'

Mabel hurried out to the shop where Harkin held his Panama hat in front of him, worrying the brim.

'Hello again, sir,' Harkin said to Reg, shaking hands. 'It's kind of you to ask me.'

'You're welcome,' Reg said, 'but the invitation came from other quarters.' He nodded to Mrs Chandekar.

'Thank you, Mrs Chandekar,' Harkin said. 'And thank you, Miss Canning, and you, Mr Winstone for... picking me up off the road.'

'And didn't Gladys help, too, Mr Harkin?' Augustus asked.

'She did,' Harkin said, and he seemed relieved to turn attention to the dog. 'She's a talented girl, isn't she?'

'She's good at chasing cabbages,' Augustus said. 'Want to see?'

'Why don't we go through?' Mrs Chandekar said, gathering

the men's hats and leaving them on the counter in the shop. 'Don't hurry, Mr Harkin.'

He did as he was told and stayed behind. Ruby hadn't quite made it all the way out of the passage and into the shop, and Mabel gave her a nod and said, 'You've got to start somewhere,' and continued into the sitting room.

Mabel wasn't sure the sitting room had seen this many people at one time outside of Christmas Eve when most of the village stopped in for mulled wine after services. Park sat at the piano teaching Augustus to play chopsticks, Tollerton stood and Skeff, Cora and Hildy crowded onto the settee. Gladys, who knew how to stay out from underfoot, sat on the bench in the window.

Reg came in without his apron – signalling the shop had been closed – and carrying a bottle of pale pink liquid. Mabel's eyebrows lifted.

'Rhubarb cordial?' she asked.

'Only the best tonight,' Reg said.

'Papa's rhubarb cordial is delicious,' she said to the group. 'Sweet enough but with a tart taste that'll pucker your lips.'

'I say, Reg' – Skeff stood to help him pass the glasses round – 'Mabel's been good enough to share your wines and cordials with us and we find them quite appealing.'

'Mr Winstone?' Reg said, holding a glass out.

Park popped up from the piano bench.

'Yes, sir, thank you.'

He threw Mabel a look. She wiggled her eyebrows at him but turned to Reg. 'Papa, you'll call him Park, won't you?'

'I daresay I'd best do,' her papa replied with resignation.

Once the meal got underway – roast chicken and ham with a mountain of asparagus browned in butter and heaps of roasted carrots, potatoes and parsnips along with a bowl of chutney – conversation was limited. The talk went no further than the weather, Cora's use of braided stockingette for a turban and a few anecdotes from Hildy about life in the women's station house, to which Tollerton listened with mild shock. Ruby spoke to her father in a tentative but civil manner at least twice, although both times it was about how fine the meal was.

Augustus nearly fell asleep over his treacle tart but woke up when it was suggested he go to bed. 'But it isn't late,' he said. 'What if I miss something?'

That was entirely the point. Mrs Chandekar oversaw the boy cleaning his teeth and getting under the covers while the others cleared the table and brought coffee and tea out. Reg poured brandy as they all settled again.

'I rang Mrs Varnell earlier,' Mrs Chandekar said when she returned. 'She's perfectly fine. She said the doctor had used her as an excuse before – he would tell Janet he'd be out on a call when he was on the golf course.'

'At least he'd do less harm golfing than he could to a patient,' Reg said darkly.

'The exchange has the records of anyone ringing in or out or through,' Tollerton said, 'and they show Risley had told Mrs Darling he'd be out on calls at the times of both murders, when he impersonated Binks and the two attacks inside the Hall – yours, Mabel, and Miss Goose's. It'll be easy enough to cross-check with his patients as well as the golf course.'

'And you've connected him to this Agatha Tyne all those years ago?' Reg asked.

'Thanks to Skeff it looks like we'll be able to,' Mabel said.

Cora beamed at Skeff, who smiled and shrugged.

'A few months ago,' Skeff said, 'a fellow rang from a paper in Manchester asking about an item Uncle Pitt ran in the *Intelligencer* five years ago. So, I rang him in turn asking him about Agatha Tyne. He passed me onto someone in Bolton who knew a fellow long retired who remembered the Agatha Tyne case in Little Lever.'

'It all comes down to making connections where you can,' Mabel said.

'And all our connections go through you,' Skeff said.

'Nothing against Scotland Yard, Inspector Tollerton,' Cora said. 'No offence meant.'

'None taken, Miss Portjoy,' Tolly said. 'Miss Canning works much the same way as we do.'

'But where has this man been before he arrived here?' Reg asked.

'It'll take time to trace his movements,' Tolly said, 'but we've got a start from Skeff.'

'Once the coroner's report had been filed and Risley disappeared,' Skeff said, 'interest died out pretty quickly in Little Lever. Ten years later, this retired fellow did a piece – "The Disappearance of Archibald Risley and the Mysterious Death of Agatha Tyne" – that sort of thing. Sent it to newspapers around Lancashire and even further along with a photograph of the young man. He had the usual range of responses – "Isn't that the prime minister?" and "The spitting image of the King" or "It's my old gaffer."

'But two letters caught his eye. One man wrote to say the photo looked remarkably like Doctor George Faber, who had the surgery in their village in Northumberland in 1901, but he left only two years later. Incompetent. The other letter came from Dorset and said the photograph was of Gilbert Furzey, the local doctor from 1902 until 1905 and that he'd been a bit of a slacker.'

'That never changed,' Reg said.

'Only his name,' Mabel said. 'He must've got hold of a handful of degree parchments and then filled in the names as necessary. How many did you find?'

'Ten,' Tollerton said. 'We've got Doctor Finlay's letter of

recommendation from the surgery and it's written in the same hand as the prescription and on the parchments. His own hand, as proved by the prescription he wrote for Miss Goose.'

That erratic script that seemed to dance above the line. Mabel heard it again – 'Flight of the Bumblebee'.

'Binks said the surgery had closed after Formby died,' Mabel said, 'and everyone shifted to the doctor in Bolton. No one bothered to follow up – they had their own troubles. But it all started with Agatha Tyne.'

'Why?' Mrs Chandekar asked. 'Why did he murder her?'

'The simple answer is because she believed she should have the right to vote,' Skeff said.

'That women should be treated as people,' Cora added.

'If Risley believed that wives were only an extension of the husband,' Mabel said, 'and Agatha began to believe differently – that she could make her own decisions and have a life in the world regardless of whether she were married or not – well, that couldn't've sat well with him. He latched on to suffragettes as the source of all his troubles.'

'There will be others who recognise this man,' Cora said, 'and that will be such a relief for everyone, but especially for Mr Binks who told the truth to begin with.'

'I'll get as many constables as I can,' Tollerton said, 'to track down other places Risley posed as a doctor. We'll put another appeal out.'

'How did he find these positions?' Mrs Chandekar asked.

'Newspaper notices of doctors retiring, vacant surgeries, the like,' Skeff said. 'Uncle Pitt runs them all the time.'

'He may have crisscrossed the country. It'll take a while to complete the picture. I'm putting Wardle in charge of that.' Tollerton tapped his empty glass on the table. 'It wouldn't have gone well for Binks if you hadn't shown up, Mabel. Risley would've finished him off and got away before we even knew where to look.'

'Here now,' Reg said to his daughter, 'I thought this was only investigating you did, not chasing down a murderer.'

'I look into things, Papa,' Mabel said, inordinately pleased at Tolly's compliment, but needing to set her father's mind at ease. 'I don't work alone. It's the entire—'

The entire London Ladies' Murder Club, but that wasn't a name she'd yet mentioned to her papa or to Tollerton. Mabel quickly regrouped her thoughts.

'It's Park and Skeff and Cora who look into matters, too. And, of course, Gladys.' Mabel thought Hildy would prefer her name not be mentioned. 'And other Useful Women, too. Their contribution is invaluable. I don't put myself in danger.' *On purpose.*

Skeff raised her glass, nearly empty of brandy. 'Well, so, here's to us all!'

It was getting late by anyone's standards. Everyone began goodbyes and Mabel carried cups and saucers back to the kitchen, but paused when she glanced up the stairs and saw Augustus sitting halfway up, his eyes wide.

'You're meant to be asleep,' she reminded him.

'Yes, going now.' He stood. 'Miss Canning, this is the very best half term I've ever had in my entire life. And there's still tomorrow left!'

Was it only Thursday?

'What will we do tomorrow?' he asked.

'We will have a quiet day of discussions about how to further the campaign for the vote for all women,' Mabel replied.

'Oh,' Augustus said, his voice heavy with disappointment.

'Or perhaps we'll go into town for an ice cream.'

. . .

Mabel and Park saw the others out. Tollerton, bringing up the rear, stopped and pulled something out of his coat pocket.

'Here,' he said. 'It might come in handy.'

He handed over his official Metropolitan Police electric torch. Mabel looked down on the small box in her hand as if it were a grand prize.

'Oh, Tolly,' she gushed, but got no further as he hurried off to catch up with the others.

'All you need now is a policeman's whistle,' Park said, slipping a hand round her waist as they stood in the dark shop.

'Can you get me one?' she asked him.

'Well, I gave my own away, but I'll see what I can do.'

Mabel closed and locked the door then put her arms round Park and kissed him.

'We work well together, you and I,' she said. 'If it weren't for your post with the diplomatic service, we could form a private investigation partnership.'

She saw, behind his glasses, a gleam in his eye.

'Well, perhaps,' he said in a low voice, 'we could form a partnership of another sort.'

EPILOGUE

Mabel squinted at the round mirror in the vestry, trying to pick out her image from among myriad tarnished spots. How could Ronald ever see if his vestments were straight? How had other brides primped and fussed with hair and veil and lace and—

'You don't think it's too many oak leaves for a wedding veil, do you?' Cora asked.

She adjusted the headpiece Mabel wore – a wreath of summer foliage and flowers that fit like a cap, causing her golden-brown curls to burst out below. Peering into the old mirror, Mabel thought she saw a forest princess peering back.

'Oh Cora,' Mabel said, 'I love it.'

From the back of the cap, a veil cascaded to the floor, ending in a puddle of lace. The veil belonged to Lady Fellbridge, and Edith had worn it at her wedding, too. When Emma offered, Mabel gratefully accepted. She would feel as if Edith were near.

Mabel's dress had been sewn by Mrs Chandekar in barely two months since Park had proposed. A June wedding – the tail end of June, but no matter – meant the church was filled with roses and the perfume so heady that one nearly swooned taking a breath. Heaven.

No one had been idle. He and Mabel went to visit his family on the Isle of Wight as soon as they could, and after that Park had been taken up with his post at the diplomatic service. Mabel's own job mushroomed nearly overnight.

She had, for the first time, allowed her name to be mentioned in the newspaper articles about Useful Women private investigations. It started with Skeff's exclusive on the suffragette murders written for Uncle Pitt's *London Intelligencer*. Other papers caught on to the story quickly. The result astounded Mabel as did Miss Kerr's reaction. After the telephone exchange had logged twenty messages from people with cases for 'the lady detective' – on the first day, the proprietress of Useful Women had decided that Mabel's Private Investigations division merited its own office. She promptly took a small space that had just come vacant down the corridor at 48 Dover Street. It would officially open after Park and Mabel returned from their honeymoon.

Cora had spent the previous two months on Mabel's veil as well as preparing to open her own millinery shop, Cora's Creations. She and Skeff had saved up, but in the end, it had happened rather fast. One day Cora noticed a small shop space on the Kings Road had come vacant and, with a bit of help from Skeff's uncle Pitt, they had taken it. The shop was to open in September and already Cora had a waiting list for orders.

While Cora adjusted an oak leaf or two, the door of the vestry opened and Mrs Chandekar slipped in along with the strains of organ music.

'You look beautiful,' she said to Mabel.

Mabel looked down at her wedding dress – silk with a square neckline and a satin-belted dropped waist. She wanted to wear it every day – were brides allowed to do that?

'It's your doing,' she said. 'I love it. And you look beautiful, too.'

Reg had specially ordered the silk for Mrs Chandekar's sari – yards and yards of a blue that seemed to change shades depending on how the light struck it. It reminded Mabel of the sky just before twilight.

'You've done so much,' Mabel whispered, her eyes filling with tears.

'Don't cry,' Mrs Chandekar said and kissed Mabel on the cheek. 'Not yet. It's contagious – if you start then I'll start then Emma and then—'

'Is Papa all right?' Mabel asked, worried that he might break down as he walked her up the aisle.

'He's proud and nervous at the same time. Now, the groom awaits – it's time we took our places.'

In years to come, Mabel would remember their wedding ceremony in snapshots and vignettes. The scent of roses and the organist playing arrangements of old English folk tunes. Reg walking her up the aisle. Mrs Chandekar sitting in the front row as Mabel's mother would have. Ronald standing before the altar, beaming. And Park waiting. As she neared, she could see that behind his glasses, his eyes glistened. He looked so fine in his slim-cut suit with that errant curl on his forehead having escaped its pomade. He held out his hands and she took them.

Behind them, family and friends filled the pews including Miss Kerr. Even Mr Chigley, the porter at New River House in London and an old friend of Reg's, had come down for the day.

Detective Inspector Tollerton – Tolly – had left all vestige of Scotland Yard behind and stood as Park's best man.

Mabel, unable to choose the dearest among her dearest friends had, with their blessing, asked Gladys to be her attendant. The dog wore a collar studded with paste jewels and a headband of daisies. She walked along behind Mabel and Reg and next to Augustus, the ringbearer. Gladys managed to keep her headband on until she reached the front of the church, at which point she shook her head so violently the headband was sent flying through the air to be caught one-handed by a leaping Augustus.

They had invited the boy because Mabel thought it most likely that he would be there regardless and this way they would be forewarned. During preparations, Deenie Pilford and Katie Darling had kept him in line, although whenever possible, he had acted as underbutler, following Binks around Fellbridge Hall.

For the ceremony, he carried a small, shallow basket lined in velvet that held the wedding rings – not only Mabel's, but a band that Park would wear, too. It was a rather new fashion for men, but he had insisted.

The ceremony ended with a kiss, the organist struck the recessional with gusto and Mabel and Park retired to the vestry to sign the documents. Everyone decamped to Fellbridge Hall for the wedding breakfast.

Several hours later, most guests still milled about the salon. Binks had just opened another bottle of champagne when Park glanced at his wristwatch. 'You should probably change into your travelling clothes,' he said to Mabel. 'It'll be a long journey.'

'Long journey?' Mabel asked. 'But I thought we were going to Margate for our honeymoon.'

'Change of plans,' her husband said and clamped his mouth shut.

Cora appeared at Mabel's elbow. 'It's all right,' she said. 'I've already repacked your cases. You have a lovely summer travelling dress to wear with its own coatee and a picture hat with one of those dramatic dips. Don't worry, it's quite suitable. You'll be properly dressed.'

'Properly dressed for what? Where are we going?' All Mabel received in reply from Cora was a secret smile. 'Park, where are we going?'

'Up to London,' he said, 'to catch the boat train from Charing Cross.'

For a moment Mabel stared at him, dumbfounded, then she whirled round and cried out to friends and family in the room.

'We're going to Paris!'

A LETTER FROM MARTY

Dear reader,

I want to say a huge thank you for choosing to read *Murder of a Suffragette*, book four in my London Ladies' Murder Club series. If you did enjoy it, and want to keep up to date with all my latest releases, just sign up at the following link. Your email address will never be shared and you can unsubscribe at any time.

www.bookouture.com/marty-wingate

In book four, it's April 1922. Mabel Canning is proud to be in charge of the Private Investigations division of Miss Kerr's Useful Women agency, but she is also delighted to be sent out of London for an assignment at Fellbridge Hall, which is quite near her home village – it's time you met her papa and the lovely Mrs Chandekar! Mabel is to oversee a meeting of suffragettes who will decide how to further the votes for women campaign. I enjoyed my research into the movement and was inspired by the women I read about who paved the way for the rights we have today.

I hope you loved *Murder of a Suffragette* and if you did, I would be very grateful if you could write a review. I'd love to hear what you think, and it makes such a difference helping new readers to discover one of my books for the first time.

I love hearing from my readers – you can get in touch on social media or my website.

Thanks,

Marty Wingate

www.martywingate.com

facebook.com/martywingateauthor
x.com/martywingate

ACKNOWLEDGEMENTS

Murder of a Suffragette may be my story, but it takes a great team to get the story from inside my head and into your hands! My grateful thanks to all of you in the mix.

My agent Christina Hogrebe of the Jane Rotrosen Agency.

My editor Rhianna Louise and everyone at Bookouture who have created a clear and easy-to-navigate publishing process. Just take a look at the Publishing Team on the following page!

My weekly writing group – Kara Pomeroy, Louise Creighton, Sarah Niebuhr Rubin and Meghana Padakandla.

My husband, Leighton Wingate ('Would you like to italicise this word?')

Continued thanks to these family members, fellow authors and dear friends who never mind listening to the latest results of my research, even if it is about the first commercial dog food in Britain: Carolyn Lockhart, Ed Polk, Katherine Manning Wingate, Susy Wingate, Lilly Wingate, Alice K. Boatwright, Hannah Dennison, Dana Spencer, Jane Tobin, Mary Helbach, Mary Kate Parker and Victoria Summerley. Cheers!

PUBLISHING TEAM

Turning a manuscript into a book requires the efforts of many people. The publishing team at Bookouture would like to acknowledge everyone who contributed to this publication.

Audio
Alba Proko
Melissa Tran
Sinead O'Connor

Commercial
Lauren Morrissette
Hannah Richmond
Imogen Allport

Cover design
Emily Courdelle

Data and analysis
Mark Alder
Mohamed Bussuri

Editorial
Rhianna Louise
Lizzie Brien

Copyeditor
Deborah Blake

Proofreader
Anne O'Brien

Marketing
Alex Crow
Melanie Price
Occy Carr
Cíara Rosney
Martyna Młynarska

Operations and distribution
Marina Valles
Stephanie Straub
Joe Morris

Production
Hannah Snetsinger
Mandy Kullar
Jen Shannon
Ria Clare

Publicity
Kim Nash
Noelle Holten
Jess Readett
Sarah Hardy

Rights and contracts
Peta Nightingale
Richard King
Saidah Graham